The Hallowed Halls

I0630402

Sara J. Kuhrman

SOVEREIGN PUBLISHERS

Erie, Pennsylvania

DEDICATION

This book is dedicated to all the people who unknowingly inspire me every day. You live, I write.

ACKNOWLEDGMENTS

First, I would like to thank my mother, Rhonda Kuhrman, for helping me build my career and supporting me every step of the way. I wouldn't be able to do this without you.

I would like to thank my father, William Kuhrman, for sharing with me your incredible legacy of knowledge, your memory will remain in my heart always.

Big thank-you to my friends Sue Dobson and Terry Hart for helping with my cover picture—you guys are fantastic.

Finally, I thank the Lord for providing me with all of my blessings, I am thankful for every day.

-Sara Kuhrman

Chapter One

Meagan Lucien rummaged through her clunky black leather bag, searching in vain for her thick five-subject notebook that she used for 9:30 AM advanced engineering mathematics class. She located the book in a short amount of time, and placed it atop her archaic wooden desk, along with her pencil, graphing calculator and textbook. After all her materials were in place, Meagan leaned back and stretched, sighing inaudibly as the morning tension worked out of her shoulders. As a hard-working, twenty-six year old grad student at Grandview Community University, Meagan often felt like hell warmed over until about 9:15 AM. By now, she was just beginning to come out of the last traces of her sleepiness. She had a long day, barely able to stagger out of bed, cat, and drive or walk from her apartment to Grandview, which took about fifteen minutes. Then, she took classes until noon before rushing off to the Laundromat to work until 5 or 5:30. After that, she did errands if necessary, worked out, studied, ate and went to bed. Masters' degrees were nothing to mess with. But then again, neither was Meagan Lucien. The room was almost deathly silent except for the rustling of papers and people murmuring under their breath, reviewing notes. It was a very small class, since most masters' students didn't want to take class at 9:30 AM. Meagan's mind just started to drift when her attention was drawn to a familiar sound. From down the hall, she could hear '*step-clack-scrape, step-clack-scrape*' of someone's determined, limping steps. "I

1

guess the Prof is coming," one of the students whispered, more to himself than anyone else.

The rhythmic scraping steps grew closer, and in a few moments, Dr. Terrence Reid, Ph.D., swept into the room, struggling to balance a bundle of papers and his coffee cup in one hand, while he carried his cane in the other hand. The professor managed to set down his supplies on his desk unscathed. Once his materials were settled, Dr. Reid transferred his cane to the other hand and moved casually to the front of the room, the cane clacking on the floor with a sound like *click-thump, click-thump.* He reached his place at the board and turned to his class. "Morning, everyone," he greeted his students enthusiastically. The class murmured a subdued collective greeting, most students not quite awake yet.

Meagan sat up a little straighter in her seat when the professor reached the front of the room. "Okay, today we are going to pick up where we left off yesterday," he instructed. "You're probably going to want to take notes."

After that statement, Dr. Reid turned and began to scribble out complex calculations and formulas on the blackboard. People called him the old-school professor, because he was notoriously attached to his blackboard and chalk.

Meagan smiled to herself as she opened her notebook to where she had left off the day before. As the professor soon launched into a lecture regarding his chicken-scrawled calculations, Meagan tried to focus but found her mind wandering. Up at the board, the professor was talking about differentiation and the relation of Green's Theorem, as if it were the most groundbreaking news in the world. Meagan found herself smiling again as she watched him teach. *Now, he's actually quite something…* Meagan thought to herself as she sized him up.

Terrence Reid wasn't exactly the California-blonde surfer boy that most girls went crazy over, but he had a veiled strength and infectious charisma that made Meagan captive to his charms. He was a wiry guy of fifty-four, dressed in a simple white shirt and tie. He had sparse, combed-over strawberry-blond hair deeply infiltrated with gray, sparkling slate gray eyes and practical wire-rimmed glasses. His right leg was partially paralyzed, hence the cane, due to a working accident he suffered in his thirties. He could move around without the cane, just used it to aid him when walking longer distances. Other than that, he looked quite fit, as if he did hard outside work often. He was sweet of disposition, soft-spoken, calm and analytical, though he let a certain brusque toughness show through when needed. Most of all, he turned math from a sequence of numbers into a magical language of the universe.

When he came to the end of that part of the lecture, the professor took the papers off his desk and began to pass them out. "Here's a study guide for your test next week," he explained, making his way around the room, handing a paper to each class member. When he reached Meagan's desk, she brushed a tendril of black hair out of her face and almost unconsciously arched her back. He set the paper down with a friendly smile and she responded with a soft thank-you and a smile that was indecipherable between friendly and coquettish. Something flickered in Terrence's eyes for a brief moment before he moved on to the next student, dispensing the paper with the same careful, gentle authority, his expression friendly and impassive.

Score, Meagan thought as she watched him make his way back to the front of the room, the vague outline of his buff biceps and muscular thighs visible through his clothing as he walked. Meagan thought she recalled seeing a tantalizing hint of a tattoo peeking out from under his short-sleeved white shirt. *Oh, my, that's perfection,* she thought to herself as she gazed at the intricate blue design winding up his arm.

Chapter Two

Later that day, at approximately 5:05PM, Meagan got out of work at Nielsen's Laundry Service. She peeled off her uniform, an ugly grey apron with the company logo on it. She stuffed the apron into her purse and waved goodbye to the owner, Aaron Nielsen.

"Have a good one, Meagan," he called affably as she left. Mr. Nielsen was a man of about sixty, with white hair and a pipe between his teeth. He was a pleasant old gentleman, and he and his wife had run the business together until she died three years ago. Meagan was relieved to be done with work for the day, so she slung her purse over her shoulder and stepped out the door into the late-afternoon September sunshine.

She had just started to walk away from the squat brick building when she heard a voice frantically calling after her. Startled and kind of annoyed, Meagan whipped around. Her frosty expression froze solid when she saw Michaelis Nielsen, Aaron's son, heading in her direction. Michaelis was twenty-seven, a broad-shouldered youth with oily blond hair and unattractive bulgy brown eyes. He was constantly trying to make a pass at Meagan, but each time, she brutally turned him down. The rejection was beginning to weaken his confidence, but he was harder to take down than most.

Meagan tossed her long black ponytail and turned on her heel, continuing on her way. But with running strides, Michaelis caught up to her.

"Meagan, please," he panted, clutching at her arm. "I just want to talk with you for a moment."

Meagan easily shook off his massive hand. She turned and faced him with her famous imperial look of intimidation. She pursed her lips and raised an eyebrow. "Talk away," she tossed off coolly, as if daring him to speak.

He hesitated for a moment. "Look, I know you've said…" he trailed off. "But, well, what do you have planned this weekend?" he asked awkwardly.

"Studying," Meagan answered shortly, then turned to go.

Michaelis caught up to her again and ran his hand over her arm. "Well, maybe I can come over and study with you," he murmured in a sleazy voice.

Instead of glaring at him or storming off in a huff, Meagan barked out a short, mirthless laugh. Michaelis stood and looked on, bewildered. When Meagan stopped laughing, she patted him on the top of the head. "Better brush up on your lines, little boy," she smirked. "Your poppa's gonna be wanting you home before dark."

With that, she turned and strode off toward her home, and this time he did not follow.

Meagan continued on her way as the Laundromat disappeared from view when she rounded the corner. That little bastard. She had already told him no and no again, and if he persisted in annoying her she would flatten his sorry ass. Meagan had a tough time in life, and she didn't have patience or energy to put up with bullshit. As she walked down the block and neared the street where she turned off to her apartment, men in passing cars stopped to give her the once-over. It didn't bother Meagan at all; she flipped her hair and continued on with brusque, saucy indifference. She was used to men staring at her, and there was no question as to why.

She was stunning, five foot seven with long jet-black hair that cascaded down her back in luxurious waves when unleashed. Her eyes were long-lashed and dark as molten Dutch cocoa, and could be alive and flaming with passion or cold as stone. She worked out every day, so she was extremely fit and had smooth, tanned olive skin. A mole on the side of her face above her lip kept her face from looking too perfect, but at the same time made her even more attractive. Her voice was low and sultry, and she walked with the confident, hip-swinging gait of a woman who owned the world. A man was walking along with his dog and stopped to stare as Meagan walked by, paralyzed by the swaying of her shapely hips. Meagan reached the beat-up white duplex where she lived and took the steps two at a time. She let herself in and carelessly tossed her bag on the floor where it landed with a muffled *thunk.* She headed into her dumpy kitchen and fixed herself a small snack before she changed her clothes to go work out. She ate a cup of yogurt and a cracker or two before washing it down with a glass of water. She figured that would get her through until she had dinner after her workout. She threw out her garbage, and after she brushed her teeth, she headed into the other room to get out of her work clothes. Meagan rooted around in her messy drawers until she found her usual workout outfit, which consisted of a black tank top and black dancer's leggings which cut off slightly above the ankles. She tossed those clothes on the bed, closed her blinds and stripped off her work clothes, leaving them in a clump on the floor. She stepped into her plain white sports underwear and surveyed herself in the mirror. After a moment, she gave a slow nod of satisfaction. All the pain and agony of daily exercise, walking, running, or dancing did her justice. She was just as gorgeous without her clothes as she was with them. She had immaculate posture, toned arms, and a nearly perfect hourglass shape. She was lean and fit but not too thin. Her breasts were voluptuous and generous of size without being enormous, her stomach was muscular as a washboard, and her waist cinched in and flowed out to shapely, curvy hips and thighs that a man would die to lose himself between. Her legs were long and strong, and she was extremely flexible, having been a faithful student of Zumba dance and calisthenics for years.

When she was finished admiring her naked reflection, Meagan continued to put her exercise clothes on. It didn't take her long to get dressed, and soon she was tying her hair back and lacing up her running sneakers. She grabbed her mp3 player and headed down the hallway to the front door. But when she got out to the door, she heard a steady pattering sound. Bewildered, she went over and peered intently through the living room window. Even though it had been perfectly sunny a few minutes ago, now it had started pouring rain and the sky was getting dark. It was late September, almost October, so she figured that by the time the rain stopped it would be dark anyway. "Damn," she muttered when she realized her workout plans were going to get canned. She was really looking forward to taking a nice evening run in the waning sun as it set. Well, she could go walk in the rain but really preferred not to. It was freezing out there, and the street would be almost flooded in a few minutes if this torrential barrage continued. If it got dark, it would be like running in a cold, pitch-black swamp, and Meagan really didn't want to try it. But she wasn't deterred for long. Sighing, she took off her mp3 and set it on the chair. Then, she turned and headed down into her basement. The basement was hers. She got half the first floor and the basement, and her flat owner had the other half of the first floor and the second floor, so they were even. But Meagan loved her basement. It wasn't fancy, just a long, low-ceiling room with a matted-down shabby forest-green carpet. She had made it into her exercise room and Zumba studio. One corner of the spacious room held the treadmill and exercise equipment, while the rest was open floor. She had hung a disco ball or two from the rafters just for atmosphere, and could turn the lights up or down depending on her liking. And of course, a huge old stereo system sat in the corner, one that Meagan had refurbished herself. Since her neighbors weren't home very often, and stayed on the second floor when they were, the music didn't really bother them much.

Meagan stood at the edge of the room for a moment, trying to decide what she wanted to do today, gym workout or dance. She considered as she went to the small, boarded-over windows and switched on the three ventilation fans to bring in some outside air. She stretched her arms above her head and decided that she wanted to dance. It was a cold, rainy grim evening outside, so she would have a party inside and get a heck of a workout while doing it. She walked over to the stereo and turned it on, flipping through the tracks. *No,* she thought. *No, no, no… yes…* she flipped through until she found a rhythmic dance song with a thrumming beat and heavy bass. She turned it up until the bass was thrumming in her veins and she dimmed the lights to a nightclub-like glow, before striding to the center of the floor to begin her routine. She sighed as she stretched the muscles in her neck and back, working out the tension. She began the standard stretch routine that she had used while she briefly taught a hip-hop class as a summer job when she was nineteen. Neck stretches, shoulder rolls, etc. It wasn't long at all before she really began to feel the music, luxuriating in the way the bass spurred her on as her muscles loosened up and she began to flow with the beat. As she warmed up, she went over her day in her mind. Stupid Michaelis Nielsen was no concern of hers. She was not afraid of him, barely annoyed. He didn't even warrant a second thought, didn't receive one. Instead, Meagan backed up further in her day. Her university classes actually weren't too bad today, she thought, though the last one before lunch had dragged a bit. She thought of the advanced calculus test and wondered if she was ready for it. No, not really, she thought, so she stopped thinking of that too. But calculus brought to mind a certain mysterious teacher, and Meagan felt the familiar rush of warmth surge through her thinking of him. She had noticed him before but every day it just seemed to be getting worse. She had no idea why in tarnation she was so hot for Terrence Reid, but she was.

Images of him flashed before her in her mind, his charming smile, strong shoulders, wiry but oh-so-strong frame… Really, it wasn't very often that Meagan wasn't in control in her relationships. But Terrence Reid was dangerous, because she didn't know how well her reserve would do. Already, it was a slippery slope. She tried to force her thoughts in a different direction, concentrating on her fluid movements as she danced and stepped along with the pounding beat. She tried but thoughts of him kept returning to her mind. *For one thing*, Meagan thought, *he is married*. But not that that would stop her. She wondered if he would cave in to her touch, and she ached to try. As she danced and stepped and spun, flashing across the dance floor and thrusting her hips in time with the music, she suddenly had a thought that left her slightly off balance. She smiled as she wondered what it would feel like to have Terrence's hands on her, the hunger in his eyes when he cupped her breasts, the feel of his hand between her legs… this thought sent a molten liquid rush through her core. She stopped and ran her hands up and down her sides and over her shapely hips, closing her eyes. *Touch me, Terrence,* she imagined herself saying, daring him to resist her. Good girls certainly didn't think those kinds of thoughts about their married calculus professors, but Meagan Lucien wasn't necessarily a good girl. She was many things; good, bad, a little of both. An obnoxious, sweet-voiced R&B song came on and Meagan danced across the room, shaking her hips and doing a complicated Latin soul- hip hop hybrid dance sequence. Her white-sneaker clad feet flashed across the room as she thrust her chest and hips, turned and stepped in and out, all with amazing grace and speed. She combined everything she knew; soul, hip hop and ballet as she crossed the room, before reaching her destination and turning, landing neatly on the weight bench. By now, she was in desperate need of release from all of her hot thoughts. The pressures were heavy to the point of aching, and so she slipped her hand down to lighten the dynamo in her core. It wasn't long before she was shamelessly splayed out on the weight bench, fighting the attraction, fighting the desire with all of her might, but eventually giving in as she brought herself to the top, hips shaking, and failing to fight the urge to murmur Terrence's name.

Luckily, her music was still pounding at top volume, and on top of that, there was no one around. She lived alone and the basement was two floors below her neighbors, so there was no audience, but honestly, she might not have cared that much at that moment. After her release, Meagan collapsed with a long, drawn out sigh, leaning back on the weight bench and staring up at the ceiling for several moments with a perplexed grimace. Finally, she propped herself up and ran a hand through her jet-black hair before getting back on her feet.

Chapter Three

"Dinner is ready, dear," Doreen Reid called down the stairs into the basement where her husband kept his study.

"I'll be right there," came the muffled reply that floated up from behind the closed door. Terrence was sitting in his office, grading the lengthy assignments that he had given his class the week before. He was a fast grader, but only if his concentration wasn't broken. He was in his swivel chair behind his desk, red tortoise-shell lamp on the table, critical red pen poised over the assignment at hand. He shook his head as he marked three problems wrong, making a note in his lesson book to review this lesson and really hit it home before the test. Once he finished that paper, he was prepared to get up when an article on his desk caught his eye. It was a magazine article he had cut out that detailed a so-called insolvable mathematical equation that no one had figured out yet. A ghost of a smile hovered on Terrence's lips as he read, and just for fun he wrote down the equation and started monkeying around with it. He had just started to let his mind wander when his thoughts were shattered by his wife's frustrated voice.

"Terrence! Dinner!"

Reluctantly, he set down his calculations, organized his papers and rose from his chair. He made his way across the room, leaving his lamp on so that he could see his way out of the room. He made his way up the basement stairs one step at a time, holding the railing and having to drag his right foot up each step. He actually got around quite well considering his disability, not needing the cane unless he walked long distances, but nonetheless, stairs were difficult.

When he finally had reached the first floor level, he saw his wife standing in the kitchen, a tired look on her face, her hands set firmly on her plump hips. "There you are," she remarked, sort of without emotion. Mrs. Reid was fifty-three, one year younger than Terrence, but she wasn't nearly in as good of shape as he was, despite his twisted leg. She was plump and dumpy with short, curly dark brown hair generously streaked with gray. She and Terrence had been married right out of high school, so it had been over thirty years.

As Terrence made his way into the kitchen, he apologized to his wife for being so late. "Sorry, Dorie," he said cheerfully. "I got lost in my work."

He followed his wife into their modest dining room and set his cane on the floor beside him as he sat down. Doreen gave him a covert frown, a mix of disapproval and disappointment.

"Work, I know," she responded unenthusiastically. "Your other wife."

Terrence sighed as he took a sip of his black coffee that accompanied every meal.
"I said I was sorry," he repeated. "Besides, I'm here now."

Doreen took a bite of her mashed potatoes and dismissively waved her fork in the air. "Doesn't matter now," she said shortly. They ate in silence for a while until Doreen's face suddenly brightened. "I've got great news, honey," she announced excitedly.

Terrence looked up from his chicken soup, interested. "Did you get the tax returns straightened out?" he asked.

Doreen shook her head, the smile still on her face. "Of course not, dear," she laughed merrily. "I mean, that is good, but the kind of thing *you* get excited about. My news is much more interesting than that."

Terrence took another drink and raised his eyebrows at his wife. "What is it, then?" he wondered.

"The news is…" Doreen began dramatically. "My niece, AnnaLeigh Rice, just had another baby! I just heard from her the other day. Her new baby is three months old, a girl. Not sure what her name is."

Terrence declined to reply to this comment. "You really should call about the tax returns," he replied. "It's not good to wait on those."

Doreen took a long sip of her water and set her glass down hard. "We aren't talking about tax returns," she huffed. "Terrence, did you even hear a word that I said?"

Terrence much more calmly took a spoonful of his soup. "I heard you," he answered.

"Well," Doreen prattled on, "Anyway, I was talking to AnnaLeigh, and she will be in town this weekend. She is low on money right now, poor thing probably can't even afford a hotel, and so I told her she and the kids could stay with us."

This comment did cause Terrence a reaction. He slammed his glass down. "What?"

Doreen sighed. "I warned AnnaLeigh that you might be resistant at first… but…"

Terrence cut her off. "Doreen," he said calmly. "I just don't understand why you do this without even asking me, always dragging in these relatives and friends of yours."

Doreen took a sharp sip of her water and glared at her husband. "I resent that," she said coldly. "First of all, AnnaLeigh is family. I don't know how you can be so cold. The only things you drag in are your math books," she let out a mirthless snort.

"I do agree with your statements," Terrence pointed out, pointing his fork at Doreen. "Especially your first one. AnnaLeigh isn't just any family member of yours, but one who I am not in favor of. And you know that."

AnnaLeigh Rice was in her mid-thirties, Doreen's niece, who lived close to town, and in truth kind of a bum. She now had four kids, no husband, and a flighty ex-con boyfriend who came and went. Every time she hit town, her kids ran wild and she pestered Terrence with unwanted advances.

Doreen shrugged. "I'm sorry, but I already invited her. It would be rude to decline now."

"I've got to finish grading my papers, Dorie, thanks for dinner," he told her blithely but somewhat stiffly. He rose from his chair and made his way into the kitchen to put his dishes in the sink. Once he had cleared his dishes, Terrence headed back down into his basement study. His study was his sanctuary, and as he reclined in his leather swivel chair he swore to stay behind his bolted office door for the entirety of the impending Weekend from Hell with AnnaLeigh and the Kids. He loved his wife, he really did, but sometimes he felt like he had been married forever.

Chapter Four

Meagan was sound asleep in her twin bed in the corner of her sparsely furnished bedroom. She lay on her side, arms outstretched, and loose, messy tendrils of black hair fanning out all over her pillow. Her eyes were closed lightly, and she wore an almost innocent expression on her face as she slept. A peaceful early-morning breeze gently ruffled the worn white muslin curtains that covered her scratched, dirty windows. Outside, the city was just beginning to wake up, and the sky was still dark for the most part, only the dishwater-grey phantom of dawn beginning to creep into the atmosphere.

Suddenly, the peace was broken by a shrill ringing sound. The sound cut the air and seemed to disturb the entire atmosphere, upsetting the harmony of the early morning. Meagan stirred faintly and murmured unhappily as the sound bored through the peace of her sleeping psyche. As it continued, Meagan finally blinked sleepily and opened her eyes, propping herself up on her elbow to see what was going on. In her sleepy haze, she realized the ringing was coming from her alarm clock. Irritated and tired, she swiped at it and squinted to check the time. "Shit," she muttered when she saw that it was 6:00 AM. She had planned to go in to the university this morning and work on one of her papers in the library. Meagan had very limited internet access at her apartment, dial-up, and besides she needed to use some of the reference books. After swiping off her alarm, Meagan collapsed back down into her bed and closed her eyes again, not wanting to get up.

It was only Tuesday, but that was often one of the hardest days of the week for Meagan. On Mondays, she had university classes, worked until five at the Laundromat, and then had a mere hour to go home and eat dinner before she had to teach a 7:30PM jazz class at one of the local dance studios. She enjoyed teaching dance, and the dance school appreciated having a weekly teacher with skill like Meagan had. Mondays were jam-packed with events for her, and she often felt dead as a doornail on Tuesday mornings. After resting her eyes for a few moments, she blinked blearily and finally, after about fifteen minutes, managed to force herself out of bed. She ran a hand through her tangled black hair and staggered down the hall into the bathroom to brush her teeth and freshen up. She numbly brushed her teeth and swabbed her face, before stumbling into the shower. She spent a good fifteen minutes in the shower as well, feeling only slightly more refreshed when she had finished.

Even though she was still extremely sleepy, Meagan managed to perk up a bit after her shower. Then, she headed back into her bedroom to pick out something to wear that day. She searched through her closet until she finally decided on a deep plum-coloured cotton shirt with adornments around the scooped neckline and cap sleeves. With it, she picked out a casual but decent looking dark denim skirt and a pair of stable flat-bottomed sensible-looking black penny-loafer type shoes. To top off her outfit, she pulled a black cotton sweater out of her closet. She fixed her hair by combing it and then clipping it back with a wooden clasp, loose strands artlessly framing her face. Even though it was just college, Meagan always thought it important to look professional and prepared. She wasn't overly extravagant or vain, but she always took pride in how she looked before leaving the house.

Still a bit tired, Meagan walked down the hallway to the small adjacent kitchen and flicked the cheerful yellow light on. The sky outside was now fully dishwater-coloured, kind of a mauve-grey, and the gentle breeze had grown slightly stronger. It was still too early to tell what kind of day it would be, but it was early October, so good chance it would be cloudy. Meagan opened the fridge and was disappointed to see that there really wasn't much in the way of breakfast options. She sighed with frustration and decided to just grab her stuff and pick up something on the way. She shrugged on her jacket and grabbed her clunky black leather bag. She shut off the lights, slung her bag over her shoulder, and stepped out the door of her apartment into the cold and rather drizzly October morning. She walked quickly across the street to her car, a beat-up old piece of crap that she had gotten for the low price that she could afford, which also was the value the car was worth. Essentially, not much at all.

She hopped into her car, stuck the key in the ignition, and started pulling out of her parking space. She felt slightly more refreshed behind the wheel, especially when she reached over and turned on the heater, closely followed by the radio. As she pressed the button, one of her favorite hip-hop songs was playing on the radio. Meagan instantly felt more energized as she turned it up and drove off down the street, tapping her fingers on the wheel and mouthing the words to herself. It was a bit of a drive to the university in inclement weather, since the traffic was slow. Luckily for Meagan, though the street was slick with rain, the traffic moved fairly quickly. She decided to swing into the Coffee Stop on the way and grab some breakfast. The Coffee Stop was a small, homey brick building on one side of the busy street. As Meagan flicked on her turn signal to switch lanes, she groaned when she saw the line at the Coffee Stop. There must have been at least seven cars backed up at the drive thru. "I knew it," she muttered, but turned into the building's driveway anyway. It was maybe about a five minute wait that she sat parked in the line, the bass of her music shaking the ground. She turned it way down when she finally reached the speaker.

"Hi, welcome to Coffee Stop, what can I get you today?" a girl's cheerful but tired voice came through the speaker.

Meagan leaned over to speak into the speaker. "One medium triple-shot macchiato, please," she instructed. She was trying to figure out what else she might want when the girl's voice broke the silence.

"Would you like to try our special today, ma'am? Today is caramel crème Danish," the girl offered pleasantly.

Meagan thought for a moment. "Sure," she agreed, thinking that caramel crème Danish sounded quite good.

"Is that all, ma'am?" the girl asked. Meagan said yes. "Okay, $6.15, first window please."

Meagan pulled up to the first window and was greeted by the girl, who looked just as haggard as her voice sounded. Meagan took out her wallet and counted out six dollars, a dime and nickel. "Thank you very much, you may go to the second window," the girl told her with a weak smile. "Have a nice day."

"You too," Meagan answered automatically, and then she pressed the accelerator and drove up to the second window. She rolled her window down and was greeted by a smiling young man maybe a few years younger than she. He grinned as she pulled up, but only in a friendly way.

"Medium triple-shot and caramel crème Danish?" he clarified.

Meagan nodded. "Yup, that's me," she answered.

The boy ducked down and retrieved her Danish in a bag and her searing-hot macchiato. He cocked his head at Meagan and gave an amused smile. "You're the first girl that has wanted to try the special this morning," he remarked with a chuckle. "All the rest of them told me they were on a diet or something."

Meagan reached out the window with a smile as she accepted her order. "What can I say?" she countered with a sly smile. "Danish for breakfast. I'm a sinner."

The boy laughed. "Nice one," he grinned. "You have a nice day, ma'am."

"You too, thanks," Meagan replied with a little wave as she floored it out of the driveway of the Coffee Stop, heading to the university. She took a sip of her macchiato and set it in her cup holder, then held the steering wheel with one hand while she took a bite of her Danish. Immediately, she was flooded with luscious caramel so deep and rich that she did a double take. "Damn," she exclaimed with her mouth full. "This is good."

It was about five minutes later that Meagan pulled into the parking lot at Grandview. She cut the motor and hopped out, her black leather bag slung over her shoulder, and balancing her Danish and macchiato in one hand while she hurried toward the entrance. She wasn't really in a rush, since she had a while before classes started, but she wanted enough time to work on her paper. It was due very soon and not having internet at home really slowed her down. She could do by-the-minute email on her phone when she had to but that was about it. The dial-up service wasn't even working right now, so she considered just scrapping it in general. She stepped into the foyer and took the elevator up to the third floor where the Baldwin Steele Memorial Library was located. Her shoes squeaked on the linoleum floor as she made her way to the library. With her breakfast still balanced in her hands, she managed to wrench open the heavy doors without spilling anything. After all, she was a dancer, so she was pretty graceful. She headed into the room with determination and took a seat at her favorite table. She set down her breakfast, and then began to pull out her laptop. When she glanced up, she saw Professor Reid sitting at the other end of the table, sort of diagonal from her. He was deeply engaged in his work, red pen poised ruthlessly over some unsuspecting assignment. He was dressed in a white dress shirt and tie as usual, and he looked fit and sharp sitting there, back straight, gray eyes focused, the phantom outline of his toned arms visible through his white shirt.

"Good morning, professor," Meagan greeted him cheerfully.

At first, he didn't answer, and Meagan thought that he hadn't heard her. But then, he glanced up from his paper with a pleasant smile.

"Good morning," he replied amiably, his grey eyes twinkling. "Meagan, right?"

Meagan felt a strange sensation, hearing her name on his lips. She looked up at him with wonder in her cocoa-brown eyes.

"Yes," she confirmed with a beaming smile. "How did you know my name?"

Terrence finally focused his gaze directly on hers and Meagan felt as if he could sear through her soul with those analytical gray eyes. She shivered slightly and had to blink to avert the overwhelming sensation. "Is that a surprise to you?" he wondered quietly, a ghost of an amused smile hovering on the corner of his lips. Then his tone became more serious. "What good is a teacher who knows not his students?" he remarked, with a more casual shrug.

"True," Meagan pointed out. "It's just that you have so many students, some professors don't know any of their students by name."

Terrence nodded. "Hence my comment about teachers knowing their students," he remarked again with a smile, turning back to his papers.

Meagan took out her laptop and started to log in. As it was booting up, she took a bite of her caramel crème Danish and washed it down with a long swig of her macchiato.

"Mm," she couldn't help but murmur out loud, still amazed at how good her food was.

Terrence, distracted by the sound, looked up from his work. He glanced over at Meagan, and then at her breakfast. "Danish for breakfast?" he smiled.

Meagan nodded. "Everyone seems to think that's weird," she replied with a laugh. "The boy at the Coffee Stop said I was the first young female to order Danish this morning. All the rest of the girls are on a diet. I took the Danish and I just told the boy that I'm a sinner," she chuckled, recalling her playful exchange with the checkout boy.

Terrence's eyes twinkled and he smiled slightly, but soon his face sobered. "Danish is good," he agreed. "I'll have to try it at the Coffee Stop."

With that, he turned back to his work, and so did Meagan. She logged into her laptop and pulled up her paper that she had started typing. After a while, Terrence rose from the table, bundled up his papers and turned to go. "If you'll excuse me, I have to go prepare for my first class," he told her with a friendly smile. "I'll see you in class."

Meagan looked up and a smile spread across her own face as well. "See you in class, Professor," she replied. "It was nice talking to you."

Terrence took his cane and tucked his briefcase under his arm. "You as well, Meagan," he responded, giving her a wave as he shuffled out of the library. Soon, he could be heard making his way down the hallway with a determined *step-clack-scrape, step-clack-scrape* until the sound faded from earshot when he got on the elevator.

As Terrence left, Meagan focused on her computer screen, but a ghost of a smile hovered on her lips. She had had a genuinely good time talking to him. He was such a kind and witty person, she just loved being with him. Though he was fifty-four, married, and walked with a cane, it made no difference to Meagan. He was in great shape, and besides, she really liked him. She had seen it, that brief flicker in his eyes when she mentioned her sinner comment. Just that tiny blip in his otherwise solid reserve. He was pretty good at keeping it under wraps, but she couldn't help but to wonder what lay beneath that near-perfect professionalism. Meagan tried to push the thought from her mind as she typed on her paper. Because she knew that once she started down that road there would be no going back. This wouldn't, couldn't just be one of Meagan's hit-and-runs. She knew that it was a dangerous game, a slippery slope; and that keeping up this kind of proceeding was equivalent to playing Russian roulette with her sanity, with herself. But Meagan, being Meagan, maybe wasn't afraid to spin the barrel just one more time…

Chapter Five

Ever since the day that Meagan had spoken with Terrence in the library, something had changed between them. She couldn't quite describe it, but it was almost as if a star had turned in the sky and cast its beams lightly on her face. When she was in class, she became notably aware of this subtle change. As she sat in her middle row seat, listening to the Professor's lecture, she realized what she had done. She had broken the barrier of anonymity. No longer could she just be one of the masses of college students swarming through the university and filtering through math class, in and out undetected.

It was a cold but bright sunny morning and Meagan sat in her seat, copying furiously into her notebook as Terrence stood at the board, scrawling calculations at lightning speed while he explained something about derivatives and quotients. As he lectured, she couldn't help but to watch him as he finished scribbling his notes and began to pace back and forth in front of the board, pointing out his work step-by-step. Though he sort of limped back and forth due to his twisted leg, Meagan found it fascinating to study him as he taught; the strong, shuffling grace of his steps, his quiet, gentle voice, and the fire blazing in his grey eyes when he talked about what he loved the most: mathematics.

The way he taught was so compelling; almost as if he was talking directly to each student. As Meagan's thoughts were wandering, the sun suddenly emerged from the light clouds and slowly dominated the sky, streaming in full-power through the windows. Meagan squinted and shielded her eyes as the golden cascade enveloped her desk, bathing her in a honey-coloured glow. She could still see, barely, but felt like she had a spotlight focused on her. As Terrence continued with his lecture, he periodically scanned the room. Meagan felt as if a bolt of lightning was surging through her veins when Terrence's deeply analytical gaze fell on hers, just for the briefest moment. She held her gaze steady for a moment, looking into his eyes until the sensation was too overwhelming and she averted her eyes back down to the page of her notebook. She was still reeling from the intensity, and it amazed her how one look from him could reduce her to shambles. Meagan Lucien was not a woman who was easily felled by a man, but this was completely different. She meekly copied her notes down for a few moments, but it wasn't long before she found her gaze drawn to him once more, like a magnet to the North Pole.

You really should just knock it off, Meagan, her mental common sense voice chimed in. *The man is married, and he is in his fifties. Who knows what kind of mess you'll cause if you're not careful.*

Just then, she looked up to see Terrence writing a long, complicated problem up on the board, having cleared off everything else. "Okay, people," he announced after he had finished and brushed the chalk off of his hands. "We've got about twenty-four minutes left today. Up here is one of the projectile velocity equations that will be on your test. I'd like someone to solve it up here and then lead the class in the explanation. It will be good preparation for your test. Any takers?"

The room was quiet for a moment, as if no one dared to speak. Terrence scanned the room and he chuckled slightly. "Come on," he encouraged. "It is very difficult, but right or wrong, just try. I need a real daredevil for this one."

The room remained silent, and Meagan's common sense chimed in again with *don't you dare…*

Shut up, Meagan told her common sense. *I'm doing this.* And with that, she tossed her long black hair and raised her hand, an impish smile resting lightly on her lips.

Terrence looked pleasantly surprised, and he tilted his head. "Meagan," he remarked with a combination of surprise and admiration. "Let's see what you've got."

With everyone's eyes on her, Meagan gracefully rose from her desk, notebook in hand, and confidently paraded to the front of the room, the heels of her black leather calf-high boots clacking on the tile floor as she walked. She was certainly glad that she had taken time to fix herself up today; she could feel the envious stares of all the other women in the class, and the longing, fascinated stares of the men. Today, she wore a royal-blue cotton shirt that accented her curves with a scoop neck and some lace embroidery on the front. The sleeves were simple and came to her elbows. With it, she wore a black skirt that was business-casual, not too dressy, but showed off just enough of her toned legs and curvy hips. She had her hair loose, and gold jewelry adorned her neck, ears, and wrists. When she reached the board, she brushed the inky curtain of her hair aside and looked over at Terrence, who was sitting behind his desk. "I'm ready, Professor," she told him with a smile, picking up a piece of chalk.

Terrence nodded, a faint smile lingering on his lips. "Good," he said with quiet satisfaction. "Take a crack at it."

She assessed the math problem and began to flip through her notes until she found the section on projectile velocity. As she concentrated and began solving the problem, she could feel Terrence's analytical gaze lingering on her. With the help of the notes and her calculator, she managed to finish in five minutes. When she had scrawled her final answer, she looked up and set her chalk down. She held her breath and stepped out of the way as she saw Terrence's eyes flying back and forth over her work, making notes in his notebook.... Meagan felt like she was going to explode from suspense while he checked her work. She really didn't want to make a fool of herself. *Shit,* she thought. *I bet I forgot to do something with the zero.* Her uncertainty grew when Terrence squinted at the board and put his chin in his hand. *Uh oh,* she thought. *Here it comes... here it comes.... Here it comes... and...*

"Your answer is correct, Miss Lucien," her scrambling thoughts were interrupted by Terrence's quiet voice. She turned, and saw the barest hint of admiration sparkling in his eyes. "Now, just share your wisdom with the class."

Meagan let out a sigh of relief and realized that she had been holding her breath the whole time he was checking her work. Composure regained, Meagan smiled at Terrence and turned to the board to begin her explanation. The explanation took most of the period, and Meagan was surprised to find that the explanation was the easy part. She walked through her problem step-by-step and ended just a few moments before the class ended.

"Nice work today, everyone," Terrence told his class. "Go ahead and pack up."

As the class members packed up their belongings, Meagan erased the board, not quite ready to leave yet. She realized that she was still standing at the board when she heard Terrence's soft voice drift over from his desk. "I'm impressed, Meagan," was all he said, and she set the eraser down and walked over to his desk. "Your work was phenomenal." His grey eyes had a soft light to them, and Meagan felt as if he could see right through her.

She smiled, warmed by his praise, and a little laugh broke from her lips. "It was tough, but I did it," she shrugged. "I was so nervous that I was going to be wrong, and…" she broke off when she noticed that she was rambling, but Terrence was still sitting patiently behind his desk, intrigued and smiling ever so lightly. "I hope you have a wonderful day, Professor," Meagan concluded, beaming at him. "I've got to get to my next class."

"Thank you and I most certainly will, Meagan; you have a wonderful day too. Everyone has the power to make their day however they wish," he replied with a grin. "Take care."

"Very wise, Professor," Meagan commented good-naturedly as she picked up her black leather bag and headed out of the room.

Chapter Six

"*Boom! Smash..... Aaaaaaah!!*" the sound echoed
heavily through the floorboards above Terrence's basement
study. As far as Terrence was concerned, this was the
weekend from hell. Doreen had indeed kept her promise to
invite utmost irksome AnnaLeigh Rice and her four kids over
for the weekend, and Terrence gritted his teeth every time he
thought about it. *She didn't even ask me*, he muttered to
himself, irritated at his wife for just inviting people over
without consulting him first. Generally, he and Doreen had a
good marriage, but there were a few things that really got
under each other's skin. They had arrived unexpectedly on
Friday evening, and Terrence was under the impression that
the dreaded guests wouldn't be there until Saturday morning.
Nevertheless, he had finished grading for the night and was
relaxing in his easy chair in the living room, deeply engrossed
in a book, his trusty cane propped next to him. It was about
eight-thirty PM, and he and Doreen were sitting together; he
was reading and she was crocheting, her hair already up on
curlers.

He had just settled into his evening rhythm, relaxed
from his warm shower and was beginning to feel the effects
of the glass of beer he had had with dinner. He put his feet up
and yawned, reading on in his book, when suddenly his peace
was broken by the sound of a car door slamming outside of

their house, followed by loud voices of boisterous children. Confused, Terrence set down his book and turned to look out the window behind him. Sure enough, that irritating white caravan was parked in their driveway and three little monsters were streaking towards the house, with their mother not far behind them. Even Doreen was a bit surprised at the rude late intrusion, setting down her crochet hook with a frown.

Terrence's grey eyes flashed and glared at his wife through the frames of his reddish-brown glasses. "Doreen, why are they here tonight?" he asked sharply. "I thought they were coming tomorrow."

Doreen sighed and shrugged. "Honey, I thought they were coming tomorrow too. I didn't expect them to be here this late."

Terrence just grunted as Doreen rose from the couch and went to the door. He tried to immerse himself in his book and convince himself that nothing was happening, but it was fairly impossible. Doreen went to the door and opened it just a crack, a puzzled frown on her face. "AnnaLeigh, I thought you were coming tomorrow morning," she said skeptically. "What are you doing here tonight?"

Terrence grimaced when he heard AnnaLeigh's annoying, bubbly voice. "Oh, Doreen, I'm terribly sorry, the drive was shorter than I expected, and we didn't have a hotel…" AnnaLeigh prattled as she dragged in three heavy suitcases. "I know it's late… but…"

"Very well," Doreen answered. "Come on in."

She held the door open, and AnnaLeigh stepped in. "Where are the kids?" Doreen wondered.

AnnaLeigh laughed. "Oh, they are out exploring the yard. It is just me and Erin for now," she stepped in and smiled down at the three-month old she was carrying on her hip.

She came in and closed the door, helping herself to a chair across from Doreen. She brought the baby over to Doreen. "Want to go see Auntie Doreen?" she cooed, handing the baby to her aunt. Doreen took the baby girl and held her dutifully.

"She is cute," Doreen remarked. AnnaLeigh smiled brightly, stretching her lips lined with red lipstick. She was a fat blonde with long, over-highlighted hair, brown eyes, lipstick-lined dry lips and coffee-stained teeth. She may have been pretty at one time, but clearly the drinking, smoking, and greasy diet had not helped her. AnnaLeigh chatted idly with Doreen for a few moments, and Terrence just continued to read, the silence occasionally punctuated by a yell from one of the kids from outside.

After a while, AnnaLeigh tired of chatting with Doreen, so she turned her attention to Terrence. Her lips spread in a wide smile as she looked him over. "Well, if it isn't the most handsome bookworm I've ever seen," she drawled. "You're looking good these days, Terrence."

Terrence barely lifted his gaze from his pages. "Thank you," he mumbled, turning his attention back to his book, as if she didn't exist at all. AnnaLeigh made many more fruitless attempts to engage him in conversation, before Doreen just told her to let him be.

"You'll have to excuse Terrence," Doreen sighed. "He's not very talkative."

"Oh, I understand that," AnnaLeigh nodded sympathetically. "I'm always telling Cristopher, my boyfriend, that he needs to be a better communicator too."

Terrence placed his bookmark between the pages and rose from his chair, gripping his cane. "Good night, Doreen," he told his wife. "I'm going to bed."

He turned and made his way out of the living room, about to head down to his basement study when he heard Doreen coming after him. "Good night, dear," she told him, pecking him on the lips. "I'll see you tomorrow."

Maybe not, Terrence thought, having planned to barricade himself in his study all weekend to avoid the annoying visitors.

So, this was Saturday morning, and Terrence could see out the windows that it was a beautiful day. He considered going out for a walk, when he heard a light knock on his door. "Yes?" he asked.

"Terrence, honey, I thought you might like to know that AnnaLeigh and the kids are going to the space museum today, so you can come out if you want," Doreen called through the door.

"Okay," he called in return. "Thanks."

He was very glad for this development, which meant that he might be granted a Saturday afternoon after all, if the pesky guests were off sightseeing all day. He waited until the white van pulled out of the driveway, then bookmarked his page in his math book and made his hobbling way up the stairs. Stepping out the door, he was refreshed with a beautiful breeze and mid-afternoon sunshine. With a smile, he decided that he would fix his car today, while they were gone. It needed to get done, he liked doing it, and besides, it would give him a way to blow off some steam from being cooped up inside all morning. He made his way to their double garage, which housed both Doreen's small silver car and his pickup truck. His pickup had been out of action for a while, so Terrence had to drive Doreen's car to work. He didn't mind, but he missed his souped-up old grey F150 that he had had for years. In addition to math, Terrence also loved fixing cars and mucking around, he often built things and repaired things when they needed to be repaired. Before he had gone to school to become a mathematics professor, he had been an engineer, out in the field. He had known all along that mathematics was what he wanted to do, but he didn't expect to be left crippled at age thirty-three. He worried that he would never be married, but along had come Doreen Carey, a sweet girl from his graduating class that he had started dating at the end of his senior year. Doreen Carey shortly became Doreen Reid, and there they were, married for over thirty years.

Shaken out of his thoughts, Terrence opened his garage door and drove his pickup out into the driveway where he could work on it. He pulled out his box of tools, and rummaged around in the garage for whatever else he might need. Squinting up into the afternoon sun, Terrence stripped his shirt off and tossed it aside, figuring he'd be hot while he worked. He turned on the radio to his favorite oldies rock station, and organized his tools, analyzing the car to see what type of repairs it needed. He hummed while he worked, and had to unbolt the back part of the truck bed, replacing the rusty screws. It felt good to be outside in the sun, hammering away on his truck. With each swing of the hammer, he felt his mental load growing lighter. Though his leg was lame, the rest of his physique was in top condition for fifty-four. His biceps were pretty impressive from all of the outside work he did, accented by his gothic cross tattoo with a Latin inscription on one arm and a blue dragon on the other. He enjoyed the head-banging physical work of repairing his truck; it cleared his mind. As he stood out in the bright sun, tinkering and bolting and hammering, his mind began to wander. He was thinking of his life in general, and how he sometimes felt that he and Doreen had grown apart over the past few years. They had been solid as gold for nearly twenty-five years; but since then they drifted apart more and more. Doreen was steadily moving on into old age, while Terrence strove to retain his youth as long as possible. He was still out pounding on his car and completing construction projects and house maintenance, while Doreen preferred to just sit inside and crochet or watch TV, always telling him that he should "give himself a rest".

Shaking his head with frustration at the thought, he twisted a washer back into place and his mind drifted off of that topic. Strangely, he found himself thinking about his teaching career, and specifically, what had happened this week. Somehow he found his thoughts on the past week, how he had taught, what he had done. Without warning, the thought of Meagan Lucien wormed its way into his mind. She was good student, he thought, and he had enjoyed their encounter in the library that day. He always wondered what her story was; and she always seemed to have a lively sparkle in her eyes when she talked to him. There was no doubt that she was attractive, and she always seemed to make sure that people were aware of that. He felt slightly uneasy as he finished tightening up one of the new bolts, his brow drawn in a frown. There was no way that he would let it get out of hand. He needed to get the situation under control, quickly, because he could have sworn he had seen it, deep in her vivacious brown eyes, that she wanted him. No problem, he told himself, perhaps she was just being nice. Having dealt before with enamored female students, his iron reserve had built up over the years and never been shaken. Then, thinking that he had resolved the situation at least for now, he focused his attention elsewhere and pushed the subject out of his mind completely.

Chapter Seven

Meagan was not having the best day. It was Monday, and she felt completely disoriented and harassed. A few moments ago, she had been comfortably stretched out between her sheets, in the midst of a delicious dream; when she was jarred awake by the shrill ringing of her alarm clock. The clock was trilling with all of its might, shrieking in her ear. She took a lazy swipe at it, only to have it fall behind her bed and smash onto the floor, silencing the blasted alarm. Meagan merely closed her eyes and sank back into her pillow, still worn out from the weekend she had had. The night before, Meagan and her friend Jennine had gone out to dinner with some other friends, and Meagan had drunk more than she should on a Sunday night. She rested in her bed for a few moments, unknowingly slipping back into blissful sleep. Sometime later, she awoke with a jolt, realizing that she had probably overslept. Her fears were confirmed when she fished the clock out from behind her bed and looked at its black face, which seemed to be scolding her with each tick of the second hand.

"Shit!" Meagan yelped, throwing off the covers and dropping the clock unceremoniously onto her bed. "Oh, shit!"

It was ten after nine. Meagan cursed again as she rooted around in her closet for something to wear. Her calculus class would be starting in twenty minutes and she had two choices; a) go and look like a bum, or, b) look okay but get there late. Meagan decided to opt for the best combination of both, and grabbed a simple outfit of a tan neat-fitting blouse, black slacks and shiny black pumps. She barreled down the hallway to the bathroom to freshen up, concluding that she would have to go without a shower this morning. Sighing in aggravation, Meagan wet a washcloth and ran it over her face, trying to scrub the crusty sleep residue off of her eyes and lips. When she had washed her face to at least a semi-presentable state, Meagan moved on to strip off her pajamas, immediately cringing at the blast of icy air that smacked her bare skin. "Damn, it's cold in here," she muttered, swabbing the washcloth over the rest of her body briefly. To make up for not getting a shower, she slathered herself with copious amounts of vanilla body lotion before putting her clothes on. Yawning blearily, she ran a comb through her long black hair, twisting it up and fastening it hastily with a wooden clasp, oblivious to the dangling strands hanging out in the back. The more she tried to hurry, the more bungled she became. Quickly, she jammed some drop earrings into her ears and sealed her lips with shiny gloss.

Smacking her lips together, she grabbed her leather bag on her shoulder and raced pell-mell out the door of her apartment, nearly tripping down the steps as she made her way to the car. As she floored it to the university, Meagan realized with chagrin that she positively would not function without her morning macchiato. "Damn!" she exclaimed, pounding the steering wheel. She switched lanes and roared through the nearest fast-food drive-thru, glad at least to see that the morning rush hour had cleared out. *Because I'm so late*, she thought as she pulled up to the window and paid for her macchiato. Although the drive-thru lane was clear, she had to sit and wait a long time at the intersection as car after car whizzed by. She slurped her coffee as her eyes flew back and forth, looking for a break in the traffic. Looking at the clock, she saw that it was already nine twenty-nine.

Finally, when the much-needed opening appeared in the traffic, Meagan gunned her engine and pulled out into the lane, one hand on the steering wheel while she sipped her drink. Unfortunately, the motion was sudden and wrenching, and a splash of searing hot macchiato spilled onto Meagan's blouse, creating a large weeping stain. She mumbled another curse under her breath and at this point didn't care. After what seemed like an eternity, she pulled into the parking lot with a screech of tires at 9:39 AM. She made a futile attempt to double-check her reflection in the mirror, before slamming her car door and hurrying toward the entrance of the university, heels rapping loudly on the concrete.

By the time Meagan got up to the classroom, it was 9:44 AM; and she was almost fifteen minutes late. A knot of anxiety struck inside Meagan's stomach like the fangs of a cobra when she glanced through the window pane in the closed door. Dr. Reid was pacing back and forth, gaily explaining some sort of complex problem, something she had clearly missed. She stood with one hand on the door, hesitating, until she gave herself a mental pep talk. *Fashionably late,* she told herself. *You can do it, Meagan. Fashionably late.* Tossing back her shoulders and taking a deep breath, Meagan pressed down on the door handle and swung the door open, announcing her presence with the staccato rapping of her heels on the tile floor and the reverberating slam of the door behind her.

The entire class fell into stony silence and everyone looked up, giving her the customary death stare for being late. Meagan tried to shrug it off as almost thirty pairs of eyes bored into her with disapproval. Terrence set down his chalk and looked up when he heard her step in. "Sorry I'm late, Professor," Meagan rambled nervously, suddenly feeling like she was going to puke under his beautifully analytical gaze. "I overslept and got caught up in traffic."

Terrence barely smiled, sort of distracted. "That's understandable," he replied absently. "Just take a seat and get the notes from someone. We're on section 3 today."

Meagan felt sort of shrugged off by his dismissive greeting and made her way to her seat, plopping down in the hard chair and pulling out her notebook. She ignored the occasional curious and disapproving glance of her classmates. Since it was a masters' class, everyone took it very seriously. Being late was a crime against nature, at least to them. Eventually, they grew tired of glancing her way and turned their attention back to the board where the professor was teaching. Meagan yawned and wiped her still-bleary eyes as she tried to concentrate on what the professor was teaching. But today, Meagan was too disoriented to even remember how to do the simplest calculations. She sat there numbly, just wanting to close her eyes and go back to sleep. As she looked down at her coffee-stained blouse, she just shook her head and gave up. The class seemed to drag on and on, and Meagan noticed that Terrence was all-business today. Of course, he was still very kind and friendly; but there was no special smile, no twinkle in his eye when he looked at her. Meagan shivered unpleasantly as a blast of icy air swept in through the open window, chilling her to the bone. Outside, the sky was dark and cloudy, and inside, the classroom provided no warmth. *Is this all because I was late?* Meagan wondered to herself. She wished it were that simple, but doubted that it was. Sure, she had been late before, but Terrence had never been this cold. Although she fought it with all of her might, Meagan found herself brooding about his absentminded greeting. She was furious with herself for thinking that. *You're so ridiculous,* she chided herself caustically. *I mean, what did you expect? You come waltzing into class late, he's in the middle of teaching, and you expect him to bow down and give you a standing ovation? Are you out of your mind?* Meagan silenced the sarcastic thoughts and tried to turn her attention to the board.

By the time class was over, Meagan was just ready to be done. As her classmates filed out of the room, Meagan hung back, packing up her stuff. Before she left, she stopped at the professor's desk, and he looked up with a smile. "What can I do for you?" he asked cheerfully.

Meagan fought the urge to just dump her stuff on the floor and tell him how she felt, but she restrained herself. "Um, I…" she trailed off, not sure of what she wanted to say. "Um… sorry I was late…" she attempted, scrounging up the first thing that came to mind.

Terrence smiled benevolently. "It's okay," he said with a chuckle. "Everyone is late sometimes. Did you get the notes okay?"

Meagan shrugged. "Erm, not yet," she managed. "But I will. Have a great day, Professor."

Terrence waved and leaned back in his chair. "You as well, Ms. Lucien," he answered with a yawn and tired half-smile.   ***

The day had progressed slowly, with the consistency of molasses. It was now four-fifteen, and Meagan was at work at the Laundromat, shoveling clothes into the dryer. Feeling hassled; she ran a hand through her now-messy black hair and sighed as she moved to the next dryer to unload the clothes and package them in a plastic bag, riffling through the racks of hangers to determine whose clothes they were. "Dalton; dryer 4," she murmured to herself, checking the last name on the clipboard. She finished packaging the clothes and walked to the desk, printing out a name slip and fastening it to the bag. Then, she tossed the finished package over with all of the rest of the bags of finished laundry waiting to be picked up. Despite the fact that it was a small family business, Nielsen's Laundry Service actually got quite a few customers and was the main launderer in town. Aaron Nielsen and his wife had run the business for almost fifty years, until Aaron's wife died. Now, he ran it on his own.

Forty-five minutes left, Meagan thought with a grimace as she looked at the clock hanging on the paint-chipped beige wall over the laundry machines. All Meagan wanted was to go home and relax; not to mention take off the damned pumps that she had foolishly worn today, not bringing her usual change of shoes. She thought that she probably looked pretty stupid in her slacks and heels with the grey apron slung over her clothes. *At least it covers the blasted coffee stain on my shirt,* she thought to herself with a mirthless chuckle. She yawned widely and went to stand next to Jackie, one of the other afternoon regulars. "Long day, Meagan?" Jackie asked with a smile.

Meagan nodded. "Heck yeah," she answered. "It's only Monday too."

Jackie shook her head as she printed out a receipt. "Tell me about it," she muttered.

Their conversation was interrupted when a car pulled up in front of the Laundromat and a frail white-haired man got out, walking shakily toward the entrance. "Hi, welcome to…" Jackie started to say, but then was startled to see that it was the owner himself. "Hi, Aaron," she greeted him.

Meagan looked up, startled as well to see Aaron Nielsen himself there. Aaron came to check in once in a while, but they hadn't been expecting a visit from him today.

"Hello, Aaron," Meagan greeted him with a smile. "Need your laundry done?"

Her face sobered up immediately when she saw that Aaron was not smiling. In fact, he looked positively lost and forlorn.

"Good afternoon, ladies, gentlemen," he said quietly, motioning all of the employees over to join him. "I'm afraid I have some news for you."

They all stared at him, waiting. Finally, Jackie broke the silence. "What sort of news?" she asked nervously.

Aaron sighed and sat down on the bench. "I'm getting old," he began. "Too old to run a business anymore. I just found out that my cancer has come back, and as much as I love you all and love this business, I'm going to have to close."

They were all silent, and there was not even a ghost of a sound in the room except for the steady humming of the laundry machines.

"Close when?" Jackie asked, her voice rising.

Aaron bowed his head. "Two weeks' notice," he said regretfully. "I already have a future buyer for the building." He looked at his watch. "I'll let you all quit early today, even though that doesn't make up for it. Again, I am sorry. I wish it didn't have to be this way."

The mood was somber as the seven employees took off their aprons and hung them up in the utility room in the back. They did not look at each other or speak to each other. Each of them waved a halfhearted goodbye to Aaron Nielsen before heading off to their respective cars. Meagan grabbed her bag and slung it over her shoulder, stumbling out of the Laundromat in almost a delirious haze. An icy rain had begun to pelt down on her and she shivered as she hurried to her car. She wrenched the door open and threw her purse in the passenger seat, climbing in and cranking up the ignition. As the heater turned on and began to fill the car with warmth, Meagan just sat there, unmoving. She pulled down the mirror on the sunshade and checked her reflection. Facing her was a ragged woman with messy black hair in a sagging bun, tired, sad eyes and a hopeless face. "Oh, my god, I just lost my job," she whispered to her reflection. "I just lost my job."

In despair, Meagan rested her head on the steering wheel. *What the hell am I gonna do?* Meagan thought to herself, mentally running though her list of financial commitments: university classes (even with financial aid), rent, car payments, grocery bills, etc.

She knew how hard it was to find a job in today's economy, and at this point she couldn't even think about where to begin. *I'll take anything to pay the bills,* Meagan thought. Although her job at Nielsen's Laundry wasn't the most exciting in the world, it wasn't a bad job. The hours were good, she had evenings to herself, the place was clean, customers weren't too demanding for the most part, and the pay wasn't too bad, since Meagan had acquired the title of assistant manager and was in charge of accounting and staff questions as well as doing laundry duties when necessary, which was about half the time. *Bummer,* Meagan thought. *Sometimes life is a real bastard.* She lifted her bleary tear-stained eyes to see that her makeup had smeared all over face. Carelessly wiping her face with a tissue, she sniffed and put the car into gear, making her sorry way home in the pouring icy rain.

Chapter Eight

After she had showered and cleaned up, Meagan sat listlessly on the couch, staring at the TV but not really paying any attention to it as it blared continuously. Instead, she turned her attention to the rain, which was still coming down in frigid sheets outside. It was October, but it felt like it could be cold enough for deep winter. Shivering, Meagan wrapped a blanket more tightly around her shoulders and sipped her coffee, which she had spiked with a shot. As she stared numbly out the window, the day's events played back to her like an irritating commercial. It hadn't helped that she and Jennine had had so much fun at dinner last night, and Meagan told herself that she would stop drinking on school nights, because it never ended well. She gritted her teeth as she thought of how badly she had made a fool of herself in class today. Even though she was just running late, she reprimanded herself for busting in fifteen minutes late with a stained blouse and toothpaste on her face. *No more drinking,* she told herself, but then let out a humorless chuckle as she sipped her spiked coffee. *Beat the bottle with the bottle;* she cracked dryly, shaking her head at the dry cynicism of her inner voice. She took another sip of her coffee and then leaned back on the couch, closing her eyes to take a brief nap and stop thinking about the day. She was stretched out on the couch in her dark and comfortable living room, drifting in a haze on the brink of sleep, when suddenly she was blearily drawn awake again by the ringing of the phone. Groaning, Meagan flipped over and grabbed the receiver. She was so tempted to just ignore it, but she figured that it could possibly be important. She put the receiver to her ear and burrowed back down beneath her blanket. "Hello?" she mumbled.

"May I speak with Meagan Lucien?" a weak male voice asked with a hoarse cough.

Meagan was perplexed. "This is Meagan," she answered. "And who are you?"

"Hi, Meagan, it is Aaron Nielsen," the voice replied. "I didn't know if you had a roommate or something… so that's why I asked."

Meagan was startled. "Hi, Aaron, and no, I'm all alone," she answered. "I must admit that I'm surprised that you called," she continued.

There was silence on the other end for a moment as Aaron drew a great hacking sigh. "I really do regret having to close the business," he began. "But I called to tell you that I have another job opportunity for you."

Meagan gave a little exclamation of surprise. "Really?" she wondered incredulously. "I mean, did you call the other employees too?"

Aaron paused. "No," he answered. "This one is just for you."

Meagan was perplexed once again. "Me?..." she asked. "Well, I'm thrilled. Shoot away."

Aaron cleared his throat with a loud cough. "Excuse me," he said, before beginning. Once he had regained his voice, he began. "Listen, Meagan, my son Michaelis works long hours as a main newspaper editor. When I told him I was closing the business, he offered to employ you as his housekeeper and cook. You'll have to talk to him more about it if you're interested, but he told me that he would like you to be live-in, and he will provide free room and board and use of the house as well as a generous salary. If you're interested, I will give you his cell number," Aaron paused.

Meagan looked at the receiver incredulously. Live-in housekeeper for Michaelis Nielsen? *Are you shitting me?* Meagan wanted to say, but decided that it might not be the nicest to say to her ailing boss. "Well… um… okay," Meagan stammered. "I'll take the number and get back to you."

She jotted down the number and thanked Aaron for thinking of her. Then, she set the note down and hung up the phone.

After Meagan had said goodbye and hung up, she placed the phone on the light stand and with some effort raised herself off the couch to go refill her coffee, which had become cold and tepid as she was lying there. She stumbled into the kitchen and filled her coffee, then returned to her spot on the couch where she sank back down onto the cushions and closed her eyes. She was thinking about what she could do about her employment situation. There was an option to race about frantically trying to apply for whatever jobs were available in town, which she may or may not get. The other option was to see what this housekeeper job entailed. Meagan grimaced as she opened her eyes and glanced down at the scrap of paper with Michaelis's number on it. She really didn't like him. Not to mention that she had a general bad feeling about the proposition. *I can just see it now,* Meagan thought with exasperation. *He hires me to be his housekeeper and tries to make me his mistress. I don't think so;* Meagan gave a harsh chuckle, imagining just how wrong he would find himself to be. She wasn't going to take the job unless she was starving to death, and even then she may not. But if she did, she would be sure to teach him a lesson if he tried any funny business with her.

Going over all of this in her mind, Meagan decided to go back to sleep. She was just about to when the phone rang again. Extremely irritated this time, Meagan lifted the receiver. "Yes?" she said shortly.

"Hey, M, it's Jen," Jennine's perky voice sounded through the speaker. "What'cha up to on this dreary Monday afternoon?"

Meagan sighed. "Laying under a blanket," she answered.

Jennine sounded like she was pouting. "Oh come on, M, is that any way to conduct yourself?" she joshed.

Meagan wasn't really in the mood. "I'm unemployed," she blurted brusquely.

There was a gasp of surprise on the other end. "Oh, that is terrible news," Jennine sounded concerned. Then, with no warning, she added, "I'll be over in ten minutes."

"Wait…" Meagan started to say, but the line was disconnected.

"Oh, brother," Meagan muttered to herself after she had hung up. She was tired and dazed and didn't really feel like dealing with Jennine's boisterous cheerfulness right now. Realizing that Jennine was coming whether she wanted her to or not, Meagan sat up on the couch and propped her feet on the coffee table with a yawn. She clicked on a lamp, picked up a magazine, and began to idly leaf through it.

Halfway through her careless skimming of the magazine, there was an enthusiastic knock on her front door. *Yup, here she is,* Meagan thought with a reluctant smile as she progressed to the door. As soon as Meagan swung the door back, she was immediately flooded with Jennine's contagious exuberance as she stepped through the door.

Jennine was petite and very slim, almost three to four inches shorter than Meagan, with softly curly light-brown hair that she often wore back, a scholarly, angular face, twinkling hazel eyes, and a wide contagious smile. She was always happy and upbeat, which was good, but she also partied as hard as she worked. As Jennine stepped through the door, she wrapped her arms around Meagan and kissed her lightly on both cheeks like a French actress. Then, she held her at arm's length. "Oh, poor babe, you look awful," she told Meagan with a sympathetic look.

Meagan barked a laugh and couldn't help but to smile as she hugged Jennine back. "Thanks a lot," she joked.

Jennine's smile softened as she touched Meagan on the shoulder. "So, what can I do for you?" she asked. "Wanna go out tonight?"

Meagan shook her head and sighed. "No, not tonight," she replied. "I had a hangover this morning and made a fool of myself in class."

Jennine gave her a curious look. "Oh, did you?" she asked with a conspiratorial smile, elbowing Meagan in the ribs. "Is there a cute guy in one of your classes or something?"

Meagan felt her face flush at this thought. *Actually, there is,* she thought. *But there is no way I'm telling Jen.* Meagan really didn't want to go around telling people that she was in love with her fifty-four year old, married, cane-wielding super genius calculus professor Terrence Reid. So, she tried to devoid her face of emotion. "You have an active imagination," she said with a sigh and a shrug. "I wish. No, I just showed up late for one of my classes and got reamed out in front of the class for not being a 'serious student'," Meagan lied, quickly making up the story as she spoke, avoiding the entire topic of calculus class in general.

"Oh, okay," Jennine replied, losing interest now that there was no cute guy. "How 'bout we go out for coffee or dinner or something and you can tell me what's up with your job? Just don't order any alcohol."

Meagan thought for a moment, but she knew that Jennine would probably end up convincing her to go anyway. Besides, it would be better than sitting around in her apartment all night by herself. "Sure," she agreed. "We can go to the A&B Diner around the corner," she suggested, and Jennine assented with a shrug and a smile.

"Why don't you let me clean up a bit first?" Meagan asked. "I should change my clothes."

Jennine took a seat on the couch and Meagan went into her room to change into an outfit that was suitable for going out. She didn't get too fancy but just put on a light-blue t-shirt, black stretch pants and a grey wrap sweater. She brushed back her hair in the mirror, wiped her face, and applied some minimal makeup. Soon, she was ready, and the two of them piled into Jennine's car.

The A&B was very close to Meagan's apartment, so it took under five minutes to get there. When they got into the fifties-style diner with red leather seats, Meagan wasn't terribly surprised to see that it wasn't very busy. After all, it was only Monday night.

A smiling blonde hostess came up to them with her hands full of menus. "Just you gals tonight?" she asked pleasantly, with a hint of a southern accent. Meagan nodded, and the woman led them to a four-top table over in the corner. Meagan and Jennine sat across from each other and placed their purses on the seat next to them. The hostess deposited the menus and told them that the server would be with them shortly.

Flipping through the menu, Meagan grimaced slightly. After her long day, she wasn't even really that hungry. She decided to start with a salad and a bowl of minestrone soup and a glass of soda, since she wasn't drinking tonight. When the waitress came up to their table, she turned to Meagan first, and Meagan recited her order. The waitress made a note on her pad and then turned to Jennine.

"Grilled chicken tomatillo wrap and a bottle of Bud, please," Jennine answered with a wide smile. The waitress noted this down as well and told them that their dinner would be ready soon.

Once the waitress had gone, Jennine leaned across the table. "Not hungry tonight?" she asked Meagan.

Meagan yawned and shook her head. "No, not really," she answered. She recalled what Jennine had ordered and always wondered how she could eat so much and drink so much alcohol and stay so rail-thin. Meagan was pretty sure that Jen had some sort of eating disorder, maybe exercise bulimia, but she had never confronted her about it. She knew Jen had a treadmill and weight set, and often worked out for hours a day.

Meagan was startled from her thoughts by Jennine's voice. "So, tell me about this job thing," Jennine began. "What's going on?"

Meagan sighed. "Aaron, my boss, is sick with cancer and he is closing the Laundromat," she answered. "That is really all there is to tell."

Jennine frowned. "Hmm, that's too bad," she replied. "But I'm sure you could get a job somewhere else."

Meagan folded her hands on the table. "Yeah, I'm sure I could," she answered. "But the question is when? I mean, my rent is due at the end of next week."

Just then, the waitress returned with their dinner and drinks, and they paused. Once she had gone again, Jennine shrugged and sipped her beer. "You have two weeks," she pointed out. "Just start bombarding with the applications. Or ask your landlord to give you a grace period."

Meagan shook her head. "I can't do that, Jen," she answered. "This *is* the grace period."

Jennine drew a breath. "Well, I can help you look, but it might be tough. Do you have a plan if you can't get a job?"

Meagan gave a relenting sigh. "Jen, I have a job opportunity," she confessed. "I just don't want to take it."

Jennine gave her a questioning look, and Meagan filled her in about the housekeeping job for Michaelis Nielsen, who she really didn't like and didn't want to work for.

Jennine listened carefully, periodically sipping her beer or taking a scoop of her chicken, and she knit her eyebrows in thought when Meagan had finished. "I know you don't want to hear this, Meagan, but I think that you should at least check it out. It might not be as bad as you think."

Meagan took a spoonful of her minestrone and washed it down with her drink. She gave Jennine an incredulous look and shook her head. "Jen," she exclaimed in frustration. "*Live-in housekeeper* for a man that I don't know and don't want to know? Really? I mean, I bet he's a date rapist or something! This whole setup sounds bogus to me."

Jennine nodded. "That is a viable concern," she admitted. "But I think we've got a slight case of your pride getting in the way, Meagan, and it isn't good for you."

"What are you talking about?" Meagan asked skeptically.

Jennine took a long drag of her beer. "How you always need to be in control when it comes to men. You always want to show everyone who is boss." She answered, not unkindly.

Meagan simply grunted. "You're getting tipsy, Jen," was all she said.

The two of them ate in silence for a while, Jennine busy drinking beer and Meagan lost in her thoughts. As they sat there, Meagan wondered what Terrence was doing right now. She smiled slightly when she thought of him sitting at his desk, red pen poised over an assignment, or writing out calculations in a notebook. She figured that he probably wouldn't hold it against her for being late today, but nevertheless the experience was quite mortifying.

After some time, Meagan snapped back into reality, feeling sort of confused by how much time had passed. It was dark outside the diner, and looking across the table, she saw that Jen had two empty beer bottles on the table and was almost through a third. Meagan looked down at her soup and saw that it was hopelessly cold, but she quickly finished it anyway. She was glad when the waitress came over to their table, asking if they would like anything else. Jennine started to say something but Meagan cut her off and turned to the waitress with a smile. "No, thank you," she answered. "Just the check."

After the bill was paid, the two of them headed out of the diner. Jennine was clearly very tipsy, because she was hanging onto Meagan's arm as they walked out and laughing when she stumbled in her high heels. Meagan hopped into the driver's seat and loaded Jen into the passenger seat. "You can just stay over if you want tonight, Jen." Meagan told her. "Then, you can drive yourself home in the morning."

Jennine just smiled and dug in her pocket, lighting up a cigarette and staring out the window while Meagan cranked up the radio.

Chapter Nine

The next day, Meagan was still quite tired, but she felt slightly better after talking with Jennine the night before, though her friend had, in all reality, offered little advice. It was Tuesday, which was usually Meagan's bad day, but this week she had had her tough day on Monday. She made it a point to get to the university earlier today, just to make up for the fact that she had been late the day before. As she staggered out of bed on this day, she picked out a simple black shirt and khaki slacks, fastening a gold-chained necklace around her neck and putting gold hoops in her ears. Her hair was up, but in a much less frazzled style than the day before, hanging down her back in a sleek French braid.

Rubbing the sleep from her eyes, Meagan finished dressing herself and applied a coat of shiny gloss to her lips to finish out the outfit. Looking at the clock, she felt pretty good about her successful attempt to get ready earlier. She would get to the university in plenty of time, and also have ample time to pick up her daily macchiato and some kind of breakfast. Checking her reflection, she felt satisfied and hefted her leather bag onto her shoulder before leaving her apartment and lightly, gracefully taking the steps down to her car.

Once she was behind the wheel, Meagan yawned and relaxed, making her way through the minimal morning traffic. Down the road, she flicked on her turn signal and pulled into the Coffee Stop, her usual morning coffee supplier. It didn't take long to move through the line, and soon she was back on the road to Grandview. As she pulled into the parking lot, she took a long, grateful sip of her macchiato, sighing aloud in appreciation as the searing liquid wound its way down her throat, spiking her pulse and flushing her body with heat. Calm and in control as opposed to yesterday's scrambled haste, Meagan casually lifted up her purse and macchiato and took her time as she walked across the parking lot, approaching the double doors. In the lobby, there were a few undergrad students hanging around in clumps, clutching their breakfasts and chattering in hushed voices. Meagan's heels rapped soundly on the tile floor, echoing across the expanse of the foyer. Some of the students glanced up nervously, but Meagan just gave them a friendly smile and walked on.

When she got up to the library, her heels no longer made noise on the carpeted floor. She looked around for which table she wanted to sit at, and she felt herself swallow nervously with a little jolt as she saw that Terrence was sitting at one of the back tables, his back turned to her. She hesitated for a moment, feeling unsure. *Should I go sit with him?* Meagan asked herself in her mind. *Or would he think I was weird?... Does he remember that my shirt was coffee-stained yesterday?* She fretted mentally. But then, she scolded herself to stop all of these crazy thoughts. *Land sakes, Meagan,* she told herself. *Stop this bullshit! Just go sit with the guy; and don't mention the shirt!*

Taking a deep breath, Meagan quietly made her way across the room and took a seat on the opposite side of the table that Terrence was sitting at. He looked up with a smile when she sat down. "Good morning," Meagan greeted him. She gave a lighthearted chuckle. "Hey, at least I'm not late today."

Terrence nodded. "You're early today," he pointed out with a light smile. "Doing a paper again?"

Meagan nodded and broke into a tinkling chuckle again. "Yes, I am, but I also wanted to make up for disappointing you yesterday," she kidded.

Terrence chuckled as he was grading one of his papers. "Don't worry, I wasn't disappointed," he reassured her. "But thanks, I'm flattered that you are so dedicated to my class."

Meagan smiled and shrugged. "It's a good class," she replied. *Good teacher too…* she thought, *stop that.*

Her brief reverie was interrupted when Terrence addressed her again. "I wonder, what is it that you want to do for a career?" he asked her. "There are many possibilities for a mathematics degree."

Meagan looked up and saw genuine interest in his grey eyes, and she found it difficult to meet his gaze for more than a few seconds at a time. "Well…" she began. "I am considering probably either architecture or engineering," she answered. "I'm taking classes in both."

Terrence looked surprised, but pleasantly so. He arched his eyebrows. "Very impressive," he said quietly but seriously, looking at her intently. "I hope that it will work out for you. I am versed in both topics if you need extra help."

Meagan's face flushed slightly. "Well, I think your knowledge is far more impressive than mine," she answered. "Man, what did you do, study everything?" she laughed.

Terrence couldn't help but to smile. "Pretty much," he answered good-naturedly. They continued to enjoy an occasional light conversation as they worked on their papers.

***

Later that day, after her university classes had finished, Meagan left the building and walked out to her car with a troubled frown on her face. She had enjoyed her day at the university, but now that classes were over, she had to face the harsh reality of her employment situation. In exactly four days, she would no longer have a job, and also have no money to pay her rent.

Today, Meagan was on a mission. As soon as she had gotten over the initial shock of the Laundromat closing, she had begun to hunt for another job. She desperately scoured the city for job advertisements and planned to interview each day at several places until one finally accepted her. Today, she was interviewing for a position at an Italian restaurant. Though it wouldn't pay much, it would be better than nothing. The night before, she had put together a résumé, but she wasn't sure if she was really ready. As socially confident as Meagan generally was, job interviews really scared her. It had been years ago when she had interviewed at Nielsen's Laundry, but that hadn't been difficult at all. She had walked in at age seventeen, told Aaron Nielsen that she was interested in a job, and *bam,* there she was.

As she drove, Meagan cranked up her music to get herself in the mood. She blasted her favorite hip-hop song at top volume, the bass causing her car to vibrate. Drivers beside her glared or rolled their eyes, but Meagan couldn't go to this interview without drowning her fears in the beat. A few minutes later, she turned the music off and pulled into the parking lot at the restaurant where she was applying, called *La Bella.* It was quite a fancy place, very upscale, and she had heard that it was generally difficult to get a job there, but right now they were really desperate for people. *Maybe my upcoming masters' in engineering mathematics will help,* she reasoned, smoothing over her hair and grabbing her bag.

As soon as Meagan stepped through the door to the restaurant, she felt rather outnumbered, out of place. The atmosphere was low of light, and soft music played in the background. Silent and elegant waiters and waitresses in black suits or black dresses gracefully and efficiently moved about with bottles of champagne and trays of elaborate, aromatic cuisine. Meagan looked around, then down at her clothes, which clearly stood out among the well-dressed crowd. She wasn't dressed poorly, but only business-casual, not business-dressy. She looked in vain for a desk to go up to, but all she saw was a sign that read *"Please Wait to be Seated"* in elegant script. So unsurely, she stood next to the sign until a waiter approached her. "May I help you, Madame?" he asked with contempt, clearly wanting her to know that she didn't belong there.

Meagan squared her shoulders and looked the man directly in the eye. "Yes," she answered. "I would like to see the manager."

The waiter barely held back a disdainful snort. "There is no manager, Madame," he responded with a heavy accent. "The owner, Mr. Bello, is in that room back there." He pointed to a closed door marked PRIVATE. "What do you want to see him about?"

"I came to apply for a job," Meagan answered. This time, the waiter made no attempt to hold back his eye roll.

"I will escort you," he sounded like he was trying to stifle a chuckle. Meagan felt like everyone was staring at her as she walked across the room, so she tried to make herself feel better by throwing her shoulders back and parading across the expanse with the confidence of a goddess. When they reached the back of the room, the waiter gave a knock on the closed door. "Who is it?" barked a muffled voice with a heavy Italian accent. A moment later, the door was opened and a short, black-haired man with a mustache and a scowl stood before them.

"Ah, Mister Bello, sir," the waiter began, motioning to Meagan. "This young lady would like to speak to you."

Bello gave the man a brisk nod. *"Grazia,"* he dismissed the man. Then, after the waiter had gone off, Bello peered at Meagan, suspicion in his bespectacled brown eyes. "Who are you?" he asked dubiously.

Meagan felt slightly nervous, but she forced herself to breathe evenly. "My name is Meagan Lucien," she explained, hoping that her voice hadn't come out too squeaky. "I, um, saw a sign that said you were hiring."

Bello gave her a cursory glance. "Well, come in," he motioned her into his office. "Have a seat."

He took a seat behind his imperial oak desk, and Meagan took a seat on the hard wooden chair on the other side. She reached into her bag and pulled out her résumé. "Here is my résumé, sir," she slid it across the desk.

Bello held his spectacles up to his eyes and scanned it, his lips pursed. After a moment, he handed it back. "Laundromat and hippy-hop dance, that's it?" he asked after a moment, not looking impressed. "You never work in *restaurante* before?"

Meagan shook her head. "I'm afraid not," she replied. "I am a student at Grandview University, I have a B. S. in engineering mathematics and I'm working on my master's degree."

Bello frowned. "So, what makes shabby girl like you want to work here at *La Bella?*" he asked. "Please. I'm just curious."

Meagan steeled herself not to react to his comment. "I will try something new, and I am a good worker," she tried.

Bello shook his head. "No, I don't want you," he replied, handing her résumé back to her with disdain. "You don't come to *La Bella* to pay the bills. You come to *La Bella* to make a career."

"Very well," Meagan replied, packing up her things. She closed the door of his office, not even bothering to thank him for his time. She streaked across the main dining room and out to her car. *Shabby girl, eh?* She thought furiously. *Stupid stuffy foreigner probably doesn't even know what a B.S. is,* she fumed. She jumped into her car and cranked up her music to top volume, before peeling out of the parking lot with a screech of tires. As she cruised down the road, she realized with a sinking feeling that she had another interview to go to today. *Time: 1, Meagan: 0,* she thought grimly, hoping that there would be at least somewhere that would hire her before her rent was due.

Chapter Ten

It was Sunday afternoon, around 1:30 PM, and Meagan was staring listlessly out the window of her apartment as the icy rain beat down relentlessly on the windows outside, turning the ground into a swampy mess. The clouds were gray and heavy and had been blitzing the city with unrelenting rain since the night before.

Sighing, Meagan wrapped the blanket tighter around herself and sipped her coffee, which had gone tepid in all of two minutes. Shaking her head, she set the mug down out of the way and turned up the TV to drown out the noise of the rain droning against the windows and the cars swishing by on the mucky streets.

As she stared at the television screen, Meagan tried to forget about what a hell of a week it had been. On Monday, she had received the news of her unemployment. Tuesday, and every subsequent day after that, even Saturday, had been packed with unsuccessful attempted job interviews. While she was snagged up in her employment dilemma, Meagan hadn't had much time or energy to study, and already her performance was suffering. *Damn,* Meagan thought to herself bitterly. *All I've managed to do this week is find out why half the businesses in the city don't want to hire me.* Some of the employers were harsher in their rejection; others hid it behind a thinly veiled mask of professionalism. But Meagan knew their reasoning was the same: they didn't want to hire a struggling grad student whose work experience consisted of laundry and jazz dancing. Besides, people in authoritative positions sometimes had trouble with Meagan because the men feared that they could not control her, and the women feared that she would take their place.

As the TV show ended with loud clapping and cheering and the anchor switched back to the news, Meagan simply shut the TV off. She rose off the couch to make herself another cup of coffee, since she was quite cold. En route to the kitchen, Meagan spotted her calculus notebook lying on the table where she had left it, planning to study the night before. *Calculus,* she thought. *Crap.* She walked into the kitchen and started brewing her coffee, then wandered into the adjacent room and removed her notebook from the table, carrying it back to her place in the living room along with her textbook.

A few minutes later, Meagan was hunched over the arm of the couch, coffee on the table, trying to figure out where she had left off and what she needed to work on. She located the current chapter and groaned aloud when she saw the menacing set of practice problems looming on the stark white page in front of her. "Damn!" she exclaimed. "I'm never going to figure this out!"

She scanned through the chapter and her notes in vain, suddenly panicked. In her daze of the week, she must have somehow missed these notes, because they were nowhere to be found on the paper or in her brain. She tried for about a half hour with no avail, until she finally gave up and closed the book. Sighing, she decided to drag out her slow laptop and shoot the prof an email, telling him why she got behind and that she needed to schedule extra help. As this thought crossed her mind, Meagan smiled. *Extra help with Mr. Hot,* she thought to herself. *Hey, I like this unemployment shit.* But her smile dissolved completely when she thought of getting too far behind to catch up. She wanted a serious degree, and really couldn't afford to futz around, as much as she might want to.

Meagan dug out her laptop and powered it on, leaning back and resting her eyes as the old hog fired up. As the computer loaded, Meagan thought with dismay of how she might fit in time for extra help. She was startled out of her brief daze by the sound of the computer logging in. She clicked to connect to internet, and was rewarded by the wheezing static of the dial-up modem. After several long, grueling minutes, Meagan was able to open her email account and draft a message. *Dear Dr. Reid,* she wrote. *This past week, I have been going through a tough employment situation, and I'm afraid I've fallen quite behind on the most recent chapter. If you are available, I'd like to request an appointment for extra help. Thank you! Meagan Lucien, 9:30 Adv. Calculus*

She clicked send and waited while the email whizzed off into cyberspace. She took an absentminded swig of her coffee, and just closed her eyes, lying back down on the arm of the couch. She hadn't laid down for long when she was startled by the ding of her computer, indicating an email. Squinting, she rubbed her eyes and checked her inbox. Indeed, there was one new message from *terrence.reid@grandview.edu* . *Already?* Meagan thought, and with a surprised look, she clicked on the email to open it. *Hello, Meagan,* the email read. *I understand your concerns. My appointments for the next week are pretty well booked, but I am at the office right now if you are available, and I would be glad to assist you. Regards, Dr. Terrence Reid, Ph.D.*

Meagan looked at the screen and checked the time. It was 2:10, and Meagan didn't have any other plans. *Wow, what a way to make the day more interesting,* she thought, and she sat up on the couch, leaning down to respond to the email. *Dr. Reid,* she wrote back quickly. *I am available, and I will be there very soon. Meagan.*

After shooting off the email, she powered down her laptop and decided to go get ready. She grabbed her handbag and stuffed her wallet along with her notebook, textbook, and keys, into it. She checked her reflection in the mirror and decided that she could probably afford to wear some better clothes. No need to dress real fancy, just better. In her bedroom, Meagan wiped up a bit and decided on a comfortable but respectable pale-blue shirt and black stretch pants. Over it, she threw a light grey jacket and brown shoes which rode the line between sneakers and boots.

As she stepped out the door of her apartment, Meagan was slapped by a gust of icy rain and wind straight to the face. Shivering, she pulled her jacket tighter around her shoulders and hurried down the steps to her car. Meagan quickly turned on the ignition and clicked the dial for the heater to come on; as well as the windshield wipers. The storm was so blinding that Meagan had to drive along at about 2 mph with the wipers frantically swishing at full speed. As she drove, the rain thinned a bit but was still coming down in quite a sheet.

It took about five minutes longer than usual to reach the university, and Meagan parked in the parking lot and checked the time. It was almost two-forty. She clicked her flip phone back into her wallet and quickly checked her reflection in the mirror before going in. She thought she looked pretty good, considering that she had to sprint to her car in the rain. Looking with a grimace at the swirling tempest outside, Meagan sighed and grabbed her bag, deciding to just get it over with and get safely inside the building.

Alighting from her car, she was only slightly more prepared for the icy blast this time. Pulling her jacket tightly around her, Meagan hurried across the slick parking lot to the double doors up ahead. They were locked on the weekends, but she pulled out her access card and slid it through the panel by the door. A moment later, a buzzer sounded and Meagan gratefully stepped into the building, taking off her soaked jacket and smoothing her hand over her weather-rumpled black hair. Looking around the foyer, she wasn't too surprised to see it deserted, since most of the students went home or worked on the weekends. If they did stay there, they would be hanging with their friends in their dorms or out exploring the city. She glanced around the foyer for a few more seconds before making her way to the stairs leading to the wing that led to the professorial offices. As she ascended the bare stairs, she felt like she was walking through a ghost town.

Every step seemed to echo through the cavernous stairwell while the rain beat down on the windows outside in full torrents and the trees swayed back and forth, straining wildly against the whipping wind. As Meagan reached the wing where Terrence's office was located, she wondered to herself why he would be here on a Sunday afternoon, working. *Why isn't he at home with his wife?* She wondered, but her thoughts dissipated as she reached his wooden door marked: DR. TERRENCE REID. Meagan didn't know why, but she suddenly felt a nervous twist in her gut. She was always hoping for something like this, but she was a bit nervous about the intensity of a one-on-one appointment. *Will he know what I'm thinking?* She panicked mentally. *Does he know I'm standing out here like an idiot?* Meagan stood indecisively for a moment in front of the door, which was opened just a crack. Taking a deep breath, Meagan steeled herself and knocked quietly on the door. "Come in," called the professor's friendly, soft-spoken voice. Meagan breathed deeply again and pushed the door open, stepping into the small but nicely furnished room. She looked over at Terrence, who was sitting in a leather swivel chair behind a large desk of dark wood. He seemed engrossed in his work; piles of papers and books neatly arranged on his expansive desk, sheets and sheets of scribbled calculations stapled and bound together, stacks of textbooks on the floor. He looked up when Meagan entered and smiled kindly, his blue-grey eyes twinkling. "Good afternoon, Meagan. You're a very faithful student," he chuckled, gesturing to the pouring rain outside. Then, still smiling faintly, he indicated a set of hooks near the door. "Go ahead and hang your coat up there."

Meagan complied and then came back over to his desk, where he invited her to take a seat. She gratefully sat down in the padded chair on the opposite side of the desk and pulled out her notebook. "I see that you are very faithful too," she said with a smile. "What are you doing here at work on a Sunday afternoon?"

The professor leaned back in his chair a bit. "To be honest, it is peaceful," he remarked. "And I get a lot of work done. Besides, it is a great place to come when my wife has all her friends over."

"That bad, huh?" she teased. "Deadly garden club or something?"

Terrence chuckled, but then his smile faded slightly and his visage turned more serious. "Not exactly," he replied quietly. "It's just that Dorie likes to fill the house with a bunch of people all the time, she is quite social. Me, I prefer quiet time to work on mathematics or think."

Meagan nodded. "I understand," she responded. "I like to be alone too; especially after a long day. I just lock myself in my basement and dance for hours."

Terrence looked intrigued. "I didn't know you danced," he observed quietly. "That is quite interesting. What kind of dancing do you do?"

Meagan shrugged and leaned back in her chair. "Well, I've done most kinds of dance," she told him. "I have a pretty solid foundation in ballet, but my forte so to speak would definitely be hip-hop and jazz."

"Hm," Terrence replied. "Believe it or not, I find dance quite interesting. I don't know a whole lot about it but I've read some books."

It was Meagan's turn to be surprised. "Wow, now I'm surprised," she laughed. "You seem to be well-versed in many topics. I never thought dance to be one of them!"

He chuckled as well and shrugged. "I guess you could call me well-read," he admitted. "I study a lot of different things." he seemed to trail off into a brief silence, staring off into space. His gaze rested lightly on Meagan for a moment before he quietly but diplomatically asked her in a light, friendly tone what she needed help with.

As Meagan pulled out her notes and began explaining to him what she needed to review, she felt like she was watching herself from above. The office was just so comfortable, and she really enjoyed being with Terrence. He had such a quiet, graceful charisma. Meagan felt his kind personality but on a more primitive level she felt his steel-hard strength, and at the right angle, she caught a hint of his tantalizing tattoos beneath his sleeve. Her reverie was interrupted by Terrence asking her if she had looked over the extra practice section in the chapter. Embarrassed to be caught staring, Meagan jerked her gaze forward. "Um, yes, but it didn't help much," she stammered, and she coughed with embarrassment when she caught the dignified but knowing look in his blue-grey eyes. A moment later, it faded, and they returned to business. They reviewed for about two hours, and Terrence retaught Meagan the sections she needed, as well as handing her some additional notes. When their session had finished, Meagan looked up gratefully at her professor. "Thank you for taking this time to see me," she told him, leaning back in her chair and thumbing through the pages of calculations he had assisted her with. "I understand it quite a bit better now."

Terrence nodded, satisfied. "Good," he replied in his quiet, measured voice. "And I am glad you came to see me; I am always very happy to help. That's what I'm here for."

Meagan looked up and saw the soft kindness sparkling in his eyes. "I'm glad too," she said, just as quietly. She looked at her watch and then back up to meet Terrence's eyes. "Dr. Reid?" she asked almost inaudibly. "I hope you don't think I'm improper, but, well, since it is five o'clock, would you like to go to dinner?" she glanced outside at the rain, which was still steadily coming down. "If you want to, that is," she added, her cheeks flushing.

Terrence thought for a moment, his brow furrowed, and Meagan held her breath in suspense. "Sure, I'd be honored," he replied finally. "Where do you want to go?"

Meagan shrugged. "Anywhere is fine with me," she decided. "There's a little diner called Murphy's; it's a few minutes' drive from here. It's a great place."

"Okay," Terrence agreed, fishing an old scratched flip phone out of his pocket. "I'm just telling Dorie that I'll be home a bit later," he explained, squinting at the screen as he texted his wife. When he had finished his message, he shoved it back into his pocket and stood up from his desk, retrieving his coat, cane, and umbrella. Meagan put her coat on and stepped out the door, waiting while Terrence brought his briefcase and locked up his office. When he was ready, they started toward the elevator.

As they glided down to the ground floor and stepped off into the foyer, Meagan turned to Terrence. "If you like, I can go get my car and pick you up at the door," she offered. "I mean, you won't have to get wet."

Terrence smiled but shook his head. "That is kind of you, Meagan, but I can get wet like everyone else," he replied. "In fact, we can walk out together and I will share my umbrella. It is big enough."

"Are you sure?" Meagan asked, and once again he confirmed.

"Well, let's face the music, then," she said with a smile, holding the door open for him as he strolled through the doors, deploying his large black umbrella. As they walked to the car, Meagan was kind of surprised that despite his slight disability, he was quite efficient in keeping up a good pace. It didn't take them long to cross the lot, and Meagan offered that they could just use her car. He agreed and they embarked. Meagan cranked up the heat and warmed her chilly fingers. "It's sure a cold day, even for October," she commented as she drove. "Feels like it's going to snow."

Terrence nodded and covered a yawn. "I know," he agreed. "At least in my opinion, too cold beats out too hot any day."

Meagan nodded in agreement. "Well said," she replied. It didn't take long for them to approach the well-lit diner, the green sign glowing like a beacon against the dreary, darkening sky. Luckily, the restaurant didn't appear to be terribly busy, so Meagan swung into a parking space near the door and cut the motor. "Here we are," she said cheerfully.

"Good choice," Terrence commented as he opened his door and stepped out.

The freezing gusts of rain were merciless, but luckily it didn't take them long to reach the door. Shivering, Meagan held the door for Terrence, who laughed softly and told her that she didn't need to do that.

Inside, the diner was quiet and sparsely populated, with only two or three other patrons. The atmosphere was subdued but not overly fancy, furnished in forest-green with light cherry wood tables. Red lamps hung from the ceiling, casting a muted glow over the tables. In the back was a small bar counter with an idle-looking bartender standing behind it in an apron. A plump forty-something blonde approached them and seated them at a table near the wall, out of the way. Once Meagan and Terrence had seated themselves across from each other, the waitress asked what they might like to drink. She rattled off the list of all the specials at the bar, but Terrence kindly held up his hand and told her he would go with tea. Meagan knew that she probably shouldn't drink much, and she vacillated for a few moments about whether to get a beer or not. Finally, with her better judgment, she decided to just have water. Usually, for her, there was no such thing as one beer. She wasn't an alcoholic, just didn't always use her best discretion on how many drinks to have. The waitress brought their drinks very soon and then she handed them each a menu. The diner offered many different types of food, from Western to Italian dishes, just all simple stuff. Meagan finally decided to go with a grilled cheese sandwich and tomato soup, and Terrence chose tortilla soup with nachos.

The waitress removed their menus and told them that their food would be ready soon. While they waited, Meagan and Terrence made small talk for a while; class, the weather, etc. When they had worn out all of the natural light conversation topics, they lapsed into silence for a moment. Meagan wanted to say something to Terrence, but she wasn't quite sure where to start. She faltered for a moment before Terrence saved her the trouble. "So, Meagan," he began, leaning back slightly in his chair. "I apologize in advance for not being a great conversationalist, since I do more listening than talking," he paused. "I'd be fascinated to hear more about you. Tell me about yourself, what do you do besides come to class?"

Meagan smiled and sipped her water. "Well," she began. "I go to class every day until noon. I already mentioned that I dance, and I teach a couple of dance classes during the week at night. I used to be a laundress at Nielsen's Laundry, but it is closing, so I am unemployed at the moment; that is why I've been behind in class."

Terrence gave her a sympathetic look and nodded deeply. "I am very sorry to hear that," he said sincerely. "Losing a job can be difficult. Have you looked anywhere else yet?"

Meagan sighed in frustration. "All of this past week," she grumbled, shaking her head. "One rejection after another. I just don't even know what to do."

"Just keep trying," Terrence advised her gently. "Don't lose confidence."

"I mean, it feels like no one in the damned city will hire me," Meagan said despairingly. "And my rent is due at the end of the week. If I can't pay it, the landlord might kick me out!" she rested her head in her hands, and then looked up at him with tear-stained cheeks. "I'm sorry, Dr. Reid, for burdening you with all of my personal problems."

Terrence took a sip of his tea. "It's quite all right," he answered kindly. "And you aren't burdening me. I am happy to help you."

Meagan lowered her eyes and wiped her nose. "Thank you," she murmured. "I really appreciate that."

Just then, the waitress appeared with a tray and set their food down before them. Delicious aromas wafted from the dishes, and the waitress smiled. "Enjoy," she said, turning and disappearing through the swinging door into the kitchen.

Once the waitress had departed, Meagan continued on her job tale by telling Terrence about the one job she was offered. "Well, I do have one job prospect," she admitted. "And there is no question that I could get it. I just really don't want it."

"What type of job is it?" Terrence asked curiously, taking a spoonful of his soup and cooling it off. "I'm just curious."

Meagan sighed and took a spoonful of her own soup as well. "It's a long story," she began, and told Terrence how Aaron Nielsen's son, Michaelis, was always hitting on her and she always turned him down. "So anyway," she continued. "Last week, Aaron, my boss, calls me up after work. He tells me that his son, who is a busy newspaper editor, is looking for a live-in housekeeper." She paused and swallowed, looking up to see if Terrence was following.

"Go on," Terrence prompted thoughtfully.

"So, I'm thinking, what the heck is going on?" Meagan continued. "Then, Aaron tells me that his son has conditions. Such as, I would have to be live-in, and generally do whatever he told me to do. I just thanked my boss and told him I would get back to him."

Terrence listened quietly, nodding and thoughtfully eating his soup. When Meagan finished her story, he paused. "I think you are wise not to take that job, Meagan," he finally said quietly, his slate-grey eyes deep and serious. "It sounds like it could be a bad situation."

They chatted for a while more about jobs, until lapsing into silence again. "Now it is your turn," Meagan told the professor. "Tell me something I don't know about you, anything."

Terrence smiled. "Well, you might be surprised to know that I like to fix cars," he offered. "In fact, I spent the past weekend out tinkering with my truck."

Meagan smiled at him and nodded. "That's very interesting," she remarked. *Not too surprised about that,* she thought to herself with a grin. *Those biceps speak for themselves.* Her smile grew when she thought of him with his shirt off, bending down to pry rusty screws from the truck bed. "I've always wanted to learn how to be handy like that," she continued when she realized that she was just sitting there grinning like an idiot.

Terrence smiled and looked impressed. "It's a good skill to have," he agreed. "The worst is to get stranded on the highway in the dark and not know how to fix your car."

Meagan shuddered. "God, I'm glad that has never happened to me," she exclaimed. "I'm afraid I'd be terrified."

Terrence nodded, and a look came over his face as if he was trying to remember something. Finally, he gave a faint smile. "It actually did happen to me once," he remarked with a grin. "Back in the college days. My friend Henri decided to sneak off campus with his two girlfriends and drive into the forest just for some fun. He basically dragged me along just so that I could stay sober and drive them back home." Terrence chuckled. "Damn, I don't know how or why I ever let Henri rope me into that one," he paused, sobering. "But if

I hadn't been there, he could have gotten them all killed, one way or another. Anyway, we were out in the middle of nowhere at about three AM in the pitch black, so I suggest that we get headed home. As I turn the car around, *Bam!* I accidentally hit a boulder and our tire goes flat."

Meagan listened with rapt attention, a smile on her face as Terrence continued his story. He went on to tell how Henri and the two girls were too wasted to do much of anything about it, all laughing and joking around while he had to go out, brave the cold and change the tire. "While I was out there grubbing around with the wrench and screwdriver, somehow one of the girls lost the keys to the car," Terrence continued, shaking his head, and telling how they had to search for the keys for nearly a half hour with no avail. "Finally, I decided that we couldn't just sit out there and freeze to death," Terrence finished with a laugh. "So I piled Henri and the girls back in, hot-wired the damned thing and drove them all home."

Meagan laughed. "That sounds like quite an adventure," she remarked. "You saved the day."

Terrence shrugged modestly. "Well, I just did my duty as a friend, I suppose," he replied.

Meagan smiled again and shot him a coy glance. "Say, where did you learn to hot-wire a car?" she teased with a little laugh. "I'm impressed."

"Oh, just a little trick I picked up along the way," he answered nonchalantly with a smile. "I always liked to figure out how things worked."

The waitress came back and cleared their plates away, asking if they wanted any dessert. Terrence turned to Meagan. "It's up to you," he told her kindly. "Still hungry?"

Meagan smiled and turned to the waitress. "Dessert might be nice," she said, feeling quite a bit better since the beginning of the evening, and wanting to spend more time talking to her fascinating math teacher. Terrence didn't reply but silently assented with a faint smile.

"Great," the waitress chirped, handing them a small laminated menu. "The special tonight is cinnamon lava cake," she paused. "Just a word of caution," she said with a smile. "It is really hot. Good though. Brave enough to try it?"

Meagan and Terrence looked at each other and smiled, then looked back at the waitress. "Sure," Meagan beamed.

"Okay," the waitress said pleasantly. "I'll be right back with that for you."

Meagan turned to Terrence, who was sitting there calmly and contentedly, strong hands folded on the table, sharp and lively wit crackling in his grey eyes, and a faint smile on his lips. Meagan was momentarily caught off guard by the muted fire in his eyes, and a shot of raw lightning tore through her to the core, jarring her bones and flaming along her nerves. Her lips parted slightly and she sat riveted to his gaze for a moment before drawing away into a noisy cough to diffuse the intensity. When she looked up again, Terrence appeared to be focused elsewhere, a distant look returning to his eyes.

A moment later, the waitress brought their cake and steaming coffee. After the waitress had departed and offered to bring their bill, Meagan took a sip of her searing black coffee, closing her eyes as the rich liquid flooded her mouth. "Ah," she sighed. "I love black coffee."

Terrence smiled, taking a refreshing sip of his own coffee. "Yes, me too," he agreed. "It is quite invigorating."

Meagan lifted her white mug. "Here's to a great evening, Dr. Reid," she beamed, her dark hair falling over her shoulders as she lifted her head.

Terrence lifted his cup as well and gently clinked it against hers. "My pleasure to accompany you, Miss Lucien," he responded amiably.

They sat for a few moments in silence, drinking their coffee and eating their cake. Finally, Meagan brushed a tendril of her dark hair from her face and looked up. "I had a really good time tonight," she said softly, wistfully. "I know it isn't ideal, but I just wanted you to know." She swallowed. "I know I shouldn't ask, but I'd love to do it again."

Terrence met her gaze with a patient, unreadable expression for a moment before he spoke. "I had a good time too, Meagan," he answered quietly, smiling. "And as far as doing it again…" his expression sobered and he shrugged. "I don't see a problem with that."

"I'm glad," Meagan said softly, and for a brief moment, the restaurant was silent, their gazes locked together.

"As long as you do your homework," Terrence joked, to lighten the mood.

They finished their coffee and Meagan decided to box up the rest of the cake and take it home. "Broke grad student," she explained with a grin, gesturing to the leftover cake. "I never turn down then opportunity for someone else to cook for me."

Terrence chuckled. "I know, I remember those days," he recollected. "Frozen TV dinners or stale bread."

They shared a laugh for a moment before the waitress returned with the bill. Meagan dug around in her wallet, trying to scrounge up enough to pay her portion of the bill, but Terrence held up his hand as he scrawled his name on the receipt. "I'll get this," he offered. "It isn't that much."

Meagan started to protest, saying that he didn't have to buy her dinner, but then she just laid down a few dollars. "I'll get the tip," she replied.

As they made their way out of the restaurant, it was pitch black. It had thankfully stopped raining but must have dropped about ten degrees, a cold mist still hanging in the air.

Meagan held the door for Terrence as he made his way to his side of the car.
Meagan hopped in, fired up the ignition, and turned on the heater. She was about to pull out of the parking lot when there was a metallic *clink* of something dropping. "What was that?" she asked.

"Oh, I think I dropped my house keys," Terrence grumbled.

"Don't worry," Meagan reassured him, and went to click on the car light, but it didn't come on. "Well," she said, in a different tone. "My light is out. Guess we have to search by hand."

They both manually searched the abyss that lay between the seats. Meagan felt a key and was just about to hand it to Terrence when their fingers brushed together. "I've got your keys," she said quietly, and for a moment they were silent, almost as if time was frozen in place. His fingers were warm and strong and Meagan had a fleeting impulse to take his hand. This moment was evanescent, quiet, both reaching for the keys, the only sounds being the hiss of the heater and the rasping of their breaths. Just as the moment occurred, it disappeared, and they both straightened up, Meagan handing the keys over and both of them returning to small talk as she drove back to the university to drop him off.

Chapter Eleven

Monday morning, and Meagan wasn't feeling too bad, despite her dreary employment situation. She awoke early, feeling full of energy, and allowed herself a long, relaxing shower. When she was done in the shower, she was humming to herself as she got dressed. She smiled when she recalled the night before, and how much she had enjoyed going out with Terrence. *I'm gonna knock his socks off today,* she thought as she leafed through her closet to find the perfect outfit. *No... no... no...* she thought as she held up one item after another. *No... no... "yes,"* Meagan said aloud, holding up a slinky deep blue V-neck shirt with a brown Indian-style pattern and beaded strings at the collar. With it, she picked a pair of sleek black slacks and shiny black pumps. Of course, under it she chose a matching black bra and black underwear. She rubbed lotion all over her gleaming olive skin, and then dressed and surveyed her reflection in the mirror with an appraising glance. The silky shirt accented her full breasts and showed a tantalizing hint of cleavage but not enough to be trashy, cinched in her waist, and flowed over her curvy hips. The pants showed the long, sleek shape of her legs and the shoes clacked smartly on the floor as she walked. She ran a brush through her long wavy black hair and twisted it up into a full-bodied bun with loose tendrils dangling down to the side. She dusted a quick hint of gold shadow on her eyelids, sealed her lips with gloss and fastened long, dangling feather earrings in her ears. With a final dab of gloss on her lips, she smiled and turned away from the mirror.

Meagan was lost in her thoughts as she was getting ready, and she almost forgot that she had to pick up Jennine and take her to work, since Jen's car was getting repaired. She remembered just as she had grabbed her keys and hopped into her car. Instead of taking her usual turn, she went the other way towards Jennine's small duplex, which was only a few minutes' drive from her own. Pulling up in front of the weathered house, Meagan parked and waited for her friend to come out. A few moments later, the door marked 315 swung open and Jennine stepped out and hurried down the stairs to Meagan's car. Brushing a tendril of her loose light-brown hair from her face, Jennine stepped into the car, tossing her small, compact, no-nonsense bag on the floor as she shut the door. "Hey, thanks for picking me up," Jen said cheerfully, turning away and fishing in her pocket. She pulled out a cigarette and stuck it between her teeth. "How's your job situation?" she asked, turning back to Meagan. "Anything yet?"

Meagan shrugged and shook her head. "Nah, not yet," she replied with a dismissive wave of her hand. "But something will come up." She turned back to the road with a smile and gestured to the sunny fall landscape. "Beautiful day," she remarked.

Jennine simply flicked her lighter, igniting the tip of her cigarette. "You're in a good mood this morning," she observed with a conspiratorial raised eyebrow. "What did you do this weekend?"

Meagan chuckled. "I studied for my calculus test," she replied. "And I think you have a big imagination."

Though Jennine was Meagan's best friend, Meagan didn't really want to talk about Terrence. She wanted to keep it as quiet as possible to avoid a lot of gossip. She had no idea how Jen would react, so she just kept quiet. After a moment of silence, Meagan turned to Jennine, who was still sitting there with a faint smile on her lips. "Hey, Jen, what did I tell you about lighting up in my car?" Meagan said matter-of-factly.

Jennine laughed and ground out her cigarette. "Sorry," she replied. "I forgot. Anyway, that's more like it. Maybe you don't have a secret love affair after all."

"Exactly," Meagan said as they pulled up in front of the accounting firm where Jennine worked. "Have a good day."

Jennine smiled and grabbed her bag. "You, too," she replied. "Call me tonight."

Meagan absentmindedly looked on as Jennine crossed the parking lot toward the giant revolving doors looming ahead. Though Jennine didn't dress overly fancy, Meagan thought that she cleaned up pretty nicely. She was petite and slim, with wavy light-brown hair that fell to her shoulders and was clipped up by a rhinestone barrette. In addition, she had flawless alabaster skin and wide, kind hazel eyes. Today she was dressed in a white cotton scoop-neck shirt, black slacks, a silver necklace and modest silver earrings.

Meagan watched as the last glimpse of her friend's pert, neat frame disappeared through the revolving doors. Lost in thought, she waited a moment before finally releasing the brake and driving out of the lot to head to the university.

On her way to Grandview, Meagan was still thinking about how Jen had chosen to live her life. Jen lived alone, had had a boyfriend once but never wanted another one. She occasionally went out on dates but it never seemed to amount to anything. Meagan couldn't help but to wonder what was going on. Then again, she herself wasn't attached, but very attracted to her calculus professor. As she entered the university campus and parked in the parking lot, she checked her reflection and clacked toward the door, black leather handbag on one arm and steaming coffee in the other.

Later, as she made her way into calculus class, heels rapping on the tile floor, she felt several people's gazes flick appraisingly over her as she set her stuff down and sat in her seat. There was no doubt that she looked stunning today, she thought with a slight smile as she pulled out her notebook and calculator. Just in case, she casually reached into her pocket and sealed her lips with an extra coat of gloss, quietly withdrawing the tube and placing it back in her pocket. She opened her notebook and began reviewing what she and Terrence had gone over, murmuring numbers to herself when she heard the telltale faint *step-clack-scrape* getting slightly louder. She looked up as Terrence strode purposefully into the room, dumping a pile of stuff on his desk. "Good morning," he greeted his class as he made his way to the board and began writing. "Let's continue with chapter three, section four today," he announced in a quiet but businesslike tone. "Referenced on pages 59-68 of your textbook."

The room was silent except for the sound of students leafing through their textbooks and the rattle of the chalk on the board. When Terrence finished scrawling his problem on the board, he turned and waited while everyone located their notes and textbook pages. "Okay," he continued. "Here is the warm-up problem for today. Ten minutes. Let's go," he announced brusquely but not unkindly, looking up at the clock. Terrence sat down at his desk and the students began copying the assignment off of the board. As he waited, Terrence occasionally glanced up to check on the class progress.

Meagan glanced up to get the rest of the problem, and her eyes happened to meet Terrence's. Meagan felt a white-hot thrill of intensity shoot through her as their gazes locked together like a spring mechanism. His eyes were so analytical, and he seemed to be studying her with his usual methodical, good-natured precision and infectious half-smile. She saw a subconscious spark flash in his eyes and her lips parted involuntarily as she lowered her gaze and brushed a tendril of jet-black hair out of her face. When she looked back up, she flashed him a little smile which he obligingly returned in a casual, friendly manner, concentrating once more on his work.

***

Later that day, after work, Terrence was sitting in the rocking chair on his back porch, deeply engrossed in a thick spy novel. It was a beautiful day, mid-October afternoon, and the sun was shining. Intermittent gusts of wind susurrated serenely through the trees send piles of colorful leaves skittering down the street; occasionally landing a leaf on Terrence's book. At the end of the chapter, Terrence gently placed a bookmark in his book and laid it down on the porch while he stretched and took a break. Leaning back in his chair, Terrence gently rocked back and forth and let out a soft groan as he stretched out his powerful back and arm muscles. Though he decided to take it easy today, he worked out frequently. Having a disability in his right leg did very little to impede his physical condition. He was not a terribly tall or big man, only about 5'9, but his frame was rock-hard and solid.

Gazing absently up into the colorful windblown leaves of the trees, Terrence let his mind wander to think about the day. It had been a good day, he thought, productive but not too stressful. When he had gotten home from work, he found a note from Dorie telling him that she was going out to her weekly knitting circle meeting at the church and would be back at dinnertime. *Fine with me,* Terrence thought as he stretched his neck. He had a good marriage with his wife, but was always grateful when he could have the house to himself and do what he wanted. It bugged him that Dorie was always trying to tell him to settle down and "act his age". She didn't think that he should be out mucking around with his truck or up on the roof, painting the garage. Also, throughout the past few years, she had aged sufficiently, putting on weight and mostly sitting around in the house. That didn't bother him nearly as much as her friends did. Man, he couldn't stand Dorie's friends. Most of them were crotchety and self-righteous, and often brought their grandkids over and dumped them on the Reids for hours. Terrence had no problem with children; he just preferred not to be around them. He had told Doreen before they were married that if she wanted children, he was the wrong man for her. She had been okay with that but later on seemed to regret the decision, and asked him a few times if he would consider changing his mind. Always, the answer had been no, but still, Doreen stuck by his side for over thirty years.

Shaking off his thoughts of his marriage, Terrence thought about what he had taught and the progress of his classes. His advanced engineering calculus class seemed to be doing fairly well, he thought. He had given them a benchmark assignment a while ago to determine their mastery of the section, and it had gone better than he had hoped. He reached down to open his black briefcase, which sat by his feet. Pulling out a manila folder, he looked over the next benchmark assignment that he had planned to get the class ready for the test. He looked over his records and was glad to know that most of the students had gotten caught up if they needed to. This made him think of, in particular, his tutoring session with Meagan Lucien on Sunday. *I'm glad she is caught up,* he thought to himself. He was devoted to his students and had been troubled when she had bombed the previous assignment, since she was one of his best. Expanding on this train of thought, Terrence found himself thinking about what a good time he had had when he went to dinner with Meagan following their tutoring session. He had known in his mind that it probably wasn't a good habit to frequently socialize with students out of class, but it was one-time, and they both needed to eat dinner anyway. *Maybe I shouldn't have started something like this,* he thought with a slight frown of apprehension. In class, he had been struck with how attractive Meagan really was. As proper and professional as he tried to be, Terrence was still a hot-blooded male, and he couldn't deny that she was beautiful, not to mention very well endowed and in perfect shape. Worst of all, he was almost certain that she might be trying to take a hit at him. He had seen it before, usually with undergrad students, but Meagan's natural cheerfulness made it hard to discern friendliness from flirtation. Despite how wrong it felt, he found a faint smile coming to his lips when he thought of their dinner together Sunday night. There he had seen it, he recalled. That night, he had seen the intense fire smoldering in her dark eyes; unbridled desire.

Getting up from his chair, Terrence went in to get a glass of water. *What a mess,* he grumbled under his breath. He was torn, because he really didn't want to jeopardize his job or his marriage, but on the other hand he really enjoyed Meagan's company and liked her as a person. There was no rule that grad students couldn't be friends with their teachers, only a rule that they couldn't be romantically involved. Terrence took a refreshing sip of his water and decided to try to just keep a friendship with her and see how things went. *I won't let this get out of hand,* he told himself. *I'm in control.*

Chapter Twelve

It was Friday, and Meagan was feeling a bit beaten down from the long week. In a way, it had been easier than the past week, and she was glad to be at least somewhat caught up on her college classes. Still, the problem of unemployment loomed over her like a dreary dark gray cloud. If she didn't get a job and get one soon, she would likely lose her apartment or not be able to pay her tuition. Sitting on the couch of her living room, Meagan put her head in her hands and tried to think about what she could do. She really didn't want to call Michaelis and let him rope her into the housekeeping job, but she might get desperate at a certain point. Meagan had no family in town, and she knew that Jen could probably take her in for a while, but not for long. Sighing, Meagan decided that she was going to have to call Michaelis and then go talk with her landlord, telling him that she had a job lined up and would pay as soon as she could. Grimacing, Meagan picked up the phone and dialed the number on the scrap of paper that she had left on the table. It rang twice before answered by a female voice. "Good afternoon, Michaelis Nielsen's office, this is Barbara," his secretary said pleasantly.

Meagan cleared her throat. "Hi, I'd like to speak to Mr. Nielsen," she gritted her teeth at the words. "Please tell him that Meagan Lucien is calling."

"Certainly," Barbara replied. "Just a moment."

There was a click and a pause, before Barbara said, "here he is," and the call was transferred.

"Hello?" Meagan asked.

There was a deep chuckle on the other end of the line. "Why, if it ain't little miss Meagan Lucien," Michaelis drawled, with another chuckle. "I've dreamed of the day when you'd call me up needin' somethin'. What can I do for you, sweet pants?"

"Cut the bullshit, Michaelis," Meagan snapped. "I have no money to pay my rent. Are you willing to negotiate about your housekeeping job?"

Michaelis paused. "Well, well," he began. "Maybe we could work somethin' out. As long as I get to see your pretty face. What are your conditions?"

Meagan sighed. "Number one," she said. "I can't be live-in. I just can't. Second, don't try to hit on me, I just need a job. Got it?"

Michaelis paused again. "Hmm," he replied. "As far as number one, for the first week I'll let you live at your place. Then we can talk about it. Second, okay, but bring me a red rose and a bottle of wine when you come over. You can start tomorrow."

Meagan felt just then like she was hitting the bottom of the pits of hell. Reluctantly, she drew a hoarse exhalation and looked down at the coffee table for guidance. "Okay," she agreed. "I'll be there at eight-thirty and get it over with."

After Michaelis hung up, Meagan slammed down the phone. *Damned fool,* she thought. *What have I done for the name of paying the rent?*

Now that she had a job, however deplorable, lined up, she decided to go try to beg for the mercy of her landlord. Figuring that she had enough to at least put a chip of the rent forward, she went to the drawer where she kept her money and took out a hundred, leaving two hundred left for miscellaneous expenses. She figured that if she at least paid some of it, maybe he would be merciful.

Straightening up her hair in the mirror, Meagan realized that she was still in the same clothes she had been wearing all day, and she was starting to feel very uncomfortable. But, she decided, she would wait until after the meeting with her landlord to change her clothes.

Meagan stepped out the door of her apartment into the frigid October air and dreary sky, and knocked lightly on the adjacent door. There were a few moments of delay before the landlord's wife, Mrs. Dolores Kent, came to the door, her hair up on rollers. "Oh, hi, Meagan," she said. "What can I do for you?"

Meagan swallowed. "Actually, I'm looking for your husband," she responded. "It's about my rent."

Mrs. Kent stopped for a moment, a slight frown on her face, thinking. "Okay," she answered. "Come on in and have a seat. I'll tell George you're here."

Meagan stepped into the Kents' apartment and followed Mrs. Kent up the stairs to their second-floor portion of the home. She took a seat on the couch while Mrs. Kent went to find her husband. A few moments later, Meagan's landlord, George Kent, stepped into the living room and took a seat across from her. He was a large, balding man with a pleasant disposition and a booming voice. "Hi, Meagan," he boomed. "Dolores told me you want to see me."

"Yes, Mr. Kent," Meagan answered. "It's about my rent. I'm very sorry that I don't have it all. I'm currently unemployed, so I brought as much as I could…" she held out the hundred dollars.

Mr. Kent strangely did not take it but gazed at her with an incredulous look. "But Meagan," he replied dubiously. "Your rent was paid this morning, in my mailbox."

It was Meagan's turn to look at him in shock. "What?" she gasped. "That's impossible. I didn't…"

Mr. Kent cut her off with a wave of his hand. "It's taken care of," he replied. "You must have a very generous friend then. Don't worry anymore."

Meagan frowned. "But, what if this is a trick?" she replied. "I hope nobody expects me to pay them back immediately, because I can't."

Mr. Kent shrugged. "It didn't seem that way," he answered. "In my account, your rent is paid. If anyone asks for it back, I will tell them that they gave it to you. Now, I hope you have a great evening."

Meagan gave him a weak smile, which grew brighter with relief. "You, too, Mr. Kent," she replied, rising to go. The entire way back down the stairs and into her own apartment, Meagan was stunned. *Who paid my rent?* She thought. She was relieved that she didn't have to worry about it. At least one of her many problems were solved and she would have her apartment for at least another month. Briefly, she thought of Terrence, wondering if it was him.

Now that that issue was solved, Meagan leaned back into the soft cushions of her burgundy couch and relaxed, closing her eyes. The situation with Michaelis was still unpleasant, but she decided to forget about it for the moment. Almost impulsively, Meagan reached for her laptop and logged onto the computer, waiting while the dial-up modem wheezed and hacked its way through the logon procedure. Finally, when the internet was connected, Meagan scrolled to her email account. *I know what will make me feel better,* she thought. *Even though I really, really shouldn't do this…* She went to her email and opened a blank message. Fortunately, she had two email addresses for Terrence; his school one and his home one as well. She just hoped that his wife didn't check his email, but she decided to take the chance that she didn't. In the subject line she typed *"Hello"*. After that, she clicked in the body of the message and began.

"Hello, Dr. Reid, it's Meagan Lucien," she wrote. *"Yes, it's a bit unconventional, but I just wanted to see how you're doing and maybe talk a bit if you want to, just since we had such an interesting conversation the other day at school. If you don't want to, I understand."*

With that, Meagan pressed SEND, and then blew on her fingertip like a smoking gun, collapsing back into her chair with her heartbeat pounding in her ears.

***

At home, Terrence was in his study as usual, researching something on the computer, when his email dinged. *Probably the phone company service tech responding to my question,* he thought, minimizing his browser window on atomic theory and opening up his inbox. To his complete and utter shock, the email showed the sender to be Meagan Lucien. *What does she want?* He thought, absolutely floored. He clicked on the message and scanned over the text with pursed lips, deep in thought. Then, when he had organized his wildly tangled thoughts, he lowered his fingers to compose an appropriate reply.

***

Meagan had gotten up to go get a cup of coffee while she waited in suspense for a reply. Would he be mad? What would happen? When she came back from the kitchen, she sat down at the computer and checked her inbox. *Still nothing,* she thought, wondering if he wasn't there or if he just wouldn't answer. She waited about fifteen minutes, adrenaline screaming through her veins, until she was finally ready to power down and save herself the trouble. Just as her mouse hovered over the SHUT DOWN button and prepared to click on it, a ding sounded and an email notification popped up. Breathing heavily with suspense, Meagan moved away from the shut-down key and opened up her inbox with shaking fingers. Sure enough, one message from *terrencereid34@unitedmail.net* waited for her. She clicked on

it and opened it up, reading the words that proclaimed her fate. The message read: *"RE: Hello.*
Hello, Meagan, thank you for your message. I am doing fine and I suppose it won't hurt to talk for a bit. How are you and how are things going for you? –Dr. Reid"

Meagan breathed out a giant sigh of relief when she read his message. So he wanted to talk after all. Though his message was rather professional and almost stiff, she knew that he would have told her he couldn't if it was a major problem.

The two of them emailed for a short amount of time, discussing rather mundane things like class, the weather, etc. as their conversation continued, Terrence seemed to be more relaxed and his emails were less stiff. Meagan let him set the tone of the conversation, but naturally they got more relaxed as they continued. When somehow they got talking about cars or something, Meagan smiled as she wrote: *"Speaking of cars, you promised to teach me how to fix cars. Are you going to keep your promise? ☺"*

***

Terrence looked at his computer screen and opened the new message he had just received. He knew that he probably shouldn't be emailing with Meagan, but he decided that a little bit of small talk would do no harm. Ever since he had gotten home, Dorie had been on his case for one thing or another. *Screw the rules,* he thought to himself, and decided to just let it go and do what he really wanted to. Almost as if daring someone to oppose, Terrence looked around and lowered his fingers to the keyboard. He typed, *"I'm planning to fix up my friend's pickup sometime tomorrow while he's out of town. You can come help if you like, bring grubby clothes for sure. I'll give you the address. Does nine-thirty sound okay?"* With that, Terrence clicked send.

***

Meagan opened the message and read it, completely astounded. *Really?* She thought. *Awesome.* With a smile on her face, she realized that her day had just gotten immensely better. Then, with a slight frown, she remembered that she had promised Michaelis that she would clean for him. Taking a breath, Meagan decided that her rent was paid, so she could take her time getting a job. Grinning, she typed back, accepting Terrence's invitation. After that, she picked up the phone and dialed Michaelis's number. He answered on the second ring. "Hey, sweet pants," he drawled. "Back for more already?"

Meagan could barely keep the smirk off her face. "Yeah," she replied. "I quit."

And then, as he remained sputtering and outraged on the other end, she smiled sweetly and hung up.

Chapter Thirteen

The next day, Saturday, dawned a beautiful, crisp autumn day with sunny skies and a strong breeze. Meagan smiled to herself as she walked from the kitchen into her sitting room, clutching a cup of steaming coffee. It was about 8:40 A.M., her hair was still wet and twisted up into a bun, and she hadn't dressed yet. Yawning pleasantly, she sat down on her faded couch and sipped her coffee, taking a cursory glance at the morning paper before setting it down. Padding across the room in her slightly worn fluffy slippers, Meagan went to her front door and opened it up so that some of the sunlight could come in through the glass door. Satisfied, she smiled faintly and sat back down, propping her feet up on the coffee table and leaning back into the familiar softness of the couch cushions.

As she sat, Meagan wondered how it would go with Terrence today. She was flattered and glad that he actually agreed to talk to her, let alone see her for a non-academic purpose! *He likes me more than he wants to admit,* Meagan thought with a smile. She sat there for a few moments until the ding of the microwave sounded, signaling that her instant oatmeal was ready. Rising, she left her coffee on the table and went to get her oatmeal. *Could be better but could be worse for breakfast,* Meagan thought as she carried the bowl of hot cereal back to her place in her sitting room. Once she was seated again, she poured milk on her cereal to cool it down and idly stirred it while she stared absently though the glass door.

Breakfast was a simple affair and it didn't take Meagan more than ten minutes to finish and dump her dishes in the sink to be washed later. When she had eaten and read the paper, she headed into her bedroom to get dressed. Terrence had told her that she should wear clothes that she wouldn't mind getting dirty. She vacillated for a moment before deciding on a grey Grandview University T-shirt and an old pair of black stretch pants. After donning her working regalia, she went to the mirror and twisted her long black hair up again, bobby pins between her teeth as she tried to fix it so that it would stay up. Looking more closely at her reflection, Meagan was pleased to note that she actually looked quite nice without any makeup. Her olive skin was fresh and gleaming, her dark brown eyes long-lashed and bright, and her lips coated with a healthy layer of chap-stick. Satisfied, Meagan put on some deodorant and lotion, and packed a change of clothes in a bag just in case Terrence wanted to do something after they fixed the car. After packing a few extra supplies and lacing up her sneakers, she grabbed the box of fresh pumpkin muffins she had picked up at the bakery the night before. She was going to bring them over for a snack.

It was a bit of a drive across town to where Terrence's friend kept the garage they would be working at. Surprisingly, the place was in a rather rural-looking neighborhood, with a few tumbledown buildings and fields visible on the horizon. The old maple trees that lined the other side of the street had already begun to shed their leaves, painting the branches brilliant hues of golden yellow, sunset orange, intricate brown, and flaming red, all interspersed with the remaining clinging green leaves. *It's beautiful;* Meagan thought as she parked in front of the place and got out. As she stepped from her car out into the panoramic fall morning, Meagan squinted up into the cornflower-blue sky as a cascade of playful colored leaves swirled merrily in the breeze. She was slightly apprehensive as she walked along the sidewalk toward the driveway, where the doors were yawning open. Meagan stood in the driveway and waited. A few moments passed with nothing but the sound of the breeze. Finally, a smiling Terrence stepped out into the sunshine, giving Meagan a warm greeting. Meagan felt immediately at ease and greeted him in return, having caught his infectious smile. *He cleans up real nice,* she thought to herself, her breath catching softly in her throat as she surveyed him. Terrence had on a pair of faded jeans, a black T-shirt, and brown lace-up work boots. The shirt showed tantalizing hints of his rock-hard frame beneath, and hints of the tattoos on his biceps were visible. "I see that you're all dressed to work," Terrence commented with a smile.

Meagan nodded. "Yup," she answered. "I am. You look pretty ready for work yourself," she commented, tilting her head to the side.

"Guilty," Terrence chuckled.

"Nice place you've got here," she remarked.

"Thanks, but it isn't mine," Terrence replied with a smile. "My friend Aaron owns it, and he lives in that white house next door," he gestured to the white bungalow adjacent to the garage. "He's out of town and asked me to come fix his truck."

Meagan smiled. "Oh, wow, that's cool," she commented. "I didn't expect it to be so pretty out here." After a pause, she addressed him again. "Will your wife be upset that I'm here helping you?" she asked, immediately wishing that she hadn't said that.

Terrence shrugged. "I don't think so," he replied. "But that's not an issue; Dorie is helping with her church fair all day until five."

Meagan breathed an audible sigh of relief, and then turned to Terrence with a smile. "Oh, that sounds nice," she said to conceal her visible relief. "You two must be very involved in your church."

Terrence smiled faintly and shook his head. "No, not really," he answered. "I don't go. Doreen goes and does the events but I think she just likes something to do."

Meagan was interested. "I don't go to church either," she replied. "Are you an atheist?"

Terrence shrugged. "Atheist, I'm not sure about that, pretty much just nonreligious." He answered. They chatted for a few more minutes until they decided to go out and take a hack at the truck. Terrence dredged up a heavy duty hose and shop vac from the squat building and Meagan dragged a can of motor oil and spray paint out into the morning sun.

Outside, they set up their equipment on the cement driveway. Meagan looked around with a smile. "So, where is the beast to be fixed up?" she asked

It was Terrence's turn to smile. He turned and opened the other garage door, gesturing to a lumpy hulking figure hidden under a tarp. "My friend dropped it off yesterday before he left town. He wanted to know if I'd like to refurbish it for him for a good price, and I said I would." Terrence gave Meagan a conspiratorial wink. "It's my side racket," he explained. "I'm more than just a geeky calc teacher."

Meagan laughed softly as Terrence pulled the tarp off of the old truck and hopped in to drive it out into the driveway so that they could work on it. "I can see that," she murmured, almost more to herself than to him, her brown eyes soft with admiration.

The engine started with a belch and Terrence managed to move it out far enough that they could work on it. He then cut the motor and hopped out. "Okay," he began. "First, let's see what we need to do with this buster," he rolled up his sleeves, and with a light grunt, jacked up the hood of the truck and bent down to inspect. "Come here," he told Meagan with a smile. "I'll show you the ropes."

Willingly, Meagan came over and stuck her head under the hood, paying attention to his detailed instructions of the different parts of the car. After he had finished critically surveying the vehicle, Meagan turned to him with a smile. "So, Doctor, what's your diagnostic analysis?" she asked him.

Terrence thought for a moment before wiping his hands on his pants. "Hm," he replied. "Engine looks solid. Maybe a little tuning up is all." He stepped back and gave the rest of the truck a critical once-over. "We'll do a little body work; and maybe have time to paint."

Meagan's interest was captivated, and she asked many questions at first, but then jumped right in. "I love this," she told him with a beaming smile. "I haven't been this happy in a long time."

Terrence smiled faintly. "I can tell," he replied quietly. "And I'm glad. I love mucking around out here too."

Meagan shared a smile with him for a moment, their eyes lightly resting on each other before they both straightened up and turned away. "I propose doing the oil change and tire change first," Meagan suggested. "That way, we will get that done."

Terrence looked impressed. "Wise decision," he replied. He headed into the garage for a moment and came out with some metal pieces. Then, he motioned for Meagan to grab a pile of bricks sitting on the floor.

"What will we do now?" Meagan asked him.

He smiled and held up the folding metal pieces. "These are jack stands," he explained. "We are gonna stick these up under here to get to the car off the ground, so we can get to the oil plug."

"Cool," Meagan replied as they prepared to set up the jack stands. "How do you know all of this? Were you a mechanic or something?"

Terrence shrugged modestly. "Yeah, I worked in a garage all through high school and college," he replied.

"Helped pay my way through school. Also, as an engineer, I've been working with machines all throughout my life."

They talked some more while they jacked up the car and set bricks by the wheels to keep the car from rolling away. It was hard work but Meagan liked it, and found the physical challenge satisfying. As the sun beat down they both began to sweat slightly, and Meagan found herself hypnotized by Terrence's strength and grace as he worked. They were silent for a moment as they finished preparing the jack stands, but something was bothering Meagan. She frowned for a moment before looking up slowly, a brick still in hand. "Dr. Reid?" she asked tentatively, not knowing how he would react to what she was about to say.

He was busy with a screwdriver and had his head bent down. "Hm?" he replied absently, focusing on what he was doing.

Meagan took a breath. "Well, since I'm not in class, well, would you mind very much if I called you Terrence?" she asked hesitantly.

Terrence thought for a moment, he finished tightening the screw and set his screwdriver down, wiping his hands on his pants again. He turned to Meagan with a smile. "I appreciate that, Meagan, but I'm afraid that's a terrible idea," he said kindly, honestly.

Meagan felt slightly stung but sort of expected it. "I'm sorry," she said quietly, eyes downcast. "I know it was a stupid question."

But when she looked up, Terrence was smiling again. "In theory it might be a terrible idea, but I didn't say no," he answered impishly. He pointed a finger at her. "One condition. Just don't slip up in class; it will get us both in unnecessary trouble. I mean that."

Meagan grinned. "Okay, Terrence, it's a deal," she replied, and they got back to work on the truck. Once they had finished jacking it up, Terrence retrieved a can of motor oil as well as a large container. "This is to catch the used oil," he explained. "We'll take this in for recycling after we're done."

After he explained, Meagan told him that she felt confident enough to get under and drain out the old oil. Terrence raised his eyebrows with slight surprise. "Great," he answered. "Just make sure you are careful," he handed her a wrench and the oil container and told her where to find the oil plug. "And if you need help, I'm right here."

Meagan flashed him a smile and took the wrench and container, getting down so that she could slide under the car. Although she had never specifically been under a car, she was a dancer, so natural grace was no problem. She enjoyed Terrence's involuntary gaze on her as she wriggled under the truck, wrench and container in hand. Her shirt rode up slightly, revealing a slice of tan, muscular abdomen. She pulled it back down and glanced surreptitiously at Terrence, who simultaneously averted his gaze and readied the can of motor oil. Under the car, Meagan located the correct nut and used the wrench to loosen it, placing the oil container under it, and quickly jerked her hand out of the way as a cascade of used oil flooded into the container. When this step was finished, she reemerged from under the car and Terrence congratulated her on her work. Next, they changed the filter. Terrence set the old filter on a piece of newspaper and they removed the remnants of the rubber seal left behind on the engine. They took some time to properly screw in the filter, and both ended up covered in grime. They filled the engine with new oil and had just emerged to give it a test run when Meagan saw a young woman with a poodle on a leash walk past, her lips pursed with clear disdain when she saw a grimy, oil and dirt stained Meagan come out from under the car. "Good morning, Terrence," the girl called daintily with a wave of her alabaster hand, smiling at Terrence. Terrence replied with a lifted hand.

Meagan couldn't help but to feel a twinge of jealousy as the girl walked past. "Who's that?" she replied casually.

Terrence shrugged. "I don't really know her, she's a neighbor of Aaron's, and she walks by here all the time. Not sure what her name is. Diana, I think."

"Oh," Meagan replied, losing interest. She realized with a bit of satisfaction that Diana was in fact probably jealous of her. Meagan was the one with Terrence all morning, not her.

Soon, they finished up with the oil, wiping their hands on their pants, and then decided to tackle the rest of the more complex problems before finally washing and painting.

Meagan helped Terrence clean up the oil change materials, following him into the garage to put things away. When they had finished cleaning up, Meagan asked Terrence what they would do next. Terrence grinned and picked up a hammer, as well as a box of bolts and hardware. "We've got some maintenance to do on the truck bed and rear fender," he explained. "That's where this comes in," eyes twinkling, he indicated the hammer.

Meagan laughed. "Sounds like fun," she replied, following him back out of the garage into the driveway to continue working.

They settled into rhythmic work, Terrence methodically prying rusty nails loose with the claw of his hammer, and Meagan loosening some of the screws so that they could repair the other side. They worked in serene silence while the sun beat down on them from above and the fall breeze ruffled leaves across the street, causing them to dance in the breeze. Meagan set her screwdriver down and reached up to retie her hair, which was sagging. She reached up and a hailstorm of bobby pins clattered to the ground, releasing her luxurious midnight-black hair into the breeze. Terrence swallowed hard and was riveted to the black cascade until Meagan turned her head. But when Meagan looked over, Terrence was set with determination as he wrenched free the rusty nails and pounded new ones into place. In the heat of the sun, he had rolled up his short sleeves, showcasing his impressive biceps and his mysterious, intricate tattoos. Meagan was frozen momentarily, screwdriver next to her on the concrete, while she watched him work. "You're very good at what you do," she breathed almost impulsively.

He was smiling faintly when he looked up and shaded his grey eyes from the sun. "Well, I must say I'm better at calculus than fixing cars," he answered with a modest shrug. But Meagan could tell that he was secretly pleased when he gave her a sideways look and added, "But I do appreciate your compliment."

Meagan smiled at him in return. "It's true," she replied softly, averting her gaze and picking up the screwdriver once more. *I love the way his eyes sparkle in the sun,* she thought. *It's like he's made of fire and steel.*

Meagan was slow in getting back to work, she got lost in a reverie while she listened to Terrence pounding and prying beside her. Finally, she broke the silence with a soft cough. "Terrence, may I ask you something?" she asked him quietly, for the first time using his first name. It felt slightly foreign on her tongue but she liked it.

"Of course," he murmured, still engaged in his work.

"Did you always want to be a calculus professor?" she asked. "And if you don't mind telling me, I'd like to hear about your accident and how you ended up at Grandview."

Terrence looked up, meeting her eyes. "Well, I must say that I didn't think that I'd end up teaching, at all. I worked in repair throughout high school and through college to pay my way. After eight years and a lot of money spent, I earned my masters' degree in engineering mathematics and I became an engineer and architect."

Meagan tilted her head to the side. "That's fascinating," she remarked. "Why did you decide to switch?"

Terrence shrugged. "I wasn't an engineer that just sat at my desk all the time," he continued. "Though I had desk work, I was generally out in the field, grubbing around with the rest of the people. I designed, but I built too," he got a wistful, almost sad look in his eyes and set down his hammer. "I loved it. Being out in the field was the time of my life." His gaze sobered. "Then, when I was in my mid-thirties, we were on the job one day, preparing to tear out this concrete walkway and build a better one. Needless to say, one of the crew members forgot to secure it and the entire thing collapsed, killed my best friend too."

Meagan looked at him sympathetically. "Oh, Terrence," she said, touching him on the shoulder. "I'm sorry I brought it up again."

He gave a weak smile. "It's all right," he answered. "I'll finish my story. Anyway, once the concrete started crumbling, we ran. Everyone got out in time except for my friend and me. Luckily, though, I was in the right place and I didn't get killed. I was spared, except for my leg. Somehow a pile of concrete landed on me and crushed my right leg. I was taken to the emergency room and the doctor said that it was a miracle that I was alive and could walk. However, the blow was so severe that I suffered some nerve damage, and my leg would be permanently crooked."

Meagan asked him some more questions, and he told her of how he couldn't work for quite some time after his accident, and had to undergo rigorous physical therapy. He had been heartbroken that he wouldn't get to work in the field anymore, so he decided to pursue a Ph.D. Grandview was just starting out, and he was one of the best known engineers in the county. So they offered to give him a scholarship if he agreed to teach and head the mathematics department. "That was exactly what I needed," Terrence commented. "I love mathematics, and I was glad that I would be able to give my gift to the next generation of young engineers and mathematicians."

Meagan was fascinated. "You have quite a story, Terrence," she said softly. "You're a special person."

They worked until Meagan thought she would drop from exhaustion, painting, washing, bolting, hammering, and more. By the time they were done, it was well after noon and Meagan was filthy, covered in sweat, dirt and motor oil. Terrence was as well, but Meagan thought that it just made him look hotter. "Hey, I can't believe you're not tired yet," she exclaimed, giving Terrence a playful elbow, and he laughed. Meagan pretended to be outraged but secretly she was impressed. She grinned at him and then checked her watch. "I'll go home and clean up, then want to meet me at that little diner called Cliff's, about one-fifteen? It's not far from here."

Terrence didn't reply at first. He dragged the shop vac back into the garage, his face set in a pensive frown. Meagan looked on anxiously, twisting her lip and wondering if she had finally pushed him too far.

"I mean, we don't have to," Meagan called over her shoulder as he went in, trying to diffuse the awkward silence. "It was a silly idea."

When he was safely out of view inside, Terrence sighed, vacillating heavily. He knew it wasn't really appropriate to make a habit of socializing with students, especially Meagan Lucien. But the way she looked out there, her dark hair blowing in the breeze, had left Terrence's reserve shaken. He sucked in a deep breath as he recalled her honeyed eyes glazing over him with admiration as he worked. Stepping back out into the sun, he saw her tensed with anticipation and decided to let it slide, just this once.

"Okay," he agreed, flashing her a thumbs-up, and her face broke into a beaming smile.

Chapter Fourteen

It was Monday again, and Meagan wasn't feeling too bad. She had had a blast on Saturday with Terrence, helping him fix up the old decrepit pickup truck. After they had changed the oil, fixed the fender and given it a wash, they went out to lunch while it dried so that they could paint it. They had gone to Cliff's Diner, which was a few minutes' drive from Aaron's garage. At the restaurant, Meagan had talked to Terrence more deeply than she had ever talked to anyone else; really clicked with him. Their conversation was deep and intellectual, but a hidden spark lurked under the surface, threatening to ignite and blow the world off of its axis. Meagan shuddered with pleasure and apprehension at the thought of that powerful feeling. She knew that if the lethal spark of attraction between them was able to get loose, both of their worlds would combust simultaneously in passion and upheaval. On the one hand, Meagan knew she was playing a dangerous game, but deep inside she longed to set the fire free.

When standing at her wardrobe, Meagan knew that she shouldn't push it by wearing a really hot outfit, but with a trace of a smile on her lips she decided to ignore her common sense, picking out her new leather jacket, ruffled black skirt, and edgy lace-up boots. Her top was cream-coloured and lacy and she finished her outfit by twisting her hair up in a dangling twist, and implementing a red wooden necklace and red earrings. Her makeup was minimal but striking, with only a bare touch of light red lipstick. *Perfect,* Meagan thought to herself as she studied her reflection in the mirror. Her outfit showed just enough skin but not too much. She looked sexy and confident but not trashy or gaudy.

On the way to the university, Meagan stopped at the coffee shop drive-thru, ordering her usual triple-shot macchiato and a pumpkin muffin. She was just in time for rush hour today, so she intermittently sipped her macchiato and ate her muffin while she sat in the slow-moving line of morning traffic. As the traffic line began to move along, Meagan sipped her macchiato and lightly pumped the accelerator. Luckily, the traffic cleared and she was at Grandview in a matter of minutes. In the parking lot, Meagan finished up and checked her reflection, wiping her face and reapplying her light red lipstick, sealing it off with a coat of shiny gloss. Ready to go, Meagan grabbed her bag and headed toward the doors.

Once she was in the building, Meagan realized that she wasn't as late as she thought she was, and she joined the stream of students making their way to their classes. She greeted a few of her advanced calc classmates and they walked into the room, most of them engaged in studying, books still in hand. Meagan had her book in her hand as well, but when she entered the classroom, she managed to catch Terrence's eye and mouth "good morning" with a little wave. He in return lifted his hand and a ghost of a smile lingered on his lips, along with a barely perceptible wink. Meagan beamed as she made her way to her seat, and sobered quickly as one of her classmates idly glanced up. Meagan didn't have to be looking at him to know that Terrence was pleased with her outfit today, especially the view of her shapely hips and toned calves from the back of her ruffled skirt. She sat down and got her notebook out as Terrence greeted the class and gave them fifteen minutes to solve the daily problem that he scrawled on the board. As she worked in silence, Meagan's mind wandered, and she couldn't help but to wonder what it would be like to make Terrence lose control. *I'd bet he's a beast in bed,* she thought, in reference to his steely frame and excellent physical condition. Halfway through the fifteen minutes, Terrence's voice shattered the silence, gently breaking Meagan's reverie. "Okay, we've got seven minutes left," he said quietly, seeming to look right at Meagan as if he knew what she were thinking. Unconsciously, Meagan's face burned red and she averted her eyes, focusing hard on her notebook.

***

Later, around 3: 00 PM, Meagan was sitting on the couch in front of the TV, garbed in sweatpants and watching the rain streak down on the windows outside. Bumming, she reached for the remote and switched channels, trying to find something that captured her interest. It was sort of a letdown day after Saturday's glorious high, and she was worried about her job situation. Just as she was about to shut the TV off and find something else to do, the phone rang. Listlessly, Meagan lifted the receiver, hoping it would be Terrence. "Hello?" she answered.

"Hey, Meagan, it's Jen," the voice on the other end said cheerfully.

Meagan was surprised, since Jennine would still be at work. "Jen?" she repeated. "What's up?"

"Listen," Jennine said seriously. "I have a job prospect for you. One of our clients just came to town and opened a little toy shop on 5th Street. She needs an assistant, and I recommended you."

Meagan was silent for a moment. "A toy shop?" she asked finally. "I appreciate it, Jen, but…"

"No buts," Jennine cut her off. "You need a job, right? It's called Toy Box, and it is on 5th Street, by the gas station.

The lady who owns it, her name is Melanie Kauffman. She's from San Francisco, part Swedish or something, so expect her to be, well, a bit feisty," Jennine finished.

"Well…" Meagan began, but Jen cut her off once more.

"She closes at five. Take it or leave it," Jen finished, hanging up abruptly.

Meagan sat, holding the receiver for a moment, before indolently pushing herself up off the couch with a sigh and heading into her bedroom to change her clothes.

The rain was still streaking down relentlessly as Meagan headed over to the Toy Box, and she could barely see the road in front of her. Wipers on full speed, she scanned the road for the little toy shop, and soon found it, as Jennine had described, in the plaza across from the gas station. She flicked on her turn signal and pulled into the parking lot, grabbing her umbrella as she stepped out of the car. Up ahead was a small little storefront with a sign that looked like blocks spelling out TOY BOX. She hurried across the rain-soaked asphalt and made it safely to the awning, pulling open the glass door and closing her umbrella.

Inside the store was carpeted, displays of toys neatly placed around in shelves. Up front there was a counter and cash register, and a busty blonde stood behind it, filling out some kind of paperwork. She didn't even look up when the chime sounded, so Meagan approached the desk, wet umbrella in hand. "Ms. Kauffman?" she asked tentatively, and the woman looked up.

"I'm Meagan Lucien," she said, extending her hand. "My friend Jennine Aaronson told me that you're looking for an assistant."

The woman shook her hand lightly. "Jennine said you'd be here at four," she replied. "It's four-thirty."

"I'm sorry, Ms. Kauffman, but she didn't tell me that," Meagan told her.

Ms. Kauffman waved her hand dismissively. "Not a problem," she replied. "Now, tell me why you want to be my assistant."

Meagan slid her résumé across the desk. "Here's my résumé," she explained. "I'm a grad student at Grandview University, getting my masters' degree in engineering mathematics. I've worked at Nielsen's Laundromat until they closed."

Miss Kauffman waved her hand again. "That's enough," she said brusquely. Looking down, she appeared to be thinking for a moment before she looked up again. "Hours are 10:00 AM to 5:00 PM, Monday through Saturday."

"Okay," Meagan replied. "My classes go until noon."

"That's fine," Ms. Kauffman replied. "But I want you here no later than twelve-fifteen. I'll explain the rest later. You're hired."

"Really?" Meagan wanted to know. "When do I start?"

Melanie Kauffman gave her a smile. "Now," she answered.

Chapter Fifteen

Now that Meagan had begun working at the Toy Box, her life had changed dramatically. She was so busy that she barely had time to think anymore. Melanie had told her that she wanted her at work at opening time, so Meagan had to push off one of her university classes to the night, only able to squeeze in some before work. She woke up early, headed to the university until ten, and then to the Toy Box until five PM. On Wednesdays, she had to make up her night class at seven PM.

Indeed today was Wednesday, also known to Meagan as the Day from Hell of every week. She was tired from the first two days of the week, and had been up since six-fifteen, and checking her watch, she saw that it was now 10:00 AM. She had to leave her last class a bit early so that she could get to the store on time, but today she was late. Flashing an apologetic smile at her professor, Meagan grabbed her bag and headed for the door. *Shit,* Meagan muttered to herself as she hurried down the hallway and down the stairs, her heels clicking hastily on the tile floor as she rushed out of the university. Jennine had been right about Melanie's feistiness, and already Meagan knew that Melanie disliked it when she was late.

She hurried to her car and made her way to the store, fighting through the heavy, slow-moving traffic. By the time she pulled up at the Toy Box, it was 10:15 AM. *Shit,* Meagan cursed again. Melanie was going to string her up to dry. Smoothing down her rumpled black hair and applying a last-minute coat of extra gloss, Meagan grabbed her purse and headed in, taking a deep breath before pulling the handle and sounding the chime over the door.

"Good morning, Melanie, sorry I'm…" Meagan began hurriedly, stripping off her coat and taking it to the room marked Employees Only.

Melanie looked up from her inventory sheet and tossed her blonde hair, peering over the frames of her red glasses. "Yes, I know, you're late. What else is new," she remarked dryly, sounding almost amused.

Meagan ignored Melanie's comment and hung up her coat in the closet, emerging a moment later and coming to stand at the desk. "So, what do you want me to do?" Meagan asked, feeling somewhat foolish with her name tag on, a little card with letters that looked like blocks, spelling out MEAGAN.

Melanie looked up, seeming disinterested. "I'm going to go in my office and inventory all of the new shipments," she answered. "So I'll leave you in charge out here. Help customers find things, check out, and most importantly," Melanie looked right into Meagan's eyes as she finished. "Most importantly, see that the little gremlins don't break anything. If I were you, I'd take a few minutes to familiarize yourself with the store before the customers start coming in."

With that, Melanie rose from her desk and went into the back room, closing the door behind her with a hollow click. After Melanie had withdrawn into her office, Meagan sighed and rose, standing and looking at the cavernous shelves which loomed before her, teeming with endless varieties of toys in all shapes and sizes and brands. *Damn,* Meagan cursed softly as she surveyed the never-ending shelves. *How am I ever going to figure all of this out?*

Meagan slowly moved around the store, trying to get a feel for the areas in which each type of toy was located. *Dolls in 2A, drums in 2B*, she recited to herself mentally. After a while, she turned back to the desk and thought that it would be smart to write down what was located where. Still unsure about how to tackle the job, Meagan had just started when the doorbell chimed, signaling that a customer had entered the shop. Meagan emerged from the maze of shelves and walked toward the desk, where she saw a mother with three little kids, two boys and a girl, standing there and looking around. The oldest boy was about seven years old, the second one maybe five or six, and the girl was maybe three, sucking on a pacifier with drool running down her face. Meagan tried to hide her disgust as she faced the customers. "Good morning," she greeted them. "May I help you?"

Meagan tried to keep her voice pleasant, but it was clear that children weren't her favorite. Meagan didn't want children of her own, and she really wasn't fond of other people's children, being even a bit skittish, not knowing how to act around them. Being an only child, she had never experienced having young children around her.

The mother was about to reply when her cell phone rang. "Sorry, gotta take this," she apologized. "I'll be right back."

With that, the mother walked out of the store, leaving Meagan face-to-face with the three kids. "So, what kind of toys do you guys want?" Meagan asked, trying to sound cheerful.

"I'll get my own," the older boy replied abruptly, darting off into the maze of shelves, with his brother tearing after him.

The girl stood there indecisively for a moment before looking up at Meagan. "I want a dolly," she announced.

"Okay," Meagan answered. "Come with me."

She led the girl to the aisle with the dolls and showed her the different kinds. Meagan felt a bit uneasy, since the mother wasn't there to approve or disapprove. "Here are the dolls," she told the girl. "Your mom will be back soon."

As she had finished that, Meagan heard a commotion in the other aisle.

"Give it to me!" one of the boys shouted, and the other one shouted back. Meagan hurried around the corner, and to her horror, found the two boys arguing over an expensive model plane, which they had taken out of the box and were hitting each other over the head with it.

"Come on, guys, be nice," Meagan urged. "There are enough of those for both of you."

She tried to intervene by getting another plane down, but the older boy turned to her and stuck out his tongue. "You're not my mother," he said sassily. "So we don't have to listen to you."

Then, he resumed fighting with his brother over the model airplane. The two children lurched against the shelves, causing a hailstorm of toys to fall down as Meagan tried in vain to break up their fistfight, finally wrenching the model plane free of their grasp and looking down in dismay at the crumpled and stomped box on the ground. "Hey, you're mean," the boys protested when Meagan took the plane away.

With the plane still tucked under her arm, Meagan walked over to check on the girl, leaving the two boys in the aisle. She rounded the corner and saw, also to her horror, that the girl had taken all of the dolls off of the shelf and had them all spread out on the floor, humming to herself as she moved them around. Somehow she had managed to get at the porcelain dolls and was thumping them on the floor. "Run, dolly, run!" she shrieked, clapping her sticky hands together with joy, and taking a drink of her grape juice box.

"Oh, no," Meagan tried to take the doll away from her. "No food around the toys!"

The juice box accidentally sprayed in Meagan's face as Meagan leaned down to take the doll. As soon as she did, the girl began to wail loudly. Panicking, Meagan turned and exited the aisle, dripping with juice, and hurried to Melanie's office. But before she could lift her hand, the door opened and Melanie came out. "How's everything going?" Melanie asked nonchalantly, not looking at Meagan's messy attire.

Before Meagan could answer, Melanie looked up to see the sobbing girl run out from the shelves, carrying a broken doll, and at the same time seeing the juice all over Meagan's face. "What in tarnation?" Melanie exclaimed. "You're a mess! Where is this child's mother?"

Meagan sighed. "She took a phone call," she explained, throwing up her hands. "Left me here with three of them!"

Melanie shook her head. "Though unfortunate, it happens," she said impatiently, throwing Meagan a disgusted look. "I'm very disappointed in you."

Within a few minutes, Melanie got the situation under control, and ordered Meagan to the bathroom to clean up. Meagan was embarrassed but glad for the excuse to leave the main floor. Closing herself in the tiny bathroom, Meagan looked at herself in the mirror. *I shouldn't be here,* she thought with despair. *If it weren't for so many damn bills, I could be an engineer by now.* Looking into her deep, purple-rimmed brown eyes, she saw the many years of hardship beginning to wear on her. Meagan Bernice Patience Lucien had been raised by a dirt-poor ailing single mother in a trailer park after her father died when she was seven, and had essentially had to take care of herself. At age fourteen she took a job in addition to school to support her mother, who had died from cancer when Meagan was almost sixteen. Meagan immediately was plunged out on her own; the only thing redeeming her was her dream of becoming an engineer or architect. Despite her desolate and isolated personal life, Meagan had thrown herself into her studies and managed to get straight A's. All she did was study, and when the pain became too much to bear, she studied some more. After her mother's death, a maiden aunt had taken her in for a while, letting Meagan live in the dark and dingy apartment at the back of her house, but leaving Meagan on her own. As soon as she was eighteen, Meagan had fled and enrolled at Grandview University, getting her own place and a full-time job at Nielsen's Laundry.

There at Grandview was the first time young eighteen-year-old Meagan had experienced some semblance of what she thought was love, when she met Kellan. Kellan Mason had been a junior, twenty-one, a vivacious lad with sandy hair and an infectious smile. Meagan fell fast and hard, but before she knew it, Kellan had stepped on her heart, broken it, and left her devastated and in pieces while he moved on. Once Meagan's deep wounds had closed and she stopped crying herself to sleep, she became flippant and callous, breaking one heart after another, as had happened to her. She loved building men up and then tearing them down again, almost as a continual revenge for what Kellan had done to her. The only exception was Terrence, who Meagan was amazed, and even rather terrified, by his power and charisma. Shaking off her thoughts, Meagan splashed cold water on her face and dried her eyes, which had begun to water thinking about her miserable past.

As she finished dabbing the grape juice stain from her blouse, Meagan bit back the last of her sniffles and walked back out into the store. She was relieved to see that the family from hell had departed, and at the moment the store seemed to be empty. Her relief was short-lived, however, because when Melanie looked up, her face did not yield a pleasant expression. Melanie looked Meagan over and beckoned with a flick of her long, blood-red lacquered nails. Meagan walked over to the desk and stood with her hands folded, waiting for Melanie to speak.

"I'm disappointed," Melanie began coldly. "I will tell you this while there are no customers in here. I understand that this is your first week, but I want to see some major improvement. I regret to say that those customers left without purchasing anything. Please keep in mind that you have a job because Jennine is a close friend and I am doing her a favor. Don't disappoint me again, Meagan."

Meagan shook her head. "I'm sorry, Melanie, I have a lot going on," she replied. "I will try my best."

"Good," Melanie replied. "Now, go straighten up whatever fell off of the shelves."

Chapter Sixteen

It was finally Saturday, and Meagan had crashed hard on Friday night after coming home from a strenuous work day, no time for university classes. She was grateful to have a job to pay the bills, but the job she could get was anything but easy. Meagan wasn't good with kids, and not to mention that Melanie was difficult to work for, very exacting, almost like a boot camp sergeant. All week long, Meagan had struggled to adjust to working there, gradually learning the store and making minute improvements to her customer service.

Now, it was very early Saturday morning, around 6AM, and Meagan was drifting in a plcasant scmi-soporific grey haze. She stretched luxuriously in her bed and murmured lightly in her sleep, thinking how great it was not to have to be wrenched out of bed at this time to rush to the university. Yawning softly, Meagan rolled over and closed her eyes once more as the calming abyss of sleep beckoned her back into its hazy depths. Her thoughts became scattered, blowing in the dreamy wind like a handful of grain, and all of the colors began to blend together, a montage of disorganized pictures drifting before Meagan's closed eyes as she returned to sleep. Just as she was breathing deeply and about to cross the border into dreamland, she was jarred awake by the harsh ringing of the telephone. Disoriented and confused, she bolted up in bed and rubbed her bleary eyes, cursing under her breath. *Whoever is calling me at this hour is gonna pay for it big-time,* Meagan muttered to herself, and contemplated just putting a pillow over her head and going back to sleep. She tried, but now she was already awake, and the phone continued to shrill at her from its perch in the living room. Grumbling with exhaustion and irritation, Meagan staggered out of bed and grabbed the phone, pressing the TALK button and silencing the earsplitting rings. "Yes?" she growled, lifting the receiver to her ear.

"Meagan, it's Melanie," the voice on the other end announced in a no-nonsense tone. "Listen, I apologize for waking you, but I need you to come in immediately."

The first thing on Meagan's tongue was *"Are you fucking serious?"* but luckily she refrained from communicating that thought to her boss.

"What? Why?" Meagan finally demanded.

"There isn't time to explain," Melanie replied tersely. "See you soon."

With that, Melanie hung up, leaving Meagan holding the receiver.

This woman is insane, Meagan thought as she stumbled into the bathroom to freshen up. *Who the hell opens a toy store at 6AM?*

After the phone call, Meagan proceeded to get dressed haphazardly, brush her teeth; jam her hair back in a reasonable bun and splash cold water on her face before lacing up her shoes and hurrying out the door. Meagan decided that she looked the bare minimum of presentable, and that was all she needed. Hopping into her car, Meagan couldn't get to the coffee shop fast enough. She was drooping and exhausted from her long week, and could barely focus as she pulled up to the drive thru window.

"Two large triple-shot macchiato please," she told the woman, slapping her money into the woman's hand. The woman procured the coffee and hurriedly wished Meagan a good day. Meagan nodded and pulled out of the coffee shop, taking a long, invigorating sip of the searing-hot coffee before she got back on the road. *Won't be long before the caffeine kicks in,* she reassured herself.

When she pulled up to the Toy Box, the sky was still dark, and she could see the lights on in the store, but the sign in the window still clearly proclaimed CLOSED.
Meagan grabbed her two coffees and her handbag, hurrying out of the car to avoid the light drizzle falling from the thick clouds.

Lifting her bag higher on her shoulder, Meagan balanced the coffee tray and pulled open the glass door. Inside, she could see that Melanie was already seated behind her desk and seemed to be filling out some kind of paperwork. Meagan hurriedly placed her purse in the back room and came out. "Morning, Melanie," she greeted her boss, expecting to get snipped at for being late.

But Melanie only smiled slightly. "Morning, Meagan," she replied, still all business, motioning to the seat next to hers behind the desk. "Have a seat and I'll explain what we're going to do."

Meagan complied, grateful for the seat, as she took another long sip of her macchiato.

"Here's the deal," Melanie began, swiveling her chair so that she was facing Meagan. "In addition to being a toy retailer, the Toy Box also hosts events. Today, at 10:30 AM there will be a birthday party that we are hosting. Fortunately, the Wharton Social Hall has agreed to partner with me, and for quite a fee, families can pay to have us host their child's birthday party."

Melanie went on to explain how they would go to the social hall and set up for the party. "We don't have a lot of time," Melanie told Meagan. "So I already bought some decorations. In the meantime, we have four hours to set up before I have to be back here at the store. So get your coat and let's go."

Meagan grabbed her purse and followed Melanie out to the parking lot. "So, you said that we need to be back at the store," she said to Melanie before she got in her car. "Are we just going to decorate, set up and leave?" *This shouldn't be too bad,* she thought.

Melanie shook her head. "Not exactly," she replied. "The family throwing the party wants an entertainer. I need to come back and run the store, so I need you to be my entertainer."

Meagan frowned. "You mean a clown costume?" she asked incredulously. "I'm not a professional party entertainer."

"Not a clown," Melanie corrected. "A princess. And I promise, you don't have to supervise the children, the parents will do that. All you need to do is talk to the kids, help serve cake, paint faces, so on and so forth. Just do the best you can."

Meagan didn't reply but instead just turned and got in her car, gunning the engine. *I've got four hours for a tornado to hit and cancel this party,* Meagan thought. She couldn't imagine being a party entertainer, having to stand up in front of a lot of children and act like a goofball. She really wasn't very good with children and often felt awkward and out-of-place.

"What if I stayed back at the store?" Meagan suggested once they got there.

Melanie shook her head. "I'd consider, but at this point I just really don't think you're prepared for that," she replied.

Meagan decided not to argue any further for the sake of keeping her job or before Melanie assigned her a more heinous task. Instead, she tried to focus her blurry eyes on the task at hand as they entered the social hall. Meagan was surprised to find that decorations were already laid out on the table, waiting to be hung up. "How did those get here?" Meagan asked.

"I brought them over before I left last night," Melanie explained. "I couldn't stay to hang them last night so I waited until this morning."

"Ah, I see," Meagan replied absently, walking over to the table and fingering a strand of decorative garland with a banner reading "Happy Birthday" attached.

"That garland gets hung around the perimeter of the room," Melanie instructed, pulling a pencil out from behind her ear. "Also, the birthday cake cutouts get hung from the ceiling. After that, we need to get cloths over these tables."

After she was done with instructions, Melanie moved off across the room to decorate the windows, leaving Meagan with the table full of decorations, lost in her own thoughts.

Still sort of zoned out, Meagan picked up the garland which she had been idly flicking through her fingers. She carried it like a fringed snake over to the wall where she was to start pinning it up. *This place is dingy,* she thought to herself, depressed by the long, low-ceilinged room with white cinderblock walls, dirty windows, vinyl tables, and tile floor. *Reminds me of my grade school cafeteria.*

Shaking off that thought, Meagan drew one of the chairs over to the wall so that she could stand on it to hang the garland up. Unfortunately, when she looked up, Meagan saw that the only way to hang the garland was by tiny hooks in the ceiling which she needed to thread through with minuscule clear thread. *This will take freakin' forever,* Meagan thought. But that wasn't the real reason that Meagan was stalling. As much as she hated to admit it, she was afraid of heights. Although she was a dancer, graceful by nature, she got nervous standing on something even as low as a chair. Taking a breath to calm herself, Meagan finished threading the garland and unsteadily climbed up on the chair. Although she was shaking and unsteady, Meagan eventually managed to establish a system of hanging up the garland.

It took Meagan and Melanie two hours to get the large room decorated. Once they finished final preparations, it looked quite festive. Looking around, Meagan didn't think that the decorations improved much at all. In fact, it just gave the room a stuffy, germy atmosphere which would soon be infested with messy children. About an hour from the start of the party, Melanie handed Meagan a box. "Here's your costume," she explained. "After you get dressed, wait by the door with the bags of party favors. The birthday girl and her family will be here first, so introduce yourself and make a good impression. I'll be here for a few more minutes if you have any questions. "

With that, Meagan headed out of the room to the bathroom to get dressed. Pushing open the door to the dusty, dimly-lit restroom, Meagan wrinkled her nose as the smell of gross hand soap and backed-up sinks flooded over her.

Opening the box, Meagan looked down into the interior, gingerly pulling out the contents. The main item was a bright pink dress that looked almost like a floor-length x-ray vest with sequins on it. It had large buttons in the back that held it on, almost like an apron. To Meagan's chagrin, it smelled slightly sweaty, as if it hadn't been washed. *Ugh,* she thought as she edged into it over her clothes. Immediately, she noticed how hot the costume was and felt suffocated in the dingy, foul-smelling restroom. After the dress came a tiara, which very luckily, was still in the box and didn't appear to be used. *At least I won't get lice,* Meagan reasoned as she looked in the mirror and adjusted it over her black hair. When she was finished putting on her costume, including cheap fake jewelry, also used, she disgustedly walked back into the main room, feeling like she was in someone else's sweaty snowsuit. Melanie looked up when she heard Meagan come in. "Oh, good, you're dressed," she remarked. Coming over, she gently took Meagan by the shoulders and turned her around, helping to fasten the remaining buttons. Now, Meagan was really stuck in the damn thing. "Sorry, I forgot about the makeup," Melanie added, fishing into her bag.

"What makeup?" Meagan wanted to know.

Melanie fished out a case of makeup. "I bought this fresh. But after this, keep it in case you ever do this again." Melanie told Meagan to come closer and close her eyes, and Meagan complied as Melanie proceeded to cover her face with layers of goop. When she was done, Meagan felt as if she had wet concrete caked onto her face. "Okay, you're ready," Melanie announced excitedly. "Here are the party favors. The guests should start arriving any minute."

As she walked with Meagan over to the decorated doorway, Meagan didn't reply. "You'll do great," Melanie assured her, lightly squeezing her shoulder. "If you really need anything, call me."

With that, Melanie turned and waved once more, leaving Meagan gazing blankly after her, with nothing to do except watch the hypnotizing sway of Melanie's curvy hips as she left the building.

***

There was a brief hiatus of about ten minutes before the birthday girl and her family showed up. As they came in, Meagan tried to smile. "Happy birthday!" she greeted the girl in her friendliest voice. "I'm Princess Meagan. What's your name?"

"It's a princess!" the girl shrieked in delight. Turning to Meagan, she looked up. "I'm Isabella," she announced proudly. "I'm five."

Still trying to smile, Meagan turned to the girl's mother, after the girl was out of earshot. "I'm Meagan Lucien, Melanie Kauffman's assistant at the Toy Box," she explained in a low voice. The mother shook her hand pleasantly, but Meagan could see in her eyes that she thought Meagan looked like a total goofball.

About three minutes after the birthday girl arrived, the second kid did, and after that, they started coming in torrents. Meagan handed out party favors and shook hands, glad that she was wearing princess gloves and not having to come in contact with a lot of people. The room filled up until it seemed ready to explode, and it got hotter and sweatier by the minute. When the last guest had arrived, one of the parents closed the door, which just made the temperature more unbearable.

Every minute felt like an eternity to Meagan as she handed out party favors, shook hands, and hobbled around the room in her incapacitating, tight, sweaty costume. She felt almost dizzy in the fluorescent-lighted room that smelled of cheap, lard-filled cupcakes, sweat, and dust. Meagan tried her best, but found herself staring almost hypnotized at the large-faced clock mounted on the wall as the minutes passed with continuous agony.

She handed out the cupcakes and tried not to watch as the kids ate them sloppily. To make matters worse, one of them reached up with sticky hands and got some of the fatty frosting smeared on Meagan's already disgusting costume.

Finally, when she thought she couldn't possibly stand another minute, some of the mothers began to extract the reluctant kids from the corner of the room where they were playing with toys and games. The exit was similar to the entrance; one kid left, two left, then a whole bunch of them left. Meagan breathed a sigh of relief as the crowd began to drain from the room. Unfortunately, the progress stalled when two or three mothers starting chatting right in front of the doorway. Their conversation lasted about fifteen minutes before they slowly moved away like a stubborn iceberg. Finally, the last guest left, and so did the birthday girl. Unfortunately, Meagan couldn't reach back to unbutton the costume, so she simply sat down at one of the cleaner tables and pulled out her cell phone to tell Melanie that the party was over.

Finally, the door opened and Melanie came in. "Hey, soldier," she said to Meagan when she spotted her sitting exhaustedly at the table. "How did it go?"

"It was terrible," Meagan said honestly, pushing herself up off of the bench. "But I did it. Will you please help me take this costume off?"

"Sure," Melanie replied, unbuttoning the costume. "Go ahead and put that stuff in a bag, we'll take it back with us."

Meagan's relief was immense when she shed the bulky, sweaty-smelling costume, but she still felt disgusting, especially with all of the makeup caked onto her face. After she had taken her costume off, Meagan rejoined Melanie. "Tell you what," Melanie offered. "The birthday girl's mother and a few others are coming back to clean up. Give them a hand, and then you can go home for the day; I'll pay you overtime."

"Okay," Meagan agreed, and looking around at the cluttered and dirty room, she thought she damn well deserved overtime.

When the other two mothers came back, they began to clean up. Meagan was disgusted by the size of the mess but just mechanically proceeded, scooping up crumb-infested tablecloths and shoving them in the garbage, spraying down tables and chairs with disinfectant, and finally sweeping the floor. Finally, around 2:00 PM, everything was cleaned up. Meagan washed her hands in the bathroom and burst from the dingy room like a cyclone was chasing her. She stood outside and took a deep, refreshing breath of the chilly November air before hopping into the car, windows down, and tearing out of the parking lot toward home.

Chapter Seventeen

On the way home, the already overcast sky suddenly, without warning, began to release a tremendous torrent of rain. At first, it was only a few drops, but then a strong wind picked up, hurling handfuls of leaves through the cold, damp air. The rain came down harder and harder, and Meagan could barely see as her windshield wipers worked at a frenetic pace. At the flat, Meagan was dismayed to find that her usual parking place across the street was taken, so she was forced to park farther back, almost a block and a half away. As she got out of her car, she was slapped by the damp and icy torrent of rain as it soaked through her grimy clothes and caused the remnants of the awful makeup to run down her face. On her way back, a car swished by, drenching her in a deluge of dirty water. Blinded, cold and dirty, Meagan stumbled down the street to her apartment, finally seeing the hallowed shape of her beat-up white duplex come into view. Gratefully, she grasped the railing and ascended the stairs. Once she got into the entryway and had closed the door behind her, she took off her soaked socks and shoes and left them to dry. Disengaging a wet leaf from her hair, Meagan stumbled to the bathroom, turned the heat up and stripped off her dirty wet clothes, leaving them in a pile on the floor. Glancing at her reflection, Meagan was horrified. Her hair was dirty, undone and plastered to the side of her face, the thick makeup was caked and running down her face, and she looked exhausted and haggard. Immediately, she grabbed a cloth and scrubbed the makeup off before hopping into the shower. In the shower, with the soothing hot water beating down on her, Meagan began to relax as the horrible day slowly melted off of her body, swirling down the drain with the dirt.

As she gradually felt better, Meagan began to think about other things. What she really wanted right now was to curl up on the couch with a blanket and a glass of wine and watch the afternoon news, maybe take a little nap.

After she got out of the shower and toweled herself off, Meagan quickly dressed in some comfortable clothes to prevent the chill that had plaguing her from returning. She wrapped her long black hair in a towel to dry it and slipped into a baggy Grandview sweatshirt and a pair of old, stretched-out yoga pants. On her feet she slipped on some colorful mismatched socks and her bedroom slippers. Finally, relaxed and comfortable, Meagan brewed a pot of tea and grabbed a handful of snack crackers with cream cheese and a cup of yogurt to go with it. To top it off, she poured herself a half-glass of white wine that she had left over in her refrigerator.

With her snack ready, Meagan poured herself a cup of tea and carried her food and drinks on a tray into the sitting room with her so that she wouldn't have to make multiple trips. Carefully, she set the tray down on the low coffee table and took a place on her favorite beat-up old couch, switching on the TV. Outside, the sky was a heavy gray, with low overhanging clouds, the relentless icy drizzle still steadily beating down on the windows, strong wind blowing handfuls of wet leaves in all directions. Shivering, Meagan sipped her tea and wrapped a light blanket around her, eyes focused on the TV but not really paying attention. Yawning, Meagan stretched out and relaxed, leaning back against the cushions. She was tired, but in a good way. After a few sips of wine and spoons of yogurt, she felt even better. Finally, switching off the TV, she curled up under the blanket and closed her eyes, drifting off into a light and peaceful sleep.

A few hours later, Meagan began to emerge from the dreamy gray haze of her nap. She shifted under the blankets and murmured lightly in her sleep. She pushed the blankets off of her head and her eyelids flickered sleepily as her dimly-lit living room began to come into focus. After orienting herself for a few moments, Meagan reached over to check the time on the phone handset which she kept on the light stand near the arm of the couch. Checking the lit-up time display, she saw that it was 5:20PM. The sky outside wasn't dark yet but looked like it would be heading in that direction anytime now. Sitting up, Meagan yawned and ran a hand through her uncombed black hair. She sat there for a moment, absently staring into space as her thoughts drifted back and forth in her mind like ephemeral ever-changing ocean currents. As the world swirled before her eyes, she momentarily rested her head back down on the couch cushion and pulled the blanket up to her chin; closing her eyes again and beginning to drift back to sleep. Just as she was about to slip back into the amorphous haze of dreamland, she was jarred awake once more by the ringing of the telephone. Disoriented and confused, Meagan groped for the handset and pressed the TALK button.

"Hello?" she murmured; her voice husky with sleep. She hoped it wasn't Melanie, calling her back to work, or some stupid telemarketer.

"May I speak with Meagan Lucien, please?" a soft-voiced male caller asked politely.

Meagan wrinkled her brow. "Speaking," she answered, not unkindly. "May I ask who is calling?"

"It's me, Terrence Reid," the soft-voiced gentleman replied, and Meagan damn near dropped the phone.

"Terrence?" she gasped, as a spark flashed through her veins, jolting her alive. "I'm... I mean, I was just surprised that you called," she stammered, already losing herself into a jangled ball of loose ends.

Terrence laughed quietly. "I apologize for startling you with my call," he reassured her. "I just wanted to see if you were okay, since you weren't in class on Friday and you missed the Ancient Math seminar today."

Meagan gasped and covered her mouth with her hand. She had been wanting to go to the Ancient Math seminar, had been planning on it for weeks. But work had hit her like a cyclone and she had completely forgotten that it was this weekend.

"Everything okay?" Terrence prompted, full of concern, when Meagan didn't reply.

Meagan drew a deep breath. "I'm fine," she replied shakily. "It's just that I had to work both yesterday and today. I've been looking forward to that seminar for weeks and I'm devastated to have missed it. I thought it was next week."

"That's okay," Terrence responded soothingly. "I can give you the papers in class on Monday if you like. Also, I've got plenty of leftover treats from the luncheon."

Meagan sighed. "Thank you," she answered. Taking another deep breath, she decided she would just go for it and ask. "Um, Terrence?" she began hesitantly.

"What is it, Meagan?" he wanted to know.

"Look, you don't have to if you're busy, but I'd love to go out for dinner again. If you don't want to think about that right now, it's okay."

There was a pause on the line as Terrence thought about it. Finally, upon reaching a decision, he released a breath. "Actually, that's not a bad idea," he replied. "I mean, technically we shouldn't, but Dorie went to visit her sister out of town for the weekend. I suppose we could go out for a bite. Any preference on where to go?"

Meagan was glad that Terrence had accepted her invitation. "Not particularly," she replied, a finger to her lip while she thought. "But I'm dying for a fresh, hot meal. I've been eating out of cartons for weeks now."

Terrence chuckled. "I understand," he replied. "Those were my college days for sure." They shared a quick laugh before continuing. "Tell you what," he said finally. "You could stop over at my house, I could give you the papers, and then we could cook something," he proposed.

Meagan's face brightened. "That's a great idea," she agreed. "Are you sure you don't mind?"

Terrence laughed. "I don't mind cooking," he replied. "But Dorie doesn't let me within ten feet of the kitchen. I never get to spread my culinary wings, so to speak."

"I'll help you," Meagan offered. "The one thing my mother did was teach me how to cook. So, what do you think? If you'd rather just go to Murphy's or something, that's okay too."

Terrence hesitated for a minute, knowing that it was a bad idea. "Let's do it," he replied finally. "We'll make something nice. I'll give you my address."

Meagan told him that she would be there in a half-hour. Then, she bade him goodbye and hung up the phone. As she set the handset back in the cradle, a smile touched her lips. *The day from hell is about to rise to heaven,* she thought to herself, and her heart skipped a beat as she pictured Terrence's handsome, patient face, twinkling gray eyes and kind smile. Her smile sobered when she realized the extent of how much she was beginning to fall for him. *I can't,* she thought with a plummeting sense of dismay. *He's married.* As much as their friendship was developing, she knew that it just couldn't go any further. But in her heart she ached for him. Shaking off these pessimistic thoughts, she turned and headed into the other room to get ready. She freshened up and dressed in a comfortable, casual, but nice looking outfit; plain black yoga pants and a soft black scoop-neck shirt with gold trim. On her feet she just wore her black boots, figuring she would take them off in the house. She fixed her hair in a bun with dangling tendrils framing her face, put gold hoops in her ears, and wore little makeup. Looking in the mirror, Meagan decided that she looked pretty nice. Her olive skin was fresh and gleaming, her long-lashed brown eyes dark and soft, and her outfit was casual and comfortable. Taking a second glance, Meagan decided against the bun and instead put her hair in a ponytail, leaving the dangling strands to frame her face.

With that settled, Meagan grabbed her bag and her coat and left her apartment.

Immediately, as soon as she opened the door, an icy gust of wind and rain slapped her hard across the face. Wincing, Meagan pulled her scarf up around her face and hurried down the steps after locking her apartment door. It wasn't quite dark yet, but the sky indicated that it would be only a matter of minutes before dusk set in.

Once Meagan got into her car and cranked up the heat, she was grateful for the contrast from the icy blast outside. On her way to Terrence's house, she swung into the little bakery on the corner and decided to pick up a treat for dessert. Luckily, they had a drive-thru, so she got in line and ordered two Danish pastries, one filled with cherry compote, the other blueberry. Smiling, she thanked the cashier and got back on the road, the pleasant aroma of fresh Danish pastries filling the interior of her small car.

The ride was about ten minutes, and the vision was pretty poor, considering the time of day and the light, sleety rain. Meagan looked for his house for several minutes before she finally pulled up in front of a neat, comfortable-looking brick bungalow. She parked across the street as not to raise questions and embarrass Terrence in front of his neighbors. Clutching the pastry bag, Meagan alighted from her car, locked it, and closed the door with a hollow metallic sound. Looking both ways for oncoming traffic, Meagan headed across the quiet street, scarf up around her neck, and walked up the sidewalk to the Reids' little brick house on the corner.

She ascended the slate stairs and ran a hand over her windblown hair before depressing the glowing doorbell beside the wooden door.

She waited a moment, listening to the faint sound of scraping footsteps coming closer to the door. A few moments later, she heard the lock disengage and the door swung open, spilling inviting light and warmth out into the dark and chilly autumn night.

"Hi there, Meagan, come on in," Terrence invited with a broad smile, opening the door fully.

"Hi," Meagan breathed, stepping gently into his warm living room. Terrence was dressed in a casual T-shirt and jeans, and his light blue-grey eyes sparkled with wit and warmth behind the frames of his reading glasses, which Meagan thought just compounded his hotness. In his hand, he was still holding a book. "I hope I haven't disturbed your reading," she said gaily, gesturing to the book in his hand.

"No, not at all," he grinned. "I was just reading while I waited. I love spy and police novels."

"Oh, really?" Meagan wanted to know. "Me too." Taking her shoes off, she handed him the pastry bag. "I brought us some dessert."

Terrence smiled. "How very thoughtful," he remarked good-naturedly. "Smells great. What did you get?"

"Danish," Meagan replied. "Cherry and blueberry. You've got first pick, I like both."

Terrence grinned. "I'm a blueberry kind of man," he remarked, and Meagan couldn't help but to break into a smile as well. They were silent for a moment. "Hey, you can have a seat if you want, or we can go start cooking. It's up to you; you're my guest."

Meagan shrugged. "Either way," she answered. "We could go get something started and then come sit."

He nodded. "Sounds good," he agreed, and together they made their way into the kitchen.

In the kitchen, Meagan looked around. "Is there anything I can do to help?" she asked.

Terrence smiled. "That's quite all right," he answered kindly. "I'll start some spaghetti. Simple but delicious. Go ahead and sit down in the other room, take a rest if you like."

"Are you sure?" Meagan wanted to know after a few minutes. "I can set the table…"

"Already did," Terrence replied. "It won't be long. Would you like anything to drink?"

"If you don't mind, I'd like a little red wine," Meagan replied. Then she laughed. "Don't worry, I'm twenty-six," she assured him.

"No problem," he answered with a grin, opening the cabinet and fetching a clear, sparkling wine glass. "I have no doubts of your legal age. Just don't drive home until you're ready."

Taking her wine, Meagan thanked him and wandered into the living room where she sank down on the couch, closing her eyes. She sipped her wine and savored it, identifying it as Cabernet. *Man has good taste,* she thought as she reclined back, resting. In the other room, she could hear the sound of Terrence humming hoarsely to himself while he prepared dinner, the scraping sounds of his shoes on the floor and the bubbling of the boiling water.

Relaxing, Meagan leaned back into the soft but threadbare couch cushions, sipping her wine momentarily before setting it on the light stand. She continued to lie there in a tranquil state, holding the Cabernet on her tongue and listening to the eclectic music of Terrence softly bustling around in the kitchen. Every so often, he would break off from his throaty humming and murmur to himself about how to prepare the meal or where to put something. Eyes still closed, Meagan smiled. She found that habit of his endearing and intriguing. It wasn't long before the delicious Italian aroma of spaghetti began to drift out into the living room. As Terrence hummed, Meagan could have sworn she knew the tune from somewhere. It was a classical piece, lesser known, and Meagan knew that she knew what it was. She became so engrossed in her thoughts and relaxation that she failed to hear Terrence's scraping footsteps as he came into the room.

"Dinner's ready, Meagan," she was startled out of her reverie by his soft voice.

Embarrassed, Meagan jolted awake, blinking. "I'm sorry, I didn't hear you come in," she apologized with a laugh.

He smiled and waved a hand. "It's no problem," he replied good-naturedly. "I felt bad waking you."

Meagan shrugged. "I wasn't sleeping," she answered. "I was just relaxing. It has been a hell of a long day."

He motioned her into the adjoining dining room where he had already set the table, and she took a seat, brushing a tendril of raven-black hair from her face. An ever graceful host, Terrence dished up some spaghetti for her and filled her water glass from an iced pitcher he was carrying. Then, he subsequently sat down and dished up his own.

The dining room was pleasant, with sort of a rustic look: reddish walls, wood trim, looking out over their yard from a picture window which had been covered with tan curtains after dark.

"I really am sorry that I couldn't help you cook," Meagan said apologetically. "I would have loved to, I'm just too tired."

"Don't even worry about it," Terrence commented sympathetically after a sip of his water. "It sounds like you had a rough day."

"Tell me about it," Meagan grumbled, dishing up some salad from the glass bowl to her right. "So, I got called in at 6:00 AM this morning. I work at a toy store, which generally opens at ten." She paused and swallowed. "Anyway," she continued. "My boss calls me and tells me we're hosting a birthday party. She drags me over to the dumpy Wharton Social Hall and we have to set up for a few hours."

Terrence looked surprised. "The toy store hosts birthday parties?" he wanted to know.

"Apparently," Meagan replied. "So, after we set up, here comes the real kicker. My boss, Melanie, hands me a box and says I'm supposed to be the party entertainer. I get out this box, and it is a sweaty old princess costume. Let's just say that it was hell."

"Mm," Terrence murmured in agreement. "Sounds dreadful. When did you get this job? Last time we talked, you were unemployed."

Meagan sighed. "I know, ever since I got this job it has obliterated everything else. Unfortunately, I need the damn thing to pay the bills. I got it because my friend Jennine is friends with the woman who owns the store. It's pretty much my nightmare job, but I'll do anything to stay at the University and finish my degree."

Terrence smiled. "You're a dedicated mathematician," he said admiringly, quietly. "That is something to be proud of."

Meagan coloured slightly from his praise, and looked down at her food with a smile. "I'm trying," she shrugged. But then, she looked up into his kind gray-blue eyes. "But I want you to know that it's you who gives me that extra boost that I need to keep going. If I didn't have you for a teacher, I probably would have fallen flat by now." She paused, took a breath, studied him sideways. "And thank you for paying my rent."

Terrence nodded, acknowledging her praise. "That's very kind of you to say, Meagan, but I don't want to take credit for your success." He looked down at the table, suddenly intrigued by the wicker placemat. "And don't mention it, I just wanted to help."

They were silent for a few moments, and Meagan thought of how good the spaghetti was. A moment or two into the silence, Meagan suddenly lifted a finger and blurted, "Beethoven violin concerto!"

Surprised, Terrence looked up from his plate. "Pardon?" he said kindly.

"You were humming a Beethoven violin concerto in the kitchen," Meagan said excitedly. "I finally recognized the tune."

Terrence looked impressed. "Violin concerto in D major, Op. 61," he added. "How did you know that?"

"My father used to listen to Beethoven all the time," Meagan said softly, sadly brushing a tendril of hair from her face. "That was a long time ago; I haven't listened to classical music for years."

Terrence looked sympathetic. "I'm sorry, did your father pass away?" he inquired gently.

Meagan nodded. "He did. I was seven years old. My mother fell ill a few years later, and she died right before I turned sixteen."

Meagan explained how after her mother died, a maiden aunt, her father's older sister, took her in until she was old enough to go out on her own. "The only thing that got me through was mathematics," she said finally. "My aunt, she cared for me physically but pretty much left me on my own. But I stuck with my dream, and enrolled at Grandview as soon as possible, moved out and got a place. And here I am," she gestured to herself. "Right where life slapped me down on the map."

Terrence nodded, twirling spaghetti absently on his fork. "That happens," he said quietly. "After my accident, I was afraid my career was ruined forever." He seemed to be gazing off into space, as recalling a distant part of his past. "But if it weren't for that accident, I wouldn't be teaching at Grandview and we wouldn't be sitting here right now." He looked at her with quiet warmth in his eyes, and still somewhat of a spacey look. "Fate is a funny thing," he murmured, almost more to himself than to her. "Each choice opens up another entire avenue of choices, like a door leading to a hallway lined with more doors."

Meagan murmured in agreement but was silent for a moment, pondering his words. It seemed that whatever time she spent with Terrence, their discussions forced her to really take a look at her life and sort of snap out of the rush and chaos of everyday life.

After they finished their meal, Meagan helped Terrence clear the dishes and put them in the kitchen sink to be washed later. Terrence then suggested that they could eat their dessert in the living room because it was more comfortable. Meagan readily agreed and followed him into the living room. He took a seat on the couch and she picked a leather easy chair across the coffee table from him so that they could have a discussion. Terrence told her to wait a moment, and he brought back plates, forks, napkins, and two mugs.

"Care for coffee?" he asked, brandishing a pot of the steaming, aroma-rich liquid. Meagan accepted, and he filled both of their cups to brimming. Then, being brave, Meagan asked if he would refill her Cabernet. Terrence complied and brought the bottle out, setting it on the table. After they were settled, Terrence leaned over and turned on the radio, which happened to be quietly playing the Beethoven symphony he had been humming earlier. Relaxing, Meagan closed her eyes and sipped her coffee, leaning back in her chair and letting her body go completely limp as the music carried her. Finally, slowly, she opened her long-lashed dark eyes to find Terrence holding his coffee cup and studying her intensely with his analytical misty-eyed look. For a brief moment, her eyes locked onto his and a spark seemed to flash between them. But just as that ephemeral moment had come, it passed. Terrence interrupted the powerful silence with his quiet voice. "I can see that you're really enjoying the music," he observed softly, with a kind but serious expression.

Meagan focused on him again. "I was," she admitted. "It is beautiful. I was just thinking about what you told me earlier about destiny and life in general." Her eyes were misty as she gazed down at the floor. "I'm not the girl people think I am, just the dumb hot college girl…" Her voice broke off. "I have dreams, I have been crushed, and all my life I've been hated for my mistakes."

Embarrassed to have poured herself out like that, Meagan sipped her coffee. "I'm sorry," she apologized. "I didn't mean to unload on you like that."

But when she looked up, Terrence wasn't upset. "That's okay," he said quietly, patiently. "I don't mind listening."

They lapsed into silence again and Meagan found herself looking longingly at Terrence, feeling the ache in her heart. All evening she had been steadily sipping the Cabernet and had grown a bit tipsy. Not drunk, just a bit tipsy. And looking across the table through muted brown eyes, she appraised Terrence's strong frame, attractive face, and his patient blue-grey analytical eyes behind the frames of his reddish-brown reading glasses. In the midst of their tranquil silence, Terrence had lifted the newspaper and began to glance through it idly and Meagan had drifted off into a serene, almost delirious state.

As if by remote force, Meagan rose on tipsy feet and walked over to the arm of the couch where Terrence was sitting. He appeared to still be engrossed deeply in the paper. "Terrence?" she all but whispered pleadingly, a mere breath over the soft music in the background.

Surprised, he glanced up but said nothing, curiosity and vitality alive in his eyes along with bewilderment.

"Forgive me," Meagan murmured, barely audibly, and before she could stop herself, she leaned down and kissed him, pressing her glossy, wine-tasting lips to his.

He let it happen, not pulling her close but not pushing her away. Finally, they broke apart and he shook his head gently. "Meagan…" he began quietly, but in her tipsy state, Meagan simply leaned down to silence his protest once more. He was stiff for a moment, as if contemplating pushing her away but soon she felt him respond more passionately, wrapping his strong arms around her and pulling her down so that she straddled his lap. Meagan felt a flood of wetness between her thighs as his tongue flicked aggressively in and out of her mouth. She moaned softly into the kiss as she slid forward to feel his erection pressing against her. She had imagined how it would feel many times, but she never even got close to how good it was. He was perfect, the perfect balance between sweet and rough, and he was so hot that he fried her nerves. Meagan groaned as she gripped his steely biceps, amazed that he seemed to literally be burning with heat.

They kissed for a long moment before Terrence drew back gently.

"I've been thinking of this for so long," Meagan whispered, trailing a finger along the side of his face. "You are amazing."

Terrence looked down. "I have, too," he admitted. "But Doreen…" he started.

Meagan's face fell. "What about Doreen?" she asked, even though she knew the answer.

When she looked back into Terrence's eyes, she could see a spark, a heated desire, and she shivered. "Doreen doesn't kiss me like you do," he murmured, pulling her close again and crushing his mouth to hers.

Meagan responded with vigor, feeling like she was finally in the right place. She gently cupped his face in her hands as they kissed and he braced his strong hands on her hips, making her squirm with pleasure and grip his shoulders. Seductively, she guided his hands to the hemline of her lacy shirt, urging him to take it off. He didn't oblige right away, but rather taunted her for a moment, gliding his fingers across the smooth bare skin right under the hemline of her shirt. After much ado, he finally allowed himself to peel her shirt up over her head. Under her shirt, Meagan's full C-cup breasts were propped up by a straining black lacy bra.

Meagan could see that Terrence was quite pleased with her appearance, the way his blue-grey eyes glowed white-hot and he roughly stroked his hands up her bare back, unclasping her bra. The garment fell open and Meagan flung it off, moaning as Terrence held her breasts in his hot work-worn hands, flicking his rough fingers over her nipples and turning them rock-hard. Soon, he lost his shirt as well and Meagan admired his impressive physical condition.

"You sure clean up nice, Professor," she murmured, tracing her tongue over his tattoo on his bicep. "It really turns me on."

"I gather that," he murmured in return, pressing her against him. Meagan murmured as he rocked against her in just the right place, and she traced her lips over his neck and collarbone before passionately kissing him on the lips once again. Oblivious of the time or condition, and both of them slightly tipsy, they were lost in each other as they explored each other's burning skin with hands and tongues. Meagan felt the throbbing liquid ache in her core grow heavier and more intense as Terrence's burning-hot, work-worn hands began to peek under the waistband of her pants, ever so slightly, while never straying below her hips.

"Please, Terrence," she whispered throatily. "Please touch me."

He looked down on her with passionate, burning heavy-lidded eyes. "Are you sure?" he murmured.

"Certain," Meagan answered in a raspy voice, and his fingers carefully dipped below her waistband, gentle but certainly in control. Meagan closed her eyes and let out a soft gasp as he slid a finger into her soaked slit, a burning sting of a blush spreading across her face like a slap. She wanted, needed this for so long, but something about having her most inner core exposed to him made her blush.

Terrence seemed surprised too by the extent of her arousal. "Meagan," he murmured hoarsely, almost amazed. "You're so wet for me."

As he began to stroke her, Meagan could only moan in agreement as flood after flood crashed over her, just when she thought she couldn't possibly get any wetter. He started out gentle, testing the waters so to speak, but he was in control, never hesitant, seeming to know exactly where to touch her.

Meagan was a slave to his ministrations, gripping his shoulders as he cradled her in his lap. The pressure grew and grew as he brought her to climax with his skilled hands, pounding harder and harder until she thought his fingers would tear her in two. Her legs were shaking as she contracted around him; she breathily gasped his name, struggling blindly amidst the roaring pleasure. He too was breathing heavily, taking her higher until the ache ruptured and she murmured his name as the trailing beams showered over her, falling limp in his arms with a final gasp. Gently, pleadingly, he withdrew and brought his fingers to her lips.

Meagan rested in his arms for a moment, and he seemed content to hold her, running his hand over her thigh. After a moment she stirred and looked up at him with desire-filled sleepy sloe eyes. "That was perfect," she murmured. "Wonderful," stroking her hands over his strong arms. Sitting up, she turned so that she faced him and looked into his eyes. "My turn," she whispered, trailing her hands down his sides to come to rest at his belt line.

"Hold on," he murmured, and before she knew it, he had risen from his chair and was guiding her towards his bedroom, his lips never straying from hers. She was impressed by how strong he was as he pushed open his bedroom door and leaned her back gracefully on the bed. It didn't take them very long to continue exactly where they had left off, and Meagan did her duty to Terrence with desire and expertise, which left him breathless and insatiable. It was a vicious battle of passion after that, hands and tongues cvcrywhcrc, hcr nails raking on his back and his plunging through her hair as he slid inside her and she gave herself to him completely. The storm raged until the early hours of the morning, when Meagan and Terrence fell asleep side-by-side in each other's arms. Outside, a full moon beamed down as an unintelligible, shadowy figure pelted across the lawn and melted away into the darkness.

Chapter Eighteen

Meagan stirred lightly in her sleep, letting out a soft moan as she rolled over, her hand brushing against something warm. The air on her face was cold and brisk, so she shivered and snuggled closer to the source of heat. Suddenly, the light of morning pierced Meagan's consciousness and she began to emerge from her sleep. When her eyelids blearily flickered open, she found herself staring at unfamiliar walls. Confused, she looked over at the sleeping figure next to her, and it was Terrence. The wonderful memories of the night before started to flood back into Meagan's mind, and she smiled, blissfully recalling the way it felt to have Terrence's hands on her, and the feeling of completeness when he slid inside her, holding her like there was no tomorrow. He had touched every inch of her and brought her to wave after wave of screaming ecstasy, she had fallen completely at his feet, and even honoured him enough to let his seed flood her mouth.

Looking at the bedside clock, Meagan saw that it was 6:13 AM. She glanced back over at Terrence, who was still wrapped in his blankets and asleep on the other side of the bed. As she did, a niggling doubt began to work its way into her mind. Now that it was morning, she had no idea how he would react. Would he think it was a mistake? Would he realize the severity of what they had done? Would he kick her out? Meagan suddenly felt a pang of sadness rip through her. She had enjoyed the hot intensity of the night before, and the tenderness with which he had held her; but she really wished she could awake next to him in the morning and make him breakfast in bed. She felt guilty for wanting more than she could have, but secretly she longed to be his wife, though she knew that wasn't possible. As she lay there, now wide awake, she stared at the ceiling and tried to decide what to do. *I really should just leave,* she thought to herself. *His wife might be getting home today; he'll probably want me to go.* She vacillated for a few more moments, silently breathing as she studied the darkened ceiling.

Finally, she decided that it would be best for both of them if she left. She decided to get him something from the bakery and leave it on his porch. *It isn't ideal, but it's the best I can do,* Meagan thought. She started to quietly rise from bed, but just then realized that she hadn't a stitch of clothing on. She was shocked as a slap of cold air hit her bare skin, and she gingerly placed the blankets back down over Terrence, who appeared to still be asleep. Then, tiptoeing around the room, she collected some of her clothes. In the dark, Meagan couldn't see very well, and she cried out when she stubbed her toe on the foot of the bed. Meagan panicked when Terrence began to stir, but he ended up not waking up. When Meagan had finally collected all of her clothing and put it on, she tiptoed through the darkened house, groping toward the door. At the entrance, she laced up her shoes and slung her jacket over her shoulders. She smoothed a hand over her hair and pulled out a travel-size vial of breath spray, spritzing it into her mouth.

In her car, she checked her reflection in the mirror. She looked totally disheveled, but there was still a faint glow to her cheeks and her eyes looked brighter than they had in days. *This was the best night of my life,* she thought in all honesty as she applied a hurried coat of chap-stick to her cracked lips.

Taking one last look at the sleeping neighborhood and little brick house on the corner, Meagan put her car in gear and slowly drove away, making her way on the main road to the nearby bakery so that she could buy Terrence a gift. Not really caring about her haphazard appearance, Meagan parked in the lot of the Carter Avenue Bakery and walked into the little store. As soon as she opened the glass door, she was flooded with warm, inviting air and the aromatic draft of fresh baked goods. Just then did she realize she hadn't had breakfast, so she decided to grab something for breakfast as well. She walked up to the counter and looked at the displays, trying to decide what would be best. Finally, she decided on all-natural pumpkin muffins with white glaze. At the checkout, she asked for a gift box, and in spirit of the coming Christmas season, the lady wrapped it in paper and put a large bow on top. Meagan thanked her, paid, and left the store.

Meagan swung her car around and exited the parking lot, noting that the time on the dashboard was now 6:37 AM. It didn't take all that long to get back to Terrence's house, where the neighborhood was still fairly dark but the first hints of dawn were peeking up over the horizon in the east. Parking in front of the house, Meagan hopped out and battled the cold path to Terrence's porch, where she set the box down out of the way and hurried back to her car. She glanced back one more time at the box sitting on the darkened porch of the little brick house and she smiled wistfully, lingering a moment before turning on her radio and turning to make her way home.

***

It was about 7:02 AM when Terrence began to stir in his bed, awaking slowly from a pleasant dream. Blinking sleepily, he rubbed his eyes and emerged from his cocoon of blankets, adjusting to his surroundings. At first he was too groggy to remember much of what happened, since he was the slightest bit hung over. He hadn't exactly gotten drunk the night before, but he had gotten a little bit tipsy and didn't usually drink. He looked over and saw that the side of the bed next to him was rumpled. There was an indent on the pillow as if someone had slept there, and he felt a strange sense of disappointment that the bed was empty now. Slowly, the night began to come back to him, the dinner with Meagan, their conversations, and then they had unwisely started sipping Cabernet. Terrence now remembered sitting on the couch when Meagan came over and kissed him. He had tried to resist at first, on principle of honoring his marriage, but her desire for him was a spark unable to be controlled, so he had given in and though tentative at first, they had ended up making love for hours upon glorious hours until finally drifting off to sleep about 3:00 AM. Terrence sighed as he remembered the vigorous passion with which Meagan had kissed him and held him; she was the best he ever had. With her dark silken hair, seductive lips, strong thighs and curvy hips she had poured herself all over him like a blanket of molten caramel, and he had nearly come undone when she took his seed in her mouth. Doreen had always had an aversion to that, so Terrence had never pushed her. Besides, it had never felt right. He and Doreen's sex life had diminished greatly in the past few years as Doreen grew older and dumpier, and started going to bed at different times. Terrence usually went to bed early and arose early, and Doreen did the opposite, sleeping in like a teenager and staying up late at night watching TV or crocheting. When they actually got around to having sex, it lacked passion and was becoming more a customary duty than a pleasurable experience.

As Terrence rose from bed and the cold blast of air slapped his bare skin, he fumbled for his robe and staggered into the bathroom to brush his teeth and shower. He still hadn't fully woken up, so he ended up steadying himself against the bathroom mirror. He flicked on the light and squinted, shielding his eyes as the blinding light speared into his eyes. When he was used to the light, he checked his reflection in the mirror. Now that he was out of his warm bed and staring at his cold, glassy reflection in the mirror, the reality of what he had done came to him. *I just cheated on my wife,* he thought to himself in horror. *Doreen, who has been nothing but faithful to me.* "What have I done?" he whispered. Not only had he cheated on his wife, but he hadn't even thought last night to ask Meagan about birth control, just praying that she had it. It would be an absolute disaster for both of them if he had accidentally gotten her pregnant. As Terrence bathed himself and began to clean up, he struggled with two conflicting torrents of emotion. On the one hand, he was deeply ashamed that he had cheated on his wife and had no idea whatsoever what he would do. Would he tell her? Would he lie? What if someone found out? But on the other hand, he couldn't help but to admit how wonderful last night actually was. *I haven't been held like that for a long time,* he thought. *She was wonderful, is wonderful.* His worries eased some as he recalled their night together, Meagan's warm skin pressed against his, the scent of her hair, the sound of her moans as he brought her to climax, again and again. After a lengthy shower, lost in thought, Terrence emerged and toweled himself off, heading back to his bedroom to get dressed. Looking at the clock, he saw that it was 7:30. If everything went accordingly, he planned to head to the airport in about five or six hours to pick up Doreen. Looking in the mirror, Terrence combed his pale strawberry-blond hair and shaved before going into the kitchen to brew his morning coffee the way he liked it, black as night and searing hot. In the kitchen he found his cell phone buried under some towels where he had carelessly left it the night before. He gave the phone its usual customary flip-check but stopped in his tracks when he saw the screen. He had twenty-three missed calls, fourteen texts and three voicemails.

"Holy shit!" Terrence exclaimed aloud. He wondered who the hell it was that blew up his phone all night long. He had been so busy with Meagan that he hadn't heard his phone, which was on vibrate and buried under kitchen linens.

He scrolled through and saw that all of them were from Sandra, Doreen's sister. Suddenly, a sinking feeling began in his gut, and he slowly picked up the phone and dialed her number, anxious to see what the problem was.

The phone was answered after two rings. "Terrence, you bastard!" Sandra screamed in his ear, not even bothering to say hello. "Why the hell didn't you answer your fucking phone?"

Terrence winced and held the receiver away from his ear. He knew that Doreen's sister had an irritable temper and anticipated her to flip out at him, as she had done many times before. "I didn't have it with me. I'm sorry," Terrence apologized truthfully. "What's the problem, Sandra, what do you need?"

"What's the problem?" Sandra screamed again. "I called you twenty-three fucking times! On both phones! That's the problem!"

Terrence sighed. "I told you I was sorry. Now, tell me what is so important."

There was a pause on the line, a long pause, and he thought he heard a muffled sniffle.

"Sandra?" he asked more quietly. "Are you okay? Is Doreen okay? What's wrong?"

Sandra drew a shaky breath, and when she got back on the line, her voice was thick with tears. "Terrence?" she said shakily, upset rather than angry, before breaking into muffled sobs again. "I have really bad news..."

Chapter Nineteen

It was Monday morning, and Meagan was late. She had laid out her clothes the night before, and stayed up late into the night tossing and turning and thinking about what it would be like to see Terrence in class. Would he pretend to see right through her? Would he be secretly angry? Give her a special smile? She had no idea. So that was all more of the reason for Meagan to look nice on Monday. Nice, beautiful, but nothing too revealing. So she decided on a black sweater with a white blouse, black slacks, and a gold-chain necklace around her neck with matching gold hoops. With it she would wear her shiny patent-leather pumps.

But none of this had gotten underway yet, because Meagan was still buried beneath the blankets. Her long black hair was spread out in all directions on her pillow, arms flung out to the side, and she was murmuring softly in her sleep as she dreamed of being in Terrence's arms again. Just then, she was jarred out of her light sleep by the roar of a passing snowplow. Meagan blinked sleepily, irritated and shaken by the sudden sound. She squinted at her bedside clock, which betrayed that she had forgotten to set her alarm and should have been up several minutes ago. Frustrated, Meagan sprang out of bed, stubbing her toe on the old wooden desk in her room. Grimacing in pain, she hobbled over to the window and pulled back the curtain. Outside, snow was falling relentlessly, and the visibility was maybe ten feet at best. Sighing, Meagan let the curtain fall back into place and quickly began to get ready to go to the university. She remembered the last time she was late for class and had no desire to repeat that experience. And today of all days would be an extremely unwise day to be late, considering her and Terrence's weekend activities and the tension that might ensue. Luckily, Meagan was used to working quickly, so she soon had herself freshened up and dressed in a record time. She brushed her long black hair into a stylish ponytail and fastened it with a headband. Looking over her flawless olive skin and mildly glossy lips, she decided that she looked pretty good. With a faint satisfied smile, she shrugged on her winter coat and put her boots on, jamming her pumps into her bag with the rest of her stuff.

The snow slowed her down considerably, and by the time she brushed off her car, got her morning macchiato, and fought her way through the slow-moving traffic, it was about nine thirty. She parked her car quickly and hopped out, hurrying frenetically toward the university's double doors as if her life depended on it. In the massive foyer, she shrugged off her boots and coat, smoothing over her hair and cramming her pumps onto her feet. With a final deep breath and flip of her hair, she started toward the elevator, her heels reverberating briskly through the empty hallway. When she arrived at her classroom on the third floor, she was nervous, and butterflies danced in her stomach as she approached the open door on the left. Strangely, though, as she came closer, she didn't hear Terrence's usual quiet voice. There wasn't really much sound at all. *They must be working on an assignment,* Meagan thought. Preparing herself, she put a smile on her face and waltzed into the classroom. "Hey, sorry I'm…" Meagan broke off when she looked up and saw that the entire classroom was deathly silent and everyone seemed to be wearing a grim expression. At the board was a stern-faced, dorky-looking young man with thick glasses and a beard. He was wearing a white coat, and Terrence was nowhere to be found. "Wait a minute," Meagan gasped, realizing that she sounded like a total fool. "Where's Dr. Reid?"

The man regarded her with unwavering owl-like eyes so light that they were almost colorless. "As I told the others, Dr. Reid will be out for a week or two due to a family emergency," he explained in a monotone voice. "I am Kenneth Follett, one of Dr. Reid's professorial assistants," he gestured to his name, which he had written on the board.

"Oh okay," Meagan said quietly, not really knowing what else to say. She turned away and headed to her seat, confused and disappointed. Terrence out for a week? What had happened? Meagan's mind was racing with so many questions that she could barely focus. Besides, Mr. Follett had such a monotone voice that Meagan was having trouble focusing on a single word he was saying. The entire lecture sounded like gibberish to her, and she didn't take a single note. She couldn't wait for class to be over, and when Mr. Follett finally announced that it was time to go, Meagan practically ran out of the room. The class had felt foreign and sterile, she missed Terrence's soft voice, the sparkle in his eyes when he taught, the scraping of his cane on the floor, and the muted, pleasant aroma of smoky leather-bound books and unscented laundry soap that always seemed to surround him wherever he went. Smiling, Meagan remembered how she had deeply breathed in his scent as she lay there naked in his arms after they were done, her head resting on his chest. She had just closed her eyes and listened to his steady quiet heartbeat as he gently stroked her back. *God help me, I, Meagan Bernice Patience Lucien, am falling in love with him with all of my heart and soul,* she thought to herself sadly, flicking a piece of lint off of her sweater onto the floor.

***

All day long, Meagan was wondering what Terrence's family emergency might be. She was curious but she didn't dare to ask him, figuring that the last person he wanted to hear from right now was her. When she got home from school and work, after five PM, it was dark outside and an icy polar wind was gusting up, whipping through Meagan's hair and chilling her to the bone. Shivering, Meagan wrapped her scarf around her mouth and nose and hurried from her car to her apartment door. *What a miserable night,* she thought to herself as a relentless barrage of wet, sticky snowflakes began to swirl around her, making her even colder than she had been. Head down, she hurried across the barren expanse of the road, ever grateful as she reached the threshold of her front steps. Shielding her face against the driving snow, Meagan fished her key out of her jacket pocket and stuck it in the lock, breathing a sigh of relief as she stepped into her dry, non-snowy apartment. It was cold and dark in Meagan's apartment, since she had not been home all day, but at least she was sheltered from the snowy blast outside. Once she was safely inside, Meagan shed her cumbersome winter gear and cranked up the old iron radiator against the wall in her living room, which began to hiss and sputter lazily as it heated up. Dumping her bag unceremoniously onto the floor, Meagan set the newspaper down and began leafing through the daily mail. A few bills and a letter from a local charity were the only papers in her mailbox. As she finished her brief survey of her mail, she set it down on the table, disinterested. She quickly headed into her bedroom to get changed into some more comfortable clothes. She peeled off her uncomfortable work clothes like shedding a second skin and immediately shivered as she was encompassed by the chill of the room. The radiator had yet to heat up the house, and was known for taking its time heating up. Unfortunately, the apartment had no gas furnace, and was heated solely by creaky old radiators. The reverse was also true – there was no air conditioning either. The only mercy from the summer heat was provided by a pair of rickety box fans that Meagan kept in the closet and blasted on high during the summer months. This apartment certainly wasn't a luxury, but it was the least of Meagan's problems. The wooden floors were scratched and the furniture was threadbare, but she found the place homey enough. After pulling on her favorite baggy Grandview sweatshirt and a pair of yoga pants, Meagan twisted her hair up into a messy bun and shoved her bedroom slippers onto her feet. Finally comfortable, Meagan headed into the kitchen to make herself some coffee and heat up a toaster pastry for a quick snack. Soon, the apartment began to fill with the inviting aroma of fresh-brewed coffee and raspberry filling, making the room smell like a quaint coffee shop. Meagan sighed with pleasure and sank back into the cushions of her couch, letting out a yawn. She was tired. It had been a long day and she was more than ready to just collapse into a soft chair and relax. The job at the toy store had gotten slightly better, but it was still very straining, having to deal with little pesky customers all day long. The kids were unruly, the parents rude and ungrateful. Meagan did her best, and Melanie seemed happy enough with her, though the husky-voiced, busty blonde's feistiness was always squarely maintained.

While waiting for her toaster pastry, Meagan took an idle sip of her still-steaming coffee and began leafing through the newspaper. *So much mundane bullshit,* she thought, glancing with overt disinterest at the many stories of plague and crime and despair. *It is such a miserable world.* Setting the paper down, Meagan suddenly felt very alone. Both of her parents were dead, and she had no other relatives in town. Even her great aunt Mary, who had provided her a home as a teenager, had died as well. Meagan didn't even have any close friends, with the exception of Jennine Aaronson. But Meagan had noticed that Jen was acting more distant lately, and it kind of hurt. It wasn't a marked difference, but Meagan sensed that she seemed to be pulling away. Jen had never trusted Meagan as much as Meagan would have wanted her to, and their friendship had always been somewhat of a disappointment. Meagan was hurt that Jen didn't talk to her about things, and always seemed rather flippant, never letting Meagan know how she really felt.

Meagan let out a deep, drawn-out sigh as she thought about the coldness of her life compared to the heavenly warmth she had felt with Terrence the other night. When he had held her, she actually felt whole for the first time in her life since her father had died when she was seven. The way Terrence had held her; she just longed to be in his arms again. She craved the gentle touches of his calloused hands, the scent of leather-bound books that surrounded him, and the way she could hear his steady, unwavering heartbeat when she laid on his chest, bare naked, just her and him. Speaking of which, Meagan thought, she had terribly missed him in class today and wondered what could have happened to him. A worried frown creased Meagan's face as she thought about what could have happened. To get her mind off of him, she once again began to leaf through the newspaper. She had just about finished with the regional news section when a brief article in the upper left corner caught her eye. It was one of the depressing quick-run events of crime or tragedy. Idly at first, Meagan began to read:

"Woman hit in snowstorm
ASHTABULA, OHIO:

According to police reports, a fifty-three year old woman was hit by a car amidst a blinding snowstorm on Saturday evening around 11:00 PM. The woman, identified by the county coroner as Doreen C. Reid, was taken to Greenlaw Medical Center, unconscious in critical condition, and passed away two hours later. The cause of death is still being investigated, but police do not expect foul play."

As she finished reading the article, Meagan froze in place. "Oh my God," she breathed in a rasping voice. She could barely believe what she just read. *This must be some kind of cruel joke,* she thought. Tears began to fill her eyes and cloud her vision, and she set the paper down. "Oh my God," she repeated. "Poor, poor Terrence."

This was terrible news. Not only had Terrence's wife died in a car accident, but it was the same night that he and Meagan had been in bed together. *This must be hard on him,* she thought. *It is all my fault. I should never have gotten tipsy and pushed his boundaries. If I hadn't drunk that damn Cabernet, none of this would have happened.* But Meagan knew that she couldn't rightly blame the Cabernet, since she probably would have kissed him anyway. The Cabernet had just given her that extra push she had needed... to simultaneously create the best night of her entire life, as well as the biggest disaster she had ever experienced.

Chapter Twenty

Terrence agitatedly paced the length of his living room, the phone pressed to his ear with a death grip. "Uh, huh," he muttered, turning to write on the calendar. "Okay, Sandra, I guess that will do... Yes, go ahead. Okay, I'll talk to you later... Bye."

Terrence hung up and placed the phone on the cradle. Turning dejectedly, he made his way into the living room and plopped down on the couch. As he sat down, he was flooded with wave after wave of despair. He couldn't believe it, Doreen was gone. Ever since he had gotten off the phone with Sandra on Sunday morning, everything had been a blur. He had stumbled about in a shell-shocked daze, alternating between sleeping, grieving, and making funeral arrangements. Ever since Doreen's death, the phone had been ringing off the hook and he just wanted everyone to go away and leave him alone. Already, practically the entire neighborhood had stopped by to give their condolences, and while Terrence appreciated the thought, he was too depressed and exhausted to give it much thought.

Groaning, Terrence put his head in his hands and rested against the arm of the couch, closing his eyes. His wife was gone. The woman he had spent thirty years of his life with. *She didn't deserve this,* he thought forlornly. Doreen had been a good wife; cooked his meals, kept his home neat and clean, and been ever faithful to him even through times of trial. They had had their minor troubles and squabbles, but generally she performed her matrimonial duty quite well. It only compounded the feeling of grief and loss when Terrence remembered what he had been doing the night that Doreen had died. On the night of his wife's untimely and brutal death, he had been philandering with one of his hot grad students. *I'm sorry, Doreen,* he thought to his wife. *It was a terrible mistake; we both had too much to drink. I'll never forgive myself.*

What a stupid idea it had been to invite Meagan over to his house for dinner! If only he had been sensible enough to take her out to a restaurant… or better yet not get involved with her at all. After all, no good could come out of starting an affair with a scorching-hot, quick-witted and charming grad student who was almost thirty years his junior. For a few great conversations and one hot and intense night, he had sacrificed his marriage and betrayed Doreen's trust on the night that she lay dying in the hospital. He pictured Sandra frantically calling, time after time, to only get his voicemail. No wonder she had been angry at him; he was angry at himself as well. So what if he loved being with Meagan? It didn't matter anymore. Even though Doreen was gone, and he was no longer legally married to her, the thought of continuing with Meagan after the stunt that they had pulled just made him sick to his stomach. *No, honey, I'll keep my commitment to you now,* he thought to Doreen. *I'll show you how sorry I am for failing you.*

At this point, Terrence wished that it was all just a bad dream. He hoped to awake any minute to the inviting smell of homemade pancakes and stumble out of bed to find Doreen in the kitchen with her favorite apron on, cheerfully humming the refrain of a hymn while she flipped the golden rounds over her plastic spatula. Opening his eyes, Terrence was dismayed to find himself still sitting in his dark and dreary living room, staring at the unintelligible gray walls and the drawn blinds that yielded a furious snowstorm outside. Shivering, Terrence rose to crank up the furnace, but found that the chill refused to leave him. For the first time, he realized just how empty the house was without Doreen. Though it was only a ranch house, it felt like a cavernous labyrinth to Terrence, cold and inhospitable, dead. From the other room, the microwave beeped, signaling that Terrence's canned soup dinner was ready, but he had no appetite. Instead, he ignored it and reached for a small canister lying on the coffee table. Popping off the top, he shook out one of the small, round sleeping pills and tossed it back with a large swig of water. Then, closing his eyes and pulling a blanket tightly around his shivering body, he collapsed into a deep and dreamless sleep.

Chapter Twenty-One

After receiving the shocking news of Mrs. Reid's death on Monday, Meagan's world seemed to be plunged into a state of cold numbness. She hadn't heard from Terrence and hadn't dared to contact him, in fear that she would be an added burden to his problems. Her calculus class was in a state of upheaval, since Mr. Follett was a poor substitute for Terrence and often got lost in his own work, making it difficult to consistently follow along with his pattern of lectures. Meagan's days were long, and on top of it all, she just really missed Terrence, and worried incessantly about what damage she may have caused by having an affair with him. It was almost hard to believe just how attached she had become to him in the past few weeks, and she was terrified that their affair would push him over the edge.

Looking at the clock, Meagan saw that it was Wednesday, and it was about ten minutes until class let out and she could wolf down her lunch while heading over to work. *Only ten minutes left,* she reassured herself. She didn't even try to pretend that she was following along with Mr. Follett's droning lecture. He scribbled calculations across the board and babbled incoherently, and Meagan mindlessly took down the meaningless figures in her notebook with little attention. Her face twisted into a frown as she looked up at the clock and tapped her foot impatiently. The weather was terrible outside, so it would take a little extra time to get to work. And the last thing she needed today was Melanie giving her hell for being late.

When the clock struck the hour, Meagan didn't even wait for Mr. Follett to finish speaking. Instead, she jammed her books haphazardly into her bag, papers crumpling as she zipped it shut. Several of her classmates gave her questioning, disapproving stares, but Meagan didn't care. Murmuring a hurried apology to the professorial assistant, she dashed out of the room and boarded the nearest elevator to the main foyer. She rushed across the barren expanse, her high-heeled pumps rapping on the tile floor. Not even bothering to change into her boots, she jammed her coat on, zipped it quickly, and opened the door to brave the icy blast. Immediately, a powerful gust of wind nearly lifted her off her feet, hurling a cloud of wet snow directly into her face. Meagan blinked and wiped the snow away before continuing her treacherous journey along the icy parking lot to her car. It took her several minutes to come to safety, but she sighed with relief when she finally hopped in and closed the door, sealing out the frosty tempest. Tired from the week and her frenzied dash from class, Meagan yawned as she put her car in gear and attempted to back out of the lot. As soon as she started the motor, she knew that this was going to be a tough drive and would probably end up taking maybe twenty minutes at best. Her predictions turned out to be accurate, and it ended up being nearly twenty minutes in slow midday traffic, crawling along the snow-packed streets at the speed of a turtle. When she finally pulled into the Toy Box parking lot and cut the motor, she was twenty-three minutes late for work. Melanie was going to string her up to dry. Grimacing, Meagan hurried from her car to the door looming ahead, not wanting to face her feisty boss's wrath. She would rather battle a tigress than face an angry Melanie. Taking a deep breath, Meagan steeled herself and burst through the doors, shrugging off her coat and wiping snowflakes from her hair. Just as she came in, she saw Melanie emerge from the back room, a stack of boxes in her hands. "I'm so sorry," Meagan pleaded. "The weather…"

But Melanie didn't seem to care. Pushing her red glasses up the bridge of her nose, she gave Meagan a disinterested glance. "Well, you're here now," she replied, not unkindly. Meagan saw a flicker of a smile on her employer's face as Melanie stacked up the boxes. *She must be in a good mood today,* Meagan thought, giving Melanie a strange look. *I thought she would give me hell for being late!*

Meagan didn't realize she was still staring until Melanie gave a throaty chuckle. "Better get to work, Lucien," she said offhandedly, pulling a cigarette out of her pocket. "I'm going out for a smoke. Finish stacking those boxes."

"Okay," Meagan replied, and walked over to the shelves to start her task. As Melanie left the room, Meagan couldn't help but to stare after her and wonder what was going on. *Maybe she got laid,* Meagan thought with a slight chuckle, but then her smile faded as she started thinking about Terrence again. Using the best of her willpower, Meagan pushed thoughts of Terrence from her mind and tried to think of something else, anything else. As she glanced idly out the storefront window, she could vaguely see Melanie silhouetted against the building, cigarette clasped between her lips, taking deep, greedy draws of the smoke. Her eyes were closed behind her red-framed glasses. As the cigarette dwindled to the butt, Melanie ground it out and reentered the store, her curvy hips swaying and massive breasts straining against her thin black shirt as she moved across the room. Meagan really didn't know much about Melanie as a person; didn't think she was married, or even dating anyone. *I wonder why,* Meagan thought, giving Melanie an appraising glance. *She isn't an ugly woman.*

Turning away, Meagan began to rearrange the boxes, but she stopped short when the radio changed to a song that she and Terrence had listened to the other night. Meagan froze as a fresh wave of pain shot through her, and she wiped her face with the back of her hand in a harried manner. Melanie must have noticed Meagan's distress because she looked over questioningly. "Everything okay?" she asked.

Meagan shrugged. "Yeah," she replied. "One of my friends just had a death in the family, and I'm a bit worried about him."

Melanie gave her a sympathetic look. "I'm sorry to hear that," she said. Apparently not having any additional comment, Melanie turned abruptly and headed over to her desk where she took a seat. That was just how Melanie was.

Chapter Twenty-Two

The funeral service for Doreen Reid was held that week on Sunday, a cold and raw winter day, unseasonably cold for late November. Meagan awoke early that day, around 8AM, partly due to insomnia. She sighed and got out of bed, feeling rather restless. Sliding her slippers onto her feet, she ambled over to the window where she pulled back the curtain to survey the weather. As she looked out, an expression of dismay settled firmly over her face. The sky was iron-gray and gusts of wind were howling through the cracks in the windows, whipping torrents of ice and snow in all directions. The ground was scattered with a light layer of snow over dirty ice, with some fallen leaves frozen into the mess. With a sigh, Meagan plowed a hand through her uncombed black hair and let the curtain fall back into its place. She had been up half the night debating with herself as to whether she should attend the funeral or not. The obituary had announced that the funeral would take place at the 10:00 AM service at Mount Calvary Methodist Church, Doreen's lifelong parish. The announcement also said that all friends were invited, and there would be a luncheon afterwards in the church hall. Meagan had deliberated for many days, vacillating incessantly, fretting about how Terrence would react. On the one hand, she really wanted to go and support him, since she really liked him. Also, there had been talk among his advanced class of attending as a group, and Meagan didn't want to be singled out for not going. On the other hand, she really didn't want her presence to distress him, reminding him of their caramel-coated sins last Saturday night.

Finally, when Meagan felt like her head would explode from the pressure, she decided that she would go and show her support, as not to make a scene in front of her classmates. She made a salad for the luncheon, and figured it maybe wouldn't be so bad if she dressed very conservatively. Meagan showered and dressed, deciding on a modest dark gray sweater, black slacks, and flat shoes. She accessorized with a delicate gold-chain necklace and pulled her hair back into a ponytail, choosing not to wear any makeup. Looking in the mirror, she decided that she looked quite appropriate for the occasion. The sweater was still attractive, but it made no immodest emphasis to her ample endowments. Her skin was fresh and clear, hair pretty but very plain. After applying a coat of lip balm, Meagan turned away and wandered into her living room to have a cup of coffee and take a look at the paper.

Sitting down on the couch, Meagan flipped through the paper, her eyes coming to rest on Doreen's obituary. With a grimace, Meagan thought of the pain Terrence must be feeling as he tried to cope with the loss of his wife. The reality struck her that she really didn't wish that on him, but now it had happened and she was all snared up in the middle of it. Glancing down, she read:

"Doreen Carey Reid went home to the Lord last
Sunday in the early hours of the morning at Greenlaw
Medical Center in Ashtabula, Ohio. She was born October 3,
1961, to the late Edward and Nora Lucille (Basler) Carey.
Doreen will be deeply missed by her husband, Dr. Terrence
Albert Reid, Ph.D., a sister, Sandra Lynn Carey of Ashtabula,
and many cousins, relatives and friends.

Doreen was a lifelong member of Mount Calvary Methodist Church, and could be found there almost every day for worship or events. During her lifetime, Doreen held a career as a secretary at a prominent oil company. In her spare time, she enjoyed reading, knitting, spending time with her family, and volunteering at her church. A funeral/memorial service will be held on Sunday, November 23 at Mount Calvary Methodist Church with the Rev. Martin Haines officiating. All friends are welcome to attend; a luncheon in Mount Calvary's Fellowship Hall will follow. Memorials can be made to Mount Calvary Methodist Church. Funeral arrangements will be handled by Carlton Funeral Home and Cremation Services, Inc."

Meagan finished reading and set the paper aside rather listlessly, taking a sip of her coffee. *Poor Terrence,* she thought. *It must be rough.* Meagan knew exactly how it felt to lose a loved one, since both of her parents had died while she was young; her father when she was seven years old, her mother when she was fifteen.

Meagan was shaken out of her thoughts by the chiming of the clock, indicating that it was already 9:20 AM. Sighing, Meagan pushed herself off of the couch and went into the other room to get her coat on, grabbing her salad and car keys on the way. Bundling herself up tightly to seal out the cold, Meagan braced herself and opened her front door. Immediately, an ugly gust of snow slapped her across the face. Shivering, Meagan locked up her apartment and hurried down the stairs to her car, careful not to slip on the icy sidewalk.

Due to the miserable weather, it took Meagan almost twenty minutes before she finally pulled up at the old wooden church. With her windshield wipers going full-blast, Meagan turned into the spacious parking lot, which was already crammed to nearly overflowing with cars. Finally, she managed to find a place relatively near the door. As she alighted and walked toward the doorway, she noticed groups of people dressed in dark clothing and speaking in hushed tones as they made their way to the entrance, fighting the roaring snowy gale. An elderly couple reached the doors and the man held the door open for his wife, and then, seeing Meagan, he waited; a rather stern expression on his face. Meagan thanked him quietly and he just responded with a gruff nod.

Inside the church, many people milled around in groups, talking quietly with one another while they waited for the service to start. Meagan had never been in this church, so she had to look around to find the fellowship hall to drop off her salad. She cautiously made her way down the hallway, murmuring "excuse me" to groups of people that she didn't know. After she made her meager offering to the luncheon, walking back to the church, she felt like an outsider. In the corner, a group of her classmates were talking, but Meagan had no desire to join them. Suddenly, through the crowd, she spotted Terrence, dressed in a formal black suit, talking with a blonde woman maybe a few years younger than him. Meagan just stood and watched as she talked with him informally, with many motions of her hands, and repeatedly touching him on the shoulder. Although she tried hard to stop it, Meagan immediately felt a flood of resentment toward the woman. *I can tell from a mile away that she's as fake as dentures;* she thought to herself, catching wind of the woman's high-pitched, over-exaggerated voice. *She looks like she's ready to crawl down his pants.* With a final scathing look, Meagan turned her gaze away from the mystery woman and followed a throng of people who were beginning to move into the sanctuary.

In the church, Meagan seated herself near the back in a vacant pew. The sanctuary slowly filled up until it was nearly overflowing with people. Meagan gathered that Doreen Reid must have had a lot of friends. The far wall was adorned with a large wooden cross and there were flowers on the altar, along with a small ceramic urn containing Doreen's ashes.

The service started with a solemn hymn and procession. The sound of the old pipe organ and the unified voices of the congregation rose and reverberated throughout the cavernous old building. Meagan was not accustomed to being in church, she had been baptized Lutheran, but her family had stopped going abruptly after the death of her father, who had been the solid foundation of her life.

Now, Meagan felt oddly comforted by the rising voices, and did her best to follow along with the hymn, her voice rusty and cracked from years of inactivity. After the brief, soaring hymn, a robed pastor stepped up to the lectern and led the congregation in some prayers. After that, he motioned for the congregation to be seated as people came forward to make memorial speeches for Doreen Carey Reid. Family members, friends, and fellow churchgoers alike all stepped up to the lectern to eulogize their beloved friend. Meagan listened for a while, but eventually the tedium overcame her and she began to let her mind drift elsewhere.

Finally, the last person sat down and the pastor stepped back up to the stand. Another hymn was sung, followed by some more prayers, and a final standard funeral blessing with an organ postlude as people began to pack up and silently head to the fellowship hall for the luncheon.

Outside of the sanctuary, Meagan stood uncertainly, watching the crowds of people mill around her. After a moment's hesitation, she gravitated toward Terrence, who was standing and talking to a group of people. Nervously clutching her purse, Meagan inched forward in the line, until the group of people moved off and she and Terrence were face-to-face. She was shocked by the level of stark exhaustion that had seemed to consume Terrence's usually handsome face. Standing there in his black suit, he looked ten years older. His face was pale and he had dark rims under his bloodshot light-grey eyes. His suit was rumpled and his entire face seemed to be chiseled with sorrow.

At first, he seemed almost stunned to see her. "Meagan," he finally said quietly, as a way of acknowledgment.

She spoke not a word, but reached out and embraced him. He was stiff at first but then sank into her arms. "Oh, Terrence, I'm so sorry," she murmured, fighting the urge to kiss him on the cheek. "I'm so, so sorry," she repeated, just holding him for a moment. And just for that fleeting instant, it was only the two of them; the dull hum of conversation in the narthex was nonexistent, the people gone. He smelled as he always did, of leather-bound books and smoke, and Meagan felt her heart ripping in two.

He let her hold him for a moment, before gently pulling away. "Thanks, Meagan," he said quietly.

As the crowd shifted, they bumped into a short, dumpy woman who may have been a few years older than Terrence. She had long blonde hair heavily streaked with gray, and was wearing a black suit jacket and black slacks. With that getup, along with the stern expression on her face, she looked like a prison guard.

The woman turned to face them, and Meagan saw that her face was streaked with tears. Terrence put his hand on the woman's arm. "How are you holding up, Sandra?" he asked.

The woman sniffled. "I don't know," she murmured, wiping her eyes. Then, she turned to Meagan. "Who are you?" she asked.

"Meagan Lucien," Meagan told her, extending her hand.

The woman was silent, and Terrence broke in. "Meagan, this is Sandra Carey, Doreen's sister," he explained.

"Nice to meet you," Meagan offered.

Sandra's eyes narrowed. "Did you say your name is Meagan Lucien?" she asked slowly, in a cold, hard tone of voice. "You're one of Terrence's engineering masters' students, correct?"

Meagan raised her eyebrows; taken aback that Sandra knew who she was. "Yes," she replied. "But how did you…."

Her sentence was left unfinished and her eyes widened as Sandra suddenly drew back and belted her violently across the face. Stunned and temporarily blinded, Meagan staggered backwards, clutching the side of her face. "You miserable harlot!" Sandra shouted at the top of her voice, her face contorted with rage. "You wretched bitch!"

Squinting, Meagan looked up at Sandra's rage-filled face looming above her, the room swaying like a pendulum. Already, she could feel the entire right side of her face beginning to bruise. She murmured incoherently, something along the lines of "What…?"

Meagan stumbled to her feet, and tried to face Sandra. "What are you talking about?" she sputtered, more out of shock than anger.

Sandra jabbed a finger at her, shoving her once more. "You know what I'm talking about," she growled. "Don't even try to play innocent. You screwed my sister's husband on the night she died, I heard all about it."

"What?" Meagan gasped; her eyes wide as saucers. "How?"

Beside her, Terrence appeared frozen, his face glazed with shock. But Sandra continued. "The source doesn't matter," Sandra snapped. "I got all the proof I needed, a whole goddamn video. It was positively sickening."

"But…" Meagan started to say, but Sandra wouldn't be stopped.

"So, how did it feel?" she asked mockingly, taking little jabs at Meagan with her index finger. "Taking his dick down your throat while my beloved sister was lying in the hospital, bloodied and dying? Do you feel good about yourself now? I sure hope so, because in the last hours of her life, you robbed Doreen of the utmost importance in her life: her marriage." Sandra paused to let her words sink in before delivering the final blow. "Furthermore," she bit off. "You were not a friend of Doreen's. Meaning, you're not welcome here. I dare you to show your face at our luncheon."

Before turning and stalking off, Sandra jabbed a finger into Terrence's shoulder. "And you," she spat in disgust. "Philandering, groveling scumbag. You're an embarrassment to the family and I'm never speaking to you again."

After Sandra had departed in a raging huff, Meagan stood, stunned. How had Sandra found out? What did she mean, video? Shaken, she turned to Terrence, who was still stock-still, a stony expression on his face. Meagan became aware of the few people curiously looking over, and she shot them scathing stares until they turned away. Looking back over, Meagan touched Terrence's shoulder. "Terrence?" she barely whispered, the shame beginning to come down on her like a waterfall. She knew she shouldn't have done it, and now it was a disaster for both of them. Tears began trickling down her face.

Terrence regarded her, his face tight, blue-grey eyes cold and numb, looking like he either wanted to take a swing at something or break out crying. His face was sheet-white and he looked stricken. "It would be best if you leave now," he finally croaked hoarsely, barely able to speak.

Meagan put her face in her hands as the tears came faster and faster. "I'm sorry," she murmured over and over. "I'm sorry."

He waved his hand. "Please go," he murmured brokenly, before abruptly turning away, muscling through the crowd, and barricading himself in the gentlemen's room.

Amidst the curious and disapproving stares of the people, Meagan shoved her way through the crowd, not caring who she pushed or how many feet she stepped on. Reaching the doors, she burst free of the old church and streaked across the parking lot, abandoning her coat, desperate to just get away from this horrible nightmare.

Once she was in her car, the dam broke and her sobs came harder and harder, wracking her whole body. She cried and cried, and as she looked in the mirror, she saw that she was beginning to develop a black eye and split lip. As she met her own eyes in the mirror, tear-filled and one rimmed with bruised tissue, she realized what a wretched level she had stooped to. Looking into her own desolate brown eyes, she shook her head and turned away viciously, breaking into uncontrollable sobs again, her vision flooded with tears as she put her car in reverse and tore out of the parking lot.

***

During the day, the already unfortunate weather grew progressively worse, until it was a full-fledged horrendous snowstorm. Meagan had hightailed it home from the disastrous funeral service and had presently collapsed on the couch at home, burying her face in the cushions and trying to forget about the awful day. She had changed into her comfortable clothes and plopped down in her seat with the TV remote and a shot glass. She hated to resort to drinking, but she figured that the alcohol would help her forget at least temporarily. Around 5PM, Meagan was sitting listlessly, making the pretense of watching the news. It was nothing exciting, in fact nothing at all, just mindless blather to seal out the memory of that cold look in Terrence's eyes, almost as if he wanted to freeze her solid. Shaking her head, Meagan demanded to herself why she had been such an idiot. And now, even worse, both she and Terrence's reputations were jeopardized by the mysterious information leak. *How did she find out?* Meagan wondered, absolutely befuddled by the fact that she knew, when no one but Meagan and Terrence had been present. Unless, of course, someone had followed her and spied on them from outside. But this was all too much for Meagan's liquor-laced brain, and so she just shook her head and focused again on the news.

Just as she was settled into a comfortable stupor, Meagan was jarred by the ringing of the telephone. At first she ignored it, but it continued to ring persistently. *Whoever it is can go to hell,* Meagan muttered to herself, reaching for the receiver.

"Hello?" she murmured in a slurred voice.

"Meagan, it's me," the caller's voice was soft and patient but cold as a polar wind, and he did not identify himself, didn't have to.

"Terrence?" Meagan whispered, a tiny flame of hope rising in her. Had he called to tell her it was all okay?

"I'm sorry to disturb you, but I called you to apologize."

Meagan couldn't believe what she was hearing. "For what?" she breathed. "You didn't do anything!"

He seemed not to hear her. "I take full responsibility for this situation," he said gravely. "It is just all around unfortunate."

Meagan cut him off. "I'm so sorry, Terrence," she whispered. "I had no idea…"

"What's done is done," he interrupted softly but firmly. "All we can do now is go forward. I apologize for getting too intimate with you as a student. And I assure you that it will never happen again. I'm sorry it had to end this way."

Meagan stifled a small cry of anguish. "Terrence," she pleaded. "It doesn't have to be like this…"

But he cut her off again. "Good night," he finished quietly, followed by a click and the dial tone.

Meagan sat on the couch, holding the phone, in a state of shock and despair. Just like that, it was all over? Outside, the wind howled and hurled gusts of snow viciously against the windows, shedding branches from the trees and kicking up sprite-like snow clouds. As she listened to the storm rage outside, all the tears that Meagan had managed to stifle earlier came flooding back to her, and she once again broke down crying. When she cried herself into a cold and numb state of oblivion, she finally burrowed under a ratty old blanket, switched off the TV, and tossed back a couple of sleeping pills.

Chapter Twenty-Three

Meagan awoke in her clothes, with her face pressed into something soft. She had no idea where she was or who she was for the first few minutes. She blinked blearily as her tired eyes adjusted to the dim light filtering in through the closed draperies in her living room. She rolled over with a groan on the narrow couch, wiping her mouth with the back of her hand to try and get rid of the heavy sleep residue crusted around her lips. She was still hazy-headed from the sedative she had taken the night before, and she felt as if her eyelids were sealed shut with super glue, since she had been sleeping since 5:30PM the night before. Grumbling to herself, she groped around in the dim light for a clock of some sort to tell her what time it was. She picked up the handset of the home phone and saw that it was Monday morning, 7AM.

Slowly, the memories of the horrible day before came flooding back to her, and Meagan sighed, sinking back down into the couch cushions, not wanting to face the day. The last thing she felt like doing was going to class, whether Terrence would be there or not. If he was, she would have to face the humiliation of seeing him after the scene that Doreen's sister had caused at the church yesterday.

Finally, after several moments, Meagan managed to rise to her feet and stagger into the bathroom to clean up. The apartment was freezing cold, and a nasty, throbbing ache was beginning to take place on the right side of her face from where Sandra had hit her. Shivering and stumbling through the darkened rooms, Meagan switched on the radiators and hit home in the bathroom, leaning heavily against the wall as she flicked the bathroom light on. Meagan winced visibly and let out a soft, muffled cry of protest as the bright light speared into her sleep-coated eyes. Squinting through the fog in her vision, as it cleared, Meagan saw just how awful she looked. Her long black hair fell in a tangled mass over her shoulders, her skin was pale and sallow, and an ugly bruise had formed under her heavy-lidded right eye. Her eyes and lips alike were crusted heavily with sleep residue, and her breath smelled of sour sleep and vodka.

A warm shower did some good to wake her up, but when Meagan stepped out, she was still tired and cold and didn't really give a shit what she looked like. She considered taking a sick day, but she really couldn't afford to miss her university classes, because missing one day would get her critically behind. She especially had to watch advanced calculus, since it was currently being taught by Terrence's quack graduate assistant, Kenneth Follett. Meagan did her best to stumble her way through her morning routine: She minimally brushed her hair and tossed it back into a bun, grabbed the first clothes she could find, skipped makeup, and plopped down at her kitchen table with a cup of coffee and two pain pills for the throbbing ache in her cheek and her hangover headache from the vodka the night before.

When she was done with her half-hearted preparations for the day, she rose and brushed her teeth, shrugged on her coat, grabbed her bag, and headed for the door. Even though the apartment was cold, at least it was dry. The moment she opened the door, Meagan was blasted in the face with a torrent of pelting, icy rain, accompanied by highly volatile gusts of wind whipping through the trees, causing a hailstorm of twigs to swirl around in the messy, freezing tempest.

Meagan shivered and pulled her coat tighter around her as she dashed down the steps to make it to her car before she got soaked. Reaching her car door, she jerked it open and hopped in, disengaging a wet leaf from the side of her face as she slammed the door, sealing out the terrible weather.

Traffic moved at a snail's pace the entire way, and the wind was so vicious that Meagan worried that her small, junky car might blow away. She gripped the wheel and squinted at the road in front of her, trying to stay on a clear path. It took about twenty minutes to get to Grandview, and then she once again had to brave the ice rain until she got to the double doors looming at the entrance.

As she stepped into the cavernous foyer, Meagan quickly checked her wristwatch. Despite the weather and traffic, she was actually a few minutes early. She let out a tremendous sigh of relief as she hung up her coat in the closet and smoothed a hand over her wet hair before heading up to class. *Maybe something will go right today after all,* Meagan thought, her foul mood lifting slightly as she boarded the elevator. Still, the day was far from perfect; Meagan's headache was better but not gone, her clothes were a mess, and she was still battling the remnants of a hangover, not to mention still in major emotional pain from the scene with Terrence.

Meagan was shaken from her disappointing thoughts when the elevator dinged and she stepped off. When she neared her classroom, she could hear the soft murmur of voices of her classmates studying before the class started. Yawning lightly, Meagan walked into the room, heading for her seat. She was maybe halfway across the room when the entire class suddenly fell absolutely, completely silent. Meagan looked around, bewildered, as she met the scathing stares of her classmates, who were now all focused on her with unbridled disgust. Meagan felt uncomfortable and averted her eyes, heading quickly to her seat with her head down. As soon as she sat down and opened her notebook, the stares dissipated and a flurry of hushed whispers broke out, accompanied by occasional curious glances and not-so-subtle pointed fingers. An icy chill raced down Meagan's spine and her mouth fell open as she realized that her greatest nightmare had probably just come true: somehow everyone had found out about her and Terrence. Not only would it cause trouble for her, but unnecessary headache for Terrence as well. He might even get fired because of her if the word got out far enough. *No,* Meagan thought to herself, her mind screaming. She prayed that her classmates were only staring because she had spilled something on her shirt or something. *Please let me have some sort of embarrassing stain on my shirt,* she thought. *That would be my salvation.* Sure, Meagan looked rumpled, but she didn't think her appearance in itself was enough to set off such an inimical reaction from her classmates.

Just to see if her disheartening perceptions of her situation were true, Meagan leaned over and tapped the shoulder of Deanna, the girl who sat next to her. Deanna was engaged in a conversation with her neighbor on the other side, a scruffy college-looking guy named Corey. Deanna, a studious, usually friendly, heavy-set blonde, completely ignored Meagan. "Deanna," Meagan tried again, louder this time. Finally, the girl turned, and the expression on her face was not very hospitable.

"What?" she snapped irritably. "Can't you see that I'm having a conversation?"

"Sorry," Meagan apologized. "I just wanted to know of you could tell me how to start number three on the worksheet. I hear you're good at the function graphs."

Deanna looked at Meagan disdainfully, and Corey stared at her in the background. "Look it up," Deanna suggested coolly, turning away once more.

Corey, though, wasn't finished, and he added one last word. "Why don't you ask your sugar daddy?" he smirked. "Maybe for a strip show he'd give you another A. That's the only reason you're here in the first place."

Meagan's eyes stung from Corey's hurtful comment, and she could feel her anger rising. How dare they think that she was sleeping with Terrence to keep her grades up? *You don't understand!* She wanted to scream. *I screwed up, okay? I made a mistake, pushed his limits, because I'm so hopelessly in love with him that I'd give him my life. So mind your own goddamned business; take the sanctimonious bullshit and stick it up your ass!*

Instead, Meagan just bit her lip and turned away with a mumbled, "Never mind." Behind her, she could hear people snickering at Corey's wiseass attempt at humor.

You'd think we're in junior high, Meagan thought. *It doesn't get any better, even when you're an adult.*

As Mr. Follett walked into the room, the whispers quieted. "Okay, get out your notebooks," he instructed, dumping his coat into his chair and picking up a piece of chalk to scrawl a complicated equation on the board. "Ten minutes to solve this," he continued. "After that, we can go over your homework. Remember, you have a test next week."

All around her, people were starting to copy down the equation, but Meagan could only sit there stone-faced and frozen. *How did they find out?* She wondered. How many of them had been at the memorial service yesterday where Sandra had slapped her? *News travels fast,* she thought. *What a disaster.* As Meagan was swamped with the reality of the monster she had created, she felt tired, and felt her pounding headache coming back. *My God, what have I done?* She murmured, just willing the awful morning to be over.

Suddenly, she was jarred out of her reverie by the sound of an egg timer. "That's time, people," Mr. Follett announced. "Let's check this over. Can I have a volunteer up here to solve it for the class?"

Several hands raised, but then some idiot from the back row mumbled, "How about Meagan?"

Please, no, Meagan thought, hoping that Mr. Follett would be merciful enough to spare her from further humiliation. But he must have been sadistic, lazy, or oblivious, because he nodded. "Sure," he agreed. "Meagan, what have you got for us?"

Meagan lifted her head off of her desk. "I'm sorry, Mr. Follett, I'm not feeling very well," she answered. "I didn't finish."

"That's okay," he replied kindly. "Just start with what you've got. I'll help you."

Meagan sighed. "Actually, I didn't even start," she admitted, and there were a handful of muted chuckles. She heard a whispered "Told ya."

Mr. Follett shook his head. "Okay, just remember that the test is next week. I hope you'll be ready, Meagan." He turned and looked around. "Okay, Matt, why don't you help us out?"

Meagan's face burned crimson as Matt walked up to the board and a flurry of critical whispered comments broke out behind her back.

This horrid torture ensued for another forty minutes, before class was finally dismissed. As soon as the time was up, Meagan grabbed her bag and bolted from her seat, wanting to get as far away from this disaster as possible.

As she burst free of the building, she noticed that the rain had stopped and the sun had come out. Hurrying across the wet, glistening parking lot, Meagan got to her car. She put her hand on the door handle but stopped short. There was a plastic grocery bag under one of her wipers like a parking ticket. Puzzled, she carefully lifted up the bag, letting the few raindrops cascade off of it. She was baffled as to why it was there, and at first thought it had just blown in. But when she looked down inside she saw a newspaper clipping crumpled in the corner. Shaking her head, she pulled out the clipping. It was a piece of the school newspaper. *Oh, well,* Meagan thought, turning it over idly as she walked toward the recycle bin. But when she glanced down, she froze solid in her tracks, realizing why the person had left this under her wipers. *"Combined Tragedy and Scandal strike Grandview University,"* the headline read in bold print. Horrified, she scanned the article and saw that it was a complete blowup of her story with Terrence- how his wife had died and he had been caught in bed with Meagan that same night. It was almost too much to bear. The obnoxious article went as follows:

> *"As many know, Doreen Reid, wife of noted calculus professor Terrence Reid, has recently passed away. In the midst of the grief over her death, information has been uncovered that adds a sordid twist to this tragic tale. Apparently, an unnamed witness found the fifty-four year old professor having sex with his twenty-six year old advanced calculus student, identified as Meagan B. Lucien. The university board is currently deciding what to do about this unfortunate situation."*

"Oh, my god," Meagan murmured. "Oh, my god!" she tore the clipping in half and threw it into a puddle. *If only I could find the sonovabitch behind this!* She fumed. Unfortunately, the author was not listed, so the bastard couldn't be identified. Working on autopilot, Meagan texted Melanie, simply telling her that she wouldn't be coming to work. Then, she pulled out of the parking lot with a wild screech of tires, feeling sicker and sicker by the minute, trying desperately not to let herself vomit in her car. The sun had just gone behind the clouds and the rain was starting up again, but Meagan didn't slow down. She cruised all the way to her home and leapt out, slamming the door. She didn't care that she had left her coat at the university. In a sick, frenzied haze, she ran up the stairs, just wanting to get away. That's when she saw the same article, cut out and tacked many times to her front door. She stood motionless on the stairs for a moment as the rain came down harder and harder. *How could someone be so cruel?,* she wondered. She ripped the soggy clippings off of her door and threw them into the bushes. Then, she burst through the door to her apartment, and made a beeline for the shower, and eventually a shot of vodka and another sleeping pill.

Chapter Twenty-Four

Michaelis Nielsen leaned back in his chair with a soft, self-satisfied chuckle. "Here's to a wonderful evening, Shelby, cheers," he said softly, lifting his glass to the lithe blonde sitting opposite from him at the candlelit table in the expensive restaurant.

"Cheers," Shelby repeated with a smile, gently touching her glass to his. She was dressed wonderfully in a black evening gown, her long blonde hair loose over her shoulders. Michaelis himself was dressed in a suit and tie, which clung to his broad shoulders, accenting his slippery, panther-like agility. He was a large, muscular man, and worked as one of the chief editors for the newspaper company. He was used to getting what he wanted when he wanted it; using either his oily charm or sheer intimidation. He was a god of the media; able to make or break anyone who crossed him.

As he and Shelby lapsed into silence, Michaelis thought about what a success he had had that day. He let out another sardonic chuckle when he thought about his latest project; blowing Meagan Lucien to shreds. *Stupid bitch,* he thought to himself. Meagan had always forcefully rejected his advances, treated him like dirt. He had wanted her for years and years, and she just threw it back in his face and stomped him into the ground. Under her disdainful gaze he had felt like less than a man.

Not anymore, sweetheart, he thought, smiling when he recalled the beautiful operation that he and his team had pulled off. True, he had pulled some strings and done some things illegally, but it was perfect. Immediately, he had set a group of goons to follow Meagan around and monitor her activity. His original plan was to perhaps kidnap her, but when one of his guys followed Meagan to her professor's house, the guy immediately called Michaelis, who told him to sit tight and get some pictures. He had some blurry shots and Michaelis had been thrilled when he thought of the scandal idea; something that would bust both Meagan and her lover, and teach her that she had screwed with the wrong man. One of his henchmen just happened to be a Grandview student, who leaked it to the school paper. A sardonic smile lit Michaelis's face when he imagined how much both Meagan and her tough-guy professor would flip out when they knew they had gotten exposed. *That guy just lost his wife,* Michaelis thought with a mocking laugh. *A press scandal like this too just might kill him.*

Michaelis's satirical reverie was interrupted by Shelby, who commented on how delicious the wine was. *Yes, yes, just wonderful,* Michaelis thought, giving Shelby a languid, disinterested smile and nodding in response to her comment. As usual, he, as one of the chief editors, had dazzled one of the lowly clerical assistants at the newspaper, with smiles and waves and the promise of a dinner date… and he smiled to himself as Shelby blabbered animatedly to him from across the table. He leaned back in his chair and stretched with a contended yawn as he mentally planned the rest of his evening: he would spring the trap; ask Shelby if she wanted to come to his house for dessert; then he would seduce her, enjoy a night of debauchery at her expense, and the next day discard her like a dirty tissue and go on the prowl for something better.

Soon, the waiter brought the bill and Michaelis picked up the check, smiling at Shelby as he signed his name. He then declined the waiter's offer of dessert and waited while Shelby shrugged her heavy winter coat on over her black cocktail dress. Michaelis too donned his coat, and when Shelby was ready, Michaelis offered his arm to escort her to the car. It was wickedly cold outside, the wind whipping snow flurries sharply against their faces, and Shelby bundled into her coat and snuggled against Michaelis's arm. He led her through the tempest to his car, where he unlocked it and gestured for her to get in. Once the two of them were in the car, Michaelis turned on the heater and the radio. Shivering, Shelby put her chilled hands in front of the heating vent and turned to Michaelis with a tooth-chattering smile as he put the car in gear and eased silently out of the crowded parking lot. "I had a great time tonight," she observed, flashing a red-cheeked megawatt smile in his direction.

Michaelis smiled lazily and reached his hand out to clasp hers. "I did too," he replied. "What could be better than spending the evening with the most beautiful woman in the world?"

"Aww," Shelby cooed, her cheeks flushing as she dissolved into a wide, shy smile. "You're too sweet."

I've got her now, Michaelis thought. That line worked every time. Every woman he had ever picked up had been the most beautiful, at least for the night. It was somewhat of a recycled line, but Michaelis was amazed at how well it worked. *Women are fools for flattery,* he thought. *Tell them they are beautiful or you love them and it is over.* He was very good at playing to and preying on the needs and responses of the female heart. Michaelis Nielsen was a professional; black-belt, stone cold. And he knew it.

Back at his house, Michaelis stopped the car in his wide, lavish driveway. "I thought I'd invite you for dessert," he said to Shelby, giving her a beaming smile. "You're so beautiful; I just couldn't bear the thought of taking you home already. If you don't want to stay, I'll just bring you some pie and I'll take you home."

Shelby beamed. "I'd love to stay," she said breathily, just as he knew she would.

He escorted her gallantly up his long, winding driveway and opened the door to his mansion. Soon, they were seated on the couch in his living room, with a roaring fire, pumpkin pie, and cocktails. Michaelis knew it wouldn't be long before Shelby would be tipsy enough to make some unwise decisions. As he reclined on the sofa, he let his eyes wander lustfully over Shelby's body, encased in her tight black cocktail dress as she rose to excuse herself to the bathroom. She was a tall, leggy blonde, with generously sized breasts and a firm, rounded rear. *What a nice ass,* Michaelis thought, contemplating taking a handful of it. As he mildly enjoyed his fantasy and found himself eagerly awaiting Shelby's return, he knew that his companion would satisfy him for the night, but tomorrow he would need to be out searching for something better. Shelby was hot but quite boring, not nearly as freaky or exotic as some of his conquests. She was a young twenty-something newspaper intern, fresh from college, inexperienced and naïve. She was easy to maneuver but he wouldn't want to keep her as his long-term plaything. His smile spread as he remembered Anisa, a dark-haired exotic dancer who he had had a long, scorching fling with many months ago. Anisa wore skintight leopard-print pants and a trench coat with nothing beneath. She had been into whips and chains, any kinky thing Michaelis's dirty mind wanted. The only secret, that no one else knew, was that he had paid her a pretty penny for it. He hated to hire a prostitute, but she was worth it.

His reverie was interrupted by Shelby's return. He rose from his chair, lifting his glass to her as he took a swallow of champagne. Then, setting his glass down, he walked slowly, predatorily toward her, clapping his hands together before placing them on her shoulders. Shelby, the wide-eyed intern that she was, did not protest but looked on him with her deer-like blue eyes as he lowered his mouth to hers and started to peel away her dress. All his cards were lined up and it was time to play. *I deserve this for my hard work today,* he thought as he molded her soft body against him.

Chapter Twenty-Five

It was Thanksgiving Day, a blustery, raw, chilly Thursday afternoon, and Meagan was struck with the jarring, heartrending reality that she had no one to spend her holiday with. Her parents had been dead for years, she had no family in town, and not many friends either. Especially now after the press scandal had erupted, Meagan had barricaded herself in, both to shield herself from the vicious blows of resentment from her peers, and also because the guilt over what she had done to Terrence was throbbing fresh and hard in her mind. The guilt and isolation, along with the deep yearning to be with him, was just about tearing her apart. Meagan hadn't gotten up until noon, just grateful to have the day off and not have to answer to anyone. Now it was about 3:30 PM, and gusts of snow were swirling violently outside, obliterating all vision for a radius of anything more than three feet. Meagan yawned tiredly and shuffled to the door to check the mail, dressed in her old gray Grandview sweatshirt, a pair of baggy sweatpants, and her navy blue polka-dotted bedroom slippers. Her black hair was tossed into a dumpy bun and she wore no makeup, only her thick black-framed eyeglasses.

As she opened the front door, she was immediately smacked in the face with a blast of icy air. Meagan cursed quietly and reached out to get the mail from her mailbox. She had just fished the envelopes from the slot and was about to retreat to the warmth of her apartment when she noticed a stout box sitting on her doorstep. Sighing, she bent down to pick it up. She carried the items inside and shut the door behind her, cranking the radiator up higher to seal out the newly chilled air. The radiator gave a slight sputter of protest as it began to pump out more heat. Meagan leafed halfheartedly through her mail- just a few bills and an ad or two, nothing terribly exciting. Setting that aside, she focused her attention on the cardboard box. *What could this be?* She thought a tad anxiously, hoping it wasn't a bag of rotten eggs or a gesture of menace from some outraged biddy. Gingerly, with a worried frown, she opened it, but then her expression relaxed and her eyebrows rose sky-high when she saw what was inside.

The box contained a box of stuffing mix, a potato, a can of sour cream, a bag of rolls and a prepackaged pie. Lifting out a handwritten note, she read:

Dear Meagan,

Here are some things to make a Thanksgiving dinner because we know you have no family in town. We are going to a friend's for dinner and wanted to wish you a happy holiday. Stay warm. Your landlords, George and Dolores Kent."

Meagan felt tears come to her eyes as she read the note. The Kents had actually taken the time to put together a dinner box for her, in spite of what had happened. There was no doubt that they had found out, but they must not have judged her like everyone else. They were the closest to family that she had in town, treating her almost like a daughter or granddaughter.

Still smiling faintly, Meagan moved deeper into her apartment and carried the box into the kitchen. "I guess I'd better make some sort of Thanksgiving dinner," Meagan said to herself. "After the Kents went to all that trouble for me."

In the kitchen, Meagan unpacked the box and set the items up on the countertop. She then reached up and switched on her old radio to the classical station, which was softly playing some unidentified clarinet concerto. Satisfied, Meagan turned it up and began to prepare her dinner. She unwrapped the potato and peeled and chopped it, humming in a raspy voice along with the radio. Once the potato was chopped, she immersed it in water and set it to cook in the microwave. She was extremely grateful to the Kents for getting her Thanksgiving started, because she never would have found the motivation to cook all of that by herself.

It took maybe a half hour for her to unpack and cook some of the things that the Kents had brought for her. When she was ready, she carried all of the steaming dishes out to the coffee table in her living room and got herself a bowl and some silverware. For atmosphere, she put one of her favorite Christmas symphonies in the CD player and brought that into the living room as well. With the music playing softly, Meagan finished setting up her dishes on the table and ducked into the pantry, a small alcove off of the kitchen, where she fetched two brand-new red candles, still wrapped in their protective plastic. She carried the candles and matches in one hand, and in the other she held a pair of ancient twin holders that had belonged to her parents.

Sitting down in the living room, Meagan dimmed the lights to lend a more subdued atmosphere. Carefully, almost pensively, Meagan placed the candles gently in the holders, and with a soft swish of the match she ignited the wicks, breathing in the festive charred scent of wax and smoke. Setting the matchbox down, Meagan sat back to admire the flickering flames for a moment before she dug in. Seeing the two candles side-by-side made her think of her parents, who were resting side-by-side in their plot at the cemetery. A single tear slipped down Meagan's cheeks as she remembered her parents and thought of how much she missed them. It had been hard to become an orphan at fifteen. Sometimes it had really taken a major toll on her. Meagan had only a ghost of a memory of a Christmas when both her mother and father were alive; she was five or six years old. Her parents, David and Patricia Lucien, had a wonderful marriage and adored Meagan, until David got sick and died when Meagan was seven or eight years old. Tricia had hung on for seven more years until she died of cancer, maybe a broken heart as well.

I love you Mom, Dad, she whispered under her breath, touching one of the candles. *I miss you.* After her brief moment of reflection had passed, Meagan picked up her fork and scooped a tiny forkful of her mashed potatoes, bringing it slowly to her lips to test it. Meagan had never been crazy about potato, but she decided to make it so that the Kents' gift wouldn't go to waste. She sampled a few scoops before setting the bowl aside and reaching for the stuffing, which she liked a lot better. She had decided not to bother with a turkey this year, because it was a lot of mess and rather ridiculous to cook an entire bird just for one person. The gift basket from the Kents was generous, but Meagan didn't think she had the appetite to eat that much food. *I'll save the leftovers,* Meagan thought. She could always use leftovers, because after her long and busy days she often didn't feel like cooking.

After a few bites of stuffing, a round of cranberry sauce, and a scoop of red cabbage, Meagan wasn't really hungry anymore. She decided to just skip the dinner and go straight to her favorite: pumpkin pie. She opened the cumbersome box and took out the prepackaged pie, which was thankfully ice-cold from being outside on her porch. Along with it came a can of whipped cream. Meagan rose to get herself a knife and a fresh cup of coffee, since her current cup had gone watery and tepid. On the way to the kitchen, she smoothed a hand over her hair and let out a ragged sigh. What a miserable holiday, she thought. Aside from physical health problems, it couldn't really get much worse. Frustrated, Meagan dished her food into storage containers and stuck it in her refrigerator to be used as leftovers for the next week. Catching her reflection in the hallway mirror, Meagan realized that she looked awful. Her hair was dull and unwashed, dark circles lined her eyes, and she had been careless with what she ate, too much junk food and not enough healthy food.

As she filled her coffee mug, Meagan sighed again. *Terrence.* She missed him. She missed his voice, his face, the way he talked to her, the way he touched her, that special smile. The last time she had seen him, his eyes had been cold and vacant as a polar desert, and he had, very nicely, essentially told her he never wanted to see her again. "What a goddamned mess," Meagan muttered, slamming her plate down on the counter. When her cup was filled, she carried it back into the other room and took a careful sip. The burning liquid seared her mouth and caused tears to come to her eyes, and Meagan shook her head, trying to clear her newly blurred vision. When she had healed sufficiently, she took a small piece of the packaged pumpkin pie and put it on her plate. Then, she shook the can of whipped cream and covered the pie in a frothy pile of the white cream. She took a small bite, and was pleasantly surprised that it tasted much better than she expected. *This is it,* she thought, and felt a bit better after a few bites. *Just one thing to make this complete,* she thought, pouring herself a few generous shots of vodka.

It wasn't long before the alcohol began to take effect and Meagan felt her head swimming, the misery of the past few days fading into an amorphous, unintelligible blur. Glancing over to the CD player, which was pumping out soft classical music, Meagan frowned. She loved classical music, but on this particular evening it just seemed to depress her all the more. With a lazy flick, she turned the music off and took the CD out. She gently laid it on the couch and hooked up her mp3 player to her mega speakers. *This party needs some life in it,* she thought, blowing out the candles and cranking up one of her favorite R&B songs. Drunk and dizzy, she shimmied out into the middle of the living room and began to clumsily dance. As the vodka burned through her veins, Meagan began to feel completely liberated. She laughed out loud as she whirled around, gyrating to the R&B artist's honey-sweet city-accented voice. Maybe it was the alcohol, maybe the music, but Meagan suddenly felt hotter than a Bikram yoga studio. She peeled off her sweatshirt and threw it, followed soon by the rest of her clothes, until she was dancing half-nude across the room, humming along with the song. She never used to drink like this, but the situation with Terrence had just torn her up. As she belted out the licentious lyrics at top volume, gyrating across the room, the walls began to spin and blur, and she tripped over her own feet before passing out on the carpet.

***

While Meagan was having a one-woman drunken fiesta of misery at her home, Terrence was on his way to his parents' home for Thanksgiving. They lived in a small home on the semi-rural outskirts of town, a good twenty-five minute drive from Terrence's own house. He carefully surveyed the snowy roads with a steely grip on the wheel, glad that he was almost there. *Shouldn't be long now,* he reassured himself as he flicked on his turn signal to turn off at the exit to the small borough where his parents lived. Driving in general made him nervous, especially in bad weather.

After what seemed like an eternity, Terrence pulled up in his pickup truck in front of his parents' one story brick home. He pulled into the driveway and cut the motor. Before he got out of the car he grabbed his precious cargo from the seat next to him, the painstakingly baked apple pie that he had made the day before. It was his contribution to the dinner at his parents', and it had taken him nearly all day the day before. Terrence usually enjoyed baking, but ever since Doreen's death, and combined with the press scandal, he had been almost out of energy. He had lost a considerable amount of weight and looked gaunt and sickly. Purplish rims lined his eyes, which were tired and unfocused. His clothes were rumpled and he had neglected to shave for a day or two, forming just a hint of stubble, which was barely visible, but still a big deal. Terrence shaved meticulously every day, and when he didn't, something was seriously wrong. Clutching his tinfoil-wrapped pie, Terrence shivered as he made his way to the door of his parents' house. He knew that his mother would fuss over him as she usually did, and his father would be quietly disapproving if he found out about the scandal.

Taking a deep breath, he pressed the bell. Behind the door, he heard shuffling footsteps before the door was swung open. The warm, inviting smell of baked bread wafted through the open doorway, and there stood Terrence's mother, wiping her hands on her apron. She invited him in and drowned him in a hug, murmuring sweet nothings to him as she embraced him.

Eloisa Hannah Reid was a spry old lady of seventy-four, white haired with sparkling blue eyes like her son's. Ever since Terrence was born she had doted on him, given him anything he had ever wanted. He was her only child and her special boy, and Eloisa loved him with all of her heart. Terrence relaxed as his mother's arms tightened around him and she gently kissed his cheek. "Welcome home, honey," she murmured. Usually, this type of overly lovey behavior would embarrass a fifty-four year old man, but Terrence was just glad to be with his mother, the one person who had never turned on him. He didn't know how she would react to the scandal, but it was clear that Eloisa Reid would always be by his side.

"Oh, Mama," Terrence murmured, kissing her gently on the cheek as well as they drew apart. "I brought you a pie."

Eloisa took the pie and lifted the foil. "It's beautiful," she commented, taking it into the kitchen. Terrence followed her toward the warmth and inviting aromas emanating from the kitchen.

"Can I help with anything?" he asked.

It was just then in the light of the kitchen that Eloisa got a good look at her son. "Good Lord, honey!" she exclaimed softly in concern, touching his unshaven cheek.

"You look terrible; so thin…" she broke off, shaking her head.

"It's been rough, Mama," he admitted, but not wanting to worry her, he put a hand on her shoulder. "I'm still here, though, aren't I?"

"Terrence," she put her hands on his shoulders, her crow's-feet framed blue eyes serious. "Honey, just go sit down and rest. Dinner will be ready soon. I want to see you eat well tonight, you need it."

Terrence obeyed Eloisa's gentle but firm words of advice, and went to sit down on the sofa in the living room. He found that his leg had stiffened from the drive and from a general lack of activity, so he had to lean heavily on his cane as he scraped his way across the room, trying to keep his weight off of his twisted leg. He sat down on the threadbare sofa in the living room and closed his eyes, letting out a soft groan. It had been really, really rough lately. Not only was he swamped with dealing with the practical and emotional reverberations of Doreen's death, but he also deeply resented the media blowout. *Whoever did this hasn't a clue,* Terrence thought bitterly, equally angry that Meagan had been swept into this mess as well. He had taken a leave of bereavement from the classroom, and he felt divided about going back. On the one hand, he knew that he had to. According to the conferences with Mr. Follett, his teaching assistant, things just weren't getting done. The class's overall grades had suffered, and all the numbers were declining. *They miss you,* Mr. Follett had told Terrence. Terrence wondered about this, if indeed they did or if Mr. Follett was just a lousy replacement. Terrence also dreaded the impending meeting with the university board, to determine what should be done about the scandal. They had said nothing about a meeting, but Terrence knew that the moment he got back, they would pounce. Terrence cursed softly to himself when he thought of how this whole situation had blown up in his face. He had never meant to cause a media scandal, or anything of the sort.

He and Meagan had shared a special connection, something that Terrence had never felt in all of his years married to Doreen. Now, that beautiful connection had been marred, tainted, dirtied and dramatized by the media; and now Meagan was made out to be some slut and he some cad. Shaking his head, Terrence contemplated how much he needed a stiff drink at the moment. He refrained, though, because he didn't want to spend Thanksgiving with his parents as a sloppy drunk.

His reverie was interrupted by his mother's cheerful voice letting him know that dinner was ready. Terrence took a moment to wrench himself from the couch, dragging his leg as he limped into the adjacent dining room. When he saw his mother's bright smile, he couldn't help but to return it. As he took his seat, he looked over the elegant feast that his mother was busily loading onto the table. She had really gone all-out as she always did, with mashed potatoes, green bean bake, glazed carrots, vegetables, homemade cranberry sauce, and a complete dressed turkey with stuffing. "Looks beautiful, Mama," he commented, and she beamed at him as she lit the candles on the table.

"Thank you, darling," she replied warmly. "Go ahead and dish up while I go get your father."

Terrence swallowed hard as he thought of his old man, who was in his bedroom watching TV. Albert Reid had not been well the last time Terrence had visited, and Terrence really hoped he was doing better.

A few moments later, Eloisa reappeared, with Terrence's father in tow. Albert Reid was a medium-height, stoop-shouldered man of seventy-six, with gray hair and just the barest hint of a beard. He had been a teacher in his heyday, and Eloisa had been a secretary until she quit her job to take care of Terrence after he was born. Though Albert's shoulders were stooped and his hair was grayed, his blue eyes still showed a spark of wit and vitality similar to his son's.

Terrence rose from the table and went over to greet his father. "Father," he said quietly, offering his arms for an embrace. Albert hesitated for a moment before solemnly clasping Terrence in his arms.

"Hello, Son," Albert greeted him gruffly, but with love. Terrence was glad to see that his father looked much better off than he had been the last time.

After the greetings had finished, Eloisa suggested that they sit and eat before the food got cold. They did, and Terrence took small portions, not sure if he would be able to eat much. The meal started with a brief prayer and they began to eat, making small talk about the weather and avoiding heavy topics. Terrence marveled over his mother's cooking, which had always been superb. He took a delicate bite of glazed carrots as he listened to his mother and father talk. *I'm glad to be home,* he thought.

Eloisa turned to him when there was a break in the conversation. "I was just thinking, Terrence, honey, if you would like to spend the weekend with us, you most certainly can. It might do you some good to get a rest for a while."

Terrence considered. His mother was right; he certainly could use a rest. And besides, spending days in an empty house was beginning to wear on his nerves. "Thanks, Mama," he said quietly. "I think I will."

"By all means," Eloisa added. "You can stay as long as you like. We know you've been through a lot."

There was a gruff cough from the other end of the table as Albert cleared his throat. "While we're on that topic, son," he mentioned. "What is all this foolishness about you and the grad student? When I saw it, I thought, surely it must not be true. My son would never do that."

"Albert, leave him be," Eloisa cut in, giving her husband a firm stare. "It's done now."

"You make far too many excuses for him, Eloisa," Albert replied calmly, taking a spoonful of potatoes.

"I'm sorry," Terrence said softly, shaking his head. "It isn't what it seems like. I can't explain it now, though."

Albert shrugged. "There's no need to apologize to me, Terrence," he replied, not unkindly. "The only one you are accountable to is yourself."

"I know, Father," Terrence said tiredly. "I know."

Eloisa shot Albert another stare. "Not a word more about this, Albert. You've upset him enough," she said firmly. Albert shrugged and took another scoop of his food, apparently accepting his orders. Terrence gave his mother a weak, tired smile, and soon the conversation switched to a lighter vein.

Chapter Twenty-Six

Meagan really wasn't in the mood for calculus class. She sat, tapping her pen softly against her open notebook, staring pleadingly at the clock. She was extremely frustrated with the way that Mr. Follett was teaching, or perhaps the way he wasn't teaching. She hadn't seen Terrence since Doreen's funeral service, and she had no idea how he was holding up. In a way, she felt that she was partly to blame for the scandal, because it had been her that had kissed him first. Since the great incident, Meagan's life had become sort of a hollow, circular conundrum; vacuous and depressing. Meagan sighed and rested her head in her hands as she thought about her dream of becoming an architect or engineer. That was the precise reason that she was in this class, and yet at the moment it seemed an unreachable goal, something she couldn't deal with.

She was delivered from her depressing reverie when the clock struck and Mr. Follett announced in his signature deep, nasal tone that class was dismissed. Meagan grabbed her bag and headed for the door, staggering backwards as she was rudely elbowed out of the way. "Excuse me," Meagan muttered indignantly to whoever had pushed her. This was supposed to be a serious adult class, but Meagan couldn't believe that it was reminiscent of middle school; getting shoved into lockers and such. After the scandal, Meagan's classmates had simply talked around her, pretending she didn't exist. She had tried to go on with her life, but apparently everyone else wasn't ready to let that happen.

Class had let out early for a faculty meeting so Meagan checked her watch and decided that she would scoot over to the accounting firm where Jennine worked and see if she wanted to go out to lunch before Meagan had to get to work at Melanie's shop. Meagan hadn't talked to Jennine since the press scandal, and she had no idea how she would react. She just hoped that her friend hadn't gone mad like everyone else. Fairly confident, she climbed into her car and made her way through the crowded midday traffic. The sky was overcast, but luckily nature had decided not to avalanche Meagan with snow or ice rain, which was quite a blessing. The weather was usually horrible, and Meagan was just grateful for a clear sky. *Maybe it will be better today,* she thought, taking the clear sky as a positive omen. In about ten minutes, Meagan drove into the heart of the downtown and pulled up to the looming, modern, glass-encased office complex where Jennine worked. Parking in the parking garage, she paid her fare and traipsed to the revolving doors at the main entrance, her heels clicking on the pavement. Meagan smoothed a hand over her raven-black hair, which was in a ponytail accompanied by a pair of chandelier earrings and matching tan cowl-neck sweater. Reaching the doors, she was sucked into the lobby of the vast corporate empire. The ceiling was high and domed, almost like a commercial cathedral. Potted plants lined the sides of the room and a sophisticated-looking dark-haired receptionist sat behind a massive marble-topped desk. Meagan approached the desk and asked for the Martin Marshall accounting firm. "Fourteenth floor," the receptionist replied smoothly, pointing one lacquered fingernail in the direction of a bank of elevators against the far wall. "Elevators are in the back."

Meagan thanked her and headed to the elevator, wondering why in tarnation Jennine wanted to work on the fourteenth floor of anything. Meagan disliked heights and was rather afraid of elevators, but she gritted her teeth and willed herself to keep walking. *I hate the city,* she thought, wishing that she could live in a quiet home on the edge of town, away from chaos and confusion. Once in the elevator, Meagan swallowed hard and pressed fourteen as the doors slid closed with a quiet, ominous rumble. She squeezed her eyes shut as the elevator lurched to a start and began to ascend the floors with a steady *click...click...click.* "Ugh," Meagan said aloud, hating the feeling of being stuck in a confined space while it rose off of the ground. Finally, after what seemed like a lifetime of agony, the elevator arrived at fourteen. There was a hesitation, and Meagan panicked for a moment before the doors slid open. Pale and shaking, Meagan released a sigh and stepped off, glad to once again be on solid ground.

As she stepped off of the elevator, Meagan entered another spacious, elegant lobby, though it was far simpler than the first. A potted plant sat in the corner, along with some chairs, and Meagan heard the quiet clacking of her friend typing away at her keyboard. She knew by the sound that it was Jennine because Jennine typed faster than anyone Meagan knew, fast and loud and brisk, almost like Jen herself.

Meagan's courage began to wane as she approached the desk. Jennine, engrossed in her work, was on the phone. "Good morning, Martin and Marshall," she said professionally. Pausing, she listened to the person on the other end before scribbling something on a notepad, swiveling in her chair. "Okay, Mr. Florence, I will transfer you. One moment, please."

While Jennine was on the phone, Meagan thought about how nice her friend looked. Jen's wavy brown hair was pulled back in a utility ponytail and her ears were adorned

194

with drop earrings. She wore a pert, businesslike white scoop-neck top and just the barest hint of mascara.

Jennine pressed a button on the phone and announced the call, before saying 'thank you' and hanging up. Meagan rested her hand softly on the desk. "Jen," she said quietly, getting her friend's attention.

Jennine looked up from her work. "How can I…" she started to say, but then she recognized Meagan. "Meagan," she said neutrally, her expression cool.

Meagan was taken aback by Jennine's frosty reception. "I… I just came to ask you if you wanted to go to lunch. We haven't seen each other for a while, and my class let out early."

Jennine barely looked up. "Sorry, I'm swamped today," she murmured coolly, in a tone that yielded no argument. "I'm afraid it has to wait."

Meagan put her hands down on Jennine's desk. She didn't want to cause a public scene, but at the same time she was frustrated with her best friend's icy reaction.

"Jen, what is this all about?" Meagan wondered. "Are you going to turn on me just because it's the thing to do?"

Jennine let out an exasperated sigh. "No, it's not that. It's just that you're a media sensation now, all up in the news and everything. All you can think about is what happened, and you've got the classic walk of shame. I simply don't want to get involved."

"Don't want to get involved?" Meagan practically screeched. "I thought that's what friends were for, but I guess that I was wrong. Jennine Aaronson, we have been best friends for eleven years, and when have I ever not been by your side?"

"I don't know," Jen murmured. She looked up at Meagan with moody, mercurial grey eyes. "I'm not mad at you, Meagan; I just can't deal with you right now."

Then, as if on cue, the phone rang and Jennine picked it up. "Good morning, Martin and Marshall," she said in the same sterile tone that she had used earlier. Meagan stood there stunned for a few more minutes before silently turning away and heading back to the elevators. Suddenly, as she got back into the elevator, she realized the stark reality that she had just lost her best friend. Now she really was alone. Shivering with a sudden chill, Meagan was too cold and numb to care as the elevator lurched back down to earth. With anger, indignation, and sadness, Meagan stalked from the corporate empire and climbed into her car, driving out of the parking lot and ripping up her parking ticket, letting the torn shards sail out the window and blow away in the wind.

It was maybe ten more minutes that Meagan arrived at work. She didn't feel like working at the stupid toy store today, but had to, since everything was so expensive. Dejected and worn out, Meagan traipsed into the store. The bell over the door dinged cheerfully as she stepped in, and Melanie looked up from her paperwork over her red-framed glasses.

"Good afternoon," she greeted Meagan with a nod, pen in her hand. "I've got some boxes that need to be unpacked, in the storeroom."

Meagan hung up her coat and went into the back room to start unpacking. As soon as she was behind closed doors, the dam broke and all of the misery and grief of the last few weeks poured over her like a waterfall. Tears began to stream down her cheeks as sadness and exhaustion washed over her, slowly at first, until her silent tears became full-blown sobs. Embarrassed, Meagan wiped her nose on her sleeve and rose to make a beeline to the bathroom when the door creaked open. "Meagan?" Melanie asked quietly, coming over with her face full of concern. "Are you okay? What happened?"

Meagan looked up at her. "I don't know, Melanie," she sobbed. "My life is a disaster."

And then, unexpectedly, through her tears, Meagan found herself being pulled into Melanie's arms. "You'll be okay, Meagan," Melanie murmured, and Meagan buried her face in Melanie's shoulder. "You'll be okay."

Meagan suddenly jerked back, almost furiously. "Why haven't you judged me?" she asked incredulously, with a sniffle. "You're the only one that hasn't."

Melanie shrugged. "Want the honest answer?" she asked, and Meagan nodded. "Truth is, your sex life is none of my business," Melanie replied wryly. "And besides, I hate when people gang up on somebody just because everyone else is."

"Thank you," Meagan sniffled with a teary smile. "I appreciate it."

"Jennine stopped talking to me today," Meagan blurted out.

Melanie looked surprised. "Really?" she wondered, a frown creasing her brow. "I'll talk to her about that," she said frankly after a moment.

"You don't have to…" Meagan replied. "I mean, if you don't know her very well."

"I will anyway," Melanie insisted. "Feeling better?"

Meagan nodded. "Well, go to the bathroom and clean up, take your time, and then come out and get back to work."

Meagan smiled weakly at Melanie. "Thanks again," she murmured.

Melanie winked. "Don't mention it," she said in her usual cheerful way. "Now enough about that, we've got toys to sell."

Meagan then broke into her first real smile for weeks and began to laugh.

Chapter Twenty-Seven

Terrence was standing at the sink at his parents' house, steadily washing dishes as he hummed along with the ballad on the radio. The song's source was an old, scratched-up handheld radio that his parents had had for years and years. Every once and a while, the music would be interrupted by a burst of static, but Terrence didn't mind. He looked around at the faded but tidy kitchen, feeling like he was back in his childhood. The house was just as he remembered, small and simple. The same faded lace curtains framed the small, south-facing window, which looked out over a little yard and the neighboring house. The adjoining dining room faced north over a small clearing and dense bramble-filled woods stretching on into the horizon. Terrence had often explored those woods as a boy, designing shelters from tree branches, doing experiments, and climbing trees. He would come back with skinned knees and assorted scrapes and bruises, and his mother would be worried, scolding him gently to be careful. He remembered walking a mile and a half home from the rural elementary school and coming home to the smell of his mother's apple pies that she would make for dessert on Friday nights. His mother, Eloisa, would wipe her hands on her apron when he came in and scoop him up in her arms with a cry of joy, raining kisses on his forehead and asking him about his school day. Then, he would have a snack of milk and cookies and retreat to his room to do his homework.

Even as a young boy, Terrence had taken his homework quite seriously, being the top of his class. When he finished his homework he would go barreling outside and play in the woods until his mother hollered for him to come to dinner. By then, his father would be home from work, his 1950's car parked in the driveway. He had had a good childhood, Terrence mused. He was very fortunate, for he knew many people who had come from tumultuous homes.

Terrence had been staying with his parents for two weeks now, and things were beginning to calm down. He felt relaxed and was glad to be out of the glaring, swirling hub of activity that was the city. Out here in the woods it was peaceful, he thought. His parents were glad to help him and he helped them as well, cleaning up the kitchen today while his father was napping and his mother had gone to the food mart on the edge of town to get groceries. Terrence offered to go, but Eloisa insisted that she needed to get out, and she would rather he stay there with his father. Terrence had told her to be careful, since the roads were somewhat slippery, and had successfully discouraged her from taking her and Albert's T-bird, borrowing Terrence's truck instead.

His general reverie and calm was interrupted by the ringing of his cell phone. Frowning, Terrence removed his dish gloves and pulled the scratched flip phone from his pocket. It was the university. "Hello?" Terrence answered.

"Doctor Reid, this is Darla, the president's secretary," a pushy female voice greeted him. "President Carlton and the dean would like to meet with you as soon as possible, to discuss your…" she paused, groping for a word. "…situation," she managed awkwardly. Clearing her throat, she continued in a professional tone. "Would it be possible for you to come into the office at 8AM tomorrow?" she asked, outwardly pleasant but the veiled undertone clearly demonstrated to Terrence that these were the President's wishes and he had no choice.

"No problem," he answered brusquely, choosing not to waste extra words on the President's smarmy secretary.

"Perfect," Darla chirped, her tone laden with heavy insincerity. "I'll see you tomorrow."

Terrence's response was a quiet click followed by the dial tone.

***

"Terrence Reid has always been a sweet peach," Darla chuckled sarcastically to the office assistant Stephanie as she came into the room.

Stephanie smirked. "I can believe that," she replied. She looked around furtively and lowered her voice. "I bet he's good in bed, though," she said with a smile. "Have you gotten a good look at him?"

Darla flipped her black hair. "Maybe, but he's too old," she pouted. "And I don't think much of his twisted leg. Who'd want to go out with a gimp?"

Stephanie nodded. "You've got a point there," she agreed, then burst into a laugh. "Apparently his grad student didn't care," she chortled.

"Apparently not," Darla replied, smirking. "I hope Carlton fires his ass. He thinks he knows everything."

Just then, the door opened and the president entered, and the secretaries immediately ceased their conversation. Stephanie scurried out of the room with an armful of papers and Darla focused intently on her keyboard, appearing hard at work. The president shot her a suspicious glare before indifferently turning away and striding into his office, closing the door behind him with a hollow slam.

***

Back in the kitchen at his parents' house, Terrence paced, his hands clasped nervously behind his back. He knew that he couldn't stay there forever, and that they would come for him eventually. His worried frown deepened as he thought of what might happen. He really didn't want to have to retire before he was even fifty-five. He liked teaching, and knew that he couldn't go back to engineering, even if he wanted to, because of his injury. Now, the only piece of his dream that he could hold onto was his teaching. He really didn't want to lose his job and have it all posted up in the newspapers. He didn't think that just because he had made a poor decision in his personal life that he should be crucified for it. *What bloodthirsty bastards,* he thought bitterly, recalling the hunter-like tone in Darla's voice, the thrill of a scandal and a destroyed reputation. He had never gotten along with the university president Jim Carlton, a pompous ass, and it was just like him to haul Terrence in at 8AM for a brutal inquisition. *Not gonna happen,* Terrence thought. There was no way he would let Carlton unnerve him. He would walk in there with a wide smile on his face and show the guy exactly where he belonged. Not to mention, he was one of the only specialists in his area. Firing Terrence would seriously dent Grandview's engineering and architecture program.

Still, Terrence was upset, his calm had been shattered. Finishing the dishes, he put the dishpan away and turned up the radio. He heard the rumble of a motor in the driveway as he was wiping off the counters and shut off the radio, heading to the back door to help his mother carry the groceries in. It was snowing light flurries when Terrence stepped outside, and the sky was the color of lithium metal. The cold didn't bother him at all as he stepped carefully off of the stoop.

Eloisa cut the motor and Terrence went over to the driver's side door help his mother step down from the high truck. Clasping her gloved hand, he helped her down. "Ah, Terrence," Eloisa sighed, smiling at him fondly. "You're so chivalrous."

Terrence smiled. "Of course, Mom," he answered. "You're my favorite lady."

Eloisa laughed, her keen blue eyes twinkling. "You're an incorrigible charmer," she chuckled. "You must have gotten it from me."

Terrence went to the rear of the truck, reaching into the bed under the tarp to pull out the heavy grocery bags. "Go on inside," he gestured to the door. "I'll carry these in for you."

Eloisa complied and went into the house, holding open the screen door as Terrence limped through it, both arms weighed down with multiple bags. It might have seemed like a lot to carry, but Terrence's muscular arms were barely strained. He still worked out several times a week, not to mention all the monkeying around he did with heavy equipment with his home and garden projects. His twisted leg was his only weakness, and as long as he had his cane, he managed quite well. After the lot of the groceries was brought in, Terrence set them on the table and prepared to help his mother unpack them. "Thank you for doing the dishes," Eloisa told him, rising on her tiptoes to kiss him on the cheek. "You're a good boy."

Terrence smiled absently at her as he began to unpack, but his mind was still preoccupied with the disturbing phone call he had received. Eloisa must have noticed his drawn look because she commented on it.

"Everything okay, hun?" she asked him, her brow furrowed with concern.

Terrence shrugged. "I'm all right," he replied. "Just a little tired, that's all." He didn't feel like getting onto the topic of his job with his mother.

But apparently Eloisa wasn't satisfied with that answer, because she looked at him more closely. "You look upset," she observed in a tone that left no room for argument. "What happened?"

Terrence sighed, knowing his mother would just keep bugging him until he told her. "The university called," he replied tonelessly. "The president and dean want to meet with me at 8AM tomorrow."

Eloisa looked concerned. "Oh, honey, why so early?" she asked. "You'll have to get up in time to drive into town."

"Because the president is a blasted asshole," Terrence growled through clenched teeth, forcefully setting down the bag of rice he was holding. Then, not to worry his mother, his face softened. "Sorry," he apologized.

"Better get a good night's sleep tonight," Eloisa commented with a smile, ignoring his apology. "So you can go knock 'em flat tomorrow. Now, why don't you go wake your father up while I start cooking dinner?"

Terrence leaned over and kissed her cheek. "You're a good sport, Mom," he said fondly before he left the room. "I don't know what I'd do without you."

Chapter Twenty-Eight

Terrence was in a dreamy, relaxed haze, reclining shirtless on a beach chair while he sipped a margarita that a busty blonde waitress had handed him at the cocktail stand a few minutes ago. He slipped his sunglasses on and surveyed his realm from his perch on the chair. The beach was teeming with activity, mostly scantily-clad maidens in bikinis and their handsome escorts. The sand was white and fine as the Caribbean, and the sparkling teal ocean waves crashed against the shore while a perfect sun beamed down from above, warming Terrence's face. He closed his eyes and relaxed in his chair, until he was interrupted by the quiet sound of his name. He looked up and there stood Meagan Lucien, stunningly beautiful in a gold bikini, her skin gleaming, and her long black hair loose and free, spilling over her shoulders. She smiled softly, almost shyly at him and handed him a drink.

"Hey," she said softly, her lips glittering in the broad sunlight. She gestured to a vacant beach chair next to Terrence. "May I sit?"

"Sure," Terrence replied just as softly, unsure of what to say to her. She looked so beautiful and her dark eyes were filled with passion, desire, and something more.

Terrence felt the familiar clench in his loins, unable to take his eyes off of her as she gracefully lowered herself onto the chair. Her tanned, ample cleavage was spilling abundantly from her gold bikini top and she smelled like sun and flowers. "So," Terrence began hoarsely, not sure what to say. "What's new?"

"Terrence," Meagan said softly, just his name, just a whisper, and leaned forward to cup his face gently in her hands. "I missed you."

He leaned forward and kissed her gently, opening to let the taste of her flood his mouth. She let out a soft sigh and melted into his arms. He lifted her up off of her chair and onto his lap and the beach was cleared out, just the two of them alone with the waves and the sun. He caressed her hot skin with gentle urgency and she murmured restlessly, squirming against him. He sighed and leaned back as she trailed kisses down his neck. Reaching up, he gently untied her bikini top and her heavenly breasts came to rest in his hands, filling them to overflowing. He lowered his mouth to her breast and was awarded with a breathy groan as she arched against him, stroking his head. She tasted like sun and ocean and woman, and he lifted his hand to cup her other breast when…

Beep, beep… beep, beep… beep, beep. A shrill noise blasted into his ear and jolted Terrence from the pleasant dream, the beach and Meagan fading away as he was thrust back into reality. "Jesus Christ," he muttered, swiping at the offending alarm clock, which read 5:54 AM. A few other assorted muffled curses followed before he threw back the blankets and climbed out of bed, dazed and disoriented. The house was cold and dark, and Terrence had a bit of a headache. Not to mention a mammoth-sized erection from his luscious dream, and it was beginning to become a burden. This was the first time since the night with Meagan that his sex drive had been evident at all, he realized. The past few weeks he had been tired and depressed, often cross of mood and preoccupied. Suddenly, Meagan had lusciously ripped back into his dreams and he had gone up like a rocket. *Damn,* he thought to himself. She certainly was attractive. And a tiny frown came to rest on his brow as he thought of the look in her eyes in the dream, almost as if she were in love. He suddenly missed her and pictured her sleeping, her arms outstretched, curtains of black hair spilling over her pillow.

But now wasn't the time to be thinking about Meagan. As Terrence thought of his imminent meeting with Carlton, his frown deepened into a scowl and he was thankful to find his erection relax. *Stupid, stupid bastard,* he cursed Carlton as he limped into the bathroom and began scrubbing at his teeth. He spit emphatically and shook his head as he shed his clothing and stepped into the shower.

Terrence was not rewarded with the hot shower that he had hoped for. Instead, he was delivered an icy blast of country water—unheated. He cursed softly and washed quickly and thoroughly, before shutting off the water and stepping out. The cold water had done him one favor; it had made him more focused and rid him of his headache.

Terrence dressed in a crisp, long-sleeved dress shirt, khaki pants and a tie. In the mirror, he shaved carefully and slicked back his graying strawberry-blond hair. With a satisfied final look, Terrence decided that he was set to go. He grabbed his briefcase, shoved on his glasses, and walked into the kitchen. He was surprised to smell coffee brewing and to see his mother sitting at the table in her bathrobe and chain spectacles, quietly sipping a cup of tea. She looked up and her aging, kindly blue eyes wrinkled gently around the edges. "Mornin' honey," she greeted him with a subdued smile. "Did you sleep well last night?"

Terrence ran a hand over his hair. "Yes, for the most part," he answered. Glancing at the clock, he saw that it was 6:30 AM. "What about you, Mom?" he responded. "You're up early."

Eloisa shrugged; a light lift of her shoulders. "I like the morning," she replied. "I like to get some quiet time before your father gets up. You know how boisterous he is." She winked at Terrence. When he only smiled slightly, her face sobered. "You look upset, honey, can I do something for you?"

Terrence poured himself a cup of searing black coffee and set it down on the table. "I'm okay, Mom," he replied. "Just not looking forward to this blasted meeting, that's all."

"Oh, I know," Eloisa murmured sympathetically, squeezing his hand. She looked him in the eyes. "You're gonna do fine. Now, can I cook you something for breakfast?"

Terrence smiled. "You're much too good to me, Mother," he said quietly. "But no thanks, coffee will do for now. I'll pack myself a good lunch."

Terrence and his mother sat in peaceful silence for a few moments, sipping their drinks with identical pensive miens. Terrence cupped his hands around his mug, warming them. After a moment's hesitation, he drained the rest of the coffee from his cup, rising to his feet. "I've got to get going, Mom," he told her, placing his cup in the sink. He held up the coffee pot. "Do you want any of this or can I take it with me?"

Eloisa shook her head. "I made it for you," she explained. "Go ahead and take it."

Terrence thanked her and poured it into his trusty metal travel thermos that he brought with him every day. Checking the clock, he picked up his briefcase and coffee cup. Bending over, he gave his mother a quick kiss on the forehead. "Bye, Mom, I love you," he told her.

"I love you too," she replied. Then, she lifted a fist in the air. "Go knock 'em dead," she said with a droll smile, amused at her own enthusiastic vigor.

"I will," Terrence laughed, waving to his mother one more time before he went to go put his coat and shoes on.

It was freezing, bitter cold outside, and the sky still held the rich purplish hue of predawn. Terrence was dismayed to see that a thin, hard layer of frosty ice had formed on the windshield and windows of his pickup truck. "Damn," he said softly, arriving at his truck in long strides. He unlocked it and reached into the driver's side door pocket and pulled out his trusty ice scraper. After maybe five minutes of tedious, continuous scraping, Terrence managed to get his windshield clear enough to adequately see through. He hopped into his cab and started the motor, blasting the defroster in hopes of shedding the remaining icy residue. He carefully navigated a few back roads until he reached the freeway. He generally was somewhat of a nervous driver, but today he was feeling better. The freeway was sparsely populated at this sleepy hour, not quite morning rush. The defroster was doing a good job clearing the ice from the windshield. Terrence leaned back in his seat and cranked up the radio, with its killer surround-sound and mega-bass speakers. An old hit rock song was playing and Terrence tapped his fingers on the steering wheel and hummed along as he sped down the highway. He was no longer feeling apprehensive about the meeting, but had established a calm sense of control. Carlton could go to hell as far as Terrence was concerned. He knew that the old windbag talked a big show but was secretly terrified of messing things up, so he left major decisions to the dean, Elisabeth Bennett. And she liked Terrence. So it was better than it could be.

But as soon as Terrence pulled in through the familiar gates of Grandview University, his macho rock moment faded away like fragments of a pleasant dream. This was their turf now, not his. Carlton freakin' owned the place, and Terrence would be stuck at the butt end of a conference table instead of on top of the world behind the wheel of his ride. He felt his gusto draining as he alighted, leaning on his cane while he grabbed his briefcase and headed for the monolithic double-doors at the university's entrance.

Terrence stepped into the foyer and was immediately assaulted by the sound of many voices. Looking around, he saw groups of students lounging in every corner, studying and eating breakfast. At first, no one paid him much mind, but at a lull in the conversation, his distinctive walking pattern of *step-clack-scrape* could be made out. The din fell silent and a flurry of whispers broke out behind hands, downcast eyes. Terrence kept his head up as he purposefully strode through the foyer, nodding a casual greeting to his persecutors. He was thankful when the elevator doors closed and he heard the chatter resume. He got off on the third floor and was absentmindedly making his way down the hall when he heard someone call his name. He stopped in time to see Carter Harland, a tall, thin, geeky gangly grad student in his advanced calc class. Carter had assisted teaching some of Terrence's lower classes and wanted to become an engineering/advanced calculus teacher just like Terrence.

"Professor!" Carter exclaimed as he bounded up and clapping Terrence heartily on the back. "You're here! Welcome back!"

Terrence smiled. "Thank you, Carter," he said. "Though this is the first welcome I've gotten," he added dryly. "I'm not too popular around here anymore."

Carter grinned, brushing his shaggy, chin-length unwashed light brown hair from his face. "Me either," he shot back enthusiastically. "But you'll always be popular with me," he added rather awkwardly, giving Terrence the not-so-subtle up-and-down eyes.

Terrence had known for some time that Carter was gay as day, but Carter had never admitted it. Terrence gave him an inattentive smile. "Hey, I'll see you around," he said to Carter, not really wanting to deal with him at the moment. "I have to go to a meeting."

Carter, oblivious to Terrence's brush-off, lifted a hand. "Okay, see ya, dude," Carter called before turning and slinking off down the hall in his striped pants and band t-shirt, his beat-up backpack bulging with books.

Terrence reached the door at the end of the hall that led to the executive wing of the building. With as much dignity as he could muster, Terrence pushed through the door to the president's spacious office. In a plush anteroom behind a large desk sat the president's dark-haired secretary, Darla, typing at her keyboard with the annoying *clickety-clack* of acrylic nails. When Terrence entered the room, Darla looked up and a fake smile stretched across her crimson-painted lips. "Ah, good morning, Dr. Reid," she said, her voice sickly-sweet like her smile. "Go ahead and have a seat. President Carlton will be with you in a moment."

Terrence's reply was unintelligible and grunted as he settled himself into a chair and picked up the paper, idly flicking through it. He became deeply engrossed in a wire report on the human brain, some new and interesting research straight from Washington D.C. He was still reading when he heard the intercom crackle on Darla's desk. "Send him in," the voice said with a burst of static.

"The President will see you now," Darla intoned, and when Terrence looked up, he found her smirking at him. "Right this way."

Terrence arose wordlessly, neatly folding the paper and setting it aside on the light stand. Let Darla think he was totally poised. It seemed to work, because she narrowed her eyes at him before returning to work.

Terrence rapped briefly on the closed wooden door marked PRIVATE, before turning the handle and walking in, closing the door behind him.

"Why, if it isn't the womanizing gimp himself," the president drawled sarcastically. Jim Carlton was seated behind his massive imperial-sized desk, reclining in his 100% real leather recliner over his burgundy suede carpet. He wore a mocking, lazy smile and an expensive suit, not to mention an asphyxiating amount of disgusting aftershave.

Terrence coughed and waved a hand in front of his face. "Jesus, Jim, care to crack a window?" he choked. "Did you take a bath in that crap?"

"The ladies seem to like it," Carlton chuckled, still smirking.

"I'm sure they're thrilled," Terrence muttered under his breath, which just made Carlton chuckle louder.

"You know, Reid, you're a funny guy," the president replied. "But you've got a way with the ladies too, just not anymore," he chuckled. "You're cold meat now."

Terrence didn't bother replying to his asinine comment. Instead, he folded his hands on the desk. "So, did you drag me in here at eight o' clock AM just to talk about ladies?" he asked, raising his eyebrows. "I've got a class at nine."

He was being quite saucy with his boss, he knew, but Terrence knew that the bag wouldn't do anything about it. Besides, it was clear that Carlton was running some sort of game this morning, so Terrence might as well join the fun.

"Ah, yes, a class at nine," President Carlton rubbed his hands together, briefly touched the tip of his fleshy chin in thought. "Speaking of meat," he piped up, a lecherous gleam in his eyes. "That Meagan Lucien's sure a beauty. Too bad I didn't get to her first," he outlined a crude female form with his hands. He cocked an eyebrow at Terrence. "Was she as good as she looks?"

"Yes," Terrence bit off crisply. "Now what's the deal here?"

Carlton smiled. "Always impatient," he mused. "That's mathematicians for you," he shook his head before continuing. "Anyway," he said in a severe tone, apparently done toying with Terrence and ready for the kill. "Look, Reid. The only reason you're still here is Dean Bennett. If she hadn't practically threatened to kill me, I would have fired your ass long ago. Which means," he continued with a sigh as if it burdened him. "One more infraction of any kind and you're outta here. Got it?"

Terrence nodded slowly. "I understand," he said with a slight yawn, as if Carlton bored him. "I'll tell Dean Bennett thank-you."

"Alright, Reid, get to class," Carlton snapped. Terrence picked up his briefcase and turned, saying nothing. He had his hand on the door when Carlton called him back. "Oh, Reid?" Carlton added. Terrence turned. "Next time you screw your girl, make her call you Jim. That's all, have a good day now."

Terrence kept an impassive face as he made his exit through the anteroom, past the smirking Darla. But once he exited the executive wing, he felt his blood boiling with rage, hands balled into fists. Carlton, the stupid, pompous bastard; he would have liked to give him a bloody nose. And damn right that Terrence could probably take him down if they got in a brawl. Jim was heavier but dumpy and flabby while Terrence was all muscle, strength and grace.

He laughed to himself under his breath as he boarded the elevator to go to his classroom. Now, he wasn't even mad anymore but just chuckling at the stupidity of Carlton. He tried to get Terrence riled and unnerved, but Terrence had matched him every tit-for-tat. He was no match.

He got off the elevator and strolled casually down the hallway, gently tapping his cane along the floor. He was once again surrounded by a hallway that fell silent as he passed. But in the distance, he made out a shape of a dark-haired woman. She turned, and he found himself locking eyes with Meagan, who was maybe seven yards away. She hesitated for a moment, and Terrence saw her eyes sparkle as he looked her up and down. She gazed at him in wonder, lips parted slightly, until she blushed and turned away. *Cold meat, my ass,* Terrence thought derisively as a punch of desire socked him in the gut. Oh, man, nothing cold at all, he thought with a sober swallow as he willed himself not to be embarrassed with a mammoth erection in public. All he had to do to remedy that was picture Carlton's smirking face, and the desire left him like a toilet flushing. *Thanks, Carlton, old pal,* he thought with a wry chuckle. *At least you're a good boner killer.*

Chapter Twenty-Nine

Meagan felt paralyzed in place as she locked eyes with him, rush after rush of molten heat soaking between her thighs. She hadn't seen Terrence for nearly three weeks but he still had the ability to get her soaking wet with just one look. *Good Lord, Terrence,* Meagan thought with a groan. Seeing him today compounded her feelings for him into one lethal fastball; her molten attraction to him as well as the softer feelings she had developed. She missed him, and she liked him. His smile, his eyes, his voice. She actually, scratch that, she loved him. She goddamned loved him, and felt like she could just melt into the floor right then and there. As he turned and scraped his way down the other side of the hallway, she just stood and stared after him, momentarily blinded by his brilliance.

"Looking for your lover boy, eh?" A mocking voice sounded close to her ear. Meagan jumped and shot a look of scathing annoyance at the broad-shouldered frat guy blocking her way.

"Yes, I am, excuse me," Meagan said coldly, stepping around the jock. She ignored his derisive laugh and simply walked away, not really caring what anyone thought at this point. Checking her watch, she saw that she had about ten minutes until she had to get to class… Terrence's class. She decided to hop into the ladies' room and check her appearance as well as take care of her business. Luckily, when she opened the heavy wooden door, she found that she was the only one in the bathroom. She sighed with relief, not really wanting to have to deal with anyone else. Stepping up to the mirror and peering intently into her own eyes, she realized how much she had changed even in the few weeks after Terrence's wife had died. She no longer wore as much makeup as she used to, in fact she wore none. But this wasn't out of exhaustion; it was almost a realization, a renaissance of her natural beauty. She had spent more time pouring herself into her studies and intellectual pursuits. She had learned to be on her own, to deal with silence around her, and it had deepened her as a person. Terrence would be proud, she thought; if he wasn't so busy ignoring her. A quick frown flickered over Meagan's face as she wondered what his reaction in class would be. The frown relaxed when she thought how electrified he had looked when they locked eyes. Maybe it would be different. Shaking her head, Meagan realized that she had probably been standing there for a good five minutes. She tore herself away from the mirror and abruptly retreated into a stall, closing the door behind her.

When she had finished in the bathroom, Mcagan hefted her bag onto her shoulder and headed down the hall to Terrence's classroom. By the time she got to the door, her hands were fairly shaking. She swallowed nervously and stepped across the threshold. Immediately, her senses were jolted to life by the energy and essence of him in the room. The air smelled softly of him, but only if one were to pay attention closely. Meagan knew his scent by heart: dusty leather-bound books, fresh, clean, masculine soap, washed linen and the occasional light, residual, earthy smoke smell, since he smoked pipes once and a while. As the painfully familiar, intoxicating scent slammed into her full-force, Meagan nearly reeled backwards, unsteady on her feet. The air seemed to be charged with a thousand volts worth of pinpricking electrons, penetrating her skin and soul. She was sure that his grey-blue eyes were studying her, searing over her curves that had once been exposed. This thought made Meagan's face turn crimson with a hot, heady blush as she remembered how gently and thoroughly Terrence had stripped away her inhibitions and taken her by silent storm, making her his forever. The class hadn't seemed to react to Meagan's arrival, still deeply engrossed in their work, pretending not to see her as if to diffuse the awkwardness. Meagan took a seat at her desk, got out her notebook, and finally allowed herself a glance at the cause of this entire delicious imbalance.

Once again, she was floored when she laid eyes on him, almost as one is blinded looking into the sun. He sat there at his desk, wearing a crisp white dress shirt and tie, his dress shirt rolled up to his elbows. His glasses rested on the bridge of his nose, his red pen poised ruthlessly over some unsuspecting assignment. His lips were pursed in concentration, maybe a touch of dry amusement, as he perused the paper. He was just so… Terrence. Meagan felt a twist of loneliness in her gut and wished that she could be in his arms again. Shortly after everyone arrived and was seated, the clock struck nine and Terrence rose from his desk. He regally limped to the board and lifted a piece of chalk. Turning and clearing his throat, he addressed his class. "Good morning, everyone, it's good to be back," he said in his quiet, low voice, friendly but always all-business. Immediately, the dull hum of chatter silenced and all eyes focused on him. "Today, I plan to do some damage repair so to speak, so that we can successfully get caught up."

This was also like him, his brusque but underlying kindly manner. He was a mathematician; wasted no words.

Meagan listened absently as he finished up his introductory announcements and took questions. She barely heard the actual words of her classmates, only their voices asking and Terrence's voice reassuring, answering, explaining. As if in a dream or soundless movie, she watched Terrence write out long strands of equations across the blackboard, his chalk rasping emphatically against the dry, dusty surface. Meagan copied down his notes, and at one moment, she happened to meet his gaze. Terrence must have done some sort of extensive mental preparation, she thought, because his initial flash of surprise and desire in the hallway was replaced by his usual calm, kind and serious mien, as if she were just another student in his class. He appeared unaffected, as if nothing had ever happened between them at all. Meagan felt chilled, as if someone had dumped a pail of freezing water over her head. Terrence's mild indifference hurt almost more than an outright rejection.

After class, she gathered her things and contemplated staying to talk to Terrence. But a cluster of students had gathered around his desk, sealing him off from her view. But she could still hear the quiet tones of his voice as he explained something to another student. Dismayed, Meagan simply turned away, deciding that she wouldn't be able to get what she wanted from him.

***

Later that day, after five o' clock, Meagan glanced up at the rapidly darkening sky as she made her way out of the Toy Box and towards her car. A chilly wind was kicking up and the air had a cold and brittle quality to it. Suddenly, a light hail began to fall from the sky, swirled about by the icy wind. Meagan pulled her collar up to protect her face and hurried to the door of her sedan, only slightly relieved when she managed to climb in and seal out the blast. Fishing her car keys from her coat pocket, she started the engine, fastened her seat belt and began slowly backing out of the parking lot. Soon, she was on the way home, making her way along the slippery and deserted roads. It was oddly quiet for 5PM; and Meagan figured that people must be getting ready for the holidays. Looking out the driver's side window, she saw luxurious displays of Christmas lights twinkling faintly in vibrant colors along the boulevard. Meagan simply inclined her head away and turned up the heat, warming her freezing hands. Meagan always found Christmas rather depressing. She always donated to the homeless shelter and tried to support efforts for the poor, but personally, she got no real joy from the season. Ever since her father had died when she was seven years old, Christmas had been dreary, a realization that she was alone in life. She clicked on the radio, hoping to drown out some of the heavy silence that filled her car. A plaintive, harmonic ballad was playing, with a catchy R&B beat and a minor key. She turned it up anyway until the bass was vibrating the frame of her car. She let herself get lost in the music, with the pounding bass and blasting heat, until she finally turned onto a side street and pulled up in front of her darkened apartment. She simply sat there for a moment, staring aimlessly at the muted lights coming from inside several houses on the block. A single, saggy bush bore the burden of bland white lights, but other than that, the street was devoid of Christmas lights. Most of the residents were cranky older folks or single, dragged-out college students like Meagan.

She parked her car, shut off the radio and heat, closed the door and hurried across the street against the biting hailstorm. Reaching into her other pocket, she fished out her house keys and approached the dark wooden door, adorned with a single, dusty wreath. She unlocked her apartment and stepped into her darkened living room, turning on a lamp as well as the old iron radiator, which gave a sleepy hiss of protest as it began to heat up. As she looked around her barren and cold living room, Meagan knew instantly what she needed. Her original thought was to get a blanket and a bottle of vodka and drown her troubles, but she decided against that and decided to do something more productive. Dance. She would put on some music and do a combination of dance and yoga until she worked out all of her stress. She left the living room and descended the steps into her basement workout room. She turned on all of the heaters in there to warm the room up while she got dressed. Up in her room, she changed out of her work clothes and left them in a pile on the floor. Rummaging in her drawers, she picked out a plain black leotard and tights, slipping on her black leather ballet shoes. She fastened her hair back into a bun and headed downstairs to get started. The radiators had done a good job warming the basement room; it was at a comfortable temperature to warm up her muscles. Meagan padded over to the CD player and hit play on one of her gradual dance mixes, starting with slow, flowing harmonies and progressing to full-on bass-heavy dance music designed to sweat out some major stress. A slow piano composition flowed from the speakers and Meagan took her place at the barre on the side of the room, breathing deeply as she stretched her neck from side to side. Checking her reflection in the mirror, she dipped into a deep *plié*, exhaling her tension as she descended and daintily brushed the floor. Then, in a less ladylike movement, she rose slowly, stretching luxuriously before bending over to touch her toes. As Meagan stretched, she focused on controlling her breathing and letting the tension of the day flow from her body. She propped her foot up on the barre and stretched her hamstrings, gradually leaning into the position to stretch out her muscles. As she stretched and concentrated on yoga-like breathing, a sudden thought came to her. The vocalist on the radio was singing about the Celtic hills and faerie lands, and an involuntary sigh slipped between Meagan's lips as she recalled her first love, Kellan, who had been as Irish as a shamrock. Those were good days, Meagan thought, but they certainly hadn't lasted long. Meagan was convinced that love in general had a lousy lifespan, deteriorating and vanishing rapidly like a volatile radioactive element. Meagan felt herself began to slip into a deep, brooding mood but tried her best to focus on positive things and catch herself before the dark mood overtook her. It had really hurt earlier when Terrence had kindly iced her, and she just felt harassed by the long day and miserable weather. Everywhere she went; she saw cheap, plastic Christmas decorations with garish paint and heard electronic remixes of Christmas carols. Again, it was a deterioration. Melanie had tried to keep her shop old fashioned for the holidays, but by now, Meagan was rather sick of Christmas. The word brought her a sickly feeling, as if she had eaten too many sugar cookies. Sighing, Meagan bent over, exhaling deeply once more. Once she felt as if she was adequately stretched out, she decided it was time to amp up the party a bit. She silently walked across the room to the CD player, still pumping out soft and slow piano music for ballet exercises. Shaking her head, she changed the CD and turned up the volume and mega-bass, pausing to change into her jazz shoes before pressing play. At once, a deep, thrumming beat filled the room as a fast-paced rhythm burst from the speakers. Immediately, Meagan felt better, and moved out in the middle of the floor to start a routine. She started simple, with deep, luxurious stretches, just flowing with the music. As the beat increased, Meagan rotated her hips and torso, letting herself go limp and supple as a sapling in a strong breeze. Her shoes made a satisfying thumping noise on the hardwood floor as she moved, mimicking the thumping beat. She caught a mirage-like glimpse of herself in the mirror, lithe and black-clad, bending, twisting, and stretching. She had to admit that she looked good. A light smile rested on her lips as she thought of Terrence standing in the corner of the room, leaning against the barre, analytical wit and heated desire reflected in his stormy blue-grey eyes.

The thought caused Meagan's smile to widen until she felt like she was grinning like an idiot. Her forehead was slick with sweat and her heartbeat matched the reverberating thump of the bass. This is why she danced, she thought. Dancing gave her a heady, healthy rush, the musky scent of sweat and a feeling of being so completely alive, undulating to a pounding beat in a hypnotizing sauna. Every nerve ending in Meagan's body was humming, pulsing to the music as sweat poured down her face. *This is it,* she thought with satisfaction. This rush was what she had spent years and years dancing and stretching for. Finally, when Meagan thought she could take no more, she shut off the music and took a gigantic gulp from her water canteen, splashing some onto her burning face and sweaty hair.

After she had showered and cleaned up, Meagan yawned and padded into the living room, clad in her bathrobe and slippers. Though it was still early, she decided to get comfortable on the couch with a cup of tea and maybe read a book. She felt completely relaxed after her dance workout and was now ready to catch some R&R after the long week. Her long black hair was still damp and twisted into a bun to dry, and her face was devoid of makeup. She shed her robe and pulled on a pair of deep gray sweatpants, a soft sweater, and fluffy socks. With another contented yawn, she settled onto the couch and lifted the mug of steaming tea to her lips, inhaling the strong scent of fresh roses that accompanied Earl Grey tea. She took a sip and then reached down to get her checkbook from her purse, deciding that she might as well balance it before starting to read. But when Meagan reached down, her purse was gone! Puzzled, Meagan rose from the couch and searched around, trying to locate her missing purse. She could have sworn that she had seen it earlier. After about fifteen minutes of turning the place upside down in increasing states of panic, Meagan came to the conclusion that she had left it at the Toy Box in the back room. Thankfully, she had had her car keys and house keys in her pockets of her coat, but her wallet, driver's license, social security information, checkbook, and about fifty dollars' worth of cash were in the missing purse. Not to mention, her class materials that she wouldn't have time to pick up from Melanie's place in the morning. Sighing, Meagan decided that she had better go get it, even though the shop was closed and it was going on 6:45 PM. Checking her key ring, Meagan saw that she had the key to the Toy Box, luckily. With a disgruntled sigh, Meagan left the warmth and safety of her living room couch and pulled on her snow boots and worn-out faux-fur poncho. Idly flipping her car keys around on their strap, Meagan steeled herself and pulled open the front door, slapped immediately by a vicious torrent of freezing rain. A strong wind was buffeting about, flinging the stinging drops of ice rain in all directions. Bare tree branches swayed and bowed under the weight of the gale, and arbor debris rained down every so often, twigs and branches scattering here and there. It was pitch black, and Meagan pulled her coat up around her face to protect her cheeks from the stinging impact. Locking her door quickly, she rushed across the deserted street to her car, which was sitting like a silent, squat stronghold in the dark. She climbed in and cranked up the heat, but still felt chilled to the bone. Even in the few minutes outside, she had managed to get freezing cold and rather wet. The driving was miserable, and Meagan had on her high beams for much of the time. *This is all for a stupid purse,* she thought, but then again, a lot of important things were in that purse. The storm had no intention of clearing up, so Meagan inched along at 2mph and was grateful for the glowing traffic lights to direct her. The only saving grace was that there wasn't much traffic on the road, almost none, so Meagan wasn't faced with the strong possibility of a collision.

Finally, when she thought she would never get there, Meagan pulled into the deserted parking lot. In the miserable weather, the store looked dark and foreboding, almost as if daring her to enter. Meagan shivered and decided to just hurry in and get it over with. At the door, her key got stuck momentarily before it reluctantly opened. Stepping in, Meagan found that it was indeed cold and dark. She groped for a light switch, but had no idea where to find one. She cursed softly to herself as she realized she would have to grope her way along in the darkened store. She was just about to call it a night and just forget the damn purse when a soft creaking sound came to her attention. Meagan froze in place and her heart pounded loudly, blood rushing in her ears. Was someone in there? She was terrified. Unmoving, mouth agape, Meagan was soldered in place, listening for another sound. A moment later, she heard the creaking repeated and the sound of muffled voices coming from the back of the store. A cold sweat broke out on Meagan's forehead and she crept closer, trying to determine who or what was causing the sounds. Were there burglars? Should she call 911? She realized in dismay that her phone was in her purse, which was in the back room. As she heard silence following, she wondered briefly if it could be a ghost. She generally didn't believe in that sort of thing, but she had to admit that this was freaking her out. Palms sweaty and breathing heavily, Meagan edged closer, unable to just turn around and walk away, the sensible thing to do. She was just too curious. Besides, she should probably find out so that she could call Melanie and maybe the police and tell them that prowlers had entered the shop. As she stumbled her way through the darkened shop, careful not to bump into anything or make noise, she noticed that a tiny crack of light was spilling out faintly from under the back room door. The door was open the slightest bit and the muffled sounds had resumed. Meagan crept along the wall, careful not to step too heavily or breathe too loudly. She steeled herself for the worst possible, expecting to see masked men bending over a dead body or something equally ghastly. But what she saw through the slim crack made her step back and rub her eyes to see if she was hallucinating. A soft, involuntary gasp slipped through her lips before she could help it.

To her disbelieving eyes, Meagan peered through the crack and saw Melanie and Jennine; both scantily dressed, locked in a fiery embrace. Jen was perched up on a low shelf and had her legs wrapped around Melanie's waist, her hands immersed in Melanie's long blonde hair as they kissed ferociously, tearing at the remainder of each other's clothing with unheeding passion. Meagan was stunned. Jen and

Melanie were lesbians? And together? She was flabbergasted beyond belief. She knew that Jen didn't date very much, but had never pieced it together. Besides, Jen had never told her, and Meagan felt hurt. She turned to leave; knowing that she had to get out of the store before Melanie and Jen knew she was there. She turned around to make a quick exit, but tripped over a crate in the dark and went flying; unable to stop the alarmed shriek that escaped her lips. Okay, Meagan thought. Now it was over. She dashed across the shop and sought the first hiding place she could find…. Under Melanie's desk. She plunged into the darkened cavern and curled up in a ball, willing Jen and Melanie to be too absorbed in their frenetic groping to notice. But to Meagan's misfortune, the noise had startled them and they emerged from the back room, half dressed, with messy hair and swollen lips. The door of the back room swung open, flooding the room with light, and Melanie's voice boomed, "Who's there?"

Meagan didn't answer. She now felt foolish crouched under the desk like this. Now they would think she had been spying on them. All she had wanted was to get her purse and leave. She hadn't planned on running into her best friend and boss locked in an illicit affair and then realizing that she would have to explain to them what she was doing there. *God, what a mess,* she thought to herself, wishing she had just gotten the purse in the morning, or better yet, not forgotten it at all.

"Maybe it was something outside," Jennine suggested in a trembling voice.

Melanie denied. "No, I heard something in here," she insisted. Reaching over to the wall switch, she flicked on the light. "Okay, prowler, time's up," she growled, stalking around the store. "Help me search the place," she called to Jen. Meagan closed her eyes and hoped to be invisible. That was before she heard a shrill scream pierce the air. Opening her eyes, she saw Jen looking down at her, eyes wide as saucers, finger trembling.

Melanie rushed over, and was equally shocked. "Meagan?" she thundered. "What the hell were you doing skulking around in the dark in here? You scared the bejeezus out of me!"

Meagan sat up, looking embarrassed. "I forgot my purse," she explained. "I heard noise in the back room, and..." she trailed off. "I thought it was a burglar," she continued. "So I looked, and after I saw you guys I didn't want you to know I was here, but I tripped and fell, then decided to hide. I know you must think I'm an idiot," she blabbered. She looked up at Melanie with pleading eyes. "Please don't fire me," she blurted. "I'm sorry."

Melanie looked at her for a long moment before she busted out into peals of robust laughter, chuckling so hard that her face turned red and she gasped for breath, slapping her hand down on the desk with hilarity, her heavy breasts straining against her black lace brassiere, shaking up and down as she laughed. While Melanie was heartily cracking up at Meagan's expense, Meagan looked over at Jen and saw that her friend wasn't laughing. In fact, Jen looked as stricken and rigid as a stone statue.

When Melanie's guffaws faded to chuckles, she turned to Meagan, who had with as much dignity as possible, brushed herself off and emerged from under the desk.

"Are you mad that I saw you two?" Meagan asked nervously.

"Do I look mad, Meagan?" Melanie asked her, grinning once more. "I'm sorry you happened to see us. It was an awkward situation." She sent a side glance at Jennine, who still hadn't moved or spoken. "No hard feelings."

Jen seemed to come out of her stupor and she stared at Meagan with unveiled hostility. "I still can't believe you're here," she hissed. "Don't tell anyone or I'll hurt you."

Meagan stepped back at her friend's icy tone. "I won't," she said quietly.

"Jen..." Melanie cut in, but Jen whirled on her.

"Stop defending her, Melanie!" Jen cried out. "Next thing you know; her little press hounds will pick this up and we'll be the latest town outcasts!"

Meagan felt herself getting upset. "My little press hounds?" she repeated in disbelief, her voice rising with irritation. "You were practically one of those press hounds; you crucified me about my situation. And now, you're caught in a similar situation and you have the nerve to blame me?"

Jen stared at Meagan. Finally, as if releasing some inner torrent, she hollered out, "I'm engaged!"

As the remnants of her anguished shriek died away, Meagan blinked at her friend. "What?" she asked softly. "What are you talking about?"

"I'm engaged," Jennine replied more softly. "To a partner at my accounting firm. We've been engaged for two weeks."

"How?" Meagan asked. "Why didn't you tell me? How did I not notice?"

"We were dating on and off for a while, and then he showed interest in me so I just agreed to go with him. Then, he wanted to get more serious, and everyone was pushing me to go the next step. I just didn't want to talk or think about it. I like him but don't love him; but I couldn't say no. But then I met Mel and…" she trailed off, shaking her head. She put her face in her hands and began to cry. "It's a mess. I don't know what to do."

Meagan put her arm around Jen's shoulders. "Will you forgive me?" she asked. "I'm sorry I upset you. Why don't you just call him and tell him it's over? If you aren't ready to go public with Melanie you don't have to."

"What a ridiculous suggestion," Jen sniffled huffily, but then she slowly looked up at Meagan. "Thank you, Meagan," she whispered. "I'm sorry too."

Jen allowed Meagan to hug her briefly before they pulled away. Meagan went into the storeroom to get her purse, ducking her head as she passed her friends. "Good night," she told them as she left, shutting the door gently as not to disturb a slumbering infant. But she heard no reply.

After Meagan left, Jennine took her phone off the counter. "I should take her advice and call him," she told Melanie.

But Melanie plucked the phone gently from her hand and set it on the counter, covering Jennine's lips with her own. "Not tonight," she whispered against Jen's lips. "Deal with him tomorrow. Get dressed and I'll take you home tonight," she scraped her teeth over Jen's lips with a rough gesture of domination and seduction. Jen sighed into the kiss and reached up to cradle Melanie's full breasts in her hands. "Sounds perfect," she whispered.

Chapter Thirty

Around quarter of five the next day, Meagan was stacking boxes in the Toy Box and she and Melanie were getting ready to call it a day. With a wry smile, Melanie went to the window and flipped the sign to CLOSED as the sky was beginning to darken. "We'll call it a day," she told Meagan. "Go ahead and pack up."

Meagan gathered her things as Melanie sat behind her desk, taking final inventory, her gray eyes critical through her red-framed glasses. "Jen and I are going out to dinner tonight," Melanie continued hoarsely, in her signature two-pack-a-day alto voice. "You can join us if you like."

Meagan turned. "Will Jen mind?" she asked, not sure what her status with her friend was.

Melanie gave a dry laugh. "Of course not, Meagan, it was her idea," she replied. "Just saying."

Meagan was stunned. "I—" she began, not knowing what to say. "I'd love to join you," she said finally. "I'd be honored."

"Very well," Melanie replied, closing her ledger with a smile. "I'm sure we'll have a fine time."

A few moments later, Meagan heard the sound of a battered muffler and the thump of bass as a dumpy white sedan pulled up in front of the store with a screech of tires. Abruptly, the motor was cut and she heard high heels on the pavement. A few seconds later, the door to the Toy Box swung open and Jennine sauntered in, swinging her car keys.

Melanie came out from behind her desk with a smirk on her lips. "Jennine Aaronson, you still drive like a high school boy," she chuckled, pulling Jen into her arms.

"You're a pretty wild driver yourself, Mel," Jennine murmured.

"Damn right," Melanie groaned as she claimed Jen's lips with her own. Jen braced her hands on Melanie's ample hips as Melanie roughly pulled Jen against her, lifting her off of the ground. They kissed hungrily, with Jen's hands tangled in Melanie's long blonde hair, taken down from her hairclip, until Jennine finally pulled back with a smile on her face. "You're incorrigible and I love it, Melanie," she murmured. "But let's not give Meg an eyeful."

"Too late," Meagan said with a chuckle. She glanced at her watch. "Listen, how 'bout I meet you lovebirds at the restaurant at six? Just tell me where you're going."

"I was thinking Nikki's," Jennine commented. "They have discounts and pretty good food."

"Sounds fine with me," Melanie said with a shrug. "See you, Meagan."

About an hour and fifteen minutes later, Meagan pulled into the parking lot of Nikki's Bar and Grille. She grimaced when she saw that Melanie's black Cadillac was already there. She knew that Melanie had won it some years ago from a broke gambler who had nothing else to give away. Meagan was late. Hoping her friends wouldn't mind, Meagan hurried toward the door and pulled it open, stepping into the dark, dusky interior of the pub. The place was moderately busy, and immediately Meagan was slapped with the dull hum of voices and the sizzling, smoky smell of barbecue. She was slightly annoyed that it was a smoke-friendly pub, but Jen and Melanie both smoked. Meagan surveyed the dim interior, looking for her friends, until she heard someone shout her name. Looking over, she saw Jen waving to her from a back booth. Meagan excused herself and made her way through the crowded diner, sliding into the seat across from Jen and Melanie, who were sitting together, Melanie's arm draped languidly around Jen's shoulders, Jen's cheeks baptized with a pretty, rosy glow.

Meagan headed over. "Sorry I'm late," she apologized to her friends as she dropped her bag on the floor.

"No problem," Jen said with a smile, lifting her glass. "We just got here. Besides, I've just been sipping on my Bud."

"Her second," Melanie coughed. She gave Jen a playful elbow. "She gets real wild when she drinks," Melanie told Meagan with a wink, pinching Jennine's thigh under the table. "It's all to my advantage."

Meagan laughed. "I'm sure she does," she replied. "And I'm sure that you're wild with or without a drink."

The three dissolved into muted chuckles, clinking glasses and smiling dryly.

At that moment, a waitress, a young, unattractive college girl, appeared next to their table. "Hi, y'all," she spoke with a loud drawl. "What can I get you?" she nodded to Meagan. "Want anything to drink?" she asked, beginning to recite a list of the nightly specials.

"I'll just have water," Meagan explained, seeing that her two friends already looked tipsy. "Somebody's gotta drive us home tonight."

The girl nodded and wrote it down. "Any dinner for you ladies?" she asked. "House special of hot pepper burger with jalapeno onion rings tonight, on sale."

Melanie looked up. "I'll take it," she turned to Jennine. "How about you?"

Jennine laughed, holding up her glass. "Sure," she agreed, high-fiving Melanie.

The girl turned to Meagan. "Make it three?" she asked.

Meagan shook her head. "Actually, I'm not that hungry," she said, deciding to order a bagel and cream cheese off of the breakfast menu. The girl took down their orders and departed, leaving the trio alone again.

"I bet you two will regret those jalapenos," Meagan said, grimacing at her friends across the table. "They always make me feel like my lips are on fire."

Jennine laughed heartily. "Doesn't matter to Mel, her lips are always on fire."

Melanie responded to this accusation with a wry chuckle and wink over the frames of her red actress glasses. Meagan glanced between her two friends, and saw a deep, stinging blush spread across Jennine's face, along with a giddy grin.

"Oh, God." Meagan rolled her eyes up to the ceiling. "Now I know why you guys needed an hour to get ready."

"We've gotta get it on while we can, before Mel heads off to law school," Jennine commented, elbowing her partner.

Meagan raised her eyebrows. "Law school?" she asked curiously. "What do you mean?"

"After Christmas, I'm going to sell the shop and go to law school. I want to become a trial lawyer," Melanie explained.

"Ohh, she's vicious," Jen sighed. "I'd both love and hate to face off with you."

Meagan pictured Melanie in a tailored suit and skirt, her ample breasts straining against her blouse, curvy hips framed by a red skirt. On her feet would be red pumps, her blonde hair in a bun, gray eyes peering over red-framed glasses. "She'll be great," Meagan agreed enthusiastically. "But I'm kind of surprised."

Melanie shook her head. "I never set out to be a toy shop owner, it isn't my thing," she explained. "I only did it until I could build up some money to put toward law school."

"Will you be staying in town?" Meagan wondered, sipping her water.

Melanie nodded. "Yes," she replied. "I'll commute, and Jen and I are going to move in together."

Meagan pointed her fork at Jennine. "Make the most of your time together, then, school can be extremely tiring. I know how that is."

Jennine laughed merrily. "Oh, there's no such thing as too tired, believe me," she replied. "Mel's got a bigger sex drive than a horny frat boy."

"And you *love* it," Melanie murmured roughly in Jennine's ear, causing her to flush red.

Meagan wrinkled her nose. "Jesus, you two, too much information," she sighed with mock exasperation and rolled her eyes. "Besides, I didn't mean just *that!"*

The conversation continued animatedly as the waitress brought their orders… hot pepper burgers for Jen and Melanie and the meager bagel and cream cheese for Meagan.

"So," Meagan addressed Jennine across the table. "How'd it go with your fiancé today?"

"Ex," Jennine corrected with a proud swig of her beer. "Well, long story short, he flipped shit, but that was expected. Needless to say, we're done."

"Good for you," Meagan told her friend sincerely, glad to see the glow of true happiness on Jennine's face as Melanie fed her a bite of burger. They were silent for a few moments before Jen looked up, a serious expression on her face.

"Oh, Meagan, I met an interesting man today," Jen said. "I was meaning to tell you about him."

Meagan smiled. "But I thought you were dating Melanie," she teased.

Jennine shook her head in frustration. "No, not like *that,"* she huffed. "And of course I'm dating Melanie."

Meagan hadn't expected a huffy response. "Sorry, Jennine, I was just kidding" she offered.

Jen calmed down. "It's okay," she replied. "It was just that I'm trying to tell you something serious. This guy, his name is Edwin Shields, and he's a new client. Just came in today, and he had a very interesting story," Jen paused to sip her beer. "Apparently, he had a daughter, and hasn't seen her since she was a few months old. No wife that I know of. The reason I brought it up is this," Jennine withdrew a faded photograph from her pocket. "He said I could borrow it. I just thought you might like to see it."

Puzzled, Meagan accepted the photograph. It was an old, faded shot of a dark-haired baby girl, dressed in a white bodysuit and standing on a stool of some sort, looking off into the distance with the backdrop of a darkened living room. Puzzled, Meagan felt the tingling sense that she had seen it before but couldn't place it. Her brow furrowing deeper, she turned it over to see the words written in faded blue ink, proclaiming *"Elizabeth, 16mos."*

"Oh my god," Meagan choked on her water, spewing it everywhere. "That's our living room. And my mother's handwriting!"

Jennine and Melanie were equally stunned. "I knew she looked like you," Jennine blurted. "Is it possible she could be your twin sister or cousin or something?"

Meagan shook her head. "I don't know," she said softly. "But I think I have the same picture. I don't know how that would be possible."

The haunting image stayed with her through the rest of the dinner, and even as they left the bar. On the way home, Meagan sat behind the wheel of Melanie's black Caddy as Jen and Mel ripped each other's clothes off and made out drunkenly, half-naked in the spacious leather back seats.

Chapter Thirty-One

It was a gray Saturday morning, and Meagan awoke at the early hour of eight-thirty. She had enjoyed her night out with Jen and Melanie the night before, glad that she could be reconciled with her friends. Melanie had never held it against her for her press scandal, but Jen had been bitter. Meagan chuckled and shook her head when she thought of her two friends. They were probably splayed out naked in bed, sleeping off a night of wild sex and body shots. They had both been pretty plastered by the time Meagan drove them home, words soft and slurred, blindly groping each other in the darkened back seat. She could only imagine the progression once they were behind closed doors. Yawning as she rose from bed and brushed her teeth, she almost felt slightly envious of Jennine and Melanie. Wouldn't it be nice, she thought, to wake up lazily to a warm house and cozy room after a long night of passion? She knew firsthand how nice it was; except with Terrence she had hightailed it out of there early in the morning as not to complicate matters. Sober and cold, Meagan shivered and cranked up her old iron radiator, hoping that the apartment would heat up quickly. The one thing she *could* be thankful for was the lack of a hangover. She had had some pretty nasty hangovers, and was lucky not to be christened with one this morning. She figured that Jen and Melanie both would probably have some nasty effects from getting as plastered as they did. She certainly didn't envy them for that.

By the time Meagan was showered and dressed and got the newspaper, the apartment was filled with some sparse heat and the acrid smell of fresh-brewed low-quality coffee. Meagan tied her still-wet hair back in a bun and went into the kitchen, where she poured a cup of the bitter brown liquid

from the ancient coffeemaker and took a seat at her scratched
wooden kitchen table. Unless suffering from a hangover,
Meagan usually awoke fairly early, completely opposite of
Jen and Melanie, who were both known to stay in bed all day
on the weekend. Meagan took a tentative sip of the bitter
black coffee and nibbled on the corner of a cracker. She never
had much of an appetite in the morning, always feeling a bit
queasy. She gave the paper a perfunctory glance but didn't
find much material of interest. Troubled, she picked up the
faded photograph that she had left lying on the table the night
before. Staring at it, she wondered why it bore so much
resemblance to her, and if the girl in the photo was a relation,
where and who she was and why Meagan never knew about
her. Flipping it over, she once more saw the inscription that
read, *"Elizabeth, 16mos."*

    Elizabeth, she murmured to herself. *Who is Elizabeth?*
After finishing a meager and bitter breakfast, Meagan rose
and decided to hunt around in some of her abandoned boxes
and see if she could solve this mystery. First thing she needed
to do was determine if that was indeed her mother's
handwriting. Part of Meagan hoped it wasn't, because then
the mystery would have nothing to do with her. She fetched a
letter that her mother had written a long time ago and placed
it next to the photograph. To her fascination and slight
chagrin, the samples matched exactly. There was no question
that Tricia Lucien had written on the back of the photograph.

    Next, Meagan opened closets, trying to find her
childhood photo albums. Finally, she stumbled upon a dusty
box that contained items from her childhood. She opened it
up and found her photo album, along with some assorted toys
and knickknacks. She leafed through the yellowed pages with
wonder. She had taken those things when she moved from her
parents' home, but never had taken very much time to look at
them. Meagan had always been too busy or preoccupied to
look at herself as a child. She barely remembered at all. And
after her father had died, life had taken a downturn, and she

didn't want to remember the years of her mother's grief before her death as well.

Meagan flipped through, feeling like she almost was entering another world. She saw pictures of a tiny baby girl, with black hair and dark eyes. There was only one album, and she turned the pages carefully, eyes scanning critically over the pages. She turned the page and froze, her eyes locked on the photo at the top right. Drawing the other photo from her pocket, she held it up, and it matched almost exactly. The toddler in the photo was in a slightly different position, but the backdrop was almost exactly the same. Meagan was stunned. Reaching farther into the dusty box, she found a small monogrammed velvet pouch. The initials on it were E. M. L. and the pouch contained a tarnished locket. E for Elizabeth, Meagan thought, now very puzzled. Looking more closely at the pouch, she saw a date monogrammed on the other side, and it was the date of her birth! Was Elizabeth her twin sister? If so, where was she, and why would she be someone else's daughter, someone she had never met?

At the very bottom of the box was a yellowed document. Meagan lifted it out of the box and saw that it was actually two documents, paper-clipped together. The top one was her birth certificate, which proclaimed the following information:

NAME: MEAGAN BERNICE PATIENCE LUCIEN
SEX: F
DOB: 8 MAY 1987
MOTHER: PATRICIA A. CORBIN LUCIEN
FATHER: DAVID N. LUCIEN
DATE FILED: 20 MAY 1987

Meagan lifted the paper and saw that the attached document was another birth certificate! This one read:

NAME: ELIZABETH MEAGAN BERNICE PATIENCE LUCIEN
SEX: F
DOB: 8 MAY 1987
MOTHER: PATRICIA A. CORBIN LUCIEN
FATHER: EDWIN A. SHIELDS
DATE FILED: 8 MAY 1987

Now, Meagan was downright astounded. Did this mean that *she was* Elizabeth? If so, why had her name been changed? And why was Edwin Shields listed as her father? Suddenly, Meagan got the uneasy feeling that her life wasn't the way she thought it had been. She took out the birth certificates and the picture of the toddler along with the one that she removed from her photo album. With a determined frown, she decided to pay Edwin Shields a visit and find out what this was all about. Had her mother cheated on her father? Shaking her head, Meagan reached for the telephone and dialed Jennine's number. It rang four times with no answer and Meagan frantically dialed again. Finally, Jen's sleepy voice came through the phone. "Hello?" she mumbled. In the background, Meagan heard a muttered curse that she assumed was from Melanie.

"Jen, it's Meagan," Meagan began.

"Jesus Christ!" Jen growled. "Why in hellfire did you wake me up this early? Mel and I are both hung over something terrible!"

"I know," Meagan explained soothingly. "I'm sorry. But that picture you gave me yesterday, that's me. I'm Elizabeth. I just found this out this morning, looking through some boxes."

She heard an audible gasp on the other end of the line. "What?" Jennine breathed. "Are you serious?"

"Completely," Meagan replied gravely. "I need Edwin Shields' address; I'm going to ask him some questions."

"Just a minute," Jennine mumbled. "I'll need to log onto the client database. Usually I can't give out client information, but in this case I'll make an exception."

***

Meagan checked the address briefly before parking her car, just so she would be sure where she was going. Edwin Shields lived on the outskirts of town, in a semi-rural community, a small ranch house set up on a high hill with a crooked mailbox out front. The house wasn't necessarily dilapidated, but it had certainly seen its better days. Meagan got out of her car and brought her bag of "evidence" and a box of chocolates as she ascended the hill and shivered against the cold. Luckily it wasn't snowing, but a thin layer of frost had formed over the night. She ascended the creaky porch and rang the bell on the right. There was the sound of shuffling footsteps before the door was opened by a man with graying hair and dark eyes that matched Meagan's. He thrust the screen door open and blinked at her with a puzzled expression.

Meagan drew her courage, hoping her voice didn't come out squeaky. "Are you Mr. Edwin Shields?" she asked.

The man gave a gruff nod. "Yes," he replied blandly. "How may I help you, Miss?"

"Well, it's a long story," Meagan began. She pulled the picture out of her pocket. "My friend Jennine showed me this picture, and I happen to have the same one. I'm Meagan Lucien."

He stared at her for a long moment. "Ah, well," he said finally, opening the door. "I guess I'd better invite you in." Inside of his sparse and drab living room, he gestured to a saggy sofa and leather armchair. "Go ahead and make yourself comfortable," he offered. "I'll bring us some hot tea."

Meagan took a seat and waited while Mr. Shields puttered into the kitchen and reemerged with a pot of steaming tea. He seated himself in the chair opposite of her with an arthritic groan and filled her teacup, then his. Clasping his hands in his lap, he looked at her expectantly. "I knew you'd find me eventually," he said, his voice rich with a smoker's cough. "I guess I owe you the truth."

Meagan slid the picture and birth certificates across the table. "Who is that?" she asked him, pointing to the picture. "Am I Elizabeth?"

"Yes," he replied. "Yes and No."

When Meagan asked him what his mysterious answer meant, he elaborated.

"It was all so long ago," he began. "You see, all throughout high school, I was in love with your mother, Tricia Corbin." He sighed and shook his head. "But she never knew I existed, not as more than a friend anyway. She only had eyes for David."

He went on to say that many years later, he encountered Tricia at a reception. "We both had too much to drink," he said regretfully. "And I'm ashamed to say that I pushed Tricia too far that night, made her do something that in her heart she really didn't want to do. Even as drunk as she was, I could see the tears in her eyes." Edwin Shields blew into his handkerchief. "I never should have done that," he murmured, wiping his teary eyes. "Even to this day I'm sorry…"

Meagan reached over and put a hand on his shoulder. "Please do go on, Mr. Shields," she said soothingly.

He wiped his eyes and continued. "Anyway, David found us and he was furious. He ran to the police and told them I raped her. Tricia was too drunk to remember what happened, so I was found guilty. I spent five long years in jail, saw horrible things. Tricia and I were in our mid-thirties at that time, I was maybe thirty-eight, and she became pregnant. She and David had tried for years to conceive, without success. Tricia knew that I was the baby's father, the baby being you, so she came to visit me in prison right before you were born. I remember her, pregnant, gripping the bars as she said, 'Edwin, it's a girl. What would you like to name her?'"

Edwin paused for breath, and Meagan looked at him with wonder. "So I said, I'd like to call you Elizabeth," he continued. "But David didn't like that name, he wanted to call you Meagan, and wouldn't have you named Elizabeth. He didn't know that he wasn't your father. Only Tricia and I knew, and I don't think she ever told him."

Edwin went on to say that Tricia had already filed a birth certificate before she talked to David, but then she had the name changed once David refused. "That's why you have two names," he explained. "Legally, it's all kind of murky now, but I suppose your true name is Elizabeth Meagan Bernice Patience Lucien. You'll always be Elizabeth to me, even though I have no right to be your father."

Meagan was astounded by his story. "Thank you for telling me this story, Mr. Shields, I know it probably wasn't easy for you to remember those painful times. And please, you may call me Elizabeth if you want to, since it was my original legal name."

Edwin sighed and sniffled, dabbing at his eyes. "Life has made me an old man, Elizabeth Meagan," he said quietly. "I'd be honored if you called me Edwin." He looked up. "How is Tricia these days?" he said. Though his voice was steady, she could see the pain in his eyes.

"She died," Meagan said softly. "Eleven years ago."

Edwin fixed his rheumy eyes on the wall and wiped his eyes again. "Oh my God," he murmured sorrowfully, a tear slipping down one of his cheeks. He looked up, staring unblinkingly at Meagan. "I'm sorry for your loss," he said quietly. "May she rest in peace."

Meagan rose and pulled her father into a hug. "My parents are dead," she said. "And I never had much of a family. So I don't see any reason not to call you Father."

Edwin replied with a loud sniffle and reached out his stiff, shaky arms to embrace his daughter. And for once since she was seven years old, Meagan felt the security of a family.

Chapter Thirty-Two

Meagan couldn't believe how rapidly the Christmas holiday had approached. She generally didn't do much for Christmas, usually buying a box of chocolates for her landlord and landlady and occasionally putting a tired wreath on her apartment door. That was about it. She usually spent Christmas Eve and Christmas Day sitting at home, stripping beds and doing laundry or some equally mundane household task to pass the time and hide the pain. Her idea of a celebration was to cuddle up under a blanket with a shot of vodka and watch the evening news, pretending that it was just any ordinary day and not that she was alone on a holiday. And now, since the day that she was old enough to drink, that had been what she did every year. As she sat thinking about it, Meagan realized what a grim existence this was and thought she might do something different this year. Looking at the calendar, she saw that it was already Christmas Eve Day, and she had no idea what she would do. She had kindly refused Jen and Melanie's invitation to go out reveling with them. Their idea of a holiday would be to light up, get plastered and dance the night away at a seedy nightclub, and then fuck each other senseless in the back of Melanie's black Caddy. No, thanks. Sure, in her younger days, Meagan would have thought that was great, but now life had changed and she had changed. Meagan gazed out the window with a pensive frown, watching as the ground was blanketed with a thin layer of frosty, icy snow. Suddenly cold, she wrapped her arms around herself and wondered what Terrence was doing. Was he with his parents? With another woman? She just hoped he was happy and wondered if he was thinking about her at all. *I wonder if he misses me,* Meagan murmured to herself, and a wave of sadness washed over her.

When her reverie was finished, Meagan walked slowly to the front door to check the mail. Opening the creaky old box, she found a handful of assorted bills and advertisements, along with a Christmas card addressed in long, loopy script with a shaky edge as someone suffering from arthritis. It was addressed to Elizabeth Meagan Lucien, which could only be from one person. Opening it up, she saw that it was indeed from her father, Edwin Shields. He had invited her to spend Christmas with him if she had no other plans. A faint smile warmed Meagan's face and she reached for the telephone to call him and accept his invitation. She dialed and the phone rang twice before it was picked up.

"Hello?" answered a familiar, shaky male voice.

"Hi, Father? It's Meagan," Meagan said, the word 'father' sounding foreign on her tongue but not in a bad way. "I just got your card today. I'd be honored to accept your invitation."

"I'm so glad," Edwin replied. He sounded genuinely happy. I was hoping you'd come; I've made a nice dinner. You may come over any time you like."

Looking at the clock, Meagan saw that it was three-thirty. "I'll be over about four," she told him. After they had said good-bye and finished up the conversation, Meagan hung the phone on the hook and decided to stop by the grocery store and get a poinsettia for her father, since he had offered to make dinner. She changed into her darker jeans and a nice sweater, freshened up a bit. Then, she took out her car keys and left the apartment, closing and locking the door. It wasn't yet dark, but overcast, with crunchy frost on the ground and light flurries drifting from a brittle, steel-gray sky. Meagan was careful as she made her way down her front steps and was glad to see that the icy frost hadn't settled on her car. There was a thin layer of flurries that blanketed the windshield, but Meagan was sure that it would wipe away once she turned the car on. As she got in and turned on the engine and heater, she smelled just a trace of a dusty aroma… almost like pipe smoke and leather-bound books. It reminded her of Terrence, and a lump caught in her throat. Until that moment, she hadn't been thinking about him, but his scent was so powerful that even an imitation of it was hard on her. She had wondered whether to send him a Christmas card, and at the end she finally bowed and sent him one. Her brief note had read: *"Terrence, Best wishes for a merry Christmas and happy new year. I think of you often. Yours, M. Lucien."*

Now, Meagan wondered what he had been thinking when he had received her note. She had faithfully checked the mailbox every day, and nothing had come. She couldn't help but to be disappointed. Flicking on her turn signal, she eased into the other lane and turned onto the road that led to the grocery store. When she parked in the lot and headed for the door, she was surprised at just how frigid it was. Shivering, she jammed her gloved hands into her pocket and hurried for the door. Inside the store was sparse, not many people were working or shopping on Christmas Eve Day. Meagan was fortunate that the selection of poinsettias was right near the door. She took a good look at the selection and took a pretty deep-red one, almost the colour of burgundy wine. She carried the plant to the cash register, and put down a ten dollar bill, smiling at the cashier, who was an older gentleman. She told him to keep the change and wished him a happy holiday before heading back out to her car, shielding her poinsettia from the cold as she loaded it into the passenger seat. The drive to her father's was about ten minutes, out into the semi-rural area of town. The sky was already darkening as she pulled into his driveway at his house on the hill. She parked and ascended the winding walk and worn porch steps, clutching the plant with both hands. Transferring it to one side, she rang the bell. After a moment, her father opened the door. "Merry Christmas, Elizabeth Meagan," he said cheerfully, followed by a hoarse cough as he leaned on his cane. "Come on in."

She smiled at him and stepped through the doorway into his small, threadbare living room. A cozy fire was crackling in the fireplace and she could smell the inviting aroma of baked lasagna coming from the kitchen. The only light in the room came from the fire and the Christmas lights wound around his cheerful tree in the corner of the room. "Merry Christmas, Father," she replied, offering him the plant she had bought. "I bought you a poinsettia."

The old man's eyes seemed to brighten as he accepted the plant and cradled it like a baby. "I love plants," he said quietly. Looking around, Meagan saw that he had several houseplants. "You will have a place in the middle of my table, dearie," he said to the plant, setting it down with care on his coffee table. He murmured to it for several moments before turning to Meagan and waving his hand. "Go ahead, take a seat," he invited. "Make yourself comfortable. I've got some tea brewing in the kitchen. Would you care for a cup?"

"Yes, please," Meagan answered. "Cream and sugar, please."

Her father let out an undignified snort. "Ah, Elizabeth," he said with a chuckle. "It defeats the whole purpose of tea if you put sugar in it."

Meagan smiled as Edwin puttered off into the kitchen. Her father was a very likable man, even if quite eccentric, but she was astounded by the way he acted so much older than he was. Though he was only sixty-five, he acted as if he were ninety. *Life must be hard on him,* she thought, seeing how prison and loneliness could age a person quickly. Meagan's reverie was interrupted when Edwin returned, rolling a tea cart with a kettle, two cups, and, much to his chagrin, cream and sugar for Meagan. He poured her a cup of the steaming amber liquid, and then filled his own cup. With much labor, he settled himself onto the sofa across the table from Meagan. Picking up his cup, he took a careful sip. "So, Elizabeth," he said, leaning back in his chair as he lit up a cigar. "Tell me something of yourself. I know very little about you."

Meagan shrugged. "Well, I'm currently enrolled at Grandview University, and I'm working on an engineering/architecture masters' program," she began. "I'm not married, never have been. I enjoy music and do some ballet and jazz dancing, that's all I can think of for now."

Edwin nodded. "Ah," he said slowly. "All wonderful things. I hope you get far in your career, Elizabeth Meagan. Grandview is indeed a fine school." He paused, adjusted his thick-rimmed glasses and took another sip of tea. "As for marriage, don't worry, my dear, I've ne'er been married either. Probably never will be." He let out a rueful chuckle. "I guess no woman wants a decrepit old wreck like myself."

"Maybe you'll meet someone," Meagan said quietly. "You never know what the future holds."

"Very true," the old man observed, and then he lapsed into a long silence, sipping his tea and staring almost hypnotically into the crackling flames in his fireplace. Finally, he turned back to Meagan. "I want to show you something," he said, rising to his feet with some difficulty. He gestured to the couch. "Stay right here," he said. "I'll be back."

Meagan waited while he shuffled out of the room, sipping her tea and sitting back in the comfortable chair. She closed her eyes and relaxed, letting the sound of the crackling flames lull her into a semi-sleep state. Her reverie was interrupted a few moments later when she heard Edwin shuffling back into the room. Opening her eyes, she saw that he carried some sort of large case that might fit a musical instrument. He sat down feebly and set the case on his lap, unhooking the latches with shaking fingers. Up close, Meagan could see that the case was very, very old and worn, and probably valuable. Finally, with a click and creak of hinges, Edwin silently opened the case, revealing a beautiful violin that appeared to be also very old. With gentle grace, he lifted it out and set the velvet-lined case on the floor. "This belonged to my grandmother," Edwin explained as he took out the bow and began to rosin it. "Which would be your great-grandmother. Luciela was her name…" he trailed off. "Anyway, she taught me how to play the violin when I was just a little boy, and I've played ever since."

"Oh," Meagan breathed. "It's beautiful." She looked up at him with shining eyes. "Please do play something for me."

Edwin chuckled. "I'm not as good as I used to be," he said quietly, the smile fading off of his face. "But I could throw together something, I bet."

"Whatever you do, you'll be better than me," Meagan said with a laugh. "I know nothing about the violin."

Edwin stopped rosining the bow and gave her a wry sidelong glance. "True," he admitted. Then, capably, he fastened the shoulder rest and plucked each string. With a slight harrumph, he tightened one of the pegs and plucked again. This time, he nodded gruffly and gingerly raised the violin to his shoulder. "Give me the name of a Christmas carol, Elizabeth," he said absently, and she suggested *O Little Town of Bethlehem*. "Ah, a lovely classic," he replied, gently placing the bow on the strings. Closing his eyes and breathing deeply, he began to play.

At once, the aging atmosphere of the room seemed to dissipate, and the soulless room was filled with the most beautiful sound that Meagan had ever heard. Looking over at her frail and sickly father, she saw that behind his violin he appeared fifteen years younger, his youth restored by his music. When the carol finally came to an end, Edwin opened his eyes, a tranquil smile on his face. Meagan leapt to her feet and applauded. "Beautiful," she exclaimed. "It was wonderful. Please do play another one!"

He chuckled. "So I wasn't too rusty, then?" he asked with a wink.

Meagan shook her head. "You were great," she told him. "Will you play *Silent Night* for me?" she asked. "It is one of my two favorites."

"One of mine too," came the answer. "And I most certainly will."

He lifted the violin to his shoulder once again, and the room was filled with the sweet, clear sound. He played the first time traditionally, but by the second time, he seemed to be completely in his own world as he embroidered on the melody by adding a double-string drone part. Meagan quietly sang along, letting the sound of her voice mingle with the music. *"Silent night, holy night... all is calm, all is bright... Christ the Savior is bo-orn; Chri-ist the savior is born..."*

After what seemed like an eternity at the same time only a mere breath in the universe, Edwin drew the last note across the strings and slowly opened his eyes, the same relaxed, dreamy look on his face. "You've a fine singing voice, Elizabeth," he said softly.

After he had run through his entire repertoire of Christmas carols, including his and Meagan's favorite, *Once in Royal David's City,* Edwin gently set the violin down in the case and wiped the strings with a soft cloth. "Well, I suppose I should call it a day and feed us some dinner," he said. "I made homemade lasagna."

"I knew it," Meagan replied. "I can always tell the smell of homemade lasagna. There's nothing quite like it."

"I agree," Edwin replied. "I just hope I haven't burnt it."

Meagan got up and followed him into the small kitchen. "Let me help you set up," she offered.

With Meagan's help, it only took a few minutes for Edwin to prepare the meal and set the table.

They enjoyed a leisurely dinner together, and Meagan was glad to be in her father's presence, for he was quiet and gentle but at the same time possessed a wry sense of humor and a sharp wit. She saw much of herself in him, and silently wondered what it must have been like for him all of those years, knowing he had a daughter but not getting to see her grow up. Along with the kindness in his dark eyes were a deep, heavy sadness and the burden of his accelerated aging. He looked tired, worn, broken. Meagan almost felt herself tearing up as she thought of the emotional pain he must have suffered; wrongfully accused and convicted of rape, locked away in jail for many years, unmarried, estranged from his family. Meagan felt a flash of anger toward her mother for not telling her the truth. *How could you lie to me all of those years?* she said to her mother silently. *Why didn't you tell me who I was, who my father was?* As quickly as her flash of anger came on, it subsided. It wasn't her mother's fault, she decided, not entirely. Young Tricia Lucien hadn't made the world, and now Meagan just missed her and longed for the family life she never had.

Meagan was drawn from her reverie by the soft *whoosh* of her father lighting the candles on the advent wreath. When she looked up, he gave her an intently concerned look. "Something amiss, Elizabeth?" he asked kindly. "You look upset."

Meagan shook her head. "I'm okay," she said quietly. "I was just thinking... about the family, and how hard everything must have been for you," she swallowed.

"Please, Elizabeth," her father finished lighting the candles and feebly settled into his chair. "Don't worry about what has happened. I've had a lifetime of tragedy, but I'm a strong man of God. What matters now is that we're together as a family once again." He paused, casting his eyes downward. "I usually say grace before meals," he explained. "You're welcome to join, but not required."

Meagan dutifully bowed her head as Edwin uttered a grace with his eyes closed and hands folded. Meagan couldn't remember the last time she had prayed over a meal, if ever, but she found it comforting. Finally, Edwin lifted his head and murmured "Amen" and Meagan echoed him. Taking a careful bite of the lasagna, she found it to be delicious and praised her father for his cooking skills. As the meal progressed, the previous sadness was forgotten and the mood became much more animated when Meagan asked him to tell her about what he loved most… his music.

***

On the other side of town, as Meagan and her father were enjoying their Christmas Eve dinner together, Terrence was at his parents' house, helping his mother cook. Eloisa Reid had always loved Christmas, and this year was no exception. Terrence's parents' small ranch home had been decked with soft white lights and cheerful pine-scented greenery with red bows, old fashioned and luminous. Similarly, the outside of the house was adorned with lights in the thorny bushes that lined under the windows, and a plaid-bowed wreath had been placed on the front door. Despite the enticing aroma from the stove and his mother's cheerful humming as she tidied the kitchen, Terrence couldn't help but to feel a bit depressed. He always did at this time of the year, though he enjoyed the stillness of winter, particularly starry winter nights. Christmas had always felt somewhat sad to Terrence, a desperate attempt to mark off the endless cycle of time, a feeble hope to keep a candle lit amidst a raging nighttime storm. The one thing he enjoyed about spending Christmas with his parents was that they were very traditional in their celebration, always had been. All candles and bible readings and quality of family time, untainted by the vast commercialization of the holiday. Whenever Terrence looked around at the advertisements offering blow-up Santas and heard the tinny, fast-paced renditions of Christmas carols that played in stores and on the radio, he felt positively sick to his stomach. He hated commercialization, the bright neon signs and cheap merchandise turning a quiet, reflective religious holiday into a fast-paced consumer commodity swarming with greed and shallowness. People were so superficial these days, he thought, nothing meant anything to anyone anymore. And he hated it. The only people who seemed to respect sincerity were himself, his parents, and Meagan. When Doreen was alive, she was pretty good to him too, though she sometimes allowed herself to get caught up in the modern fast-paced life, when Terrence would rather barricade himself in the basement and do math.

After a festive and blessed Christmas dinner, Terrence had helped his mother clean up the kitchen and to stash the leftovers in the refrigerator. Now, it was around 11:00PM and his parents had already gone to bed. Giving the counters one final swipe with the rag, Terrence shut off the kitchen light and padded silently through the empty dining room to the darkened living room, where he let himself sink into the couch cushions with a soft groan. The entire house was silent, the only sound being the soft crackling of the remaining embers in the fireplace, the living room illuminated by the soft flames and the twinkling, muted white lights on the Christmas tree. Terrence flicked his lighter and lit up a pipe, taking a deep drag of smoke as he leaned back in his chair. It had been a long month, and he was tired, just wanted to be alone for a while. So he gazed out into the darkness with half-lidded eyes as the twinkling lights faded in and out and he watched the muted flames and their shadows dance on the walls of the fireplace. As his pipe dwindled to a stub, he took a final draw and ground it out. After a few moments of aimlessly yet contemplatively staring into the blackness, Terrence fell asleep against the arm of the couch, curled up as if he were still a little boy, with his head against the pillow and one arm flung over the side.

Chapter Thirty-Three

Terrence was more than ready to get back to work. He had indeed had a wonderful Christmas vacation, but he was ready to go back to his classroom and start the second semester with a bang. He chuckled as he straightened his tie in the bathroom mirror, hoping that his students hadn't forgotten everything he had taught them. He had found that the advanced classes were usually pretty good, but college students were college students and in the excitement of Christmas, calculus was often set to the side. Which was fine, Terrence thought, because everyone deserved a break.

When he finished tying his necktie and had his black leather briefcase all packed, Terrence shrugged on his coat and went out to scrape ice off of his truck. As he opened the door, he was met by a blast of icy wind. Squinting, he could see that the landscape was in complete whiteout, the range of visibility was maybe five feet at best. Terrence cursed softly, extremely dismayed at the thought of having to drive into town in this horrible weather. He hopped into the cab and blasted the defroster, fishing his ice scraper out of the pocket on the side. Terrence's muscles bunched as he scraped with determination at the thick, crusted ice that had settled itself over his windshield. He cursed again as he managed to dislodge a particularly tough sheet of ice, the shards falling to be swept up by the wind.

When the windshield was as defrosted as it would get, Terrence put the scraper away and hopped into his cab, sealing out the icy blast and cranking up the heater and radio in equal measure. The drive into town was treacherous and slippery, but luckily, there wasn't much traffic on a sleepy Monday morning, at an hour before the morning traffic began to set in. He had the windshield wipers on full blast and he drove carefully, gaining control as the heavy snowfall began to lessen and the visibility improved.

***

On the other side of town, Meagan finished putting her hair up in a neat bun, with artful strands hanging down to frame her face. She hung a pair of onyx drop earrings on her earlobes and checked her reflection in the mirror. So far so good, she thought, assessing her gray stretchy boat-neck sweater, form-fitting black skirt and matching onyx chain hung around her neck. The outfit would have looked too schoolgirl if it weren't for the chunky-heeled black leather boots with silver buckles. Turning to the side, Meagan assessed her tight, curvy figure and she smiled. She didn't work out six days a week for nothing. Once she was ready to start the second semester in style, she jammed her calculus book in her leather tote bag and shrugged on her heavy winter coat, slinging her tote over her shoulder. So far, the morning was going well. All she needed to kick-start it into a kick-ass day were a triple shot macchiato and maybe a smile from Terrence. By the time she left her apartment, the snowfall had lessened enough so that she could fight a path to her car. A cold, light mist of snow was falling, thrown about every so often by a mercurial gust of wind. She unlocked her car and climbed in, cranking up the heat and the radio. She drove carefully through the slippery streets, time marked by the steady *bumph, bumph* of the bass. She swung into the coffee shop drive-thru and ordered her usual, before continuing on her way to Grandview. As she parked in the parking lot and looked up at the old brick building, she realized that she was happy to be back. Most of her Christmas break had been spent either working or sitting alone at her house. She had, though, spent some quality time with her father, and she really appreciated that. Shaking out of her reverie about the break, Meagan lifted her bag and pulled her hood up as she stepped out of her car and hurried toward the door, leather-gloved hands shoved deep in her pockets.

Inside the massive foyer, the university smelled as it always did, a combination of dusty tile floor, the old heating system, and fresh coffee and cinnamon buns from the cafeteria. Meagan hung up her coat in the closet and inconspicuously checked her hair in the mirror before heading up to class. She was both ecstatic and terrified at the thought of seeing Terrence again, and she wondered what it would be like. Ascending the stairs, she hoped that the New Year would bring a fresh start. So far, no one had commented on the press scandal, and Meagan was very glad. She was tired of being treated like a criminal for surrendering to her passion. Shedding last year like an old coat, Meagan stepped up the landing and onto the floor where Terrence's room was. She couldn't believe how nervous she was, and just to go to class. As her stomach turned wild somersaults, Meagan steeled her nerves and approached the open door. She stopped momentarily and forced herself to breathe, before she finally got up the nerve and strolled through the doorway.

Immediately, she was hit with an intoxicating rush of Terrence's scent, and she looked up to see him sitting serenely at his desk, his ever-present red pen scribbling notes on a sheet of paper. Meagan allowed herself a good, long look at him. Damn, he looked good, she thought. The Christmas break had evidently done him some justice, for gone was the pale, sickly figure he had been before, and in its place was a healthy, strong, very male man. As Meagan took a seat at her desk, she let her gaze wander over Terrence's sinewy biceps, hidden by the rolled-up sleeves of his white dress shirt. She knew that beneath that white linen, lurked the outline of his tattoos… as well as much more danger. She felt a twinge of desire as she noticed his glasses resting haphazardly on the bridge of his nose, his analytical grey eyes critically assessing the document he was reading.

Almost as if he felt her gaze, Terrence looked up and a ragged spark of attraction flashed between them as their eyes met. Meagan smiled and lifted a hand in a discreet wave. Terrence, in turn, smiled warmly and shot Meagan a wink that sent a trail of fire searing through her nerves. She got out her calculus notebook, trying not to grin like an idiot as the remainder of the class took their seats and Terrence stood up to begin the lecture. With a sense of easy grace, Terrence made his way to the front of the room and picked up a piece of chalk. "Welcome to the second semester, folks," he began. "We're going to go slow and easy for the first few days, just to get back into it."

Meagan felt her cheeks burn and she lowered her gaze, her mind flashing to that night in Terrence's bed. Slow and easy, she thought, and imagined them both naked, skin burning as he lowered himself over her, the wet, white-hot friction as he slid inside her again… and again. *Holy Lord,* Meagan thought, and bit her lip to keep from moaning aloud. Her face was so crimson that she hoped no one would notice. Terrence regarded her briefly as his gaze swept the room, his expression neutral, a flicker of a smile tugging at the corner of his lips, as if he knew exactly what was on her mind. *Bastard,* she muttered good-naturedly under her breath, looking on admiringly as Terrence began his lecture with a sequence of chicken-scratch calculations on the blackboard. "Let's see what you remember," Terrence was saying. "It's been almost three weeks. I'll give you ten minutes, and then we will review. Any questions?"

In the front row, Carter, the geeky over-enthusiast, shot his hand in the air. "Dr. Reid, I just wanted to say that I studied every day, even Christmas day!" he blurted when Terrence nodded to him. His cheeks were flushed and he eagerly awaited his teacher's praise like a drooling puppy.

Terrence smiled tolerantly. "I must say I admire your dedication," he responded sincerely, leaning casually against the wall. A genuine flicker of amusement sparked in his eyes, but his tone was serious. "But I hope you gave yourself a rest, too, because we've got a long semester ahead of us."

Carter nodded imperceptibly and lowered his eyes. Meagan knew that Terrence hadn't been purposely harsh, but Carter had a major crush on Terrence and had been crushed by even the gentlest rejection. Meagan knew exactly how he felt; Terrence had such a nice way of turning someone down, it unconsciously made the blow ten times worse. Meagan almost wished that Terrence would just buckle down and be a jerk about it, so that it would be easier to be mad at him. Meagan's thoughts flicked to Jen and Melanie, who settled their accounts by a fierce sparring match followed by searing make-up sex when their anger gave way to passion. Terrence never flamed with anger, Meagan noted, he was always quietly in control, just like the firm but gentle grip he held on his steering wheel when he drove his truck.

After class, there was quite a crowd around Terrence's desk, people jabbering away with questions about the long-forgotten material. Meagan felt irritated and slightly dismayed; she wanted it to just be her and him. She hung back at her desk, pretending to look over her notes, until the crowd had cleared out. She packed up her things and softly approached Terrence's desk, her boot heels clicking quietly on the floor. He looked up and smiled warmly at her, his grey eyes twinkling behind the square frames of his glasses. "Hi there, Meagan, what can I do for you?" he asked pleasantly, setting his pen down on his desk.

Suddenly, Meagan was rendered speechless. She didn't feel like she could just walk up and start a conversation. "I have to work," she finally said abruptly. "Do you have an appointment this afternoon or evening? I, uh, need some extra help," the lame excuse rolled off her tongue before she could stop herself.

Terrence looked at her kindly. "Okay, how about five thirty?" he suggested. "I'll be done by then for sure."

Meagan bade him good-bye and thanked him before hurrying out to her car. Melanie was packing up her stuff so that she could get ready to sell the shop, and Meagan had said that she would help her. In return, Melanie agreed to help Meagan get another job, since for some reason her charisma pulled a lot of weight in town.

When Meagan got to the store, she parked her car in the lot and hurried through the wind and snow to the door. Grasping it one-handedly, she jerked the handle back and stepped inside.

Inside the former Toy Box, boxes and crates lined the wall and Melanie was perched on a ladder, in the process of stripping the shelves, a pen stuck in her messy blonde up-do and an unlit cigarette between her lips. When the bell above the door chimed, Melanie turned around and gave Meagan a wave, motioning her over. Meagan quickly complied, and took the armful of goods that Melanie handed to her, holding them steady as her boss shimmied down the ladder, curvy hips swaying as she descended. When Melanie reached the floor, she took back the armful of goods and packed them efficiently into a box, which already contained another load. Taking a breath, she turned to Meagan. "You have no idea how stressed out I am," she sighed, shaking her head. "I need to get this stuff out of here so I can see about selling the building." She closed her eyes briefly. "It's a mess."

"I'm sure," Meagan murmured sympathetically. Looking around, she asked what she could help with.

Melanie gestured to piles of goods on the floor. "Pack those into boxes," she instructed with a wave of her hand. She leaned back against the wall. "Forgive me, Meagan, but I need a light."

Meagan shrugged. "Go right ahead," she told Melanie. "I'm sure you deserve it."

Melanie gave a throaty chuckle and reached into her pocket. With a sharp flick of her lighter, she ignited the tip of her cigarette and stuck it in her mouth, taking a deep drag. "Oh, hell, that's good," Melanie groaned, leaning back against the wall with her eyes closed, blowing a wayward cloud of smoke to the ceiling. As Meagan packed boxes, she stole a quick glance at Melanie, and could instantly understand why Jen was so attracted to her. Even to Meagan, who was straight as a board, Melanie was on fire. She wore a lacy red V-neck that hugged her curves and cut a deep dip in Melanie's straining, ample cleavage. Beneath the lacy material, her breasts jiggled seductively, held in place by a racy black lace brassiere. Against the wall with her eyes closed, her messy, beachy blonde hair spilling in tendrils out of her up-do, and cigarette between her blood-red nails and blood-red lips, Melanie looked like a screen siren from an old movie. Meagan was all for men, particularly one, but she admitted that Melanie was quite nice-looking. Melanie regarded Meagan through half-lidded eyes and blew another cloud of smoke in the vicinity of the ceiling. "How was the U?" she asked casually. Melanie called the university "the U". That was just the type of thing she did, saved words.

Meagan smiled as she packed another box. "Well, it was all right, I guess," she answered. "I have a meeting with my prof at five thirty."

Melanie raised her eyebrows. "The one you're sweet on?" she asked with a wink, and Meagan nodded. "Well, have fun, charm his pants off," Melanie responded. She lowered her voice conspiratorially. "Jennine and I have our own plans tonight."

Meagan laughed. "I can only imagine," she replied, smiling at her boss. Then, her face sobered. "You know, Melanie, I'm really going to miss you when you go off to law school," she said with a slight frown.

"I'll miss you too, Meagan," Melanie replied. "I really mean that. But don't worry, we'll stay in touch. The only difference will be I won't be the one to write your paycheck anymore." She winked. "But if you break the law, I'll be your gal."

Meagan looked up at Melanie, clad in fire red, and smiled. "You will be one kickass defense attorney, that I am sure of."

Melanie chuckled throatily as she stubbed out her cigarette against the wall. "Damn right," she replied.

After Melanie had stubbed out her cigarette, she threw it away and emerged from the back room with an enormous crate in her arms. Approaching Meagan, she set it on the floor with a slight grunt and a heavy *thud*. Meagan looked up incredulously at her boss, who didn't appear to have even broken a sweat. "Jesus, Melanie, how do you lift shit like that?" Meagan laughed. "I would have broken my back."

Melanie stretched sinuously, smiling as she sat down to unpack the crate. "Practice, I guess," she replied. "I'm not a weak woman."

"I can see that," Meagan said smilingly as she sealed up a finished box. 'I'd almost feel bad for anyone who tried to mug you."

Melanie just chuckled and reached over to the shelf where the beat-up portable radio sat, and she shot Meagan a sideways look. "Screamo or R&B?" she asked with a wry smile.

"Are those the only choices?" Meagan countered good-naturedly.

Melanie shrugged apologetically. "Sorry, it's all I've got," she answered.

Meagan shifted some items around in the crate and paused to wipe her face with the back of her hand. "R&B, I guess."

Melanie cranked the dial and pressed play, and the room was filled with the soulful, thrumming beat of an R&B

song. Meagan discovered very quickly that Melanie's CD was quite uncensored; and she watched as Melanie made her way methodically around the room, her ample hips swaying as she shamelessly sang along with the verses that would make a trucker blush. As she studied her vivacious blonde boss, Meagan was suddenly curious about her past. Later on, when Melanie came by with an armful of garbage bags, Meagan looked up from the shelf she was unloading. "Melanie?" she asked. "I've a question for you."

"Hmm?" Melanie mumbled, unceremoniously dumping the garbage into the can, unlit cigarette clamped between her lips.

"How did you and Jennine meet?" Meagan wondered. "Did you always know you liked women?"

Melanie finished packing the can and turned to Meagan. "Jennine and I met at her accounting firm," Melanie explained. "We just hit it off, right from the beginning. We got to be friends, but the spark of attraction just kept growing." Melanie paused. "Though I'm with Jennine right now, I'm actually bisexual," she continued. "I had a boyfriend in high school, lost my virginity at sixteen in the back of his '92 Buick." She smiled when Meagan raised her eyebrows. "Hey," Melanie said with a dismissive wave. "I never said I was dignified."

Meagan laughed. "Don't worry," she replied. "When I was sixteen, I was an orphan, living at my great aunt Mary's. At nineteen, I fell hopelessly in love with the biggest jerk of all time. We've all had our trips in the road."

"You've got that right," Melanie replied soberly, pulling a cigarette from her pocket. She waved her hand, gesturing to the boxes. "Good work," she told Meagan. "Go ahead and take a break, I need to smoke again."

By quarter of five, Meagan and Melanie had gotten the whole shop stripped down and packed into boxes. Melanie explained that she was boxing up the unused inventory and selling it to another shop, which was just starting and had agreed to pay her a handsome price for it. As Meagan finished up dusting one of the shelves, Melanie leaned against the wall, smoking through her third cigarette. As usual, her eyes were closed and she periodically released ghost-like clouds of smoke toward the ceiling. The R&B CD had reached the end of its track long ago and now the shop was in silence. Outside, the sky was beginning to darken and turn a beautiful indigo color as the daylight faded into the horizon. Suddenly, the quiet was broken by a screech of tires and loud pounding bass as a dumpy white car hurtled into the parking lot, slipping and sliding on the ice. The brakes squealed as the driver parked abruptly, and a moment later the driver's side door flew open and Jennine sauntered toward the door with her short, wavy brown hair bouncing and a bright grin on her face.

"Hey, gorgeous," Jennine purred, flinging herself into Melanie's arms. It didn't take long before they had their tongues down each other's throats and hands in each other's hair, gripped with a searing fit of passion. After a long, intense, crushing kiss, they finally broke apart, breathing heavily.

Meagan took this opportunity to tell Melanie she was leaving. "Have fun, you guys," she said with a smile, gathering up her purse as she shrugged on her heavy fur coat. "I'm gonna hit the road."

Melanie and Jennine waved, and Melanie wished her luck with Terrence. Before she was even out the door, Melanie was half-carrying a topless, messy-haired Jennine toward the back room, their lips soldered together, Jen's nails raking down Melanie's back, both of them moaning loudly.

"Careful not to burn the building down," Meagan chuckled as she stepped out into the chilly winter evening. The sky had darkened and the landscape was peacefully silent, the only sound of cars swishing by on a distant road. Meagan walked out to her car, breathing in the fresh night air. Tilting her head back, she could see stars twinkling in the vast indigo sky above. *What a lovely night,* she thought as she unlocked her car and slowly pulled out of the parking lot. Shaking her head, she thought that Jen and Melanie must be naked by now at this rate. She found it funny that the two of them acted like a pair of horny teenagers, at twenty-seven and thirty.

Meagan turned on the heat and radio as she pulled out of the parking lot and turned onto the main road. The roads were relatively clear, and at the moment it wasn't snowing, it hadn't all day. In a good mood, Meagan followed the road to Grandview and parked in her usual spot. Looking up at the university, Meagan could see that it wasn't very populated at this time of night. This observation was confirmed when Meagan swiped her student ID card and stepped into the foyer, which was dimly lit and completely deserted except for a pair of bespectacled girls in the corner, quietly going over terminology, nose-deep in their thick books. Meagan walked across the spacious room, her heels tapping loudly on the floor, echoing off of the cavernous walls. The girls were too busy engrossed in their studies to look up, and Meagan made her way up the stairs to the Terrence's office. The third floor corridor was as deserted as the foyer, with reduced lighting in the hallway, with many closed doors. From a distance, Meagan could see that Terrence's door was open just a crack, spilling a thin column of light out into the darkened hallway. Meagan's heart pounded with anticipation as she approached the door.

As she neared, Meagan could hear strains of soft music coming from behind the door. Looking through the crack, Meagan saw Terrence deeply immersed in his work, humming to the soft alternative rock ballad that flowed from the speakers. His head was bent intently over his work, and in his hand he held his red pen, making notations on a piece of paper. His tortoise-shell glasses were perched haphazardly on the bridge of his nose, and his sleeves were rolled up, exposing a hint of his tattoo. He had loosened his tie and looked artfully messy and relaxed, perfect. Meagan's heart skipped a beat and she swallowed hard as she knocked on the door and gently eased it open. Terrence looked up from his work and gave her a sincere smile. "Ah, Meagan," he said softly, reclining in his leather swivel chair. "Come on in."

Meagan smiled as she stepped into the cozy office, shutting the door behind her. "Terrence," she breathed, taking off her coat. "I sure hope I wasn't interrupting."

"Not at all," Terrence replied, looking her on with twinkling blue-grey eyes as she hung up her coat. "I was expecting you." He waved his hand. "Go ahead and hang up your coat, then you can have a seat."

Meagan felt conscious of his eyes on her body as she turned around to hang up her coat, and she felt herself getting hot. When she turned around, they locked eyes and a fierce spark flashed between them for the briefest moment, before Terrence returned to his usual serene smile, watching her with kindness as she lowered herself into the chair.

"How were your holidays?" she asked him, trying to start the conversation off in a breezy, casual manner.

Terrence smiled and leaned back in his chair. "Good," he answered, leaning back in his chair, idly fingering his red pen which lay on his desk. "I went out to my parents' home on the edge of town, in one of the rural counties. Christmas itself was a small affair, just the three of us out there. I've been staying with my parents, helping them out..." he trailed off, fixing his gaze out the window. "It's been really nice."

"I'm happy for you," Meagan said sincerely. "And if I may say so, you look well rested. I think it has done you some good."

Terrence smiled faintly. "My mother would be happy to hear that," he said. "She worries a lot." He regarded Meagan with a nod. "And may I ask how your holidays were?"

Meagan explained to him the ups and downs, how she had discovered her biological father and spent the holidays with him. She told Terrence about Jen and Melanie and their crazy reveling, and Terrence was well entertained. He was surprised about her father, and expressed his sympathy for her situation, as well as gladness that she and her father had been reunited.

"Hey," Terrence said quietly when they had a lapse in conversation. "I'm sorry I never answered your Christmas card. I was at my parents', so I didn't get it until yesterday." He regarded her with sincerity and seriousness in his blue-grey eyes. "But I wanted to let you know that I appreciate the thought," he said as he withdrew an envelope from his desk. "This is for you," he explained. "I apologize for the timing."

Meagan accepted the envelope and opened it carefully, revealing a navy-blue card with a gold-coloured embossed city pattern on it. Opening it up, she read the message, written in Terrence's nearly illegible chicken-scratch handwriting. It said, *"Dear Meagan, I wanted to take the time to thank you for the wonderful card. I hope you had a merry Christmas and New Years' Day. I always enjoy our engaging meetings. –Terrence."*

Though the note may have seemed a bit stiff and impersonal, Meagan felt a stir of warmth. She knew that as a mathematician, Terrence was conservative with words, and even a note of this length and content was a great compliment. She beamed at him, brushing a tendril of raven-black hair out of her face. "Thank you," she breathed, looking him on with luminous eyes. "You asked how my holiday was, and I tell you that it just got about ten times better."

Terrence smiled, and Meagan saw his cheeks colour ever so slightly. She didn't expect Mr. Handsome to be bashful, but she found it even cuter. He simply studied her for a moment, still smiling, before he finally folded his hands on his desk. "So, what is it that you're struggling with?" he asked, opening up his calculus book.

Suddenly, Meagan was lost for words as her ruse fell through. "I—" she began, not knowing how to explain that she had lied to him, even a minimal lie. Suddenly embarrassed, she looked at her hands, feeling foolish. "I don't need help," she said quietly. "I just wanted a chance to talk to you."

"So you understand everything fine?" Terrence asked, as if he were just checking up. Meagan nodded. "I'm glad," Terrence commented, and Meagan looked up to see him smiling faintly.

"So… you're not mad?" Meagan wondered incredulously. "I can leave if you have other students waiting."

Terrence surprised her by chuckling. "I must say that your underhanded approach impresses me," he joked. "But I've got time today."

Meagan visibly relaxed, and the two of them settled into a pleasant conversation, every so often accentuated by a peal of laughter. Terrence leaned back in his chair, and Meagan abandoned her ramrod-straight posture in favor of a more relaxed stance. The hours ticked by and they talked and laughed until they were distracted by the ding of Terrence's phone. He excused himself and bent down to flip it open. "It's my mom," he explained. "She wants me to pick up a carton of milk on my way home tonight."

Meagan looked at her watch and saw that it was almost eight-thirty. "Do you have to go?" she asked.

Terrence closed his phone and stood up. "I probably should, yes," he replied. "But it was wonderful talking to you today. Come in anytime you want."

Meagan smiled at him, her eyes shining softly as she looked up at him. "Thank you," she said quietly. "I had a great time."

Terrence rose and went over to the mini coatrack at the same time as Meagan, and they reached for their coats at the same time. Like a match on a scratch pad, their fingers brushed and a white-hot surge of electricity shot up Meagan's arm and flooded throughout her body, weakening her knees.

She nearly sighed as her knees threatened to buckle under, and she was forced to grab onto Terrence's hand for support, his hot hands searing her flesh. Alarmed, she looked into his eyes, and saw that he was equally startled. Neither one of them moved to jerk their hands away, instead paralyzed in the moment, almost in disbelief that it happened. Meagan searched Terrence's stormy grey eyes with hers, seeing them darken ever so slightly with depth and the first stirrings of desire.

Suddenly, Meagan felt a surge of emotion and passion rise in her throat, threatening to cut off her air supply. "Terrence…" she choked out, her voice raspy and barely audible.

He made a step to untangle himself from her grasp, but she could sense the white-hot passion smoldering beneath his collected demeanor. He wanted her, she could feel it. "I don't think this is a good idea…" he started to say, his voice husky, but before he could finish, Meagan cupped the side of his face and covered his lips with hers. As soon as the contact occurred, Meagan felt the breath get sucked from her lungs as their passion exploded and the dam broke along with Terrence's resolve. He groaned softly and Meagan felt her back hit the door as he cupped her buttocks in his hands and held her against him. Meagan moaned into the kiss and rocked against his steel-hard erection, which was wedged intimately between her legs. She trailed her fingertips lovingly over the sides of his face while her tongue explored his mouth and his strong hands roamed over her shapely hips and rear end. She arched her back under his touch and pressed her ample breasts into his heavily muscled chest. She slipped her hands under the collar of his shirt, letting her hands trail over his hot skin. Lowering her head, she kissed his exposed collarbone. In turn, she felt his hands slide up her shirt, searing her skin.

Reaching her bra clasp, he undid it with a light grunt and Meagan felt her heavy breasts spring free. Meagan reached up and slipped the bra through her sleeve, tossing the black garment onto his desk. "There," she whispered. Terrence slid his hands around to the front and suddenly her breasts were in his hands. Meagan bit her lip to keep from crying out in pleasure as Terrence squeezed the heavy globes in his hands, pinching and rubbing her nipples as he studied her with his hot, tempestuous grey eyes. Conversely, she molded herself more tightly against him and reveled in the dual pleasure of his hands on her bare breasts and the weight of his erection pressing into her most sensitive core through their clothes.

***

Meagan. Terrence's mind swam with her heat, his mouth flooded with her taste. One moment they were standing there putting their coats on, the next moment she was in his arms and kissing him senseless. His resolve had shattered like glass the moment their lips had touched and he had become ravenous for her, his vision clouding with the need to be deep inside her and hear the sweet sound of his name on her lips as he made her come. He loved her care and sensitivity as she traced his tattoo with her tongue, her almost innocent yearning to lick every inch of him clean. Progressively, they moved away from the wall, and one of them accidentally sent a sheaf of papers sailing off the bookshelf with a careless arm movement. Startled by the noise, Terrence opened his eyes and gazed down at the mess on the floor. He would have disregarded it if it weren't for the clipping that lay close to the top of the pile. Terrence stiffened as he recognized Doreen's obituary, and he swallowed hard as he was swamped with a heavy feeling of guilt. Summoning all of his strength, he gently pushed Meagan away.

"What is it, Terrence?" she whispered, pressing a soothing kiss to his shoulder. "What's wrong?"

He said nothing, but hurried to shrug on his coat, not even bothering to button his shirt. "I have to go," he murmured in a strangled voice. "I just have to go."

***

Meagan watched, bewildered as Terrence haphazardly gathered his things, jammed a stack of papers in his briefcase, and moved toward the door in a zombie-like trance. Ignoring the mess on the floor, he breezed past Meagan and out of the office, leaving her topless, confused, and crushed. With wilted dignity, she pulled her shirt over her head and stuffed her bra in her bag. The office still smelled like Terrence, but it lacked the humming vitality of when he was in it. She stooped down to pick up the spilled papers, and she stopped short at the sight of Doreen's obituary. With a knowing frown, she stacked the papers and put them back where they belonged. So that was what had upset him, she thought, gathering the rest of her things with a sinking heart. Though she understood, it didn't make it hurt any less. After she straightened Terrence's papers, she sadly looked around one more time before she left, gently closing the door and turning the lights off as if tucking a small child into bed. Wordlessly, she left, a deep shadow of hurt covering her soul.

Chapter Thirty-Four

It had been two and a half days since the disappointing evening with Terrence, and Meagan had sunk into a deep, brooding depression. The problem with Terrence, Meagan thought, was that he dealt with things by cooling off and putting up a pretense of nonchalance, hiding his emotions and making it downright impossible to negotiate or move his heavy barriers. Sometimes, Meagan wished he would just be angry about it, because sometimes anger yielded to resolution. But this cold silence, she couldn't take it; there was no way out, no loophole. In class, he was perfectly neutral, treating her with the same gentle, sincere kindness as he displayed to the rest of his students. He never let it show that they had anything more in common than that she was learning calculus from him. Both days, she had held her head up and tried to pretend she was okay, whilst dying inside. She was torn between missing him and feeling guilty for pushing him beyond his boundaries… yet again. She needed to stop doing this to him, and to herself.

Rolling over in bed, she checked the clock which resided on her bedside table. The solid black square face projected a solemn readout of 4:15 PM. After class, she had come home, tossed down a couple of shots, and collapsed into bed in her clothes, pulling the covers over her head and sinking into a deep, messy sleep.

Now, at nearly 4:20, she felt like a complete slob. Her breath smelled of sour alcohol and her hair was an untamed, sweaty mess. She had had fitful dreams and woke up with sweat pooled under her arms and between her legs. Disgusted, she threw off the heavy covers and plowed a hand through her unruly hair. Then, sitting down at the foot of her bed, she swung her feet and tried to decide what to do next. At that very moment, she heard an insistent banging on her front door. Grumbling a string of expletives under her breath, she went to the door and peered out the peephole, not in the mood to receive company. Looking out, she saw Jennine and Melanie standing on her porch, looking concerned and impatient.

With a sigh, Meagan disengaged the lock and swung the door open.

She had barely opened the door when her friends barged in. "What the hell is this?" Melanie asked, gesturing to Meagan's dirty clothes and hair and unkempt surroundings.

Jennine wore a worried frown on her face. "Are you okay?" she asked.

Meagan shrugged. "I could be better," she sighed. "Obviously."

"You haven't contacted us for two days, Meagan, we started to get worried," Jennine explained.

Melanie gave Meagan a suspicious frown. "This doesn't have to do with Terrence, does it?" she asked.

Meagan shifted uncomfortably. "Well…" she said, and heard Melanie mumble something under her breath that sounded vaguely like the word *bastard.* Seeing Melanie's frown, she held up a hand. "It wasn't his fault," she explained. "It was mine."

"I don't care whose fault it was, Meagan, but you need to get cleaned up. No more sulking. We'll be back in twenty minutes."

"All right," Meagan sighed, knowing that Melanie meant business. She was glad that her friends thought enough to come check on her. "Thanks, guys."

"Twenty minutes," Melanie warned, and they left.

***

Freakishly true to her word, Melanie showed up exactly twenty minutes later, and Meagan could hear the screech of tires and thumping of the bass as a car parked in front of her house. In twenty minutes, Meagan had speed-showered, washed her hair, and dressed in a sweatshirt and jeans. She still wasn't in the mood for much, but she figured if she didn't agree to the girls' night, she would probably be dragged against her will anyway. The one thing about Jennine and Melanie, she found, was once they had an idea there was no stopping them. Meagan grabbed her purse as Meagan stepped out the door of her apartment, fishing around in her purse for her keys. "I'm coming!" she yelled, even though she was sure that Jen and Melanie couldn't hear over the pounding music.

Bundling up against the chill, Meagan hurried down the steps and pulled open the back door to Melanie's shining black Caddy, sliding herself onto the smooth leather seats. She had barely closed the door and hooked her seatbelt when Melanie slammed on the gas pedal and roared off. "Woo-hoo!" Jennine hollered. She turned to face Meagan. "Welcome to the party!"

Meagan winced as the car lurched sideways. The seats were heated and the stereo was pumping out a sleazy rap song, which Melanie was belting out the lyrics to while she kept a leather-gloved grip on the wheel. When they were at a stop light, Meagan leaned forward and turned the music down. "Dude, Mel," she said. "Could you slow it down a bit? I'm not used to driving the way you and Jennine do."

Once Meagan had made her request, Melanie turned out to be a reasonable driver. Jennine, on the other hand, couldn't be helped no matter what.

A few minutes later, they pulled up in front of the Kool Kat Lounge, a family-owned establishment about ten minutes from Meagan's apartment. Meagan followed her friends into the warm diner, where jazzy lounge music was played by the live band on the stage. Immediately, she felt more relaxed and at home, with the deep forest-green walls, pine trim with wooden ceiling fans and dim red lamps over the tables. Looking around, Meagan saw a pretty sizable crowd for a Thursday night. The trio found a table in the back and was soon approached by a thin Goth-looking waitress with short, spiky black hair and a ring in her nose. She gave them a wide, purple-lipstick smile and asked what they would like to drink. Melanie and Jen both ordered large tumblers of beer. Meagan had resolved not to drink any more, but she resigned herself and ordered a beer as well. After their drinks and food came, Meagan settled into the flow of the conversation as the buzz began to set in. *Ah,* she thought to herself, leaning back in her seat. Sometimes all one needed to do was go out and drink with the gals.

When they were almost done with their food, the bandleader, a young, strapping black guy, took the mic. "All right, y'all," he announced. "Let's have some couples out on the floor. Get it hot in heerrre!"

Immediately, the people sitting at the tables began to cheer, as some of them made their way to the center of the room with their partners.

"Let's dance," Melanie said with a flourish, yanking Jennine to her feet. Melanie winked and waved to Meagan as the two of them joined the forming crowd. Meagan didn't mind being left behind at the table, she simply stretched back in her chair and settled into her buzz, grooving to the music. She smiled as she watched Jennine and Melanie slow-dancing, bodies pressed together, eyes intense, and could practically feel the sparks flying between them. Reaching for her beer, she took another sip and swallowed, enjoying the fresh, cold taste.

"Excuse me," Meagan heard a deep male voice beside her and her eyes flew open as she practically choked on her beer. Bewildered, she looked over at the handsome black-haired gentleman, maybe in his early thirties, standing at the foot of the table.

Setting her glass down, she stared at him. "Who are you?" she spluttered with a suspicious frown, immediately regretting her rudeness when she saw how nice-looking he was.

But the man just smiled and extended his hand. "Daniel Kincaid," he replied with a sincere grin. "And I apologize for startling you. It's just, you looked so pretty all alone over here; I had to talk to you."

Meagan shook his hand and smiled. "I'm Meagan Lucien. Go ahead and have a seat," she gestured to the open chairs across from her.

Daniel took her up on her offer and seated himself comfortably across from her. "So, why are you sitting here alone?" he teased good-naturedly.

Meagan gave an embarrassed cough. "Well, my friends are out on the dance floor," she pointed to Jennine and Melanie.

Daniel raised his eyebrows with a smile. "Well, they're burning up the floor, those two," he commented. Giving Meagan a sideways glance, he extended his hand. "Care to join them?"

Ordinarily, Meagan wouldn't have agreed to dance with a complete stranger, but she had had a couple beers and was feeling like she had nothing left to lose anyway. So she clasped his outstretched hand and let him lead her out onto the floor. Meagan felt light-headed and dreamlike as Daniel gracefully waltzed her around the dance floor, and she found that he was actually quite charming, not to mention that he was a phenomenal dancer. "Where did you learn to dance like this?" she asked him as he gently spun her around.

He smiled down on her. "I took ballroom lessons in high school," he explained with a laugh. "All of my friends thought I was a dork… until prom night, when all their girlfriends wanted to dance with me."

Meagan laughed. "I bet," she agreed.

As they talked and danced, Meagan found out that Daniel was thirty-two, unmarried, and a successful self-published author. He was an engaging, entertaining, and charming gentleman, and Meagan was having a great time with him. Even if it was only for the night, she was able to push down her feelings for Terrence. But aside from her tipsy bliss, she couldn't ignore the deep, stabbing loneliness that Terrence's void had left within her; it had simply been muted for the night, like a painkiller.

Finally, at 2AM when the club closed, Daniel agreed to drive the three women home, since he was sober and they were not. Jen and Melanie were very drunk, and Meagan was only a bit buzzed. On the way home, Meagan leaned against the window, trying to ignore the awkward fact that Jen and Melanie were completely plastered, and drunkenly making out in the back seat, with whispered slurred words and clumsy kisses, tongues shoved down each other's throats as Jen groped Melanie's breasts and Melanie had her hands all over Jen's butt. She turned to Daniel with a grimace. "I apologize on their behalf for the eyeful," she said. "They are devils when they get drunk."

"I can see that," Daniel chuckled. He shrugged. "Don't worry, I've seen it all. My best friend is gay. He and his boyfriend are exactly the same way."

Meagan reached back and pushed a button, sliding up the panel between the seats. She noted with a chuckle the slight look of disappointment on Daniel's face. Guys were all the same, she thought, but tonight she didn't mind.

Chapter Thirty-Five

    Terrence was sitting at on his living room couch, with the idea to grade papers, but he hadn't gotten that far yet. Soft rock music flowed from his beat-up portable CD player that rested on his nightstand, and he had folders and papers spread wide in every direction. He had his red pen in his hand, but rather than focusing on the assignment at hand, his gaze was absent as he stared moodily towards the far wall and curtain-concealed window. This was the first week he had been back home from his parents' house and the house felt empty and lonely. Tonight he felt tense, a deep crease between his brows. The incident with Meagan had troubled him greatly, because he really enjoyed her company and could see in her eyes that she was simply crazy about him. But he couldn't shake the clinging guilt about Doreen, feeling like he had betrayed her and it would be disrespectful to her memory to continue on with Meagan. Every night he lit a fire in his fireplace and would spend hours staring into the flames as visions of Doreen's face clashed with a sensuous flash of Meagan's ardent kisses. Feeling a tension rise in his gut, Terrence realized that he desperately needed a light. He felt in his pocket and extracted a half pack of cigarettes. Carefully, with sophistication, Terrence ignited the tip of his cigarette with the lighter and stuck it between his lips, closing his eyes with a deep, greedy draw of smoke. As he exhaled, a halo of smoke ringed the air around his head and Terrence remembered how he had quit smoking years ago, but after Doreen had died, his habit had flared to life like the flame itself. She had always kept him in check, but now, he craved nicotine and he couldn't help himself. Taking another deep draw, he leaned back on the couch and sighed with pleasure as the chemical filled his lungs. Damn, how nice guilty pleasures were, he thought. All he needed were two things: a nice, good light, and Meagan Lucien in his lap. As soon as his flash of lust came on, it dissipated, and he felt once again a deep sorrow. He took another deep puff, this time holding the smoke for a moment before creating another smoky halo around his head. *I'm sorry, Doreen,* he thought. *I hope you know I'm really sorry.*

Suddenly, Terrence sensed a change in the air, almost as if a new air current was flowing in. Bewildered, Terrence opened his eyes, wondering if he had forgotten to put the insulator bar under the door. Then, before his tired eyes, he saw Doreen standing before him, dressed in a white floor-length robe, almost as if she had been at a spa. Her hair was up on rollers, but her image was blurry, almost as if he could have imagined her. Before he could react, he felt the cigarette snatched from his lips. His hand flew to his mouth, and he looked up to see Doreen giving him a sympathetic look.

"Terrence, you have to stop this," she said firmly, extinguishing it with her being.

Terrence blinked up at the image of his dead wife. "Are you really here?" he asked shakily. "Are you a ghost?"

Doreen shook her head. "No, I'm with the Lord," she answered. Then, she gestured to his papers. "Look at these, honey, you're a mess."

Terrence rubbed his eyes. "Did you come back just to tell me to straighten my papers?" he wondered.

Her response surprised him. "No, Terrence, I don't care about your papers. I came back to talk to you about love."

Terrence raised his eyebrows. "Love?" he wondered. "Why?"

"Look, I know the chemistry you have with Meagan Lucien," Doreen said quietly.

Terrence winced. "I'm sorry, Doreen," he said softly, finally glad he was able to tell her. "I'll never forgive myself." He groped for his cigarette, but remembered that Doreen had taken it. "Damn, if we're going to have this conversation, at least let me smoke," he pleaded.

Doreen held up her hand to stop him. "No, Terrence, you didn't let me finish," she said softly, and suddenly, Terrence missed his wife. He felt his eyes blurring as he looked up at her. "What I meant to say," she continued. "Is stop blaming yourself. You were a wonderful husband and served me well. But now I'm in heaven, and anyone would be crazy not to see the potential you have with Meagan."

"I…" Terrence didn't know what to say, he was at a loss for words. He shrugged.

"She loves you," Doreen continued. "Take her as your wife. I know she will do much better than I did."

Terrence wasn't sure what to say, but he lowered his eyes. "Thanks, Doreen," he said quietly. "You've always had a good heart."

"So have you, Terrence," she responded. "I loved you but it's time for me to leave you. Just know that I give my blessings to you, and someday we will meet again as friends." she made a wide sign of the cross over Terrence and leaned in to softly kiss his cheek. "Goodbye, Terrence, God bless you," she whispered, and then with a soft squeeze of his hand, she faded into his dreamscape.

Chapter Thirty-Six

There were no university classes on Friday, so Meagan had spent her day sleeping off her hangover from the night before. Daniel had called, asking when he could see her again. Honestly, Meagan didn't know how to respond. Yes, she had liked him at the club; he was a very nice man, exceptional conversationalist, and terrific dancer, but deep inside, her heart still belonged to Terrence. She just couldn't see herself falling for Daniel, he was great but he would never be the one she wanted. So Meagan had stumbled through Friday, downing a couple seltzer tablets and sleeping on and off throughout the day. Saturday morning, Meagan awoke at 7:45 AM to bright sunshine streaming in through her filmy curtains, unusual for mid-January.

Meagan rose and showered, dressed in black low-rise yoga pants and a black long-sleeved crop top. She toweled off her still-wet hair and threw it back into a bun, with dangling strands hanging down in the back. Stretching with a luxurious yawn, she walked into the kitchen and poured herself a stout glass of orange juice, removing a container of low-fat yogurt from the refrigerator. Meagan wasn't exactly a morning person but she often liked to get up early on the weekends to exercise, whether she ran on the treadmill or did dance or yoga. After she swallowed down her meager container of yogurt with a handful of nuts and washed it down with orange juice, she brushed her teeth and headed into the living room, deciding to warm up with some easy stretching exercises before going down to her basement gym for a more hard-core workout. She scooted her coffee table over so that she had room on her carpet, and she stripped off her shoes, padding across the carpet to turn on the boom box, which was hooked up to her mp3 player. She pressed play and a California-boy-band alternative rock song came on. The song was fast and driving, but almost hypnotizing. She turned it up and did some jumping jacks and running in place to get her blood flowing, whilst beginning to preliminarily stretch her leg and arm muscles. When the blood-pumping California rock song was over, the next track on her mp3 was flowing and soothing... perfect for yoga. Meagan dropped to the floor and breathed deeply as she spread her legs in a perfect straddle, sighing with pleasure as she leaned from side to side and stretched her leg muscles. Meagan became lost in the music, flowing gracefully with the melody, letting it carry her as she seamlessly transferred positions, contorting lithely on the floor. She was so immersed in her meditation that she failed to hear the insistent knocking on her front door. Finally, the sound pierced her consciousness and her eyes flew open. Listening intently, she shut off the music and hastened to the door. She gave her armpits a quick sniff just in case it was Terrence, but luckily she hadn't sweated yet. Her heart flip-flopped in her chest at the thought that it might be him. She checked her reflection in the mirror and took a deep breath before opening the door. But as soon as she did, her face fell when she saw Daniel standing on her doorstep, an expensive bundle of pink roses in his hands. "You look beautiful this morning, Meagan," he said, handing her the roses. "These are for you."

Meagan accepted the roses with a neutral expression. "Thank you," she replied evenly. Cocking her head sideways, she gave him a look. "What brings you to the neighborhood?" she asked casually.

"I came to see you," he answered, looking deep into her eyes and confirming her worst fears.

"Um, well, I was kind of in the middle of my exercise routine, but…" Meagan stammered.

Daniel looked so crestfallen that Meagan had to feel bad for him. "I can come back later," he said quietly, turning to go. "I'm sorry."

Meagan felt so guilty about his crushed expression that she grudgingly opened the door. "I guess you can come in if you want to," she said, attempting to force a smile. She held the door open and motioned him in. He hesitated, and then stepped through the door, his face brightening. Meagan gestured weakly to her old faded armchair in her living room. "Feel free to sit," she sighed, trying to be a good hostess. "Can I get you anything to drink?"

Daniel shook his head. "I'm good, thanks," he replied. "In fact, I'd like to make breakfast for you."

Meagan's eyebrows shot up and she barked out a hoarse cough, choking on a lump in her throat. "What?" she spluttered, unable to conceal her shock. "Why?"

Daniel shrugged. "I make really good crepes," he explained. "It will only take me about fifteen minutes. You can keep exercising; I'll have it ready for you. I even brought my own can of whipped cream and fresh berries." He opened his bag and grinned at her. "And I'll do the dishes, don't worry."

Normally, Meagan would have refused, but she loved crepes but didn't know how to make them, not to mention that she felt bad about all the trouble that Daniel had obviously gone to for her. "Thanks for all your trouble," she told him sincerely. She pointed in the direction of the kitchen. "Kitchen's back there. Make yourself at home."

Daniel shot her another wide, sincere smile, and as he headed to the kitchen, Meagan admitted that he was really a sweet guy, clad in dark jeans and an argyle sweater, with black dress shoes. Yes, he was a bit of a geek, but a really nice person. *Maybe I should give him a chance,* Meagan thought, as she continued to stretch, listening to the sounds of him bustling around in the kitchen and humming to himself.

True to his word, Daniel had the crepes made, coffee brewed, and table elegantly set about twenty minutes later. He had found a vase for the roses and placed them in the center of the table. Though Meagan was a bit annoyed that he hadn't asked for the vase, she couldn't help an admiring gasp as she surveyed the beautifully set table. "Oh, Daniel, it's beautiful," she breathed, and he beamed at her.

He moved behind her and pulled out her chair like a perfect gentleman. "Madame," he intoned, gesturing for her to sit down. With a nod, Meagan sat down as Daniel lit two candles for festivity. Being Catholic, Daniel said a brief grace over the meal and they began.

Meagan sampled the crepes and found that they were melt-in-your-mouth delicious, Daniel was a genius cook. Also, as the conversation progressed, she found herself loosening up to him and actually beginning to enjoy his company.

"I'm sorry if I was too forward," Daniel was saying with a bashful laugh, his brown eyes sparkling. "I hope I didn't offend you."

Meagan took a bite of her crepe and washed it down with scalding coffee, savoring the sweet raspberry compote. "Of course not," she reassured him. "I was a bit surprised that you came, but I'm glad you did."

"I'm glad too," Daniel said, looking relieved. "Because when you first answered the door, you looked very dismayed to see me."

Meagan shook her head quickly. "Don't be silly," she lied. "I was just startled. You must have read my expression wrong."

"Oh," Daniel replied, sipping his coffee. His expression softened. "I can't explain it, Meagan, but I have this feeling when I'm with you," he confessed.

Meagan swallowed hard. She didn't want to be having this conversation with him. "What sort of feeling?" she asked suspiciously.

"It breaks my heart," Daniel continued. "Because every time I see you, I fall more in love. But it almost feels like I can't have you..." he broke off, shaking his head sadly. "You don't want me," he said quietly.

This train of thought was interrupted by the slam of a car door across the street. "Who's that?" she heard Daniel ask. Looking up, she saw a steel-gray pickup truck parked across the street, and Terrence had just alighted from the driver's seat and was walking efficiently towards her door, though slightly dragging his right leg as always.

"That's... Oh, God, oh no..." Meagan mumbled, feeling like her throat was closing up. Before she could think, she heard a knock on her door. Moving on pin-like legs, Meagan staggered to the door and thrust it open like she had seen a ghost. Wide eyed, she stared at the smiling Terrence, dressed in ripped blue jeans and his winter coat, clutching a bouquet of carnations. Seeing him here broke her heart. "Oh, Terrence," she breathed.

"I came to make up for the other night," he said, handing her the flowers. "I'll explain what happened later." He raised his eyebrows. "I saw a car in front of your house. do you have company?"

"I... no, yes..." Meagan stammered, flustered. Just then, as if right on cue with this nightmare, Daniel appeared behind her.

"I'm Daniel Kincaid," he said cheerfully, extending his hand to Terrence. "I'm Meagan's friend. We met the other night and were having breakfast together."

Terrence's eyes turned cold as ice and Meagan felt the pain cut her in half like a knife to the very soul. Her eyes filled with tears as Terrence suddenly turned wordlessly and left, striding toward his truck in large paces, moving quickly despite his bad leg.

"Terrence!" Meagan called; her voice hoarse with pain as she sprinted after him. But Terrence got a head start as a car whipped by, blocking Meagan's path and sousing her with slushy water. But she didn't care. "Terrence, wait!" she screamed as he climbed into his cab and slammed the door, gunning the engine and roaring off down the street. Once he was gone, she sank down on her porch steps and put her face in her hands as deep sobs wracked her body.

Daniel clapped a hand over his mouth, his eyes wide with shock.

"I'm sorry, Meagan," he said softly. "I didn't realize..." but Meagan cut him off and held up her hand.

"Just go, Daniel," she choked out weakly, her eyes rimmed red and brimming with tears.

"But I..." he started.

"Get out!" she yelled, her shrill screech so forceful that it nearly shattered the windows of her apartment. "Get out," she repeated more softly, her voice crumbling into sobs. Then, turning, she walked into her apartment and slammed the door, collapsing on the couch in her soggy clothes, reaching for the canister of sleeping pills on her light stand.

***

Terrence was barreling down the freeway in his truck, blinded with hurt and rage, white-knuckled hands on the wheel, slipping and sliding on the icy streets as screamo rock blasted from his speakers, so loud that the car vibrated and his teeth rattled. He had never driven like this in his life, always being overly cautious, but he had never experienced this kind of humiliation either. Women, he thought. Blast the feckless, fickle creatures. Never again would he dare to trust a woman with his heart. Being a man of great pride, it had taken a lot of sacrifice for him to go show up at her door and bare himself to her like that. But he didn't mind, because he loved her, or thought he did. But what had he found? Some jerk in a goofy plaid sweater with a cup of coffee in his hand and a smirk on his face. "Is this your twisted way of retribution for my infidelity?" he demanded aloud to Doreen, pounding on the wheel for emphasis. He couldn't help wondering if she was behind this ridiculous disgrace. "Screw you."

He was furious. Furious with the argyle-clad prick at Meagan's place this morning, furious at Meagan for making a fool of him, furious at Doreen for lying to him, and most of all he was furious at himself for being stupid enough to trust someone else. Love, he thought, was the most meaningless word in the English language. With his jaw clenched in determination, he regained control of his grip on the wheel and vowed to himself that he would never be foolish enough to believe in it again.

Chapter Thirty-Seven

Several hours later, Meagan awoke, groggy from the sleeping pills she had taken. At first she just felt dissociated, as if she were floating in a cold grey mist. As she brushed a sticky lock of hair out of her face, she realized that her face was wet with tears. Looking down on the couch, she saw a dark stain where she had wept. Suddenly, the day's events begun to come back to her. Looking out the window, she could see that the sky had grown heavy and gray, and cold, crystalloid flurries were floating aimlessly from the bleak strata, blown about by restless wind. As she remembered the look on Terrence's face, the pain in his eyes, she buried her face in her hands and sobbed once again. Now he was really gone. She had really done it now. Silently, she cursed herself for letting Daniel in. It wasn't his fault, she knew, but still, she couldn't help being mad at him. Why had he chosen today to come stop by and chat? And why had he emerged from the other room and introduced himself like he was a member of the family? Meagan pushed herself off of the couch, wet and shivering from her damp clothes. With a surge of fury, she yanked the roses out of the vase on the table and thrust open the window, tossing them out in the street. Then, with a bang, she shut the window and stalked off. After she had disposed of the roses, the fight seemed to go out of her and she sank down onto the couch once more, reaching for the bottle of whiskey she had left out on her lamp stand. She feebly poured herself a shot with shaking hands as she tried to control her sniffles. She had just lifted the glass to her lips when she heard a knocking on her front door. She was startled out of her daze by the noise, and she accidentally splashed her shot all over her lap. She cursed colorfully and rose to pour herself another. The knock sounded again, and Meagan ignored it. But a second later, she heard a key rasp in the lock, and the door swung open. Jennine and Melanie rushed in, their faces drawn with concern. Meagan felt the shot glass and whiskey bottle yanked from her hands. "Jesus, Meagan, how much did you drink?" Melanie asked.

"None yet," Meagan grumbled, and she saw her friends relax. She lay her head down on the couch arm and felt the tears start to flow once again. Melanie and Jen both embraced her, and Meagan lost it, blubbering all over their shoulders like a baby. "How did you know to come?"

"Daniel called," Jen said soothingly, rubbing Meagan's back. "He was frantic, and told us everything that happened. We came over as fast as we could."

They continued to murmur soothing words and stroke her hair as she cried for Terrence. Finally, when she felt as if she could cry no more, she looked up at her friends, her face streaked with tears. "What am I gonna do now?" she sniffled, wiping her eyes on her shirt.

Melanie and Jen looked at each other. Then, deep into Meagan's eyes. "Do you love him?" Jen whispered. Meagan nodded, and almost began to cry again.

Melanie wiped her face with a tissue. "Stop crying," she told Meagan. "What you're gonna do is get him back."

Meagan barked out a hopeless laugh. "And how can I do that?" she asked.

"That's for you to figure out," Melanie said softly. She rose. "If you want, Jen and I will stay with you tonight," she offered.

Meagan gave a weak smile. "Thanks," she whispered, glad that she had such good friends.

***

It took Meagan a while to figure out what she would do, but eventually the idea came to her. She decided to do something that would take time and effort and really demonstrate to Terrence how much she cared for him. She decided to make him an apple pie, so she went out Saturday evening to the grocery store and got some supplies. She bought apples, as well as a houseplant for Terrence with pretty, diminutive white blossoms on it. While it was true than women didn't generally get flowers for men, she figured it would be different, because it was a whole potted plant. Besides, Meagan didn't care about the restrictive rules about who did what anyway. After purchasing the apples and the plant, she headed home and got started on her project. It was frustrating at first, and she had to redo the crust about three times. All afternoon, she was elbows-deep in flour and apples, but finally the timer dinged and she took out a pretty well-done latticework-topped pie, even though she had limited experience as a baker. She wrapped it in tinfoil and stuck a curl of turquoise ribbon on it for decoration.

By the time she was finished with all of her preparations and cleaned up, it was about six o' clock. She went to her closet and decided to dress up, picking out a sparkly black dress, elegant but not too revealing, since she didn't want to give the wrong impression. It was a sequined, tea-length V-neck gown, with a matching shawl and gloves. With it, Meagan wore nylon stockings, black pumps, and silver chandelier earrings. Jen and Melanie helped her curl her hair, and prettily pinned it up to the side. When she was dressed, it ended up being about six forty-five. But she couldn't stop now. Glancing out the window at the darkened sky, she saw that a light snow was falling. She put a bag over the plant to protect it from the cold and shrugged on her coat. Jen and Melanie stood at the door and wished her good luck.

Meagan thanked them, but as she walked out to her car she was extremely nervous. What if it really was too late? Would Terrence scream at her? Close the door in her face? Or would he just be his usual calm, collected self and pretend that nothing had ever happened between them? As she navigated the darkened, icy streets, the snowfall began to thicken, but Meagan didn't turn back. She needed to do this. Her very life depended on it. Without Terrence, she found, she really didn't want to live at all. She eased her way through the storm at about two miles per hour, feeling like she was groping blindly along a darkened wall. Finally, she recognized the neighborhood and the little brick house on the corner. When she saw that house, she suddenly felt a rush of déjà vu. The last time she had been inside that house, she and Terrence had made passionate love all night long. She pulled into his driveway and saw that his steel-gray pickup truck was parked in the driveway. Inside the house, a muted light shone through the curtains. Taking a deep breath, with her heart in her hands, she grabbed her plant and pie and alighted from her car, fighting the blizzard as she made her way up the steps. She was grateful that Terrence's porch provided a cloak of darkness.

Summoning up all of her courage, Meagan leaned forward and pressed the bell, which was glowing a serene peach color amidst the snowy darkness. At first there was complete silence, so she pressed the bell again. This time, she heard the muffled sound of Terrence's scraping footsteps as he approached the door. With a soft click, Terrence opened the door and flicked on the porch light, causing Meagan to wince under the harsh glow. He looked haggard and tired, and after giving Meagan a cursory once-over, he turned away wordlessly and closed the door. Meagan was shaken but she wouldn't give up now, couldn't give up now. With desperation, she pounded loudly on the door until her fists were sore. Finally, in resignation, Terrence came to the door once more. "What are you doing here?" he said in a hoarse, barely audible voice, sounding as if he hadn't spoken in five years.

"Please, Terrence, I just want to talk to you," Meagan pleaded, her voice cracking.

Reluctantly, with no change of emotion, Terrence opened the door and gestured for her to come in. "Very well," he said coldly, but she could hear the pain in his voice. "The roads are dangerous out there. I'll drive you home when the snow eases up."

Meagan stepped into his cozy, dim living room, and took off her coat. She took the bag off of the plant, handing it to Terrence, and set the pie down on the table. "These are for you," she said softly, looking into his stormy grey eyes. She leaned over and kissed him on the cheek. "I'm sorry," she whispered.

Terrence didn't move, simply held the plant, standing there stock-still. He finally sat himself in a chair and nodded for Meagan to sit. He picked up his cup of tea and sipped it thoughtfully. It was clear that he wasn't going to say anything. The silence was making Meagan nervous. She fidgeted in her chair. Finally, she locked eyes with him. "I made you an apple pie," she said meekly, gesturing to the foil-wrapped package on the table. She swallowed. "Because I want you to know how much you mean to me."

Terrence lifted the foil. "Did you make him a pie, too?" he asked, his voice icily calm and just as quiet.

"No," Meagan said softly. "I met him at the club the other night, he's a friend of my friends. He showed up at my door and wanted to make breakfast for me, so I let him." Terrence was silent. "He's a great guy, great cook, and superb dancer, but I turned him down," Meagan continued, tears beginning to spill from her eyes. She grabbed a tissue from the coffee table and wiped her nose. "As soon as you left, I screamed at him to get out." She paused and dabbed her eyes. "I never want to see him again."

Terrence looked confused. "Why not?" he asked.

"Because he isn't the one I want," Meagan replied through teary eyes. She looked up into his thunder-clouded grey eyes. "The only one I want is you."

Looking up into Terrence's eyes, she saw that they too were misty. Meagan felt such a surge of love for this man that she rose off of the couch and knelt at his feet, clasping his hands. "I love you and only you, Terrence Reid," she whispered, looking up into his eyes, into his soul. "And I want to spend my life with you, through sickness and health. Marry me."

Terrence sat quietly, her hands clasped in his, gazing into Meagan's pleading, tear-filled brown eyes for a long moment. She could see the currents shifting in his eyes as his thoughts swirled in his mind, and for that moment, she held her breath. *Let me make it up to you,* Terrence heard Doreen's voice in his head. *Just trust her, Terrence, she won't hurt you.*

Finally, Terrence took a deep breath. "I will," he murmured, and Meagan felt as if she was finally complete, for once in her lifetime. He grinned at her. "Are you always this forward, Miss Lucien?"

She beamed and tears of joy moistened her eyes. "Only when it matters," she replied, lifting Terrence's hand to her lips. "I love you," she murmured. Looking deep into her eyes, he reached down and gripped her hips, lifting her up into his lap. As their lips met, Meagan felt that Terrence's cheeks were damp. Gently, she lifted the corner of her shawl and dried his eyes, before they sank into a deeper kiss, the flame of their passion obliterating all sadness and regrets.

The kiss deepened and Meagan melted into Terrence's arms, feeling his hot, strong hands trail up her sides, searing his name into her curves. He slid his hands up to cup her breasts through her dress. With gentle pressure, he eased the straps of her dress from her shoulders, trailing his hands all the way down her arms as they kissed. Then, his hands returned to her breasts, this time unhindered by any material. Meagan moaned aloud at the glorious sensation of his hot, work-worn hands on her bare skin as he held her breasts, tested their weight, and gently squeezed them in his hands. "Oh, God, Terrence, I love your hands," she moaned when their kiss broke and he continued to massage her breasts, gazing at her through heavy-lidded grey eyes, a different kind of storm brewing in the depths of his soul.

He smiled. "You think this is all my hands can do?" he whispered, keeping one hand on her breast while he slid the other up her nylon-covered leg beneath her skirt. Lowering his head, he leaned down and his lips grazed her other breast. "Well, you're wrong." His voice was low and husky, filled with sinful promises. Meagan stroked his head as he sucked her nipple and squeezed the other. There was no way to stop the little breathy whimpers that came from her throat, and they seemed to egg Terrence on all the more. She could feel his hot, steely erection pressing against her thigh as he slid his hand up under her skirt. With her free hand, she reached down to stroke him and heard his sharp gasp when she clasped her hand around his strong shaft. In turn, she spread her legs farther as his hand moved up her thigh. Her underwear was soaked and her breasts had turned hard and heavy under his expert ministrations. He touched her through her pantyhose and she arched her back and held him to her. With molten eyes, Terrence stood her up and stripped off her pantyhose, followed by her black silk panties, throwing them in a heap on the floor. Then, Terrence moved the houseplant, pie, and newspaper from his coffee table with a methodical determination. As she realized his intentions, Meagan felt another rush of wetness flood between her legs, and with smoky sloe eyes, she stepped out of her dress, letting it slither to the floor, now completely naked. She saw the flames flash in Terrence's eyes as he trailed his hands over her body and gently eased her back on the table. Terrence knelt beside the table and trailed his hands up her thighs, gently but firmly spreading her legs. She was shocked when he clamped his mouth over her most sensitive place, parting her slick folds with his tongue. He raised his head and gazed over the expanse of her body, his eyes blazing with desire. "I'm going to make you come, right here on the table," he whispered hoarsely. Meagan let out a sharp gasp as he slid a finger inside her, and then two, stroking and filling her.

"Oh, Terrence," she moaned, moving with him as he stroked her sensitive core. "Don't stop," she whispered as he plunged deeper, stretching her limits. Meagan felt the pressure building and she began to squirm around his hand as he increased the pace, driving into her deeper and harder, until she felt that he would tear her in two. She began to gasp and writhe on the table as he lowered his mouth to her. Wave after wave of pleasure swamped her as she cradled his head between her legs and screamed his name, over and over. Finally, when she collapsed, she rose off the table, which was now damp where she had lain. She stood and went to Terrence, feeling as if she wanted to worship him for what he had done to her. With ultimate gentleness, she peeled his shirt from his shoulders. "Let's go to your bedroom," she suggested in a seductive whisper, taking his arm in hers. "I won't make you lay on the table."

In the bedroom, she helped him strip off the rest of his clothes and gently pushed him back on the bed, admiring his fit, muscular body. "You're beautiful," she told him, stroking a hand down his chest as she propped herself over him. "I want to taste every inch of you."

"I promise, you can," he murmured hoarsely. "But I have to have you first. Top or bottom?"

"Bottom," Meagan whispered. "I want to feel all of you all over me."

Terrence liked this idea and agreed with a soft groan, flipping Meagan over on her back and pinning her between the soft mattress and his hot, steely weight. Meagan murmured restlessly and spread her legs, guiding him with her hands to her slick opening. "Take me, Terrence," she whispered, trailing his hands down his biceps. Her words turned into a gasp as he slid inside her, filling a long-empty void. He moved on her slow and deep, each thrust feeling like she could take no more. He gazed down at her with stormy grey eyes as he ground his hips into hers and she trembled and cried out under him. It didn't take long for the pressure to build, an intense, sweeping sensation that had them both racing to finish. Meagan bathed him in her wet heat and quivered around him as she reached her peak, stars exploding in front of her eyes as she murmured his name. Terrence thrust deep one more time, filling her with his seed. Then, he rolled off of her and lay quietly beside her, spent. His eyelids flickered sleepily and he feebly held her hand. Naked, with the heat of their fluids still slick between her thighs, Meagan snuggled up to Terrence and trailed her lips over his collarbone, propping herself up as she explored his steely biceps with her tongue, her loose dark hair brushing his chest as she leant down to lick his tattoo. Only then did she notice what it was… a Celtic cross with chains on it and the Latin inscription, *'fides vincit omnes'*. Also, at the foot of the cross was written the word "Brooklyn" and a date.

"Who is Brooklyn?" Meagan whispered, brushing her lips over the tattoo.

For a long moment, Terrence didn't speak. Finally, he replied. "My accident," he murmured quietly. "The job site was at Brooklyn Avenue in Ashtabula. I got this tattoo because only by a miracle of the Lord did I survive that bridge collapse," he closed his eyes, seeming deeply disturbed.

"I'm sorry," Meagan murmured, sliding up to kiss him gently on the lips. As Meagan painstakingly explored every inch of him with her tongue, Terrence felt himself getting rock-hard once again. This time, he spread her wide from the back and buried himself deep inside her, where he belonged. They made passionate love for hours, time after time in every way, until they finally collapsed together, falling asleep in

294

each other's arms, completely entwined in each other and so deeply immersed in the kind of love that lasts forever.

Chapter Thirty-Eight

Meagan awoke just as the darkness of the January morning was beginning to fade. It was about 7AM on Sunday morning and the sky had not yet lightened. She was curled up naked next to Terrence, her dark hair fanned out over her pillow, her arms entwined around him. She was still immersed in her dreamscape, but became aware of a delicious heat radiating towards her. In her dream, she was laying on a beautiful beach, basking in the glow of the sun. As she awoke, her dreamscape began to dissipate, and she flicked her eyelids open, almost not believing the sight before her. There he was, in all his glory, Terrence Reid, and she was in his bed. A joyful grin spread on her face and she sniffled, wiping happy tears from her eyes as she looked down at her sleeping soon-to-be husband. In sleep, Terrence looked younger than his fifty-four years and more carefree, his arms flung out to the side as he breathed deeply and evenly. She brushed back a wisp of strawberry-blond hair from his face and gently bent down to kiss his forehead. "I love you," she whispered.

As she gazed upon the sleeping Terrence, she felt love for him flowing out of her like an overturned cask of wine. She touched his face once more and silently slipped out of bed. Though it was cold, she decided to go into the kitchen and make breakfast in bed for her fiancé. Smiling, she tied her hair back and shivered as she walked over to the closet. She just realized with a faltering smile that the only clothing she had was the black cocktail dress that she had left on the floor in the living room. She thought that Terrence probably wouldn't mind if she borrowed something from the closet. She opened it up and found that he had two robes. Picking one, she covered herself with it, though it was a little bit too big. Then, she put a pair of heavy-duty crew socks on her feet and padded into the kitchen. She wasn't the world's best cook but she did know how to make pretty good griddle cakes. Looking in the refrigerator, she saw that Terrence had all the necessary ingredients, including buttermilk. Buttermilk griddle cakes were always the best, Meagan thought, especially topped with maple syrup or raspberry jam. She quickly located all the necessary equipment and got out a flat skillet, dabbing some oil on it to preheat it. At the same time, she got out all of the ingredients and began to combine them in a large mixing bowl. She smiled to herself when she thought of how pleased Terrence would be when she went to wake him and had breakfast all laid out. She hummed to herself cheerfully as she whisked the batter and when the skillet was ready, she began to pour the batter into neat little rounds on the hot frying pan, waiting with a spatula in hand for thcm to turn a crispy golden-brown.

Meanwhile, as Meagan was downstairs making breakfast, Terrence had just begun to arise from his dreams. At first, his senses were blurred together, and his eyelids flickered sleepily as he struggled to familiarize himself with his surroundings. Suddenly, the memories returned to him like the flood of a waterfall, and he was blinded to everything except Meagan, her dark silky hair, gentle kiss, and sweet scent. He groped for the pillow next to him and found that the space beside him in bed was vacant. Now fully awake, his eyes flew open and he felt a cold trickle of terror down his spine as he realized she was gone. Had she promised to spend her life with him and then disappeared the next morning without a trace? Terrence scrambled for his robe and slippers, not even caring that he was stark naked on this brisk, freezing morning. As he reached for one of his robes, he realized that the one he usually wore was gone. Confused, he parted his clothes, but it was nowhere to be found. Sighing, he put on his other robe and his slippers and padded out of his bedroom. As he emerged from behind the closed door, he could hear the sound of a sizzling skillet and smell a delightful aroma wafting from the kitchen. Terrence was suddenly choked up as he realized that Meagan hadn't left him but was in the kitchen making breakfast for him. He arrived in the kitchen and was amazed by how beautiful she was, standing there in his robe, her dark hair tied back from her face as she flipped griddle cakes with her spatula.

Meagan looked up and her eyes softened when she saw him standing in the doorway. Setting down the spatula, she billowed towards him and folded him into a passionate embrace, kissing him softly and sweetly on the lips. The robe parted, revealing a tantalizing glimpse of her bare cleavage, and Terrence felt a tightening in his groin. He reached down to untie the robe and peeled gently it from her shoulders, admiring her statuesque beauty. Then, he untied his own robe and pulled her to him under the cover of his cape, the kiss becoming more passionate as they melted into each other. Terrence tightened his hold on Meagan's hips and held her against him as her knees turned weak and she sank into his arms with a soft sigh of surrender, cupping his face with tenderness. The sweet, tender embrace became hot and vivacious as Terrence pressed Meagan back against the wall and broke the kiss, trailing his lips roughly down her neck to her shoulder while he gripped her toned buttocks in his hands, grinding against her in a slow, sensual dance. Meagan gave a breathy moan and let her hands roam freely and gently over Terrence's hot, muscular frame, wanting to touch every part of him. They gazed intensely into each other's eyes, and Meagan felt the hot burn of a blush flush her cheeks as Terrence's analytical gaze seared over her every curve. Her lips parted slightly and she lowered her eyes coquettishly, unable to meet Terrence's blatant, scorching scrutiny head-on. With a burning ache pooling between her thighs, Meagan locked her gaze onto Terrence's, letting her robe spread out in a billowy fan on the floor. Then, she reached up and untied her hair, letting her dark locks spill over her shoulders. Slowly, she trailed her hands over the planes of his chest, and looking like some exotic moon goddess, she sank to her knees in front of him, gently clamping her lips around his shaft. She heard him gasp sharply and felt him tense beneath her as she sucked him slowly and thoroughly, drawing pleasure from him like from a straw. He gasped and moaned hoarsely, plunging his hands through her silky hair as she sucked him off, quivering on unsteady legs. "Holy Lord, Meagan," he gasped, tensing above her, moving in shaky thrusts. She could tell by the fluid appearing at his cleft that he would come soon. Lifting her head, she met his gaze. "I'm going to make you come, Terrence," she whispered. "And this time, I want you to call me by my first name, Elizabeth."

Terrence seemed surprised but had no problem with it, just grateful when she returned her attentions to him. He rocked against her frenetically, on the brink of climax, and as he pitched over the edge he deeply groaned, "Elizabeth… oh, Elizabeth," fisting his hands in her hair as he released his scalding torrent of passion in her mouth.

When they had finished, Terrence let out a soft sigh, holding Meagan close. "That was the best thing I've ever felt in my life," he murmured. "I just can't believe you'd do that for me."

"I'd do anything for you," Meagan whispered back.

They spent a few more quiet moments just holding each other, until Meagan glanced over at the stack of griddle cakes. "Damn, our breakfast must be cold by now," she remarked, looking up at him. "We'd better get some clothes on and eat. I didn't make this feast for nothing."

Terrence laughed. "You're right," he replied. "And man, I am hungry, too. Having you make love to me is hard work."

Meagan shared a smile with him. Her eyes glinted playfully. "How 'bout we take a shower, then eat breakfast?" she suggested, slinging her arm around his shoulders. "We've got engagement ring shopping to do today."

***

Back at Meagan's place, Jen and Melanie had spent the night in a similar way. "Wow, Meagan didn't come home at all," Jen remarked. "I wonder what happened."

Melanie gave Jen a conspiratorial wink. "I think the same thing that happened here last night," she chuckled.

Just then, Melanie and Jen's phones went off simultaneously. Jen reached for hers first, and opened the screen. "Ahhhh!!" she screamed, turning to Melanie. "Meagan and Terrence are engaged!"

Melanie smiled and reached for a cigarette, lighting it up and drawing it to her lips. "Whaddaya say we join them, Jennine Aaronson?" she asked.

"Leave it to you to propose to me while you're lighting up," Jennine joked. Then her voice softened and she leaned in to kiss Melanie's cheek. "But I love you anyway."

Chapter Thirty-Nine

March 21, about one year and two months later:

Meagan couldn't believe that it was her wedding day. The past year had been such a rush, and she and Terrence were finally going to be married. Neither one of them liked big, lavish parties, so they decided to keep it simple and beautiful, like their relationship itself. The ceremony was set to take place at 11:00 AM at the town's rose garden. Naturally, the rose garden was beautiful, so extra landscaping really wasn't needed. The "aisle" that they set up actually included a quaint bridge over a pond. Up front in the field near the gazebo, the minister waited with Terrence, who was dressed in his Sunday best. Naturally, they wanted to be married on Sunday, because it was their favorite day of the week, both of them.

In the bridal chamber, which was the rose garden's gift shop, Jen and Melanie finished fixing Meagan's veil and smoothed her dress. Her two best friends were her bridal attendants, and would also be getting married soon, possibly in May.

Meagan was struggling to wipe tears from her eyes as she heard the beginning of the wedding march from outside. They had chosen to have a recording of the wedding march played on the pipe organ, traditional and elegant. A slender college girl with a headset, dressed all in black, gently smoothed Meagan's veil over her face and helped her line up at the door. "Go," she told Jen, the first attendant.

Jen and Melanie were dressed in matching knee-length metallic taupe gowns, sprinkling rose petals as they walked. Jen was cued first, then Melanie. Finally, the girl nudged Meagan to go forward. As Meagan opened the doors to the recreation center, she was flooded with bright morning sunlight. Outside, her frail father stood waiting to escort her over the bridge, dabbing his eyes with a handkerchief. She took his arm and they fell in step with the music, drawing closer and closer to her groom.

Meanwhile, Terrence stood up by the gazebo, trying himself not to get choked up as he saw Jennine and Melanie processing down the aisle, carpeting the grass richly with pink and white rose petals. His breath caught in his throat when he saw his bride bringing up the rear, holding her father's arm as he shakily marched along. Meagan looked radiant, the most beautiful that Terrence had ever seen her. She wore a one-shoulder ivory gown with an embroidered rose on the decorative strap. The dress fell to just above her ankles, with matching flat white sandals and a filmy, net-like chin-length veil with a flower pinned in her hair on top and a flowing swath down the back. Even from far away, Terrence could see that she was positively glowing with happiness. On her other arm, she carried her bouquet, comprised of Queen Anne's lace, pink gardenias, and stargazer lilies, tied together with a taupe ribbon that matched her attendants' dresses. Finally, as the music swelled, Meagan reached the platform and her father let go of her arm as Terrence helped her onto the stage. The minister began with some opening talk before it was time to make the vows. "Today, we have gathered here to celebrate the holy marriage of Dr. Terrence Albert Reid and Miss Elizabeth Meagan Bernice Patience Lucien. I will now ask the couple to state their vows."

He turned to face them and gestured from his book. "Do you, Terrence, take Elizabeth to be your beloved wife, to honor, love, and cherish for the rest of your life?" he intoned, looking up at Terrence.

"I most certainly do," Terrence said softly, looking on Meagan with love.

The minister turned to Meagan. "Do you, Elizabeth, take Terrence to be your beloved husband, to honor, love, and cherish for the rest of your life?"

"I most certainly do," Meagan echoed fervently.

The minister smiled. "Then, by the power vested in me by the church, I pronounce you man and wife," he said solemnly. In the front row, Meagan and Terrence could hear Eloisa Reid blubbering loudly into her handkerchief. "You may kiss the bride."

With gentle grace, Terrence lifted Meagan's veil and drew her to him. "You're so beautiful," he murmured, gently cupping her face in his hands. She returned the gesture and he kissed her sweetly on the lips. "My wife."

They at long last broke apart, and the crowd cheered, throwing rose petals and rice into the air. Meagan turned her back to toss her bouquet, and all of the ladies lined up, hands outstretched eagerly. On a count of three, she let the beautiful flowers fly into the air. She heard a squeal of joy when it was caught and turned to see Jen and Melanie both holding it. A recessional was played and they all went off to a delicious soup luncheon with wedding cake. That night, they had an outside reception with dancing, and as Meagan whirled around barefoot in Terrence's arms, under the stars, she knew that they were the happiest man and woman in the world, and that their love would last forever.

The End

If you enjoyed *The Hallowed Halls,* check out:

My Sweet Vermont

Sara J. Kuhrman

Pretty, quiet banker Araminta Cullen lives out her days in a landlocked, dreary New Jersey town. An exacting, straight-laced perfectionist, she dedicates all her time to her career, refusing to make time for leisure or romance. But when she works herself too hard, she is firmly encouraged to take a vacation.

By a stroke of luck or fate, Mindy vacations to quaint and sparkling coastal town of Burlington, Vermont. There she encounters old-fashioned shops, picturesque sunsets, and a mysterious, charismatic man known only as B.

From the moment she meets B., Mindy's world is rocked off its axis. He's thoughtful, charming, and strong as steel. But it soon becomes apparent that B. is different, and his life is shrouded in a fortress of secrets that he fiercely defends. In order to get through to him, Mindy must have incredible patience and determination, and allow her perceptions of reality to be changed forever.

*coming soon in 2016

Lost & Found

By: Sara J. Kuhrman

Practical, impatient secretary Cindy Washek has always bumbled her way through life, stubborn and surefooted as a mule. But when she finds a woman's purse in the grocery store, she has no idea how it will change her life.

When she goes to return the purse to its owner, she is immediately struck like lightning by the mysterious, dark-haired authoress Teela Grant. The two women become friends, and soon Cindy finds herself falling deeply, completely in love.

Cindy soon learns that Teela harbors dark scars and secrets, and that she is constantly on the run from the shadowy terrors of her past. As these evils begin to reemerge, Cindy finds her strength and wits tested past the limit as she fights to defend herself and frail, restless Teela from their enemies. When the harrowing danger reaches its fever pitch, Cindy must carry out a dramatic rescue... and prove to Teela that love conquers all.

Released August 2015

Virgins of Death

By T. W. Frederick

JOHN TANNER: Special Agent, Criminal Division, FBI.

KARIN MILL: Operations officer, Deputy Directorate of Operations, CIA.

He's experienced, tough and resourceful. She's smart, career-minded, and beautiful.

When a senior CIA officer is assassinated near CIA headquarters, Tanner and Mill team up to stop the assassins before they strike again. Their only clues to the killers are a baggage claim ticket from Hamburg, Germany, and a mysterious fragment of paper.

With Tanner and Mill closing in on the terrorists, the game turns deadly as they find themselves being stalked by the assassins that they have set out to find. To make matters worse, Tanner and Mill find that the danger is not only in Europe, but at home as well. For waiting in the shadows for a single mistake is the branch chief of the CIA division, Arlene Masters, ready to crush them if they fail. She's out for the glory herself and will destroy them if they get in her way.

From Washington to Hamburg to Rome and back again, Virgins of Death takes the reader on an action-packed chase for terrorists in a mission of lurking danger and high-powered suspense!

Karin Mill returns in her next adventure!

BRIGHT FLAME IN BAGHDAD

By T. W. Frederick

Superstar CIA operations officer Karin Mill is back in her latest high-powered adventure! Her mission: to stop an international conspiracy to sell top-secret U.S cryptographic software to Iraq. Join Karin as she travels to the mountains of northern Africa to meet with a secret Iraqi agent. Contending with the bloodthirsty Iraqi secret service is only part of the difficult task. In the wilds of Kenya and Ethiopia, Karin battles ferocious wild animals, roving mobs of bandits, and a tribal liberation army intent on killing her for her golden blonde hair. In the end, Karin must emerge from Africa and track down the secret software before it ends up in Iraqi hands. Will she survive a fight to the death with the arms dealer who has it and his hulking hired gun? Will she recover the software before it's too late? Find out as Karin calls on her extraordinary talent and hard-earned experience to outwit her ruthless adversaries in another great, action-packed thriller from T.W. Frederick!

About the Author

Sara J. Kuhrman is a witty, eccentric young lady who is known for always making her own way in life. She loves writing, especially melodramatic stories of people bonding in spite of tragedy or criticism. In her free time, Sara enjoys reading, taking walks and analyzing the ways of the world, always dreaming up another story line.